steel toes

also by Eddie Little

Another Day in Paradise

steel toes

Eddie Little

An
LA Weekly Book
for
St. Martin's Press
≈ New York

LA Weekly Books is a trademark of LA Weekly Media, Inc.

www.stmartins.com

Book design by Lorelle Graffeo

Library of Congress Cataloging-in-Publication Data

Little, Eddie.
    Steel toes / Eddie Little.— 1st ed.
      p. cm.
    ISBN 0-312-28291-5
    1. Fugitives from justice—Fiction.   2.
Boston (Mass.)—Fiction.   3. California—
Fiction.   4. Art thefts—Fiction.   5. Prisons—
Fiction.   6. Escapes—Fiction.   I. Title.

PS3558.E14 S74 2001
813'.54—dc21

                               2001041807

First Edition: November 2001

10   9   8   7   6   5   4   3   2   1

To my beautiful genius daughter, Rita.
Never go where I have gone.

Love, Pops

There are a few people who had the faith and courage to stay on my side through the good times and the very, very bad ones. I want to thank them:

Patti Felker

Chuck and Ellen Aydelotte

Sean and Cotty at A-ville

Frank and Dottie Clayman-Cook

Coup DeLeo

My poor mother and
 her saintly husband, Don

Big Nate

The Fabra Clan

Sue Horton

Trevor Miller, who is MIA

Rita Senior

My girl, Brandi

and

David, Mike, and Jason at
 Vigliano Associates

steel toes

The thing about trying to escape is that trying really doesn't cut it. Getting caught is a real drag.

In solitary now, ricocheting between rage and numbness, watching huge flakes of snow drifting through the night sky, floating past the bars, then through the chicken wire, and sticking against the heavy screening in front of the Plexiglas window. Each flake unique.

Snow swirling, reflecting all the colors of the rainbow as it melts . . . sometimes just tinted misty pink, blurred with the blood dripping from a cut that keeps reopening over my eye.

Spotlights glaring behind the flakes, the cold coming through the walls and into my bones. Each breath sending a visible plume of mist from my mouth to fog on the Plexiglas, only to recede to nothingness.

Gray world, gray concrete, grinding pain, throbbing, fading from one wound to call attention to another. Every move smashing through my kidneys, reminding me of where the steel toes did their work.

Beyond the snow, the concertina wire fence the only break as empty cornfields stretch to eternity. Coming through the floor the vibrations of the train that rockets by every night, too far away to see. The sound of freedom, audible now, vibrations and noise. The train whistle shrieks across the Indiana farmland, echoing through the concrete room that contains me. Growing fainter, now gone like the snowflakes, like the condensed breath on the Plexiglas.

Escape.

This is my second attempt in God's year of 1975. Twice tried, twice failed, this time after being chased for miles across snow-covered farmland, thinking that running across frozen streams, breaking through the thin ice, would make my pursuers as wet and miserable as it made me, that they would tire of the chase, give up. I'd get away.

Wrong.

When the trusties finally trapped me this time, they beat me senseless.

Eight of them caught me, circled, and started punching and kicking till I hit the ground. Then they went to work with their boots. Did such a good job that I felt a flash of gratitude when the guards finally arrived and called them off, saving me for Indiana's quaint custom of the strap.

Bruised, bloodied, regardless, you still have another beating coming when you try to escape. After you've had the strap applied, you think twice before running. Or don't think about it at all.

Or, if you're like me, the need for freedom is with you like a bad tooth, no respite. Constantly reminding you that this is an unacceptable situation, making you apply every brain cell you have to solving the problem of getting away. Not trying. Doing it.

Turning from the window, I take in my world. Four feet by eight feet. Toilet and sink combined, chipped gray porcelain. Steel door painted brown. Bunk with the springs so shot out that the weight of the paper-thin mattress brings the middle to the concrete floor. Walls made of brick, with names and dates carved into it going back way to before I was born, all of eighteen years ago.

Never occurs to me that eighteen isn't much. For me, it's old, an eternity of criming and drugs and cops and prison.

The accessories: A green wool government surplus blanket. A roll of toilet paper that doubles as a pillow propped on top of the New Testament *Good News for Modern Man,* the only reading material allowed. Issued when you enter along with the blanket and toilet paper.

Lots of time to think here, to feel the pain of the beatings you got, the first by your peers who actually ran you down. That's one of the things the red cap trusties are for in this particular institution.

The second beating by the man with the strap.

Now solitary, an opportunity to read the "good book" and contemplate your sins while freezing. Plainfield, Indiana, temporary home to John Dillinger, Charles Manson, and now me.

Pulling a piece of spring out of the bunk and resuming the work that's kept me entertained for the last few days, I keep carving the words "No hope—without dope" into the brick wall.

This is one poem I won't sign. Doesn't matter; it's signed in my soul. Dope was the answer to all the questions. The thing that kept me alive. Salvation. But damaging state property is rewarded by corporal punishment, the strap.

The piece of spring steel starts to rip through the ends of my fingers, tearing open the blisters already formed by the constant friction, and I quit my artistic endeavors for the night.

Do push-ups until my body is shaking from the effort and collapse on the bunk that folds in the middle and watch the steam rise from my mouth.

Staring at the ceiling, thinking of all the things I would be doing if I was out, getting loaded, getting laid, getting rich, it seems like it's all in the getting. Not being. Getting. The knowledge that whatever you get you're gonna lose has been there since I was a small child.

For a year or so leading up to the bust that landed me here, it had been so good—a drug run and crime spree that hit the sky, with a high of being in love and on top of the world, rolling so hard that I felt like Genghis Khan, like Elvis Presley, like Billy the fuckin' Kid.

Like I was blessed with a state of grace beyond comprehension. And the spree rolled down until I was so lost in my own inner pain that the only answer was death.

And I did my best to achieve that. The wonders of modern medical science brought me back from a massive overdose. Now I'm paying the price for my lifestyle.

Being very young and not overly smart, I have no concept of consequences, don't know that I and the people I loved were statistics, cartoon characters waiting to be taken off the page.

Junkies don't live long and I know of nothing except better living through chemistry. I still don't understand that the narcotics that kept me sane also doomed anything other than the ongoing pursuit of more narcotics. And prison.

Now, in solitary, wanting to go back, and do things different somehow, knowing I can't, wanting to touch the ghosts that populate this tiny cell and knowing I can't do that either.

They took the only love I knew with them when they died.

Mel, my mentor, my coach, my guide, taught me how to be a thief, how to be a junkie. And he taught me that someone actually could care what happened to me. And Rosie—I never knew I could love someone, never knew how to say it, never knew she could be taken from me just like that, but that's the way it played out. Welcome to reality, pal.

The end of this last run, the death of people I loved, only set the feeling of hopelessness in stone. Losing my freedom is nothing new, but acceptance is a concept I don't understand, and people dying, getting busted, all these things make me mad, beyond mad. On the edge of berserk.

I know I'm guilty as Satan himself, that the situation I'm in is self-created, but that doesn't change the desire to destroy everything I can before I'm destroyed.

Guilt and pain and anger rolling through me like the Union Army rolling through the South, burning and pillaging everything in its path, no pity, no prisoners . . . my own brain doing Grant's march through my soul. "The Night They Burned Old Dixie Down" playing every second and every minute that I can't keep the volume low enough to make it inaudible.

Pulling the cover around me, wrapping my feet; rolling as tightly in it as possible to try and contain a little warmth. The toilet paper on top of the Bible doesn't make much of a pillow but it's better than nothing. Feeling the rage, not tired but gonna get to sleep eventually. Beat these sons of bitches out of a few hours.

Listening to Mr. Washington, the fat little black man who runs the night watch on solitary row, boning Candy as the sounds come through the walls.

First the squeaking of bedsprings, then Candy's falsetto voice rising louder and louder, sounding just like a girl coming, finally Washington's loud groans, then silence.

Candy's a punk who caused so much trouble on the yard that they pulled her/him out of population so he/she wouldn't be getting sodomized and causing fights.

Now Candy's warder has fallen in love. A time-honored tradition of victims getting further victimized by their protectors.

The word is that Candy isn't a punk voluntarily, Candy was once named Charlie. After about the hundredth rape he became Candy. Femme fatale, heartbreaker extraordinaire.

Now the joke is on the man. Ray Charles could have seen the wreck coming. For those of us on lockdown their nightly sessions break up the monotony.

The next thing of any interest is breakfast and that's a long way away, listening to my stomach growl and doing my best to ignore it.

Back inside my head, trying to stay warm, willing my mind to shut down and shut up and finally drifting to the edge of sleep.

The first rays of the sun turn the absolute blackness into pewter. The distant rumbling of the morning train rattles through the cell, and the sound of steel wheels precedes the howling of the whistle, and from the back of my mind comes a memory of a book by Kerouac or London or somebody and I settle into sleep knowing how to escape. Make it over the razor wire, run like hell, and just jump the train as it flies by. Nothing to it, right?

Waking up at noon, eating the cold oatmeal from breakfast and the sandwich that is lunch at the same time. Full.

Stare through the window at the grainy dismal sky and again revisit the crime spree that landed me here till the age of twenty-one. Three and a half years to go, longer than forever.

Wondering if I could have made things different, somehow; wanting to be living like a high-rolling, rock-and-rolling, dope-shooting, pistol-packing, Teflon-coated fool . . . then my reality, the concrete and steel surrounding me and my complete aloneness, comes crashing back, like an instant replay from hell.

Still seeing Rosie on that stretcher, dying from pain and a life of abuse and infection . . . bitter, failing, losing her. Grieving all the friends lost and the unnameable emotions that tear through my insides shut my brain down, screaming to itself. Stop it . . . leave me alone . . . shut the fuck up . . . and I smash my forehead into the wall, letting the physical pain cancel the hole in my soul.

Sitting on the bunk staring at my bare feet and directing my thoughts into safer channels, searching my memory for what it was I read about jumping trains and coming up with no useful knowledge.

Just knowing that it's been done before is enough. It's only a matter of time, getting over the razor-wire fences and making it to the train tracks before my pursuers; it's what I'm living for. Picturing it, seeing it work, feeling my freedom, is the ray of hope that is going to keep me breathing in and out till I put it together.

Now I know I was using what they call visualization, although I'd never heard the term then. I thought of it as daydreaming, seeing myself catching hold of the flying train, making it to whatever city it first stopped at, stealing a car, then picking up some money and a new ID from friends outside of Chicago. East Coast bound, going fast. New faces, places, dissolving my past, leaving no traces. That my pain would go wherever I went is something I didn't realize. The going, getting, doing seemed like the way out. *That's the trap.*

Time expands and contracts, goes slow, goes fast. The one thing you can count on is that it passes. Good or bad it ain't gonna last . . .

When they bust Washington and Candy it becomes spoken history at Plainfield. Word had gotten out, as it was bound to. The superintendent and three guards lie doggo, hidden in one of the empty cells, waiting, and when the creaking springs and groaning start echoing through the cellblock they close their trap.

Washington's denials and Candy's shrieks ring through the concrete corridors. The superintendent's bellowing drowns them out: "Perverts, goddamn perverts! Disgusting animals!"

Washington's crying now, and even as his tears have no effect on the outcome, Candy's psychotic break goes directly into reformatory legend. The voice that booms through the cells is that of a woman gone insane: "I'm gonna kill ya, motherfucker, gonna kill ya!"

The sounds of battle echo through the concrete rooms, screaming and flesh striking flesh. The fight lasting far longer than it should have with four grown men trying to subdue one skinny little boy.

My hands are laced under my head, the words "Sock 'em up, Candy, put one on the sons of bitches" running through my mind, and without thought I'm on my feet screaming for a miracle.

The cellblock explodes with the yells of every kid in there. "Kill 'em, Candy, beat the motherfuckers down, boy! Go, go, kill!"

As the yelling fades the only sound remaining is Washington crying and the whispering of the guards. Like whispering will wipe out the screams of seconds before. Finally the echoing footsteps of the trusties taking Candy/Charlie out on a stretcher. So much for the meek inheriting the earth.

Sunup to sundown time slips by. Read the Bible, masturbate, and do push-ups. Every Wednesday morning you get biscuits and gravy for breakfast, something to look forward to.

Solitary.

Eventually you reach a state of Buddha-like nonexistence, need nothing, want nothing. Floating behind your eyes. People pride themselves on getting there through meditation.

I think it's harder to come back. Reentering the world after enough time being your own universe is brutal, being reborn with no skin, flayed nerve endings screaming.

The sound of locks turning tears into my sleep, the spotlights outside have been turned off, so morning must be close as the light from the corridor slices into my cell. Smith, the day guard for the row, yells, "Rise and shine, give God his glory, motherfucker. Get your skinny butt movin'."

Fighting my way back to consciousness, swinging my feet to the floor and staring up at the balding, inbred, potbellied cracker who cackles like the half-wit he is. He spits a stream of tobacco juice onto the floor and throws the mud-caked khakis I ran in, now wrapped around my combat boots, at my head. Jerking my face out of the way and catching my clothes, grunting, "Thanks, Smith," as he relocks the door and proceeds on his rounds.

This means that my lockdown time is finished. Now it's time to get back on the yard, time to kick it with the fellas, time to learn about hopping trains, time to put my brain back into gear.

two

The toes of my boots look like obsidian. Spit-shining shoes is an art. If you're about anything you have got to have your bonaroos, pressed khakis, clean T-shirt, and shoes or boots shined till they look like black mirrors, and your hair greased back tight. Ready to kick ass, immaculate.

Polishing my boots is soothing, lets me shut the noise of the eighty other fools in the dorm I'm locked in out of my head. After enough time in solitary a whisper sounds like thunder.

I'm trying to listen to myself, drown out the yelling of the blacks, the Spanish babble of the Puerto Ricans, the drawling slow speech of my guys, the paddies, peckerwoods, white boys, all soon-to-be killers and convicts in training, and my steel toes are almost perfect.

One more layer of polish to go when my road dog, Red, squats and stares at me. Says, "Got a polish on, boy, lookin' good for a skinny fuckin' wood. Sad they caught ya, but I'm glad to see your sorry-lookin' ass."

Looking up from the boots and into Red's gray eyes, already tired and burnt at eighteen, carrot hair and freckles covering his face, Pop-eye arms with jail ink over the freckles. Red's sloppy, doesn't care if he's bonarood or not, another kid that aspires to criminal greatness, he can talk a burglary with the best of them. In here everybody talks a big game. With Red most of the time I believe him, he's my closest friend in this joint. And for all those Irish freckles, he somehow missed the Blarney stone. He shoots straight.

I laugh and say, "Go press your pants, dog, ya look like shit. Fucked my boots up runnin', took me two hours to get 'em lookin' right."

"Crap, Bobbie, y'all jist gonna fuck 'em up again. Why bother . . . gonna scuff 'em up anyhow."

"Why am I gonna scuff 'em up, Red? Next time I run I'm gonna make it. Hit the street and buy some new ones, maybe polish these and buy a glide so they last forever."

"Gotta tell ya, dog, things gettin' fucked up. Got some pruno brewin', the man busted our last batch. One a' the niggers, Monkey Man's punk. Lester fuckin' Liplock himself ratted on Joe Moppa's last batch and his people won't take care of it. I tried talkin' to Big George and you know me and him don't get along too good anyway. He says he's gonna cosign Monkey, we move on his guy we gotta move on all of them, and ya know they got us outnumbered. Anyhow I say that to say this . . . you got a good line of shit, you and Big George get along good. I want you to talk to those porch monkeys, see if ya can get George to act right, give us his guy; shit, I'll sling with Monkey one on one. What they should do is let Moppa and Liplock do the thumpin'. Moppa was doing the cookin' anyhow. And Liplock did the tellin'. We can't let the motherfuckers get away with this crap. If it works, no problem . . . me and the Monkey go head up. Or Moppa and Liplock. If it don't, ya gonna scuff those shiny boots all up kicking those sons of bitches in their melon heads. What's up, dog? Ya down?"

Look back at my boots, dab another glob of polish out of the can, spit on the toe and start rubbing the polish in until it's shining, gleaming, burning like a black fucking diamond, and I don't want to get involved in any of this.

Me and Big George are as close to being friends as a white and a black can be in gladiator school. The only thing I want to do is catch my train, blow out of this little nightmare.

Looking up into Red's eyes and feeling the rush of friendship, knowing that if it was reversed he'd be down with no hesitation, feeling lost for a second, not knowing what's important.

Not wanting to go back to the hole for being involved in a riot, not wanting to hurt anybody, and sure as hell not wanting to get hurt. Realizing that all that really matters is getting out and then feeling an overpowering rush of shame for being less than a hundred percent down, for hesitating for even a second, not only do I feel like a coward, what kind of friend am I?

The anger comes, at myself, at George, at Red, at the state of Indiana, hating the universe . . . and I smile and say, "Stupid question, my brother. Twenty-four/seven ready to kill, ready to die, motherfucker. I'll talk to George as soon as possible. Chill. Either they'll act right or it's on. When's the brew gonna be done cookin'?"

The rules that count, not those imposed by the man but the ones that mandate survival, remain constant in all penal institutions, be they county, state, or federal; adult or juvenile.

Never show weakness. You have no reverse, only the forward gears; any backup can get you killed. Once a confrontation starts it has to be finished, signed in blood.

You stay with your own. Color lines are as solid as the penitentiary steel that surrounds us. You eat with, get loaded with, exercise, gamble, live and die with your own. Cross those lines and you're out of the car, roadkill.

Cliques, gangs, crews, cars . . . cut to the chase and what you have are guys that are scared to death, and willing to fight to the death to deny that fear. Respect is the most important thing in life because that's the only thing we got left, the way we view ourselves, defined by the reactions of our friends and enemies.

A chink in your self-image can be fatal. Anything other than total confidence allows the feeding frenzy to start and you become dinner or worse.

Survival mandates that you have a commitment to your car more serious than marriage.

I don't like doing time. Never got used to it, never want to. But right or wrong, the world I'm in is all that exists. Anything else is fantasy until I'm out of here.

I hope this thing can be chilled. That train is calling my name.

Filing into the chow hall, getting my tray loaded, my partners on the serving line giving me double issues because we all know that hole time means half servings and no meat. Almost nothing but potatoes, bread, and oatmeal, a diet designed to sap your strength.

Four-man Formica-topped tables, gray tile flooring, bilious green paint on the walls, plastic chairs at the tables, the room divided into three parts, white, black, Latino . . . whether this has been manipulated by the system so that we stay broken into groups fighting each other instead of channeling our aggression at the institution that holds us is a moot point.

This is the way it is.

If you crave martyrdom, sit at the wrong table, you'll get your cross, crown of thorns, thrown in for free. What a deal. Me, I want to get out. Don't care about politics. Just survival. Make my time as pleasant as possible, get out as soon as I can, get on with life, not that I have any idea what that means, but I have a mission and doing time isn't part of it.

Time does heal all wounds . . . except when the wound is time.

Hitting the white side of the chow hall, sitting down with Red, Cross-Eyed Phil, and Joe Moppa, digging into the pork stew with gusto, fat gristly meat, carrots, potatoes . . . could have been Beef Wellington and not tasted as good.

There's no time to talk, I'm shoveling the slop into my mouth as fast as possible, my ears and brain absorbing the hum around me as my body is ripping the nutrients it's starved for from this lovely repast. Wiping the last of the gravy up with a piece of white bread and finally looking up to pay attention to the conversation around me.

Cross-Eyed Phil has a mouthful of stew and bread, sandy brown hair, both eyes stuck against his nose. A big corn-fed farm boy in here for multiple GTAs, and one count of involuntary manslaughter. A regular car-stealing fool, with a real bad temper. Definitely the toughest white boy on the yard, naturally strong and fast. He grew up throwing bales of hay around and hand-plowing the rock-filled fields of his people's truck farm on the Indiana–Kentucky border. Drinking moonshine whiskey and beating the hell out of anyone willing to fight or, as he called it, roll and tumble. Until he beat his stepfather to death and went on the run, ending up hiding with his real dad in the ghetto in Gary. Got apprehended when the Feds busted his dad for bank robbery. Phil was at the house when it was raided and his fugitive status came up. Some of the black kids in here know him from there and give him a wide berth. He doesn't talk about it and they don't either. Grudging respect from both sides. The ultimate sign of toughness is when your enemies show fear. Phil inspires that.

He's waving one of his plate-sized hands in the air and has got food all over the table around him, talking around the mess in his mouth.

"Tellin' ya, boy, a calf is the ticket. Slap your pecker into its mouth and it thinks it's mama's tit, starts suckin' and won't stop till it gets a gallon. God ain't made the woman yet that can suck a dick better than a new calf. Shit howdy, don't got no fuckin' teeth, just keep on gummin' at your organ till you're howlin' at the sky."

Me and Red glance at each other, trying not to react, look over at Moppa, who's got a mouthful of stew and can't hold it, he busts out laughing, spewing food all over the table, and we're all losing it, Red pounding on his leg with his open hand, guffawing so loud he's howling at the ceiling, and I'm laughing so hard it hurts.

Joe Moppa's got tears rolling from under his glasses and down his cheeks and gasps out, "Ya sick fuck, if it didn't stop till it got a gallon it'd pull your brains out the end of your dick . . . which, in your case, probably wouldn't be too hard 'cause ya don't got no brains, ya fuckin' pervert."

Phil's chuckling with us and says to Moppa, "Shit, you four-eyed motherfucker, it wouldn't be too hard 'cause I got one of those monster white boy dicks. Drive a truck up inside it. Suckin' a brain through it would be easy as pie . . . ya fuckin' assholes."

Looking around the chow hall and the whole room is frozen and staring at us, anything loud attracts attention because loud usually means violence on the way.

The white guys laugh at us and resume eating, the Puerto Ricans ignore us, and the black kids are mad-dogging us . . . what the hell are we laughing about? Who do these white assholes think they are?

I can feel my back getting straighter and the adrenaline starting to run through my veins when Red says, "Ya know, fellas, I'll bet every freckle I got that Joe Moppa spat more food out than he ate, whatcha wanna bet? Spittin' good food all over the place when people are starvin' to death, right here in Indiana, as a matter of fact. . . . I say that to say this: Ya still awful skinny, Bobbie." He shoves his half-full tray at me and says, "Finish this, killer, get some meat back on your bones."

The noise level has returned to normal, the electricity in the air has dropped. I look around the chow hall and things are cool, look at the tray of food and pull it in front of me, grab the spoon that is the only implement issued and say, "Thanks, Red."

Joe Moppa points at Red with his spoon and starts in. "Ya fuckin' asshole, spat out more than I ate, whatcha talkin' about, ya freckle-faced, carrot-headed fuck."

It feels good to be back with my peers enjoying pleasant dinner conversation.

The sound of snores and sleepers' raucous responses to bad dreams feels like sandpaper on my nerves. All that hole time left me what you might call noise-sensitive. Real aware.

It's an eighty-man dorm, four rows of ten double bunks. At one end the rest room and showers spilling light into the larger room. Next to the head the guard's "office," Plexiglas and chicken wire to protect him from us.

Wind cuts through chinks in the walls, the radiators that dot the walls make an occasional noise, but the last time they carried heat was so long ago that the families of spiders living in the coils go back for generations.

Knowing that me and the night guard are the only ones awake in the whole universe. The state-issue blanket seems to be keeping the cold in rather than providing warmth as I wait for the whistle of the train. Watching the second hand on the clock above the guard's cage.

The glow from his cigarette going up and down as he earns his money and I wonder what kind of person can voluntarily sit in a cage eight hours at a time, doing nothing except hoping that nothing happens.

The guard won't come out of there.

Not if a kid is getting raped, or having an epileptic fit, or appendicitis, not if one of us goes staggering up to the bars with a shank buried in his chest.

His job is to watch us and if the shit hits the fan, pick the phone up and call for backup. My thinking is if I do a good job with the file he won't know I'm gone till one of my peers tells him I skyed.

Hopefully that will take five, maybe even ten minutes. Anyone that thinks there's some kind of operative code about keeping your mouth shut hasn't been exposed to anything other than movies and the bullshit that's always talked and never walked.

The saying "Why do time? Drop a dime" isn't a joke. That's the way it is.

No one but my crew can know what I'm planning till my feet clear the razor wire.

The whistle finally tears through the night. I clock it at eleven fifty-five, feel myself starting to relax when my rack starts shaking as the dude in the top bunk begins jacking off. I realize that I'm not the only one awake.

I wonder if I'll even have a five-minute head start before my escape is called in.

The diluted sun sends tendrils of weak light through the darkness to highlight the garbage I'm emptying into the back of the pickup truck that will take it to the hog pen.

The garbage crew is me, a half-witted hillbilly known as Pin because of his pinhead, and three Puerto Ricans. Juan and I are doing the lifting, Flaco and Roberto are dumping the crap into the truck, and Pin is moping along behind the truck muttering to himself.

Once we get all the stinking leftover food from the previous day loaded it's transported to the hog farm, where we shovel it into the troughs for the pigs.

Recycling. Yesterday's garbage. Today's pig. Tomorrow's bacon. Vocational training. Another fucking day in paradise.

And after slinging the garbage, another day of building my body back to speed. The gym is falling apart, all the equipment is rusty and battered. Grimy skylights and hundred-watt bulbs hung from the pigeon-filled rafters create shadows, slicing the barnlike building into sections. The floor concrete is pitted by years of sneaker-clad feet streaking across it.

The clanging of iron hitting concrete, the basketball echoing off the boards, the jump rope tattooing the floor, the speed bag and heavy bag singing their songs, all mingle with the smell of sweat and the yells of the different crews echoing through the air.

"Push it, motherfucker, nothin' to it."

"Pass dat ball, punk. Foul, mo'fucker. Foul."

"Jab, jab, now hook offa the jab, maricón . . . hit 'im, barboso . . . you here to fight, not fuck."

"Your set, wood, get your money."

And it's my turn on the bench press. I'm weaker than puppy piss, no stamina and no power. We're halfway through our routine and I'm running out of gas. I weigh 140 and there's two hundred pounds on the Olympic bar, and I know there's no way once I get it out of the rack that it's going to come back off my chest. I look at Red and he says, "Shit dog, raise your hand if you scared, lotta weight there for a skinny little fuck like you, don't wanna try it don't make you a bad guy. . . ."

Moppa cuts in with the rest of the line: "Don't make ya a guy at all."

One of the oldest tricks in competitive sports is to get angry, allow anger and adrenaline to kick your body into overdrive. Sometimes it works. I open my mind to the hate that lives inside me, always there, just below the surface, bubbling like nuclear sewage. Let visions of my father kicking me in the face and memories of what it felt like fill my mind and my hands start shaking and these motherfuckers don't think I can lift this fucking thing? Unbidden ghosts and demons come, shit that hurts so bad I didn't summon it, wouldn't summon it, want to deny my own ghosts and pain but here they are behind my eyes, with people that meant more than my own life who died and I'm alive and want 'em back and there's no way, no number of prayers or sacrifices. The good die and those of us that are left bear the guilt of living and the bar is coming out of the rack, smashing into my ribs and shooting back into the air like a feather. By rep seven I'm screaming and on ten the bar slams back into the rack and I'm swinging my feet off the bench gasping for breath and looking at Moppa, saying, "Your turn, motherfucker, get ten . . . if you can."

Red smirks and says, "Good set."

Moppa laughs and raises his hand in the air, saying, "That's right, I'm scared. Take fifty off, ya fuckin' idiot. That shit would cave my chest in. Just 'cause you like gettin' hurt don't mean I'm gonna get a hernia to keep up with you maroons."

The endorphins are kicking in and I can feel the competitive edge.

Thanks, Moppa.

* * *

Moppa's real name is Joe Rosen. He's called Moppa because he's the mop man, has control of one of the few areas in this place that an inmate can run: the utility room.

That's where we cook our pruno, raisin jack, and my favorite, the beverage made from fermented tomato puree with fruit juice added for flavoring.

Moppa now owes. If he'd tried to get the two hundred I would have waited for him to mention it. Since he's choked it's all right to fuck with him.

"I'm spottin' ya, if ya can't get the deuce ya gotta pay rent, when are we gettin drunk . . . asshole?"

"Be done cookin' tonight. Pull fifty, shithead."

Joe, otherwise known as Moppa, grins, flips us off, and hits the bench. "Guaranteed if I damage myself I'm drinking it without you motherfuckers."

Red and I laugh and each pull a quarter off the end of the bar.

The brew in the mason jar is as red and cloudy as our futures, the smell of fermenting puree and rotting fruit as distasteful as our pasts. The oblivion it brings the only thing that matters now.

I chug the first tumblerful and feel it burn like turpentine all the way down my throat and my stomach flips. The sour odor of the hanging mops and antiseptic cleaner combines with the putrid taste of the alcohol and I get the last of it down without stopping.

Raise my tumbler to Moppa in a toast and say, "Delicious fuckin' shit, dog. Gimme another."

The sixty-watt bulb that illuminates Moppa's kingdom reflects off his glasses and his dirty blond hair. The scrawny mustache that is his pride and joy has got home brew dripping from it, and he says, "Why, thank you sir, vintage Plainfield, a light bouquet offset by a pleasant vinegar flavor, catsup with a kick . . . Indiana champagne."

The alcohol is creeping through my system, easing the pain in my muscles, dulling the ache in my head. The more we drink the more shit we talk, voices starting to slur, vision starting to blur.

Cross-Eyed Phil is perched on a mop bucket, tumbler in hand, looking like a psychotic college football player with all the education removed, crossed eyes now shot with red, saying, "Road Runner, maybe a fuckin' GTO, gonna get one, boy. Fuckin' license to fly. Make parole this time, find me some little old country gal. Get married and make babies . . . never gonna do time again. Go to work, maybe get a job at one a' them big plants, RCA or somethin', make good money, benefits, all that shit. Come home, play w' my young-uns. Get drunk, watch TV, love my honey up."

Red's squatting, his back to the wall, drinking out of an old tin can, holding the can with both hands like it might escape. Popeye arms bulging as he squeezes the tin out of round, then back to can shape.

Moppa's sprawled on the floor, glasses lopsided now, saying, "Fuck all that bullshit, get outta this fuckin' trap. This white boy is going to college, smoke pot, take acid, and fuck every bitch on campus, fuck 'em bowlegged. Fat ones, skinny ones, tall ones, short ones, midgets, all of 'em."

Red's got the can bent into a square, looks up from his endeavors for a second to ask, "Midgets?"

Moppa drags himself up into a sitting position, takes a hit from his brew, lights a cigarette, and gives this some thought, making a noise. "Hmmm."

Hits his Camel again and says, "Hell yeah, fuckin' right. Midgets, let 'em lick my belly button while I'm going up inside them. Gonna specialize. Midget master, maybe I can find a midget college. Bone nothin' but midgets. Fuck yeah, talk about being big man on campus. That's me . . . midget master . . . Joe Moppa, king of mops, master of midgets, maker of the finest tomato jack in da world. You ain't lived till ya boned a midget, Red."

Red sets his can down and asks, "Tell the truth, ace, have ya ever really fucked a midget?"

"Sure, of course I have. I been locked down since I was eleven, I'm eighteen now . . . had plenty of time for fuckin' . . . long as a motherfucker likes young boys. What kinda question is that?"

Moppa stands up from his sprawl on the floor, face turning red, the alcohol kicking in insanity, talking in the hard whisper that precedes mayhem. If you get loud it brings heat, if you're serious about violence you stay quiet, and Moppa's not loud-talking at all.

Red picks his can off the floor and takes a drink, saying, "Easy, hoss, easy."

"You know I'm state-raised. Motherfucker . . . when the fuck am I supposed to of had any pussy . . ." Moppa starts laughing. "Let alone rare exotic midget pussy?"

Red's back to bending his can, tosses it to Moppa for a refill, the violence put on hold. In here the things you don't say mean as much as what you say, what you don't do is as serious as what you do.

Moppa is different from the rest of our car, not quite as physically dangerous, meaning that he'd avoid using a weapon if possible. Not as guarded, much funnier, more of a kid than any of the rest of us ever were.

Turned over to the state by his parents. In Joe Moppa's case, "incorrigible" meant he ate too much. Not a felon. Just a kid that got thrown away, who was consequently more easily offended and, win or lose, more than willing to sling 'em with anybody to prove that he was one of the fellas.

We hang together and cosign each other's lies, learning how to survive. Red's question leaves Moppa vulnerable for a second, in his own eyes only; but when image is part of continuing to breathe in and out you keep it well fed and fortified.

Taking the can back from Moppa and downing a long slug, Red says, "Come on, hoss, we your dogs. Like the four fuckin' musketeers. Don't plex on me. Shit, man, kick it off with me and after I get done cripplin' ya I'll feel bad for at least five, six minutes. Let's save it for the bad guys. Besides, ain't nobody can make crazy catsup like you."

Raising his tin can in a toast, Red says, "To Joe Moppa, certified fool and the finest bootlegger in Indiana."

The jack is smoothing all the edges, life is great. I raise my tumbler and say, "Cheers, Moppa, and by the way I need a metal file."

Red starts squashing the shit out of his can. Moppa raises his tumbler and asks, "A file, huh?"

Phil shoots his drunken, red-rimmed psychotic stare at me and says, "They catch ya again you're on your way to Pendleton, no more gladiator school, go right to state fuckin' prison. Last time they gave ya maximum hole time, plus the strap. Give it up, dog, jist do your time. Quit trying to sky. This ain't that bad. Shit, bro, I did my whole nickel and I'm getting out the end of next month. It goes by fast." Phil's smarter than he looks.

"Ain't gonna get caught this time. Gonna go at night. File the window dividers a little bit at a time, get 'em thin enough to kick out, then lay dead for a foggy night. Soon as the parole dust rolls in I roll out. Head for the tracks. That train that goes screaming by every night at eleven-fifty is gonna take my ass outta here. Gonna jump the motherfucker. Let's see 'em chase a train down. Fuck this shit, dog."

I look back at Moppa and ask him, "So what's up? Gonna get me a file?"

Phil's shaking his head. Red and Moppa lock eyes for a second and Red shrugs. I can feel my shoulders tensing and the settling-in feeling that comes before a confrontation starts, the alcohol upping the madness factor because anything other than getting a full cosign is not acceptable. I need the goddamn file to do this right.

Take a hit from the tomato jack and light a Camel, watching Joe Moppa, who finally says, "It's your ass, pal. Gimme a couple days. One metal file coming up. If they catch ya you're gonna wish I'd never got it for ya. You sure about this, Bobbie?"

"They ain't gonna catch me, Moppa. I got it wired."

Red sets his can down and asks, "Eleven-fifty?"

The excitement is building in my chest like storm clouds forming across the sky, I can observe them but have no control over what's going to happen; the grin on my face is so wide it feels like my cheeks are going to split as I say, "Eleven-fifty, give or take ten minutes either way."

Red picks his can back up and gestures with it. "That could be as much as twenty minutes dead time, dog. If I was gonna try that I'd get it narrowed down some." Takes a slug from the can, points at me, and asks, "Know what I mean, ace?"

"So you guys are down with me on this?"

Moppa starts laughing and sputtering, says, "Shee-it, ain't none of us running nowhere. Whatcha mean, down with ya, fool? You know we'll help, but you make it over the wire and as far as the tracks, you gonna be jumpin' that train all by your lonesome."

I pass my tumbler to Joe Moppa and say, "Stay down, Moppa, I'll bone a couple of those midgets for ya. Let me get a refill."

When the tumbler comes back the crazy catsup tastes better than the finest wine and I toast Moppa: "De-fucking-licious."

* * *

It's time for evening count. Each dorm forms lines and we all get counted to make sure no one has escaped; when count is complete you march back to your dorm, not shamble. March in lockstep.

I'm so drunk the guy in front of me keeps fading in and out and every third or fourth step I'm running into him doing my best to maintain and not doing a very good job of it.

Red's two guys over from me and stumbling like his legs are made out of rubber. My whole focus is on putting one foot in front of the other when the words "Get up offa my ass, ya drunken fuckin' cracker" are screamed at top volume, the sound of a fist striking flesh punctuating the word "cracker."

As my eyes rise from my feet I see the guards already running towards our unit, steam billowing from their mouths, chasing the yells directed at us. "Hit the ground, you motherfuckers. . . . Unit Three, lay down. . . . Fight, fight in progress."

As the black dude who was yelling at Red sucker-punches him and one of his partners jumps in, it's on, adrenaline and crazy catsup have me moving. It's all a speeded-up blur, sound and vision melting into action, throwing the guy in front of me out of the way and plunging into the middle of the fight and slinging with everything I got.

Kicking one of the negroes that are rat-packing Red in the middle of the back, knocking the air out of him and grabbing his hair in both hands, running forward and throwing my weight into a dive, not letting go of his hair, our combined poundage and momentum stopping as his face smashes into the concrete walkway like a bug into a windshield. See ya.

Rolling to my feet, seeing Cross-Eyed Phil lifting a black dude over his head and another one tackling Phil, all three going down in a pile and now Red kicking the pile with both feet while screaming like a berserker as I get tagged, start to go down, catch myself, and come back swinging with both hands.

Getting knocked back down, feeling the kicks to the head and noticing vaguely that my sight has gone from the double vision of drunkenness to so many images it's like staring into a funhouse mirror, a mirror showing hands and feet flying at each other.

Black against white, white against black. All so consumed by our differences and own fears that there is no thought, no hesitation. Only the hate we have all learned, or maybe got genetically programmed with when we were all varicolored monkeys swinging through the trees, primates whose priority was to kill any simian creature different from ourselves, and, true to our natures, in a tradition dating back to the dawn of mankind, under the fading winter Indiana sun the dance of death is replayed one more time.

The foot that's been kicking me in the head hesitates for a second too long and I get it trapped, both my hands locked around the ankle, twisting; feeling the leg start to break, hearing the popping of ligaments and tendons separating as I throw all my weight against the knee.

Pulling the owner of the foot down and getting a grip on his jacket, smashing an elbow into his eye and leveraging myself up as his partners put the boots to me until I can fasten my teeth into his cheek, as the thick coppery taste of blood fills my mouth and the riot siren drowns out the screams of the guy getting his face bitten open and the goon squad is on us.

Like the good programmed animal I am I keep grinding my teeth through his flesh as his guys are kicking my ribs in, not gonna stop till they kill me and that's what they intend to do when the goon squad hits all of us and a police baton smashes me into the concrete. The walkway feels warm as I melt into it, thinking, This was really stupid, man, really fuckin' stupid.

Handcuffed to the hospital gurneys, whites on one side of the infirmary, blacks on the other. The overhead fluorescent lights flickering and the smell of disinfectant, blood, and puke mixing with the adrenaline hanging in the air combine with our muttering at each other. Hostility and anger escalating like a grand mal seizure.

Monkey Man is black as tar against the white sheet on the gurney he's cuffed to. He's all the way nuts, got his nickname from the way he looks and acts. Built like a gorilla, muscle-bound without being a weight lifter, an intimidating dude who's the main shot caller for the colored car when Big George isn't around.

Monkey Man and George don't get along at all. George is a guy who takes care of business. Gives respect and gets it. Monkey is a racist to the bone, willing to victimize anybody regardless of race, creed, or color but consumed by his hatred of whites. The only thing that keeps him in check is fear, and right now he's got the upper hand. His crew has us way outnumbered. But that's nothing new, they have their car, we have ours, and a wreck is on the way.

Monkey hasn't got the brains God gave a turnip but is a very dangerous guy, looks us each in the eye—Phil, Red, a new white guy named Burt, and me—says, "Gonna kill you fuckin' cracker motherfuckers." Points at me with his free hand and says, "You gonna go down first, mo'fucker. Sendin' yo blue-eyed devil ass back to hell."

My first day in Plainfield I had walked into the head as Monkey and a couple of his partners were raping a Puerto Rican kid.

Walking past the showers I heard grunting and turned to see what was happening. The kid was on his knees, Monkey straddling him, pumping into his mouth as the kid gagged and puked around Monkey Man's dick.

There was blood all over the place. This youngster hadn't given it up without a fight. Not that it did him any good.

For a second I paused, thinking that maybe I should try and be a hero. Then walked on, pissed in the urinal. Washed my hands and strolled out, doing my best to look like I didn't care, like I was so tough that walking over corpses to get to breakfast wouldn't affect my appetite, but so scared and sick to my stomach that when I got into the TV room I puked into the waste can.

When Monkey tried to jack me for my Camels later that day I was in a state of terror, I knew it was coming and didn't know how I was gonna act.

I was so scared that as soon as he started talking shit I head-butted him, grabbing his shirt in one hand and his hair in the other, smashing my forehead into his face, flattening his nose and hearing teeth break, trying to kill him.

In the fight that followed I sustained plenty of damage but Monkey Man ended up hurt, bad. And I kept my Camels. That insane fear saved my ass.

But the missing front tooth in his demented smile reminds him that he doesn't like me every time he looks in a mirror.

Now I can feel that fear rising in me like rock and roll, like intravenous methamphetamine, like rabies in a pit bull. Hammering itself into full-on rage, vision blurring from adrenaline and hearing my voice sounding like it's running through an echo chamber, saying, "Ain't nothin' between us but air, pal. What's up, Monkey; is your killer broken?"

Monkey is sitting up and all his guys are moving with him, he gets his feet on the floor and says, "Broken? My killer ain't never broken, peckerwood."

Burt is a tall, rawboned white boy, stringy muscles and pale blue eyes. He spits on the floor, looks at the blood and mucus that comes out, and drawls to the room in general, "Cut your hearts out, ya chickenshit watermelon-eating toads."

Monkey's road dog, Willie, a big pimply negro who's so fat his belly hangs halfway to his knees and his arms look like balloons filled with cottage cheese, starts on Cross-Eyed Phil: "Been fuckin' your momma, peckerwood, gonna go all up in you next."

Phil's swinging his feet to the floor, handcuff dragging the hospital bed behind him as he rushes Willie, saying, "Shee-it, come on with it, nigger, rip the eyes outta your head and skull-fuck ya, just like I did your daddy."

The gurneys are tipping over, my heart going like a jackhammer, hurtling across the room the handcuff ripping into my wrist as the bunk drags behind me. It's an instant replay, once again me and Monkey are doing our best to kill each other. As he grabs my throat with his free hand one of my steel toes makes contact with his shinbone and I can feel the bone and steel impacting through my entire body as I get set to kick him again.

Around us bedlam reigns, everyone screaming "Peckerwood" and "Nigger" and, almost in harmony, "Gonna kill ya," all doing our best to get out of our restraints and at each other, and the guards come running in, not only ready but enjoying their work. Each of them holding a can of Mace in one hand, a billy club in the other.

Spraying the blinding streams of chemical fire on us till there's no chance of resistance when they start in with the clubs.

For the moment the only thought any of us have is getting air past our swollen-shut throats and the burning searing pain that goes from the bottom of your lungs down, making your legs spasm and your bowels loosen and ripping back up through your eyes and forehead like rusty, acid-dipped concertina wire through your flesh.

The sound of the guards laughing at us when they go to work with their batons. Registering through the pain and inside my head I'm screaming the words "I'm really, really fucking stupid."

three

Smith swings the door to my cage open, says, "Judgment time, boy."

My stomach is in knots but the thing is you can never show fear. You have to look and act like no matter what happens you don't care.

I know I'm facing exclusion as a juvenile. Going to the pen scares the shit out of me. I have no control over anything. I want to get loaded so bad that I feel like screaming. Stand up as straight as I can, puffing my chest out. Trying to look as tough as possible. Face deadpan. Show no emotion. Practice makes perfect.

Stroll into the hallway and take in the endless line of locked doors, lunch trays sitting in front of them. It's a full house.

Anywhere you go you need a trusty, called a red cap, to escort you. Big George is the head cap for the whole institution and he's here waiting. I know this is no accident.

If George is one of the caps there to escort me to my exclusion hearing, then he asked for the assignment, or maybe I should say assigned himself. He's the number one shot caller for the black car. Six feet plus of light-skinned, hazel-eyed, dangerous negro. The other cap is Mario, one of the Puerto Rican cats I know from the gym.

I wonder if George is gonna try and move on me. In here not only is blood thicker than water but color is much more important than friendship. I know I got no chance of beating George in a fair fight. I got no weapon.

Fuck it.

As we hit the yard and start the walk to the administration building I ask, "So what's up, do we got problems?"

George laughs, says, "Yeah, motherfucker, they exclude your ass, who am I gonna play chess with? You a fool motherfucker, bit that nigger's face all the way open, looks like he got a pussy growing out of his cheek. I guess when your dogs call ya 'dog' they mean it."

I just look at George and shrug, saying those all-encompassing words "Fuck it." Then, "I think I got a shot. Maybe I'll be here for another minute or two. Teach ya how to play."

George raises one eyebrow. "Seems like I play as good as you do, fool. If they don't roll ya up it's on like Vietnam, two outta three for a pack."

I smile at this fool and feel good that friendship is more important than warring, at least for this second in time. I tell him, "On like Vietnam, long as I'm here."

He slips a pack of Camels and a book of matches to me and as I stuff them into my pocket says, "These from your boy Cross-Eyed Phil."

"Thanks. Tell Phil thanks. That's a good motherfucker."

George laughs and says, "Yeah, ain't bad for a white boy. Good luck."

Mario's face is blank as he says, "Yeah, good luck, carnal."

I just grin, knowing I look confident. My guts are in knots as I say, "Gracias."

The table is oak, polished to a high gloss, the chairs actually upholstered; the six correction officers and the shrink are staring down the table looking at me to try and determine if I'm crazy. Like they think they're so perceptive it would show through the bruises on my face, like I'm so stupid I'm going to tell them that all I want to do is get the hell out of here and get loaded.

As they're looking through my jacket and whispering to each other my mind is running scenarios, imaginary conversations with these guys to keep itself amused: "A little heroin, some coke, a taste of whiskey. You understand, don't ya, fellas? Take the edge off. Know what I mean?" . . . "You're an idiot with no moral fiber. You're not only stupid, you're crazy, nuts, bona fide looney tunes. First you participate in a riot. Now you say you want to use illegal drugs." . . . "What riot? Shit happens, fellas. Don't see how I had any choice. Do you, fellas? Like I said, I just wanna take the edge off, just a little teeny speedball. Breakfast of champions. What the hell do ya mean I'm nuts?" . . . "Did I stutter? You are insane. Top your sentence out in state prison. Asshole. Then do the additional time you get for participating in this little conflict that got you back in front of us." . . . "Bad idea, fellas. Escaping is hard enough from IYC, it's damn near impossible from Pendleton. Gonna stay here if I can, fellas."

The voice of Fred Reynolds, the superintendent, cuts through the voices bouncing around in my head as he reads my file out loud.

"Robert Prine, arrests going back to ten years of age. . . . Vandalism, Theft, Grand Theft, GTA, Possession of Controlled Substance, Burglary, Strong-arm Robbery, Burglary, Possession of Heroin for Sales, and Concealed and Unregistered Firearm. Got arrested for this last one after you overdosed shooting a heroin-cocaine combination."

He pauses and swipes his hand over his balding head, trying to neaten hair that isn't there, directs his stare at me, brown eyes behind thick glasses, thin face on a sprinter's body, the suit that he's wearing worn and baggy. He flips the page and shakes his head, purses his lips, and makes a humming noise.

"Uh-huh, hmmm . . . The State of Indiana has had you in custody for a little over a year, Mr. Prine. . . . You are not what one would call a model inmate, sniffing glue . . . fighting . . . sniffing gasoline . . . escape attempt . . . drunk . . . used a weapon on another inmate, hit him with a mop wringer it says here. Hmmm . . . another escape attempt . . . And now involved in a riot, racial at that. You have managed to go from our school program, to a unit clerk, to barber, and are now working on the garbage detail. Hmmm, a steady downward spiral if you will. Some men are determined to succeed. You are obviously driven to fail. My initial reaction is to help you with that goal, waive your juvenile status. Ship you to Pendleton with the idiots who are doing life on the installment plan. Do you have anything to say, Mr. Prine?"

I'm tongue-tied, have no idea how to tell this guy what's really up. I don't have any desire to be a badass or a hood. I just want to get loaded and be left alone. The only time I fight is when I've got to. The guy I hit with the mop wringer was twice my size and scared the shit out of me. As far as escaping goes . . . I got to get out of here. Simple as that. I have got to get out of here. The thing is that nothing matters. These guys are going to do what they want regardless of how eloquent I am. The only thing I can do is make my situation worse. Excuses don't cut it.

I say, "I made a lot of mistakes. . . . This last thing, it wasn't a riot. It just happened. I was just there."

Reynolds turns to Dr. Pike, the shrink, and asks, "Any input on this, Doctor?"

Dr. William Pike, a roly-poly, happy little guy. We have a good rapport, actually like each other. I'm hoping he'll go to bat for me. He tamps his pipe and refers to the file in front of him, saying, "Definitely. As you may know, Fred, this inmate has shown incredible potential. Mr. Van Horn, who runs our school program, gave young Bobbie the highest recommendation possible. Of course he quit school. But his potential is great. His IQ extremely high."

Referring to the file, Pike smiles at Reynolds and continues, "As we both know, Robert is no longer in school. As you observed, he's now on the garbage detail. A desire to fail. Very well put, sir. By the time this lad was ten his father had broken almost every bone in his body. We have here a very bright individual who's been programmed to self-destruct. Sending him to Pendleton would only compound the problems already existing."

Dr. Pike sighs, frowns, and goes on. "Many of his difficulties stem from his dependence on drugs and alcohol. While there is no real treatment for this problem, he has been making progress in therapy. I would urge you to leave him here."

Reynolds looks around the table and gets a couple of shrugs. No one really gives a shit one way or the other. Except me. He focuses back on me and asks, "What do you think, Mr. Prine, can you overcome your need to fail? For once, attempt to succeed? Work on your drug problem?"

I'm staring at the table, thinking that it would be nice to be able to tell Reynolds what's really up. He isn't bad people, he just wants to do his job.

And I just want to do mine. Get the hell out of here and get loaded. Looking directly into his eyes I say, very respectfully, "Yes."

The word comes out like my throat was sandpapered. Before the goon squad rushed us, Monkey Man had done a good job of crushing my larynx. The Mace had finished the job. I'm thinking that I hope that Monkey's leg is broken, wishing that I'd had a chance to use my boots on his head. Realizing that the silence is hanging, and focusing on Reynolds and the questioning look on his face, I wheeze, "Absolutely." Meaning the opposite of what he's thinking, but feeling good about not lying. Absolutely . . . next time I run I'm going to make it. Absolutely I'm going to work on my drug problem . . . I'm going to consume all I can get.

Reynolds stares at me for a second and asks, "Absolutely what?"

My stomach sinks. He's going to back me into a corner, and one of my personal rules is don't lie. Evade, sidestep, whatever. Don't lie. If I have to define "absolutely" I'm finished. I hesitate and say, "Absolutely . . . sir?"

He looks at me like I'm a laboratory experiment gone awry, says, "Two more weeks solitary. One more infraction of any rule and you are on your way to the big house. Do you understand this, Mr. Prine?"

"Absolutely, sir."

Red's working the heavy bag, looping rights and lefts, they have plenty of impact but every time he throws a shot he drops his hands. I'm holding the bag and yelling at him, "Leaving your head open, wood. Keep your hands up, Red."

As he modifies the way he's holding his hands he's got both feet planted and now I'm yelling, "Dance, motherfucker, gotta move those feet, think they're just gonna stand there? Dance in and out, dog, sling 'em."

Red runs out of gas, strips the bag gloves off, and throws them to me, saying, "Your turn, motherfucker. Let's see how the Great White Hope himself does . . . son of a bitch."

I got my hands up shooting lefts, dropping down and getting right crosses off and then hooking after the cross, got my hands up and feet moving. Feeling good, everything is working right. The bag jerking on its chain and knocking Red back with every power shot. Even the jabs are connecting with a lot of force, and Red sticks his head around the bag and yells, "Look pretty like a motherfucker, but ya hit like a little girl. What's up wi' that, wood?"

I shoot a double hook and finish with a right cross that knocks Red and the bag back a couple of feet.

Winded, drunk on endorphins. Gasping for breath, I manage to say, "Little girl with brass knuckles maybe. Carrot-head motherfucker."

Walking to the wall and both sliding down it, ending up squatting side by side. Covered with sweat and breathing hard. I pull the last Camel out of my pack, split a match in two and light it, take a drag and hand it to Red.

As we pass the smoke back and forth, Red asks, "So what's up? Big George and Monkey are ready to kill each other. George is fed up with Monkey's bullshit. He fucks his own people over more than anybody else, and Big George don't like it a bit. This is the time—are ya gonna talk to George or what? Only reason I'm askin' is, I can't and Phil won't, he says him and Big George got an understanding. What the fuck is an understanding? He's the only white boy in here that could take that big old nigger one on one. He don't mind breakin' Fat Willie's jaw, he's down for murder one if he's gotta be. But him and George got some kinda fuckin' understanding. What kinda shit is that?"

I stare at Red for a second, wondering if he thinks I'm brain-dead, like maybe I don't know the last little dance was only a prelim and realize that if Red had any idea how to talk to Big George without escalating the conversation into murder one he would have already done it.

I grin at him and say, "Yeah, man, I kick it with George pretty often. What's up is Phil's on his way home, he don't wanna blow it. I'd steer clear of this crap too, if I was him. I just got outta the hole. Gimme a day or two. Try and get this bullshit squashed. If him and Monkey are warring, it gives us a better shot. The PRs hate Monkey, I hate Monkey, shit, everybody hates that fuckin' Monkey Man except his baby-raping partners."

Red mutters, "Oh, yeah."

"If George wants his ass," I point out, "Monkey and his road dogs are dead fuckin' meat. Big George is a reasonable human being. If Monkey fucked up, George won't cosign his bullshit anymore . . . I hope."

Red takes a toke and blows the smoke out through his nose, hands me the Camel, and says, "I don't know, dog. First, last, and always, George and Monkey are both black. I think that is gonna count for more than who's right or wrong. Know what I mean?"

Truth is, I don't know what George is gonna think or say. I do know that if we can't get this shit resolved, life is going to get real unpleasant. Strategically, I can enlist the Puerto Rican crew, just on the basis of giving them a shot at Monkey. There are a few different white cars and the tension is so high any squabbles we had have gone by the wayside. Like Red said, I got a gift for gab; now that gift has got me stuck right in the middle of the madness. If George won't cosign some kind of treaty, the shit is on like Vietnam . . . and guaranteed, I'll miss my train.

I say, "I know whatcha mean, ace. Believe me, I'm gonna do everything I can to get this chilled. The beef started with the one dude that gave the pruno up. Lester Liplock, am I right?"

"Yeah, but Liplock is Monkey's punk. The whole thing is a fuckin' mess. Somebody's gonna end up dead behind this. I don't want it to be one of us."

"You ain't lying, dog." The Camel is burnt down so low that it's singeing our fingers, and as I flick it into the middle of the floor, I repeat, "It's a fuckin' mess . . . certainly is, Red. It's a motherfuckin' mess."

As we're walking out of the gym I spot Big George playing basketball. We nod at each other. That's as far as communication can go except under special circumstances.

It's Big George's move, I have his king in check with my knight, he's only got one way to go that I can see. He reaches for the Kool burning on the edge of the table, takes a huge drag, and says, "Think ya got me, huh?" and moves out of check.

I'm studying the board and George at the same time; there's something wrong but I'm not sure what it is. We've been chess competitors and have swapped books ever since I came in. George is one of the few other compulsive readers in this institution. Our shared addiction to the printed word was what initially overcame the hostility we would have normally had for each other in this little piece of reality we share.

Over the months of doing battle over chessboards and exchanging books it was inevitable that a friendship, however guarded, would develop. Being aware of the rules and the limits of our relationship has let us tell each other things about ourselves that we couldn't talk about with our own cars.

Knowing that your friend is also your enemy is almost freeing. The lines are clear. We talk so much shit about each other's race that as individuals we don't need to keep up our normal image.

So it's OK to ask, "What's up, pal? I know this shit we're trying to get squashed don't got ya this down in the mouth. Shit, if Monkey's fuckin' with your own people, just hit him. Him and his little boyfriend are who started this shit anyhow. I gotta tell ya, George, it seems like there's somethin else fuckin' with ya. What's up?"

He looks over his shoulder, then back at me, says, "Your move, Bobbie."

Red is strolling by, on patrol. George recognizes the move and smiles. He's not going to say anything in front of his guys or my guys. We both know this. I put him back in check with my knight. Once Red's out of earshot, I ask, "So what's happening, big man?"

"I'm thinking about skying. I been hanging in here 'cause my girl wanted to get married when I got out. My pop's in da pen, and Moms went missing, anyhow my grandma was gonna put us up. Get on up outta here and get me a job. . . . Two weeks ago, Grandma passed away. Yesterday I gots a letter. My girl's goin' wid some college-educated nigger to St. Louis. I still got two years to go here. Shee-it, Bobbie, I run, ain't a one a' dese mothafuckas gonna chase me. Catchin' me be they worst nightmare."

He slides his bishop across the board and takes my knight, asking, "How you like me now?"

"No better than I liked you before. . . . Makes sense to me, skying that is. First chance I get I'm gone like a chicken to fuckin' corn. Make a plan, George, don't just run. Even being boss cap, what'll happen is five, ten, shit, twenty of these motherfuckers who you think are your friends will climb on your back. Don't matter how bad you are, they'll drag ya down. Make a plan."

"I got one."

I study him for a minute, ask, "What is it?"

He looks up from the board and laughs at me, saying, "Shee-it. Tell you, I be woke up some morning and find out your white ass is all the way gone. And my black ass would still be stuck here. Play chess, fool."

I shoot my castle down the board and nail his bishop, then say, "So what we gonna do about this situation? I'm gonna sky, you gonna sky. But till then we're both stuck here. Are ya willing to let Monkey or his punk sling one on one with one of our guys? Try and get this shit chilled?"

"One on one?"

"Yeah."

"You know it's gonna be the Monkey Man."

"Check it out, Moppa was the one got busted with the brew Lester gave up. How about Moppa and Lester one on one? Ain't neither of them killers, but they both can brawl. Nobody gets hurt real bad. Everybody's happy."

"Joe Moppa?"

"Yeah, man, him and Lester Liplock, why the fuck not? The question is, can ya get Monkey to chill?"

"Shee-it, the battle of de year. Fuck dis Monkey Man, I'd pay to see that fight. I'll handle Monkey. Joe Moppa and Lester Liplock, huh? It's on, Bobbie. That Liplock is one tough fuckin' faggot. He goin' kick your boy Moppa's ass. I'm down with it. Long as you-uns leaves it one on one."

I roll a smoke, state tobacco. Split a match. Say, "Shee-it, my man, Moppa will knock all the kink outta Lester's hair. Hit him with so many combinations he thinks he's a Mosler fuckin' safe. Beat his ass so thoroughly Liplock will think Vietnam is a love-in."

Light the rollie. Tastes like cancer. Ask, "Long as *we* leave it one on one?"

The cans of slop are freezing cold, if they make contact with your skin it rips away. The only good thing is that the hordes of flies that would be buzzing around us in warmer weather are absent.

Me and Roberto are working the truck, standing in the sloshing swill as the cans are handed up to us, emptying them, doing our best to minimize the amount of slop that splashes all over us. Throwing the empty cans back down to Flaco and Juan.

It's a four-man crew now. Pinhead finally got shipped to the nuthouse.

We finish the last set of cans and sit on the sides of the truck inhaling the pleasant aroma of the breakfast we'll shortly be serving to tomorrow's bacon.

As the pickup truck bounces over the dirt road leading to the farm and, more specifically, to the pigpen, Roberto pulls out a bag of tobacco and rolls a smoke. Passes the bag to me.

Tell him, "Thanks, bro."

I'm following suit, filling the paper, tamping the brown flakes down, rolling it tight and licking the edge, crimping the ends, and lighting it off Roberto's smoke. He says to me, "Hey, carnal . . . my people are saying that the thing with the niggers ain't gonna get squashed. Monkey and his boys are gonna take Big George outta the box. Monkey wants to call all the shots. And even if George is there, Liplock is sayin' if Moppa wins it's all about swords and shields. They gonna bust a move. On the serious. Right now they got the big car. You white boys got a few hitters. We gonna be there, and we got some hitters. I want some of Monkey. We gonna roll with ya."

I look up and Flaco and Juan are nodding their heads. They both look as serious as slow death. Flaco is a featherweight, his army coat is so big on him he looks like an eight-year-old wearing his dad's clothes. As I catch his eye he pulls a sharpened piece of rebar halfway out of the sleeve of his coat and smiles.

I look at the rust-covered, razor-sharp piece of iron and say, "Yeah, that's a bonecrusher all right. Maybe ya won't need it."

Juan is darker than most of the so-called black guys in this joint, almost the color of tires, hence for about one day his nickname was Ilanta. The nickname was dropped after he broke a guy's jaw for using it. He's Puerto Rican and proud of it. Juan doesn't have a real great command of the English language yet, but he knows what's up. He smiles ear to ear and says, "Yea, mang. Chongo muerte." And starts laughing so hard tears are rolling down his face.

I take a drag off the rollie and shrug, look down and watch the slop swirl around our rubber boots. Feeling in my guts that I have as much control over this situation as I do over the tornadoes that sometimes hit Indiana. That I'm as trapped in the events unfolding as a guy whirling inside that tornado, feeling his limbs breaking and tearing off, waiting for the wind funnel to drop him from the height of the storm clouds feeding into it to the ground waiting below.

Looking up and smiling at my PR friends, unable to express any of this and saying, "Fuck it. Whatever happens . . . just fuckin' happens."

Taking another hit off the rollie and then flipping it into the pigs' breakfast. Tripping on the slowly drowning ember.

Strolling past Monkey and his crew when I come out of the chow hall that afternoon and he starts shadow boxing, watching me. He's trying for intimidation. As I go past them one of his partners makes a kissing noise and I look into his muddy eyes, leaving my face completely blank. Filing him away for future reference. Knowing that I got no backup and if I give these guys any excuse I'm gonna get mobbed right here and right now.

Looking around for something to use as a weapon, seeing nothing.

Now figuring the best route to take if I have to run. I'm not going to try and fight ten guys. I keep my face blank, moving, putting one foot in front of the other. Heart trying to jump out of my chest.

Monkey shooting combinations into the air saying, "Um-hmmm, goat ropers, klansmen, sodbusters, nazi motherfuckers . . ." And his guys muttering around him, mad-dogging me.

Think if I have to I'm going to stab this motherfucker. You can't escape if you're dead. And if it kicks again it won't be about fistfighting this time. Kill or be killed.

I'm on the way to dig up my bonecrusher. A piece of insurance I made and then buried, hoping that it would stay beneath the ground, unneeded. A homemade sword. Eighteen inches of rebar filed down to a needle point. Club 'em or stab 'em, an excellent weapon.

I keep my face blank and keep walking. When I'm almost out of earshot I hear Monkey loud-talking, announcing to the whole yard, "Big George ain't shit. That cracker ain't shit. They gonna go down. Yeah, man. The devils goin' down."

* * *

The snow is falling so thickly that it piles on your shoulders if you stand still, fills your eyes and goes up your nose. Would bury you, given the chance.

Giving everything a softness and a look of purity. Past hip-deep, so much snow so fast that everything is on lockdown. The guards can't go home, no shift change.

Sandwiches for breakfast lunch and dinner, the snow's too deep to get real food from the kitchen to all the different chow halls.

I'm staring out the barred window, almost able to feel the peace that exists just on the other side of it. The wind blowing flurries of virginal white powder through the gathering twilight like ghosts or spirits rising towards the sky. And the bonecrusher stuck inside my boot is freezing cold. It has its own life, and its own temperature. Cold.

The point scraping against my heel, the tape-wrapped handle stopping right below my knee. The top of my boot laced tightly enough to hold the steel securely, loosely enough so I can fill my hand with no hang-ups or hesitation.

Every time I move it talks to me, saying, "You're boss now, they mob ya, you got me. I'll stop their hearts, ruin their lives. Fuck it. Get busy now. Why wait? Do it."

And I'm more scared now that I got it. Praying that it stays in my boot. That things will chill out. That I can bury my homemade sword unused.

But at the same time there's that part of me that listens to it, the part of me that is terrified. That knows that violence and blood will quiet the madness running through me.

That part of me that's going to survive no matter what.

Staring at the snow falling like a white wall, feeling the cold radiate through the glass, hearing the muttering behind me, everyone talking low. Don't know if the tension running through my body is really part of the atmosphere or if it's self-created.

Am I the only one that feels like screaming, going berserk, spilling blood just to get it over with, or is it a virus in the air that has infected us all?

*   *   *

Sweat is running down my sides, collecting in the small of my back and mixing with the snow hitting my face to form ice. The knit cap is pulled all the way down to my eyebrows. Got a towel wrapped around my throat and lower face to keep as much heat in as possible. The army coat and khakis I'm wearing are soaked and one minute I'm freezing and the next burning up from exertion and fever.

It looks like crystalline cotton, light and fluffy. Soft.

Got news for ya, pal. It's shaved ice, frozen fragmented water. Each shovelful has a real, tangible, weight. After bending, scooping, and throwing tons of it, each of those shovelfuls rips into your back and shoulders. The skin under your arms starts to chafe and the gloves covering your hands don't stop the blisters.

After a few hundred more yards it feels like you've been stabbed, or maybe baseball-batted in the lower back. The chafed skin under your arms becomes raw seeping wounds, the blisters oozing holes burnt through your hands.

But the deal is you don't snivel and you don't complain.

The guard put me, Big George, and Roberto on the front shovels, breaking the ice, clearing the walkways leading all over the institution. Making the load light enough for the guys coming behind us with the real snow shovels and scrapers.

Ethnic balance, one white, one black, and one brown, all competing to see who's going to fold first, shoveling as fast as possible. The ethnically balanced racially correct mix from the front of the line going all the way through to the end. And at the front we're all working our asses off to make sure we don't look bad. None of us is going to let anyone outwork us. Not unless it's one of our own.

After what seems like eternity, reaching the main count area between the school and vocational buildings and the guard yells, "Break for ten, smoke 'em if you got 'em."

I've been smoking rollies for a while now and my hands don't feel steady enough to roll one. Catching my breath, watching Big George take a pack of Kools out of his jacket and light one.

He lifts one eyebrow and offers the pack to me. The number one rule in the book of unwritten rules is: you don't talk, give or take smokes, or in any way fraternize with anyone from the enemy car. Except in clearly defined situations. This is *not* one of those situations.

George knows this, I know this. Which is why I do a double-take to make sure that I am not confused. Feel the pressure of eyes on me as I'm looking at George's pack.

Glance up and Monkey is staring at us. Behind him Red, open-mouthed, next to Red, Flaco. Take the smoke extending from the end of the pack and split a match, light it. Say, "Thanks, George."

Look back at the line and Red's removed his knit cap and is scratching his head, still open-mouthed. Flaco's watching Roberto. And Monkey is spinning and spitting onto the frozen cement.

George looks as serious as a guy can get. He has thought this out. He extends the pack to Roberto and asks, "Want one?"

Roberto freezes for a second, looks over at Flaco, who shrugs. And then Roberto reaches for the pack and shakes one out. Extending his hand to get a light from my smoke, he stares at George for a second and then says, "Thanks . . . amigo."

George smiles, takes the pack back, puts it into his jacket, and says, "Ain't no thang."

Roberto heads for Flaco and the rest of his car. I glance at Red, who's now conversing with Phil. Behind them Monkey is cliqued with a group of his dogs, glaring at us. I take a hit off the Kool and say, "I gotta tell ya, I think ya lost your motherfuckin' mind, George. Monkey's gonna use this against ya. You know that . . . right?"

Big George flips his smoke into the snow, looks over at Monkey and spits on the ground, says, "This shit ain't racial, ain't about movin' on a bunch of klansmen or some kinda shit. Monkey wants to play all that race shit. It's just an excuse. It's about him and me. I already called the shot. He don't like it. Fuck him in his nasty black ass. Send him and alla his dogs to the pound, put their asses to sleep if they ain't careful."

As he's saying this, George is standing talking to a white guy. Me. Most of his car is grouped around Monkey, mad-dogging us, and I got no idea what to do. The rules that we live by don't have this situation anywhere in them. All I know is I'm not walking away.

Take a hit off the Kool and flip it away, say, "Those fuckin' things taste like shit. Why do ya smoke 'em?"

" 'Cause badass niggers smoke Kools, and believe me, Bobbie . . . I'm one badass nigger."

I check out Monkey's crew, look at my crew—who are busy ignoring me talking to George—and I say, "Yeah, you one badass nigger. Ya got balls, that's for sure."

"Like a Christmas tree. Like a mo'fuckin' Christmas Tree. You kinda tough yoself . . . peckerwood."

"Uh-huh."

As the guard yells for us to get back to work I grin at this fool and say, "If your escape plan is so great maybe we oughta kick it around. Sky outta this bullshit."

"Shee-it. I like ya but I don't trust ya. Nope. That's my ace in da hole, ain't sharin' it with nobody. I run alone. Came in alone, leave alone. My daddy always said, 'Trust no man that ain't blood, black, white, or brown.' And you ain't blood."

"Don't blame ya a bit. Your daddy sounds like a wise man."

My shovel cuts into the ice and snow. Lifting it up and throwing it through the air is a relief from my own confusion. The pain cutting through my hands and shoulders a welcome distraction. Focusing on outshoveling George and Roberto gives me a temporary escape from my mind.

four

Moppa's eyes are homicide red, a line of drool going from his mouth to a viscous pool on the concrete floor of his kingdom, the utility shed. He crouches rocking back and forth and the trail of spit twists and turns in the air while he's visiting whatever planet or alternate universe the gasoline fumes have transported him to.

The gas can seems to be miles away as my arm stretches like Silly Putty towards it, finally making contact, and my hand drags it to me, not in slow motion but in the fragmented reality brought on by inhalants. It's like being stuck in a poorly working movie projector, life reduced to a series of black-and-white still photographs and you're jumping from one picture to the next. The ticking of dying brain cells so loud you can hear it. Tick, tick, tick, tick without beginning or end . . . ticking forever and finally the rich rush of the fumes filling your lungs and shutting your brain down, dreaming stronger and more vivid than life could ever be, and I'm breathing as quickly and deeply as I can 'cause I got to get out of here. Here being my head and the body that transports me around, here being Plainfield State Reformatory in the state of Indiana, here in the USA, here on planet fucking Earth, and I got no IDEA how much time has passed but the front of my shirt is covered in drool and the can is now in front of Red, who is talking a mile a minute, eloquently and persuasively, making points and closing deals in a language that no one could possibly understand but him. He's looking at and gesturing to the empty space in front of him. The audience as enthralled as it's invisible. Red's a happy kid.

Moppa drags the can in front of him, looks at me for a second or a century, I still don't know which, and says, "My family loves me." Puts his face into the can, takes a few huffs, and continues.

"They in the can. Soon as I get the tick, I can hear em. Tellin' me. They love me. They really do."

Moppa smiles and the drool is already starting to drip off his chin and he buries himself in the fumes until he's all the way gone and now it's my turn.

Recreational therapy.

The thing about filing through the bars is it takes time, lots of time, and time is one thing I don't have. This place is going to go off like World War Three and if I'm still here I'm going to participate. And end up with all the time in the world. Mandatory on the participation. No ifs, no ands, no buts; either you're in or you're out.

Red is spotting for me and I'm filing bars like a machine, blisters coming up, breaking and burning like hell. We have a total of fifteen minutes on dorm cleanup that I can work without getting spotted or interrupted.

The file has cut about a half inch into the first bar, got another quarter inch left and two bars to go. The idea is to get them filed to the point that I can just kick them out and dive for the ground. At the rate this is going it will take another two, maybe even three, months to get them to that point.

Red whistles and I shove the file down the front of my khakis. Blow the metal filings out the window and apply the soap, cigarette ash, and shoe polish mix to the cut in the bar to disguise it. Look at my endeavors and feel like screaming because it's going to take too long.

Red saunters over, pushing a broom, says, "Let's roll, dog. Man walking."

I grab my mop and finish mopping just as the day guard hits the top of the stairs. We stand and watch him as he inspects lackadaisically.

He hitches his pants up almost to chest level, coughs up phlegm and spits it on the floor, says, "Seems like you boys missed a goober." Laughs at his own vast wit and says, "Clean that snot up, then get your asses outta here."

As soon as he's out of sight I flip the drain protector in the shower open and attach the file to the wire holder that it hangs from. Not perfect, but a good hiding place. No guard will stick his hands into a slimy, germ-infested drain. Close the protector and finish cleaning up the cracker bull's spit.

Red grins at me and we grab our brooms, mops, etc., and get our asses out of there.

Kicking it in Joe Moppa's kingdom, the smell of freshly cooked meat filling the air, and I can feel my stomach rumbling, staring at the steak sandwiches that I stole from the officers' chow hall for the occasion, and we are all smoking Camels.

Joe has a gourmet batch of pruno that he made for today, life is grand. Tension is letting up at least for the minute and our crew is waiting for Red to show up to start Phil's checkout party.

When a guy gets released, if he's no good, checkout consists of an ass-beating that he'll never forget. When he's one of the fellas, a guy from your car, it's a sad thing, with the sadness left unacknowledged. For a friend, checkouts can run from a casual "See ya" or "Good luck" to a full-on spread. A spread is where you pool your resources—contraband food, cigarettes, drugs, alcohol—and you kick it. Talk shit. Almost a party. You're happy that your partner is getting out but you know you'll never see each other again unless it's in another institution.

You don't show pain, or sadness. The thought that you could care enough about another human being to miss him is not one that you can entertain. Emotions other than hate are counterproductive. So our faces are hard, the conversation the usual bullshit, just a little bit strained. Sort of forced. The focus is on the bite and kick of the Camels, the steak sandwiches, and the alcohol high on the way.

Red rolls into the utility room and the smoke halos him as he pulls the door shut. He grabs a Camel out of the pack that's on top of the upside-down mop bucket we're using for a table, does a spin, and says, "Check it out, fellas."

Pulling a red cap out of his back pocket, putting it on, and tilting the bill back, says, "Motherfuckers done gone crazy, made this white boy a trusty. Like a license to steal. We gonna be havin' thangs, the joint's thangs, other people's thangs, all kinda fuckin' thangs. Lettin' me work the hospital, how's zat, fellas, drugs . . . real drugs."

Reaching into his pocket and pulling out four Doriden and twelve codeines, says, "Almost a full load apiece, party's on, fellas.

Send this cross-eyed fool out in style, get him so fucked up if he makes it to the gate it'll be a miracle."

Joe Moppa's latest batch mixes with the loads, the steak is delicious. A spread worth writing home about if you had a home to write to.

And for a little while we create the illusion that we are real human beings with some control over the world we live in.

Loads have a vicious hangover, homebrew leaves you wanting to die. Put them together and what you get has got to be as close to hell as you'll ever want to experience. The cold from the floor cuts from my feet to the top of my head, the mess that comes out of my stomach feels like sulfuric acid on the way up. This is all before morning whistle. A great way to start the day. Doriden leaves you groggy, so not only are you in pain but you have no coordination. Making it to the chow hall is not a pleasant experience. Sitting there smelling the grease is worse. Feeding the pig's a joy. Going to the gym unavoidable, every movement awkward and painful. The only thing that makes the day bearable is the looks of agony worn by my friends. Misery does love company.

Razor is going from dorm to dorm delivering mail. He's one of the trusties that works as a runner. Got his cap on backwards so that the words "Fuck You" tattooed in Old English script across his forehead show clearly, his face set like rock in a homicidal frown 24/7, khakis pressed so sharp that the creases look like the razors he tapes to the ends of his fingers when fighting.

As he walks into Unit Three he throws the hand sign for "White" at me and motions with his head. I set the science fiction book I'm reading down to mark my seat in the TV room and wander in an indirect line towards him.

If you get spotted cliqueing the man knows that something is up, and I don't want any heat, I'm focused on getting out of here. Not being a warrior. Being fucking Houdini. Fat chance.

Razor's built like a bulldog, all chest and shoulders. As I roll up he says, "Yo, wood. It's kicking in the gym after dinner whistle. You,

Red, Cross-Eyed Phil, Moppa, and the rest of your crew be there."

"I'll be there. Phil don't need to come. He made parole. Going home tomorrow morning. Cut him some slack. The rest of our car is down. The PRs will ride with us. Leave Phil outta it."

"He's the only white boy on the yard that could go head up wid George. He's gotta be there."

"Nah," I say. "Big George ain't backin' Monkey. It's supposed to be Moppa and Liplock slingin' one on one."

"Shee-it, wood, were you born stupid or did ya have to work to get this way? Don't matter what George says, Monkey ain't gonna let Liplock get beat down, and if Liplock takes Moppa we gonna move anyhow. Tell Phil to be there or we green-light him."

I stare into Razor's eyes and know that he means what he's saying. He doesn't care if Phil made parole or not. A green light means that you have a hit on by your own people.

Razor is the head of the biggest white crew in the place and has the juice to do this. Hitting one of your own is easy, and every group victimizes its own people the most.

We're outnumbered and outgunned and this maniac is threatening to move on one of our own guys because he'd rather go home than take a chance on getting a new case, or getting killed.

I tell him, "Razor, you fuck with Phil, you got our whole car aimed right at ya. I'm the one that hangs with Roberto's crew. Without our guys ya lose them too. Fuckin' with Phil is a losing situation. You such a bonafide killer, hit Monkey yourself, save us all a lot of grief. Shit, if ya don't wanna razor-blade his ass I'll have Moppa make ya a bonecrusher. If we can chill it with a one-on-one we should go for it. If Monkey moves it's on. Otherwise we leave it one-on-one. That's the deal."

Razor scares me, that's a fact. He likes doing time, picking up a murder case is no big deal. Probably something he aspires to. The thing is that Razor isn't dumb, he's certifiably insane but he's got burning intelligence that is evident the first time you talk to him. I know that this is like handling nitroglycerine. If I play my cards wrong, make him feel like I'm disrespecting him, the only way I'm going to avoid getting cut to ribbons is to hit him first.

I tell him, "Save it for Monkey's car, give Phil a pass. At least one of us oughta make it outta here. Just 'cause you ain't had pussy since pussy had you don't mean we all gotta do life fuckin' young boys."

Razor laughs, then points to his forehead and says, "Read that, motherfucker. It says, 'Fuck You.' Ain't had pussy since pussy had me, huh? Shit. Fuck it. You and the rest of your car . . . be there. Monkey looks like he's gonna sneeze and we move. Period."

He points over my shoulder and says, "Leave the cross-eyed lame home. If he thinks getting laid is more important than representing his race, fuck him."

I turn my head and see Phil has been standing behind me. He's staring at Razor, says, "Sho-you-right." And walks away.

I feel the bonecrusher inside my boot cold against my skin. Keeping my face blank, say, "Don't sweat it, the rest of us will be there. Ready."

The sky is like burnished steel, the barren trees cutting into the horizon as naked as skeletons, concertina wire framing the picture as soot-colored clouds drift across the weak gray sun.

The garbage that we're shoveling into the troughs is being fought over by the walking pork that we feed every day. The biggest and by far the most aggressive pig in the pen is nicknamed Elmer. We watch as he knocks the other pigs out of his way, gobbling as much as he can and throwing scraps all over the pen as he shakes his head and bites at any hog audacious enough to come within reach of his teeth.

The smaller pigs get the scraps, unless they are hurt or crippled. Then their fellow swine eat them alive. The bigger pigs each have their own little segment of trough. Flaco points at Elmer and says, "Like Monkey Man, he'll eat the little pigs, starve his partners. The harder he fights the more he eats. The more he eats the sooner he's fuckin' bacon."

Roberto laughs, spits on Elmer, the pig, and says, "Oye, Flaco. What's up, so you saying your new handle is gonna be Farmer John?"

Flaco looks younger and smaller than ever, the adrenaline that's charging all of us flushing his cheeks and putting a crazy light into his eyes. He takes a drag from the cigarette he's smoking and says, "Yeah, mang . . . gonna make bacon, sausage, ham. Motherfuckin' Monkey Chops instead of pork chops. Farmer Flaco, fuck a whole bunch of Farmer John. Cut that Monkey from asshole to appetite. Cut him deep and cut him wide. Up and down and side to side."

I'm staring off into the distance, it feels like I'm watching a movie, like there's an invisible wall between me and the rest of the world, the words "You won't ever get out" going through my head like a chant, feeling a scream building in my chest that can't be released. Telling my brain to work, to try and talk this thing into something less than a full-scale riot. Knowing that it won't do any good and trying anyhow, saying, "Slow down, carnal, if Moppa and Liplock go one on one you don't gotta be Farmer Flaco. Let somebody else make the motherfucker into Monkey Chops."

Flaco looks at me with eyes as empty as the soul of the bonecrusher he's packing, as cold as the one I got in my boot, and says, "If you scared, lock up. Monkey's mine. Now's the time."

I know that there's nothing more to be said. The kid that Monkey was raping the first day I hit population was Flaco's little brother. He's waited till a time right for revenge. That time is now.

Roberto throws a right cross at my chest, pulls it, and asks, "You down, ain'tcha?"

My hand speed has always been good, I get off a jab–double hook combination at his chest, pulling all three shots short of contact, and say, "Yeah, dog. I'm down."

The chow halls are so quiet you can actually hear the sound of the spoons we eat with hitting our trays. Moppa looks all the way insane, twirling the end of his malnourished mustache spastically, his tray sitting in front of him untouched. Phil won't look up from his tray, hunched over it like paying enough attention to the slop in front of him will make everything else fade away. Red is eating slowly and methodically. As he gets to the cherry-filled paste that is dessert he mumbles, "You about a lucky motherfucker, Phil. What ya gonna do first? Get drunk or get laid?"

Phil keeps his head in his tray and grunts, "Uh-huh, fuck, shit."

Moppa can't let this pass, even as sprung as he is he's still on. Still talking shit, pokes Phil, and says, "Yeah, makes sense, fuckin' redneck is gonna fuck and then shit, make one hell of an impression on whatever poor broad is his first victim. Then again, if he sticks with barnyard animals he should be OK."

Moppa points at me and says, "You awful quiet, killer, whatcha think—will he go for the calves or graduate to full-grown cows?"

I rearrange the mess on my tray and do my best to laugh, saying, "Sheep, he'll do so many fuckin' sheep that when they see him coming the whole flock will go da-a-a-a-a-dy."

Phil finally looks up from his tray, takes a deep breath, and says, "You guys know I'm down, I ain't runnin' out on ya. It's time for me to get outta here. I got an obligation. I gotta keep it. It's about blood. Kin. When I beat my stepdaddy down I didn't mean to kill him. He wouldn't stop beatin' on my mama. I did what I had to. Did my time. Now I'm gonna do what I have to. I got somethin' I gotta take care of, and I can't do it from in here. Big George will handle his end, ya don't need me."

Red nudges Moppa and says, "If you ain't gonna eat that shit, slide your tray over here."

As he starts in on Joe Moppa's leftovers, Red says, "Don't know, boys, color is all that counts in here. I don't think George will stand up if Monkey's drivin' the car now. They both black, ain't gonna matter what's right. They gonna roll together."

Phil actually sits up straight and says, "Don't bet against Big George. That nigger don't got no backup in him. He's down for whatever he says. Got enough backbone for ten motherfuckers."

Red smiles and says, "Hope so, old wood, hope so. Fuck a couple sheep for me."

Moppa laughs his stuttering laugh. "I really fuckin' hope so. This skinny white boy's gonna be right in front, slingin' with that goddamn Liplock. If you wrong about George it's gonna be a fuckin' mess wid me in the middle. Keep your ass away from my midgets. Got it, redneck?"

As we get up to dump our trays I nudge Phil and say, "Good luck."

Phil whispers, "I owe ya, pal. Gettin' Razor offa me is what's lettin' me outta here on time and in one piece."

I wink and keep walking, thinking this is the last time I'll ever see Phil.

The stainless-steel mirror distorts my reflection, blue-gray eyes that hide the fear behind them, the waves in the steel making my nose appear more crooked than it is, the scar tissue showing more around my right eye than my left. Beat up a little, but the face don't look bad. Hair loaded down with Tres Flores, first choice of greasers and hoods nationwide.

Moppa's next to me brushing his mustache and Burt next to him checking to make sure he's bonarood.

Red walks into the head, puts his hands on his hips, spits on the floor, and says, "Ain't goin' to a beauty show. You silly motherfuckers look like it's visitin' day or checkouts. What-zup. It's time for glory or the graveyard, boys. Let's roll. Be there and represent, let 'em know these white boys are about somethin'."

Burt lifts his T-shirt to show Red the shank stuck in the front of his pants and asks, "Do what? Do who? I know ya ain't talkin' to me."

Red laughs and says, "Sho-you-right. Stay down, wood."

And we're two deep, shoulder to shoulder. Red and me in front, Burt and Moppa behind us, marching in lockstep to the gym.

Life is beyond real. So right here and overwhelming that I can hear the breath going in and out of us in four-part harmony, our feet crunching on the snow-dusted concrete, fabric scraping, hearts hammering. See every individual flake of snow, each barren twig on the bushes and trees, every grain in every brick. Smell the hair oil and cigarette smoke from hours before, even the odor of fresh shoe polish on my spit-shined boots, and feel every molecule of cold hard steel radiating from the bonecrusher stuck in my boot up my leg and through every cell in my body, and I want to start screaming.

I want to have a spike jammed into my arm pumping a chemical lobotomy into my bloodstream and there's no fucking way out.

As we roll into the gym, warmth and the smell of sweat hit me like a wall that is overlaid now by the rank odor of fear and adrenaline.

And the madness that we have worked so hard to create. Or that we are forced into.

Or that just appears like black magic, like we're all voodoo dolls waiting to get stuck.

Whatever causes the madness between races and religions and countries and neighborhoods.

It doesn't matter who's right or wrong or who did what to who.

The one thing I know is that every one of us there is trapped by a tangible force that you can feel like the bass coming out of the hugest speakers ever made, rattling through your bones and shaking your soul, setting up its own rhythm that is going to make you dance.

If you got two left feet. If you're on crutches. If you're in a wheel-chair. It doesn't matter.

You are going to dance. Like Nureyev, like old Bojangles, like Gene Kelly, like Fred Astaire.

You're going to dance, motherfucker, because your life depends on it.

There are small groups scattered through the gym, three, four guys per car. As we come drifting in, the small groups separate and flow back together as if choreographed, slowly forming into two masses, one white, the other, bigger mass black. In the front on our side, Razor, me, Red, and Moppa. Burt and Razor's guys fanning out behind us, mixed with the other white cars. Staring at us, Big George, standing next to Liplock with Willie next to him. Directly behind George, Monkey Man. The different black crews stretching deep into the gym.

As we face off, George and I nod at each other and I feel a rush of relief. Maybe, just maybe, this will stay one-on-one. If it does, my money is on Moppa. The best of all possible worlds, no riot, no se-rious bloodshed. If Moppa wins we look good, and even if he loses I know Liplock is in for a battle because Joe will sling 'em till he drops.

As they face off I notice the Puerto Rican crews and one Cuban car drifting in from the sides and Liplock starts loud-talking Joe Moppa, saying, "Fuckin' nazi, klansman motherfucker, this nigger is gonna kick yo white faggot ass."

Moppa raises his hands, says, "Faggot, huh, Liplock? Klans-man . . . who ya tryin' to bullshit?"

Pauses and looks around like he's trying to figure out who Lip-lock is yelling at, says quietly, "Nazi? I'm a Jew, you fucking moron." Then spins and hooks in one fluid, textbook motion, catching Lip-lock in the mouth, knocking him back. Now Joe's rushing him, throwing combinations as fast as he can, hands blurring as he bulls into Lester, driving him back until Liplock's going down, blood flowing from his mouth and nose, with Joe over him, kicking him in the head and ribs as Liplock's rolling away and Big George is stepping between 'em, hand at Joe's chest level, saying, "Slow down, Moppa, let da boy up. This a fistfight, not a . . ."

And everything comes apart as Monkey blindsides Big George with a piece of pipe, knocking him forward, and when George starts to spin, Monkey Man using the pipe like a ball bat and smashing it into George's face, making a sound like a home run hit in hell, and as George is crumpling, kicking him in the head and screaming at Liplock, "Do it, bitch, do it now or I'm gonna kill ya."

Liplock is on his feet now with a cutter in his hand, a toothbrush handle with razor blades melted into it, and Moppa's backing up trying to keep Liplock off him with jabs and we're getting rushed. As the bonecrusher fills my fist I see Razor slinging with both hands, fingers extended, razor blades cutting a swath into the mass of bodies that are rushing us, blood flying into the air like little red geysers till he folds in half, and Willie is pulling a sword out of Razor's guts and swinging it into the side of his head and screaming.

I'm using my bonecrusher like a club, feeling the steel rebar smashing into a skull and vibrating like a tuning fork, trying to get to Liplock to get him off Moppa, when one of Liplock's slashes catches Joe's throat and Joe Moppa is hemorrhaging a river down the front of his bonarood blues and I'm almost on Liplock when Burt catches him in the eye with his Arkansas toothpick, twelve inches of spring steel with a needle point. Monkey is rushing me, pipe held behind his head like a tomahawk, I can't spin fast enough to block and it hits the side of my head, I hear it more than feel it echoing through my entire body and my knees are buckling and I'm fighting for balance, watching Monkey coming around from the floor with his piece of pipe with enough force to take my head off, when he stops like a fly caught in aspic and starts screaming, suddenly standing on tiptoe and hopping convulsively, as his feet come off the ground seeming to levitate, hanging suspended, whirling.

Now I see Flaco behind him, both hands under Monkey's ass, lifting him into the air, blood running over Flaco's hands and out of the cuffs of Monkey's bonarood khakis, and Flaco's thrusting upwards lifting Monkey higher and then ripping both hands down to the floor. Dropping Monkey and revealing the blood-covered bone-crusher that he'd used as a handle to impale the guy that raped his little brother.

Two hitters from Monkey's car have got Red and are stomping him into the ground and Willie is spinning from stabbing one of the Puerto Ricans and has his shank raised above his head, bringing it down towards Red's chest, when I catch him with a downward shot.

The reason that a bonecrusher is called a bonecrusher is that it will go through bone, gristle, whatever . . . and as it tears through the top of his shoulder and deep into his chest, I rip, putting my full weight behind it, and the sharpened rebar opens him up like a fish getting gutted, tearing through his collarbone, the top of his ribs, and everything between. And I can't stop screaming and the world is soft and blurred and as I go after one of the guys who is holding Red, my foot slips in the blood that has turned into a wading pool and something, I don't know what it was or who holds it, catches me in the mouth and through a filter of copper-tasting, thick liquid I feel my front teeth on my tongue, as blood fills my mouth and washes them down my throat, then whatever it is hits me again and the world strobes and rainbows so quickly that the colors all run together, red into blue, and it hits again, feeling like it's cushioned, blue into green into yellow, and now it's like getting hit with a pillow and back into red and blue into swirling purple. Hearing the blow distantly but feeling nothing and finally red, blue, yellow, green into a soft, welcoming black. Thinking, Th-th-th-that's all, folks.

Probing the hole where my front teeth were and trying to whistle. The stitches holding my top lip together making it impossible. Limping from the bunk to the toilet-sink combination and pushing the chrome button set above the sink that works the water. Filling my mouth and spitting into the sink and there's only a light red film. Good deal. I'm healing.

Using the chrome button as a mirror, studying my blurred miniaturized image, wondering how I could look this bad and live. Head swollen up and stitched up. Poor head, an awfully hard head and one that is definitely no longer real good-looking. The expression "young and pretty" won't ever apply to me, getting older and more beat-up to go with it. Check again to see if the image swimming in the chrome has miraculously improved and laugh. Here's to you, old skull with a new face.

Cheers, motherfucker, you can take a beatin' and keep on tickin'.

Drinking and staring at the concrete wall, the feeling of doom that is always present when there's nothing to cover it filling my chest. Knowing that I'm on my way to the pen, but I'm too spent and burnt to feel anything other than resignation. Like I was a freight car in a train that had been going full speed around the railyard, circling, chasing its own tail uselessly and endlessly. Finally, inevitably, put into a siding, left to rust.

Moppa's foolish laugh echoing in my head, and wondering why he weaved instead of bobbed, didn't duck in time, why he kept fighting, knowing that he should have run like hell; only a madman goes head up against a blade unarmed. Knowing that he was more scared of looking like a coward than he was of dying. Saying a prayer that he'd survived getting his throat cut. Wondering if they had midgets in heaven. Tripping on the balls it must have taken for Big George to represent, stand up right in the middle of the madness jumping off, and attempt to keep it a one-on-one. Wondering if the last shot from Monkey Man's pipe killed him or if he was blessed with a head as hard as mine. And trying to figure out why it all happened.

But I find no answers. None of us has any answers; we never knew what the question was or even that there was a question, for that matter. We've just paid the price while exacting a toll. Pain and suffering all the way around. Hurt me and I'll hurt you.

Victims and victimizers.

Why?

How can I know that there are no answers to questions like that? Why some die and others live. Why kids like us are trapped in a whirlpool of shit. Years later, I learn that social workers and shrinks *think* they have answers and try to help, and that cops and district attorneys have other answers and do their best with what they believe.

But living through the nightmare, an eighteen-year-old tough guy, I don't even know the theories. I can't imagine that someday I'll write and make speeches, saying that it comes down to individuals, one person stopping one cycle, accepting responsibility, not having children who are doomed to be state-raised, welfare babies. I haven't yet even thought of the cliché, true as it is, that you have to take an exam to get a driver's license but the only requirement for parenthood is having reached puberty. I can't imagine getting out of the trap, let alone that I will someday talk to earnest, well-meaning audiences, saying that the one thing you can take to the bank is that every one of us in that joint came from a nightmare background, that of course there is no excuse—if you break the rules obviously you have to pay the price—but the fact is that the more babies brought into the world by people who have no business having children, the more problems we as a society will have.

Most of these kids who become outlaws are just chronic fuckups, irreparably damaged emotionally by their short lives and doomed to grow up to be professional convicts and felons, addicts or alcoholics. It seems as if there must be a better answer than gladiator schools and group homes that perpetuate rather than solve the underlying problem.

Long years after my own days in gladiator school, I'll try to point out to my readers and listeners that the largest growth industry in the United States, and probably the world, is penal institutions. And I say to you, "Think about it."

At eighteen, in Plainfield, right now, I examine my wounds and grieve for my friends. More dead, more ghosts in my short life.

Biscuits and gravy, my favorite. This is the second time they have been served since I got locked down; that means I've been in here a little over two weeks. The time is dragging like a dull tattoo needle, leaving its mark but so slowly that the progress is undetectable.

The nightmares that come every night are more intense than normal, the sleep that would offer a temporary escape from solitary something that now gives more pain than relief.

I've been exercising like a hamster on its wheel, moving frantically and going nowhere. Push-ups till I'm shaking, to sit-ups until my abs are burning like dry kindling, to jumping jacks until the fire in my legs and shoulders meets the flame in my midsection, then shadow boxing till I drop. As soon as I can breathe starting over, getting as ready as I can, because one thing is beyond doubt: while I may get greeted with hugs and kisses when I get to the pen . . . they won't be friendly.

I plan on making the foreplay so bloody that no one is going to want to pay the price. Glory or the graveyard. Fuck 'em all in the neck. I'm terrified and making that terror work for me like a whore works for a coathanger pimp. Nonstop, go for broke, pushing past any limits that make sense. Going to survive. You can't expect any mercy and you can't give any . . . especially to yourself. Keep on working till your entire body is screaming and then push harder. All day every day until it's show time.

When the door swings open it's right after breakfast and I know that any break in routine is bad news. Smith sticks his head in the cell and says, "Here's your clothes, boy."

Tosses the bundle to me and shakes his head, saying, "Don't got the brains God gave a turnip, stupid motherfucker, aren'tcha. They gonna send ya to the big house and you too light in the ass to be messin' with them boys. They gonna fuck ya bowlegged. That's if the niggers don't kill ya. This shit made the news, made this place look real bad. Guess you deserve whatever you gonna get, but I still feel bad for ya, boy. Good luck. Say your prayers."

Then he laughs, scratches his stomach, and finishes with, "Maybe ya can jist stab a few of 'em when ya get there and they'll leave you alone."

I've been praying my ass off and so far no lightning has come down and blown a hole in my cell wall, no angels have descended to rip the door off its hinges, no heroin already cooked and in the outfit has magically appeared. Shit, the tobacco that I wanted hasn't even materialized.

I stare at him as I pull my khakis on and say, "Prayin' don't seem to be helpin', Smith. Got a shank ya can loan me? Or how about giving me a five-minute head start? Sky the fuck outta here."

Cackling now and slapping his knees, looking at me askance and saying, "Well, shit howdy, don't you beat all. You jist might make it up there, boy, come out in one piece. You one game little motherfucker. I got to give ya that. Get ready, they excluding ya and that's that."

The cold air hits me like Methedrine, the bubble that had surrounded me seems to burst and the electric blue sky is as clear as a moron's conscience, not a cloud or a hint of pollution.

The caps escorting me are two white guys, one a hulking redneck with the personality of a wart who I don't know but who obviously takes his job real serious. Thinks he's a cop, not a cap. And he'd love to get the brownie points for stopping me or calling in the alarm if I tried to run. The other cap is a low-profile kid who stays out of the way, does his time in the library and the chapel. I know him because he reads, but we've never had much conversation.

I ask Low Profile, "So what's the score, ace? Who won?"

"The man. Who else? Goon squad and state police came in and cleaned up, beat everybody down, the whole joint's been on lock-down for over two weeks. Moppa's dead. Razor is still in the hospital. Monkey died. Flaco got a murder case. Willie lived, lucky for you; bad news is he caught a murder for shankin' Razor so you two be hittin' the big house at the same time. Red's back on his feet. Big George had his head all bandaged up, but he's all right. Neither of them caught a beef. Burt's dead and so is Liplock. Whole buncha dudes hurt bad. Everyone they got with a weapon, or with witnesses saying they used a weapon, got beefed. You in big trouble, man."

I say, "No shit. I thought they were gonna give me a medal. Gimme a smoke."

The redneck squints his eyes like he's trying to scare me and says, "You can't smoke. He gives you one I'll tell. You assholes got us all locked down."

I stop walking and spin to face him, ask, "What are they gonna do, lock me up? Want some, get some, pal. Otherwise, let me have a smoke."

He drops his eyes like a yelled-at dog and Low Profile laughs at him, then hands me a filter cigarette. I rip the filter off and split one of his matches to light it, say, "Thanks."

The smoke hits my lungs like a brick and we keep walking to-wards the administration building.

five

The table is the same, the faces the same, except this time there is no Dr. Pike, it is not a kangaroo court, the rules have been laid down, and I've fucked up. We all know what is coming. Superintendent Reynolds has my folder in front of him and when I sit down asks, "Do you have anything to say for yourself, Prine?"

"Nope."

He stares at me for a second, shakes his head, and says, "Inmate Robert Prine to be returned to court for exclusion as a juvenile. New charges of assault with a deadly weapon and attempted murder will be lodged against you. That should be good for at least another ten years. Add that to the new adult sentence on your original charges and you'll be out before you're forty. Have a pleasant day."

The caps doing escort duty on the way back are two Cuban guys I know from the gym and around the yard. As we walk away from the administration building the taller one says, "Listen up, pecker-wood, your friend Red has a message for you. You wait till they take the trays after supper tomorrow night, then you start screaming your ass off. Act like you're dying. He's on escort duty then. That's what's up. You down with it?"

I look from his face into the sky. The day is gorgeous, huge soft clouds with a pinkish tint like cotton candy are now drifting across the burning blue sky, the wind has the first hint of spring in it, and you can almost sense the plants getting ready to push their way through the thawing ground, birds hiding, barely out of sight, waiting to break into rock-and-roll song. Life is just around the corner and almost here, like a lovely woman stripped down to nothing but panties and starting to roll them down her legs while smiling into your eyes, and my heart picks up its beat, my blood flowing strong and elation running with it, and I look back from the sky at the Cuban cap and say, "The Lord does work in strange ways his wonders to perform, amigo. Tell Red that right after evening chow tomorrow I'll be screaming so loud they'll be able to hear me in fuckin' Russia. Thanks, commandant. I owe ya."

"Got that right, carnal."

I'm stuck in glue, trying to run, and my feet will barely move, the cops chasing me transforming into wolves wearing police uniforms. Finding safety, swinging into a tree, climbing to the top, and looking down on them howling up at me. Seeing a hypodermic growing out of the tree like a fungus filled with poison and pain, knowing that if I pull it off, the tree will deflate like a punctured blow-up doll . . . then ripping it free anyway. Trying to get it into my arm and there's no needle, just the barrel with blood-colored liquid in it bouncing off my vein, and the tree sinks into the ground and I'm running again, back on the treadmill, lungs ready to burst, getting nowhere.

The treadmill opens up and it's jungle now, dodging trees and vines. Head pivoting as I run, looking for a place to hide, finding a cave, running inside, looking around and seeing all the people in my life who have died, all looking at me. Moppa and Monkey intertwined somehow, the jumble of limbs and faces that are part Joe Moppa and part Monkey Man standing in front of the crowd of decaying friends and enemies and all the nameless dopefiends that have fallen by the wayside. Joe and Monkey separating into two torn and bloody bodies and the one that was my friend, Joe Moppa, saying, "About time, pal, you can't cheat us. It's your time. You made your choices, we died and you still live. It's all your fault. Everything. You gotta pay now, killer."

The wolves who are now a mix of canine and lizard are filing in behind me and the dead from my past, both recent and not, are in front of me, circling, smiling through rotting faces and fangs, tired of waiting for my arrival. Here to hasten my demise.

When my eyes open there is no hesitation, no thought. Roll off the bunk and start doing push-ups, then slow because if I understood the message correctly I'm going to want to be rested tonight. Ready for a marathon run. Stop the push-ups, climb back onto the bunk, staring at the ceiling, and try to nap with as much success as if I'd tried to fly.

Time moving so slowly that I start counting, "one, two, three," etc., forever . . . until I lose count, then start over so that I know the day is really passing. Incapable of stopping my brain's erratic jaunts all over the universe, tracking the progress the sun has made across the horizon by the tiny increments the light and shadows have changed until it is the soft feel of twilight and finally, years later, finishing the supper tray and starting to scream with everything I have, beating the tray on the door and yelling, "Help, I'm dying! Help me!"

And the seconds are passing like weeks. It's taking way too long for a response, so long that I know they can tell it's bullshit, they must know that I'm faking. That there's nothing wrong with me except everything and the door is swinging open as I'm hitting my knees and grabbing my stomach, letting drool run from my mouth and looking up at the guard and, when he turns away to yell for the trusties, jamming my fingers down my throat and puking all over the cell. Puking so hard that it splashes onto his trousers and all I can see is feet and bile-covered concrete as the caps come running in and one of them yells, "Get a stretcher . . . dis boy's dying." And I let myself collapse.

The guard is yelling about having puke all over him and the caps are back and rolling me onto the stretcher. Holding the end with my feet is my road dog, Red, and I almost grin, let my eyes travel up to see who's got the other end. Almost as tall as the doorway, face still a little puffed up from getting piped, Big George is looking down at me, and I damn near go into shock when he gives me a half-wink. I'm so surprised that I stop thrashing for a minute and feel my mouth drop open but George doesn't miss a beat as he yells at the guard, "Gotta get him to da infirmary. Outta da way. Move it, Smith. Unlock da gate, you fuckin' hillbilly. He's dying . . . da boy can't breathe."

Taking my cue, grabbing my throat and thrashing like a guy in the electric chair. George is bulling past the guard and rushing down the hallway, Red at my feet carrying his end and babbling, "Just hang on, partner. You'll be in the hospital in no time. Tough guys don't need air anyhow."

As Smith unlocks the gate leading out of isolation into the main yard, Red looks directly into my eyes, sticks his tongue out and crosses his eyes, then blows a raspberry at me before continuing his babble as we pass Smith on our way out.

Headed toward the infirmary and Big George saying, "You about one lucky peckerwood. I always pay my debts and if I'd squashed Monkey when I shoulda you'd be goin' your way and me mine. Plus you did me and mine a solid you don't even know about. Got a set of clothes and your boots stashed behind da chapel. It was a righteous pain in da ass slippin' that shit outta the property locker, but you can't run barefoot. Anyhow, I'm takin' your sorry ass wid me. We gonna bruise your boy Red here up and he'll report us in a bit."

As we come abreast of the chapel, Red says, "This fuckin' gorilla has one hell of a plan. I'm goin' with you guys. Ain't got no friends left after you gone anyway. Let's do it, George, I'm in. You ain't bruisin' me up none without fightin' to do it."

They freeze with me suspended on the stretcher watching the words fly back and forth over my head like a tennis ball over the net.

"Whatchoo mean you in, dumdum?"

"Just what I said, foolio. I'm goin' with ya. Skyin' the fuck outta here."

"I don't remember invitin' yo white ass. Might bruise ya up right now. How ya like that?"

"Either get busy bruisin' or let's roll. If you'd kept your mouth shut about how ya were gonna get outta here I never woulda known you needed me. I'm magic with locks, you fuck. I'm worth taking, you'll see. I'm in or we can set this fuckin' stretcher down and start slingin' right now."

Finally George spits on the ground and says, "Redheaded fuckin' cracker, if you comin', let's dump your dog. He too heavy to carry."

And like it was rehearsed they start swinging the goddamn stretcher and on the count of three heave me through the air and into a snowbank, both laughing and slapping each other high fives.

Wiping the snow off my face and trudging through the snow towards these chuckleheaded morons, the snow burning into my bare feet and legs, starting me shivering so hard that my whole body is shaking and they're both laughing till they're crying and I say, "Couple of slaphappy motherfuckers, giggling like little girls. I'm gonna freeze to death, ya cocksuckers. Let's roll."

Of course that makes them laugh harder, till George wipes the tears off his face and gasps out, "Come on, we hiding out in the chapel's basement till about midnight. My half brother is gonna pick us up down the road a taste. Been plannin' this for a while. Just wasn't plannin' on you two. He normally don't cotton to white folks . . . then again he don't got much use for colored either. Can't wait to see the look on his face when he sees you-uns. Or the look on your faces when you see him, for that matter. He's got a bad skin condition, looks freakish, poor motherfucker, but he's my bro. Try not to stare at him, he plexes easy. Let's get busy."

Dashing through the snow, every step burning like it's fire instead of ice, following George and Red until we reach the back door to the chapel, where George hands me the bag with my clothes in it. Pulling my pants on and before I can even get anything else out of the bag, Red's done loiding the lock with such speed, skill, and finesse that I'm caught by surprise. Doing it so well that Big George says, "You slick, Red. You real good for a white boy."

Red just grimaces at him and shakes his head, saying, "Silly fucking negro. Toldya I was a burglar."

Then he grins like a junkie in a pharmacy, just as happy and proud as possible.

I'm starting to feel frantic, and beyond cold, frozen to the bone, and all of a sudden these two are old pals. Talking shit and probably getting ready to play the dozens. There's a time for everything and right now it's time to go, my entire being is focused on getting out of here, and the longer they gab and high-sign the longer we're exposed and the colder I get. My teeth are chattering so loud they can probably hear it in Japan. I say, "I thought you two didn't like each other. What's up? Let's get inside. You can swap spit later."

The door squeals as Red pulls it open. Sliding through in single file and we're inside on mouse feet, the room dark and musty, long wooden benches taking up the middle and sides. The threadbare rugs running down the aisles muffle any sound our feet make as George leads us to the basement door hidden behind the choir rows. Above the choir section is a stained-glass window showing a graphically bloody crucifixion scene, the last rays of the setting sun reflecting softly through Jesus's eyes and I swear it feels like he's watching and cheering us on.

Red slips the lock on the basement door in seconds, slides the door open and relocks it behind us. Going in single file, we're now feeling our way down the stairs through the cobwebs into pitch blackness, broken only by the hissing blue flames coming from the furnace.

Getting as close to the furnace as I can and pulling the rest of my clothes on, feeling the dried blood from the riot crackling on the shirt and jacket, the electric feeling of circulation returning to my arms and legs, feet and hands and face stiff and burning like they're made out of wood and set on fire.

The smell of mildew, rot, and fuel oil overwhelming as we settle in to wait for the institution to shut down. The time in solitary dragged, but this is way slower. Low-level adrenaline mixes with equal parts of hope and fear.

It seems that we are in that basement long enough for cities to have been built, prospered, withered, and blown away. Time for Adam and Eve to have met, eaten the apple, fallen in love, bred, had children, grandchildren, and great-grandchildren all the way up to the present. Plenty of time for all that to have happened while we're sitting watching the dancing blue flame in that furnace, letting our eyes adjust till we can make out shapes.

At one point we're listening to echoing footsteps and shouts above us as they search the chapel, and the noise the basement door makes as they try it to see if it is locked sends my whole system into emergency overload. The sound of the search moving on and the upstairs doors slamming behind the caps and guards. The mounting excitement as the possibility of really making it out of here increases.

Sitting in a semicircle, whispering occasionally and listening to the gradually fading yells as the hunt for us waxes and wanes. Waiting.

The whistle of the midnight train drifts weakly into the basement and the adrenaline builds from low-grade to fever pitch, all the way on.

George stands up, making a darker shape against the vague outlines in the boiler room, the sound of him rubbing his hands together coming through the darkness as he says quietly, "Let's roll, fellas. I got a blanket to throw over the razor wire. As soon as we out the door I'm blazin'. If ya can't keep up, shame on you—keep up wid me and we all got a ride outta the state. Fall behind and you on your own."

We hit the ground running full out. Eyes wide open, heads panning back and forth with every step, watching for trusties or guards. Plumes of condensed breath trailing us as we dash away from the chapel and administration buildings.

The snow's knee-high once we hit the open ground between the main body of the yard and the least-used part of the compound, Company 13, the graveyard where the kids who die in Plainfield are buried.

George hits a headstone and goes flying, lands on his shoulder and rolls to his feet so fast he is still in front of Red and me.

My breath is starting to hit my ribs like a hammer and Big George is moving faster than ever, flying through the graveyard directly at the razor-wire-topped chain-link fence.

We reach the base of the fence and George gasps out, "Yo, Bobbie, you the lightest. I'm gonna cradle my fingers, boost ya up there. Throw the blanket over the razor wire. Me and dumdum here will be right behind ya."

George cradles his fingers together, I put my foot in the cradle, and as he lifts I jump as high as I can, catching the chain link and flying up, hand over hand, the last few feet to the top of the fence where the chain link and razor wire meet.

Figuring the best way to cover the incredibly sharp wire and then holding on to the chain link with one hand, leaning back as far as I can and grasping one corner of the blanket, I fling it over the rolled concertina. Crab-walking along the chain link until the cloth is pulled taut, pulling the blanket with me, using the hand holding the blanket, I grab one of the Y-joints holding the wire in place and swing up onto the blanket and, as the wire cuts through it into my legs and hands, roll over and clamber down the other side, George and Red right behind me. Halfway down saying to Big George's descending feet, "Lightest, huh? Most cut up, that's for sure."

Red muttering all the way down, "Dumdum my fucking ass. Dumdum, huh? You fuckin' gorilla."

"Dat's right, you a dumdum, old redheaded peckerwood. Let's see ya catch my ass."

George is fast, fast enough to tweak Red's nose, spin, and have a running start of ten feet before we are right on his ass. Sprinting to keep up.

Flying across the deep snow, legs burning, lungs fighting for every last particle of oxygen, and the stars are shining through the crystal-clear Indiana night like high-voltage diamonds, the clouds that had been blocking the half-full moon gone like a junkie's fix, gone like the concertina wire that is now behind us and letting the moon sparkle softly from the snow and light our way like a silver dollar that's been cut in half and imbued with a soft mystical light.

Coming out of the fields, climbing a regular barbed-wire fence, one made to stop animals, not men. Scrambling up a drainage ditch to a dirt farm track that looks like it hasn't been used in years, slowing to a jog and George wheezing, "Almost there, not far now, boys. Jus' a couple more miles."

It feels like every breath is cutting through my lungs and dripping like acid into my guts, got charley horses in both legs and my heart wants a vacation bad.

Accelerate.

Running forever, our feet thudding, thudding on the snow and in our ears, our adrenaline-pumped minds not knowing if the sound of running is our own or caps and guards onto us and ready to beat us into good little prisoners, knowing we'll never let them take us alive, never go back.

Looking behind us, seeing nothing but crystal-white country trail, no guards, no caps, no living thing, we hit a small, tar-paved road and George staggers across, collapses in the drainage ditch running alongside it. He's lying flat on his back, looking up into the sky, and gasps, "We here, boys. Taxi be pullin' up any minute."

Red is breathing too hard to talk, and all I can get out is, "Praise God, ten more feet woulda killed me, motherfucker."

Drunk on endorphins, cold air reviving me as the sweat dissipates into the night air.

Red falling into his customary squat, wiping the sweat off his face and parroting, "Praise God, motherfucker."

And we're laughing and gasping. And I'm wondering why I

didn't think of a variation of this a year ago and laugh harder.

Red breaks out a pack of Camels and passes it, lights a match and holds it for me and George. When he lights his he says, "Three on a match, fellas, don't feel like bad luck to me."

The smoke does exactly what it's supposed to, it doesn't just taste good, it tastes like a celebration, like cocaine and champagne, like victory. George is sprawled on one side of the ditch, I'm on the other, and Red is squatting in the center. George takes a huge drag off his Camel and asks, "Where you two headed?"

Red looks at me and then shrugs, saying, "Don't know." Points at me and continues, "My dog always said once he made it back to the world he had shit wired. I'm just along for the ride."

George pulls his coat tighter around him and raises his chin at me, says, "So what's up, ya got somewhere to go? Or are ya just goin'?"

Take a hit off my smoke, blow it out, giving myself time to think and put it together, say, "A ways over the Indiana–Illinois border, one of my partners has a farm, sort of. Ain't no problem with him putting us up. Plus he owes me some dough, a lot of dough, as a matter of fact. Probably going to kick it there for a taste, then head for the East Coast, Jersey and Boston. Sooner or later gonna exit stage west, go back to LA. I like it there. How about you, George? Where ya headed?"

"Shee-it, who knows. Just down the road a ways, down the road. Get outta this fuckin' state, anyhow. Maybe Florida, Georgia, down South, somewhere warm. If my half brother has any good ideas, just gonna head off with him. Do something and get a bankroll together. Stay free and live big, at least for a while."

Red looks up from the ground and says, "Just rollin', huh? I thought ya had the whole thing planned out."

Big George laughs. "We sittin' here smokin' cigarettes, aren't we? Ain't locked down, not that I can see. Are we? Just rollin' with no place to go is a hell of a lot better than not bein' able to roll but havin' gangs of places to go. Shee-it, da Queen of fuckin' England could invite your redheaded ass over to visit and if you locked down . . . you ain't goin'. Are ya?"

Red laughs, catches my eyes, and as I nod at him, says to George, "Stay down, pal, you sure got that right."

I know Red well enough to know what's going on behind that freckle-covered, cold-as-stone face, so I think about it for a second and tell George, "Check it out, man, where I'm headed you'd be more than welcome. Your brother, too, for that matter. These fools would dig having us show up. These people are kinda strange but as solid as they come. Us showing up won't rock 'em a bit. It ain't no thing. You and your bro tag along, be a hell of a lot better than heading cross-country with nothin' in your pockets but air and nothin' to put in your hand except your dick. Who knows? Might be real cool. Can't hurt ya none. Whatcha think?"

George looks at Red, who shrugs, and then he gives me a look of appraisal, shakes his head, and says, "Thanks . . . but I can't be staying on no farm, let alone a farm of nothin' but strange white folks. My ass would get picked up the first time one of the local cops saw me. Do I look like a farmer? Naw. I think my way is the highway."

"Think about it, George. My partner who calls the shots is black and sure ain't no fuckin' farmer. It's kickback, they're like born-again maniacs."

Big George does a double take on this one, looks at me askance, and says, "Let's see what my bro thinks. Ya say a nigger is running this place? Might be all right then."

Red's mouth is hanging open, and he's shaking his head. Looking at me, squinting in the moonlight to see if I'm joking, and when he realizes that I'm for real, he asks, "You serious? We're lamming from a riot and a black guy is gonna hide us out? What the hell you gonna come up with next, dog?"

I guess I've caught him by surprise, but this night is full of surprises for all of us. I nod my head, tell him that I'm as serious as solitary, and ask him for another Camel. It tastes like success.

The sound of straight pipes and a heavily cammed engine growls across the fields and down into the drainage ditch. George hops up from his sprawl into a crouch, saying, "Sounds right, he's a fuckin' gearhead. Tie off till I talk to him. If it's him."

When the rumbling engine and headlights reach the intersection of the dirt and tar roads the car stops and the engine and lights go out.

The sound of a car door opening cuts through the night and George is scrambling over the lip of the ditch and onto the road. Me and Red stay behind and listen to the muffled voices and laughing that goes on for a long time. Finally George appears at the top of the ditch and says in a regular tone of voice, "Let's go, fellas, and remember what I said about his skin condition, it's kinda scary."

I'm rushing, the elation so strong that it feels like I'm going to start floating while Red and me are jogging towards the two shadows that are George and his bro, getting close and seeing that his half brother is as big as he is and wearing one of those hooded parkas. As Red and I reach the car, Red gasps, "Wow, bad piece of equipment. Hemi Cuda, ain't it?"

George cuts in, real serious, has that tone people use when they really want to get a point across, saying, "Don't let the way he looks scare ya. What he's got is a terrible, terrible skin condition, but it ain't contagious."

The driver says, "Yeah, Red, Hemi Cuda. Fastest thing smokin', motherfucker."

Flips his hood off, opens the car door, and when the interior light comes on I understand the skin condition and the solid that George said I did him and didn't know about.

Surprise. Surprise.

Red's stuttering, "Uh-uh-uh-uh."

George is busting up laughing, slapping his hands together and saying through the laughter, "And ya can't catch what ya already got."

I tell Cross-Eyed Phil, "Shoulda figured it out, bro. You two look like gorillas, just different-color pelts."

And Phil smiling like a jack-o'-lantern, saying, "Toldja Poppa was a wandering sorta man. My momma left him for that fool I had to sock up, long time ago . . . when I was only two and he wandered down the road and met George's momma. Look close and you notice we sorta look alike. That's my baby brother."

Snaps his hand out and pushes George, saying, "Except for that nappy fuckin' hair. Skin condition my ass, foolio. We both know I got the good looks, not to mention the brains."

George is still laughing when he pushes Phil back and says, "Yeah, hear you tell it. Cross-eyed motherfucker." And we're piling into the stolen Cuda, accelerating like a rocket towards the highway and out of Indiana.

Cross-Eyed Phil and Big George in front arguing about whether the radio is going to be set on country-western or soul.

Red's still shaking his head and muttering to himself.

Me, I'm planning out my next move, thinking that I have to choose a new name, the name and false ID problem reminding me that I'm sucking my top lip through the space that once held my front teeth and wondering what will be involved in getting false ones. Hating the idea of seeing a dentist.

Staring out the window at the fields and small towns flying by, sensing the wheels eating up the miles, listening to the hemi engine growl over the sound of the radio and feeling safe for the first time in a long time, rolling down the highway with my friends, knowing that sanctuary is just down the road.

Bouncing over the back roads of rural Illinois, rock and roll having been settled on as a reasonable compromise by Phil and George. I'm sipping on a Styrofoam container of coffee and digging the sun breaking its way over the horizon. As we approach the fence around the compound, Phil hits the brakes and shoves the four-speed into neutral.

George looks into the backseat, turns the radio down, and says, "So if this is da place, it's time to decide what's up. Me and Phil will check this shit out, if everything is cool we'll hang. If it ain't we rollin'."

Phil is now looking over his seat at me deadpan, jailhouse hair-cut grown out a little bit, making the hair stick out from his head in clumps, crossed brown eyes rimmed in pink from driving all night, showing no expression, and asks, "What makes ya think this dude is gonna welcome us with open arms? Seems like anyone with a lick of sense would lock their doors and call the cops as soon as they see us comin'. Know what I mean, killer?"

I laugh, thinking about these folks calling any cops, saying,

"Slow down, dog. That's about the last thing they'd do. Blow us away, maybe, but never call the cops."

Phil and George look at each other. Red tries to read me, wondering if I know what I'm doing.

I guess I have to tell them more, but I'm hurting from the old memories, already feeling my ghosts around me, some crazy rooster crowing into the cold air and reminding me of my introduction to this place, the pain of my broken jaw hanging, Mel carrying three bullets, Syd and Rosie holding us both together until Ben could fix us up.

"Look, you may be weirded out by these people," I say. "They're even weirder than you are. They're a bunch of ex-junkies, fuckin' born-again crazies . . . farm together here, take care of each other, all that shit, used to follow a guy called Jimbo or Reverend James Cook, depending on whether he was saving souls or selling firearms, until he got blown away. They saved my life, me and Mel's. . . ." I fade off, remembering Mel and Syd and Rosie, getting that empty-gut feeling.

Phil pulls his brows together over his crossed eyes, making him look even more like a cartoon in an underground paper, says, "Mel? That's the guy taught ya how to be a badass? Ain't that right, badass?"

I say, "Yeah, right, that's Mel. And Ben put the last score I was on together. We stole a sackful of cash and another sackful of drugs. It got messy. Real messy. Anyhow I ended up overdosed. That's how I caught the cases that got me in Indiana Youth Center."

Flashing back too hard now, no time for it, I don't want to talk about it anymore. Time to go in. Or not. Saying, "Flash forward a year and a little bit of change and here we are. He should still have my end, or most of it. If there's a problem I'll handle it. Don't sweat the small shit, fellas. Anyhow we're here now, you may as well come in for a minute or ten."

As we roll through the gateway a big, plain-looking girl wearing thermal clothes and a hooded parka steps in front of the Cuda with a flashlight in one hand and an M16 in the other, both pointing at the center of the windshield.

When Phil hits the brakes she walks around the car and says, "Kill the engine and the lights, big boy. Where the hell do y'all think you're goin'?"

Phil turns the lights and engine off, moving slowly, staring at the girl. She hits each of us with the light, while keeping the M16 pointed into the car, and then drawls, "Mental giants, huh? If that one was too tough for y'all, try tellin' me who ya are and what the hell you doin' in our driveway."

I lean forward slowly, keeping both hands where she can see them, and say, "I'm a friend of Ben's. Name's Prine, Bobbie Prine. He'll want to see me. Check it out. Go ahead."

She sneers and the cold makes the air coming out of her mouth look like smoke as she says, "Well now, maybe he will and maybe he won't. Just pretend I'm the police and get outta that there vehicle real slow and easy. Y'all keep your hands visible and then assume the position. You know the drill. Right, boys?"

We know the drill.

Red looks at me and says, "Yeah, dog, this is real cool. Last time I ever listen to your peckerwood ass. This bitch looks fuckin' evil."

Big George and Phil are spread over the hood, me and Red have our hands planted on the roof, and all three of them are staring at me. The looks on their faces are what you would call a little bit upset.

Big George shakes his head and says, "Don't sweat the small things, the man says. Now I gotta ask ya, Phil, is a M16 a small thing or a big thing? Hmmm? Whatchoo think, Red, he's your fuckin' dog. Seems like a pretty big goddamn thing to me."

Before Red can answer a voice comes from behind us, saying, "Took you long enough, Bobbie. Let's get in out of the cold."

The tunnel vision that had set in when I realized we were getting jacked opens up, the adrenaline that had overridden the bone-deep tiredness lifts, and my heart slows and as I turn from the car, still moving slowly, I see that the farm is lit in soft red fire by the rising sun, the main house huge, smoke drifting from the chimney and framed by the empty fields of winter, the trailers scattered around the main yard, a new addition since the last time I was here.

Staring at me from less than ten feet away is Ben, afro grown out and shot with more gray, gold-starred eyetooth glinting against his plum-colored skin and a look of appraisal on his face. Less than the warm welcome I was hoping for but certainly a step forward in the journey.

Not that I have a clear idea of where the journey is to, or any real goal except going, getting away from where I am. Staring back at Ben, and when he starts to smile feeling the grin split my face in return.

When Ben asks if we are hungry, Phil's the first to respond, telling him, "Starvin' like Marvin, ready to eat anything that can't outrun me."

Walking through the front doors of the main house and the aroma of frying bacon and baking biscuits combine to make my stomach growl and remind me that not only am I hungry but it has been well over a year since I've had real food.

The awkwardness of our showing up out of the blue is still present in Ben's stilted movements and my hesitation to let my guard down.

By the time we're on our second helpings of bacon, eggs, grits, and biscuits the conversation is no longer forced. In between helpings the girl who was on the gate joins us, stripping out of her parka and sweater and settling down to eat. Across her nose is a sprinkling of freckles and the hair that was under the hood is bright red and curly, the sun beaming through the kitchen window making a red-gold halo around her head.

As the rest of us are eating and talking Red has frozen, fork halfway to his mouth, staring at the girl, who finally laughs and says, "Whatcha starin' at, Red? My name's Lily. Close your mouth before ya get a fly in it. What's your handle?"

And she gives him a thousand-watt smile that makes her unremarkable face more than pretty.

Red snaps his mouth shut so fast the click of his teeth hitting together can be heard across the room and mumbles, "Red, they call me Red just like you did. Pleased to meet you, Lily."

Ben and Big George are cutting it up, Red is blushing so hard he looks like a freckled tomato and keeps peeking at Lily while pretending to have his attention focused on the plate in front of him. The biggest giveaway that he's trying to be cool is that he's eating like a human being, one small bite at a time, not shoveling the food in like we normally do.

Phil jerks his thumb at Red and puts his hand over his heart mimicking a drum and we both start laughing as Red mad-dogs us. After wolfing enough food down to make movement almost impossible, Ben does a slow take of all four of us and says, "You boys look tore up from the floor up, all got your eyes at half mast. Got a room for ya upstairs, get some sleep. Then we'll figure out what to do with your raggedy asses."

SIX

We take up residence in one of the upstairs rooms, four mattresses thrown on the floor, real blankets, pillows, and the ability to come and go. Freedom. It feels really strange. The four of us stretched out, smoking and contemplating the future with full bellies, when Red says, "Pretty as a speckled pup. She's even redheaded, all the better. She sure is, pretty as a picture. Just held that machine gun as natural as if she was born with it. Lily . . . even got a pretty name. That girl is naturally fine as wine."

George is already snoring, Phil and me glance at each other, then at Red. Say "Uh-huh" simultaneously and fall out, soft mattresses, soft pillows, clean soft blankets, full bellies, and sleep coming on like a tidal wave as Red's babbling on, "She is, boys, fuckin' beautiful. . . ."

Real eggs, bacon, biscuits, grits, potatoes or pancakes, and hot black coffee every morning . . . with variations but always all we can eat and always good. Compared to the powdered-eggs-and-reconstituted-milk breakfast at Plainfield, it is a feast every morning.

The daily routine at Ben's compound isn't much different from that at Plainfield, although the quality of life is as different as life and slow death.

Red and Phil right away get into the whole thing, working around the place, hitting the church/political-type meetings that Ben holds every evening after supper. Me and George are lazier or maybe just not cut out for voluntary manual labor. But Ben's right-hand guy, name of Ross, drafts us anyway.

It's the second day in the compound as the plates are being cleared from breakfast, and this Ross, a Georgia cracker who walks, talks, and acts blacker than any black man any of us have ever met, asks us to help him clear out one of the barns. How hard could that be for guys who have gathered the slop and fed the pigs at Plainfield?

Harder and messier than we thought. The hay and flotsam that had been sitting in the place since the turn of the century was knee deep and held together by old horseshit and mold. As soon as we start shoveling, Ross is gone, out of there like a chicken to corn.

Me and George look at each other and laugh at the dude, because one type of guy that gets no respect from anybody on the inside is a cat who acts like and wants to be anything he's not. George says, "One stupid fuckin' white boy there. Bet his mama and papa wished they'd drowned him when he was a baby."

I just grimace and say, "Yeah, man."

This is not my idea of fun. Halfway through I'm covered with grime from top to bottom, and I look up and notice that me and Big George are doing all the work. Red's outside smoking and talking to Lily and a real pretty black chick with cocoa-colored skin is deep off in conversation with Cross-Eyed Phil.

I pause to catch my breath and light a smoke. George walks over and puts his hands on his hips, spits into the hay and shit surrounding us, and says, "Motherfucker. Cross-eyed son of a bitch is covered with ancient fuckin' cowshit and still don't miss a beat. You and me is in here bustin' our asses and your dog and my goddamn half brother is chasin' pussy."

He pauses, takes a drag off his Camel, looks the girl that's talking to Phil up and down, and continues, "Fine fuckin' pussy at that. At least Red is stickin' with redheads. Phil's just like our pops, loves dark meat, fuckin' asshole. Why's that fine sister wanna talk to an ugly fuckin' paddy like him anyhow?"

I can't let it pass. I laugh and say, "Can't help herself, dog, she must know white is right."

As I'm dodging the shot George wings at my chest we're both laughing and Red, Lily, Cross-Eyed Phil, and the mystery girl walk in to socialize.

The motes of dust hanging in the barn are shining from the light slicing in from the open door, outside the snow is starting to melt and turning the frozen ground into mud. As we form into a loose circle I notice that the chick with Phil is beyond pretty, she's a knockout. Even in a thick parka with mud-soaked work boots and filthy jeans she's feminine as a runway model, she's got a shy demeanor that's real attractive, and I can see why Phil's shooting his best shot. He says, "Fellas, this is Jazz, short for Jasmine. Jazz, this is my little bro, George."

Then he jerks his thumb in my direction and says, "And this is Bad Bobbie," and as she looks at me I notice that her eyes are such a light brown they're almost gold.

She smiles at me and then looks back and forth at Big George and Phil, starts laughing, and says, "The family resemblance is amazing, I'd of thought you were twins." Focuses those cat eyes on me and asks, "Why are you bad . . . Bobbie?"

I'm tongue-tied, got no snappy repartee, just smile and shrug. Rosie was my last relationship with a girl and that had kinda a sad ending and doing time doesn't prepare you for small talk with pretty females. Especially pretty females who are already flirting with one of your road dogs.

George says, "Pleased to meet you." Then tells me, "Come on, dog, you and me on the labor side, let these lames slither on outta here." George is in a foul mood through the rest of the day, muttering to himself and occasionally spitting.

From that point forward I do my level best to avoid getting dragged into work projects. Phil and Red, on the other hand, are working fools, digging holes, planting fence posts, working on equipment, whatever. Showing off their manly skills for their girls. I get the feeling these Indiana Hoosiers are both farmboys at heart and pretty comfortable with honest work. It makes me uneasy. Me and George kick back as much as possible, reading, exercising, and visualizing a future of high living and drugs. I'm a lot happier in that vision than in one populated by pigs and chickenshit.

On the eighth day there, George and I are in the now-immaculate barn working the heavy bag we've rigged out of burlap sacks and dirt, using cotton gloves inside heavy canvas work gloves so we won't rip all the skin off our knuckles. When it's my turn to hold the bag he's hittin' hard enough to knock me and the bag both into the air. George has gotten madder by the day that Phil and Jazz dig each other and with every shot he's saying, "Cross-eyed motherfucker."

A few days into this routine and we're smoking between rounds on the bag, doing push-ups and talking shit, me about getting loaded, him about broads in general and Jazz's insane poor taste in particular, when Ben walks in and says, "Big George, I'm headed into

Chicago to deliver some hardware to the South Side. Wanna ride shotgun?"

I'm the wrong color to be delivering illegal guns or anything else for that matter to the South Side of Chicago . . . I'd get noticed real fast. I know this and I know I shouldn't take it personally but my feelings are hurt and it's just me and the heavy bag till lunch. Even with the double gloves my hands are dripping blood when I go in to clean up for chow.

Lunch is gourmet shit, thick sliced ham and lima beans, rice on the side, and Coca-Cola. Watching Red and Lily, Phil and Jazz giving each other those corner-of-the-eye looks that are supposed to disguise how hot and heavy things are getting. Doesn't fool anybody at the table.

And even though the food smells great I can't eat, sitting in a civilized chow hall with twenty other people and lonely as a motherfucker. I can't figure it out, I'm sad all the way to the center of my soul, remembering Rosie, missing the sense that somebody loved me no matter what, the sureness that I'd fight dragons for her, walk on the moon for her, take care of her . . . the feeling I could see Red had for Lily and Phil had for Jazz.

I know what would make it all better quick and in a hurry-up, though. Just a little teeny squirt of opiates and life will be beyond OK. Now I just have to get them.

Phil's working the bag with the intensity of a jackhammer, left jab, hook off the left, then throwing a series of overhand rights that are literally splitting the bag and letting the dirt run onto the floor. George is holding the bag for him and talking around it, "Hit harder, motherfucker, throw both hands, get it out on the bag 'cause ya can't afford to kill that motherfucker right now. Sling em, bro."

I walk in as Cross-Eyed Phil accelerates the pace of his shots, throwing chunks of torn burlap and clods of dirt all over the place. Red is squatting, watching and smoking, he looks up at me and shakes his head, saying, "It's always some fuckin' thing, dog." Then hands me his pack of smokes. I light one and blow the smoke out, watching it disappear into the twilight that is descending on the farm rapidly, making the barn a place of shadows mixed with pitch black.

I light one, my adrenaline already up just from the anger in Phil's shots, and ask Red, "What's up? Who can't Phil afford to kill? What the fuck's going on?"

Red's staring at the dirt between his feet and without looking up says, "I reckon Phil will run it all down to ya. It's about him and Jazz."

The first thing I think is someone else is trying to move in on her, knock him out of the box, and I know if for some reason he can't move on the guy I sure as hell can 'cause I'm not staying out here with the chickens and goats any longer than I have to.

When the bag is finally completely destroyed, Phil strips the gloves off and says, "Guess it's all planned out, I'm out and you in, George. Motherfucker told me he didn't believe in race mixin', said he could see the devil in me and ain't gonna let his niece fuck around with white trash like me. Fuckin' cocksucker."

George is looking everywhere except at Phil, catches my eye and says, "Bobbie, what's up? What do you think about this shit? The girl don't even wanna be wid me. This shit ain't my fault, old Ben got this shit in his head that me and Jazz would be a good thing. I dig Ben's style but I didn't put no moves on the girl, told Ben that even if I get a girlfriend it ain't worth losing my goddamn brother. You got history with him, how about getting his head right about this."

I take a toke off the Camel, fill my lungs with as much smoke as they'll hold, and to gain a minute to think, I say, "Looks like we gotta rig another heavy bag, seems like termites got that one."

Red looks up from the ground and stands up from his squat, saying, "Cross-eyed termites."

Me and Red laugh but Phil and George look serious as nuclear waste; a joke isn't gonna change the subject.

I ask Phil, "What happened? What kicked this shit off?"

He looks all the way 51/50, certifiably insane, his crossed eyes as red as maraschino cherries. He grunts, gets his voice under control, and says, "Fuckin' Ben rolls on me after chow. Says he's got to talk to me about Jazz, tells me she's his niece and he can't let her fuck her life up. Like I'm some kinda fuckin' psycho or somethin'. So I tell him I won't fuck her up, I really dig her. The motherfucker don't miss a beat, before I'm even done talkin' he starts going off about Kahlil Gibran or some kinda shit, says the pillars of the temple of God are equal but must stay separate like I'm supposed to know what the fuck he's talkin' about, starts quotin' shit outta the Bible I never heard of, and I read the Good Book every time I get slammed into solitary like we all do."

Phil stops to take a breath and choke down the bile rising in him. "Anyhow, I say all that to say this: I finally tell the motherfucker that I don't know what he's talkin' about, all I know is I dig the shit outta Jazz, and I'm gonna stay with her unless someone kills me. He says it can be arranged. That you and me, Bobbie, are outta here. . . . Red and George are down with his program, but he said you're a junkie and won't ever change . . . and then he looks at me all fuckin' nuts and says some kind of shit about he can see Satan behind my eyes. If you can talk sense to him that's all good. If not, anytime he's ready to start killin' I'm right here. Know what I mean, dog?"

Me, I'm confused trying to reconcile all this data with what I thought I knew about Ben. Not understanding that the most reasonable of human beings suddenly become fools when it comes to power, family, race, and money and the fact is that we were affecting Ben in every one of these sensitive areas. Many years later I will understand the rage he must have been feeling, but now I just think he's gone nuts.

I'd like to tell Ben he's full of shit . . . including his interpretation of Kahlil Gibran and the Bible . . . and that Phil's probably the best thing that could happen to Jazz, but I now suspect that Ben's basically a dry junkie with a madman itch. I sense that my persuasive powers with Ben are worth about as much as they were with the trusties at Plainfield.

So I study Red and George for a second and ask them, "So what's up? Do you guys dig this scene or do ya want to travel?"

Red looks away for a second and says, "Shit, dog, Lily ain't gonna take it on the hop, runnin' cross-country, robbin' and stealin'. I wouldn't ask her to. I reckon I'm gonna stay right here and work on those redheaded babies. Ya can't blame me . . . this is the real world, not the joint."

"George?"

"Ben's takin' me under his wing, showing me moves that are slicker than snake snot. I dig it. As long as we can all part friends

I'm gonna stay. Red's right. This is the real world. Know what I mean?"

"Phil?"

"I'm just a stupid fuckin' cross-eyed country boy, we all know that. Ben don't want me here, and if Jazz don't want to swing outta here I can understand that. I don't fuckin' know, maybe go get that factory job, I just don't fuckin' know. Only thing I do know is I gotta talk to that girl before I make my mind up about anything. You go on ahead and talk to Ben, Bobbie, see if he might reconsider. Shit, I'll marry her if that makes him happy. I just don't know about all this race shit. If he really believes all that crap—and me with a half brother as black as he is and as white as I am—he ain't gonna change his mind."

I stare at the fellas one by one and know the feeling of eternal friendship is slipping away, and that what passed for my childhood is coming to an end. The only thing you can count on is change.

Ben's leaning on the top strand of the barbwire, got his old pipe stuck in the corner of his mouth at a forty-five-degree angle and doing the best he can to ignore me. Around us stretch empty fields ending in woods knee-deep in snow and slush, the sun breaking through the clouds and shining off the snow with enough power to make you squint.

I'm watching a rabbit who has decided to leave his nice warm burrow and nose around in the snow. I light a Camel, take the smoke in as deep as I can, and focus on the rabbit. Doing time teaches you how to wait. Ben wants to pretend we're not having this conversation, that's fine with me. One way or the other this shit is gonna get settled. Halfway through the second smoke and the rabbit is long gone.

The sun is back behind the clouds and Ben takes the cold pipe from his mouth, tamps it on his hand, and says, "Spring's comin', Bobbie, it's a big country. Whatcha gonna do?"

I flip the burning smoke into the snow and watch it die and say, "Probably head east, look up Syd, maybe Billy. Get laid, get good and loaded, you know. The standard shit." A deep breath, steady voice. "I need the dough you owe me, Ben, I'm not plannin' on another cross-country crime spree, from here on in anything I do is gonna be planned. Go down like clockwork, I've had plenty of time to think. I ain't leaving the game, but I'm not gonna blaze a path to either coast again. Fuck that. You got my dough? Or not?"

He stands up straighter and has his chest stuck out, playing with the pipe, and asks real slow, "You threatening me, son?"

Ben's got probably eighty pounds on me, and it's a safe bet he's packed, and I feel the fear that is always with me growing like Jack's magic beanstalk and with it comes the rage that fear always produces in me. The terror of being scared that drives all rational thought right out of my head. But another thing doing time teaches you is to hold your emotions in check, if I push this to a showdown right now I'm gonna lose . . . even so, I'm measuring the distance from the toe of my boot to his kneecap, just in case he decides to rush me.

I can hear my voice shaking anyway, as I say, "You owe, pal, you set that shit up and me and my partners went in. Al got shot, Cloud bought the farm, I got busted. You had my end, it had to be thirty or forty grand any way ya figure it."

Ben's eyes are like slits in his face, making it look like an old walnut, dark brown, wrinkled and hard as hell. He whistles and says, "Shit-fuck-damnation, boy. You got a crocodile mouth if I ever heard one, forgot how bullheaded ya are. Here's the deal. That dough's gone, long gone. Been spent on things that were needful. Now ya can try and down my shit here and now in which case I'll just beat ya senseless and leave ya lay till ya freeze or develop some common sense. Or ya can bide your time and kill me when I ain't lookin' for it, 'course it'll be a cold day in hell when I ain't lookin' for it. Or you and your buddies can kick it here for a little while and I'll get ya what I can and we'll part friends. Whatcha wanna do? It's your play, killer."

His leg hasn't moved, and I figure I can kick a field goal with his kneecap if I don't like the answer. I blow out the breath I find I was holding and ask, "How much? When?"

He looks down, catches my eyes, and smiles, saying, "Sayyy, ten grand. Two weeks. How'zat?"

"Fifteen and we part friends. Whatcha think, hoss?"

"Deal, Bobbie." As we shake hands he says, "Never would have connected, kid."

"What?"

"The kick, stupid. You fuckin' white boys always telegraph your moves."

I shoot a fast right cross at his solar plexus and pull it, then ask, "How about that one?"

He laughs, slaps his hands together, says, "Let's hope we never find out, Mighty Mouse. OK, now, what else is botherin' ya, might as well spit it out, I know it's coming."

"What's up with tellin' Phil and Jazz they can't hang out, and all the bullshit ya ran down to my man Phil about he can't be with Jazz 'cause he's white. Tell me true, Ben. That don't sound like you. What's up with that?"

"Ya better be clear on one thing, son, this is my operation. I call the shots, answer to nobody but the man upstairs. Got it? I don't hold with white folks and black folks being romantic. We different, God made us that way. Now your boy Cross-Eyed Phil is a good worker, no doubt about that, but he ain't just a normal, nice little white boy, he's like you, pure peckerwood fool, he's got the devil in him and bullheaded, and big as a goddamn bull on top of it. Jazz is my kin, my blood, and ain't no way I'll countenance her race mixin' with a boy who's got trouble wrote all over his face. Crossed eyes, ugly as sin, nothin' but heartache for either of 'em. I'm doin 'em both a favor. I read Jazz from the Good Book, and what she didn't understand I explained with a razor strap. Spare the rod and spoil the child."

My gut clenches, memories flooding me of the fear and pain and rage that seized me when I'd hear that strap whistling through the air, the old man swinging it with such savage pleasure, feeling it now, and seizing up with anger at the picture of this beautiful girl being beaten just because she dares to love Cross-Eyed Phil.

Ben must see the rage in my eyes, because he backs off a foot or two, softening his tone to say, "She understands now, so don't you bother your head about it. Once you and your buddy are outta here it'll be better for all of us."

I take a deep breath, try to remember all Ben's done for us and why I'm in this conversation at all. "I don't know about all that, Ben. Phil's not gonna be a real happy guy."

"I talked to him this morning with Jazz in hand, Bobbie, and once she told him that this is the way she wants it he understood that this is for the best. Come on, I'll kick ya a few hundred to go shoppin' with, get you and your crew some new threads. Your boy Red seems to've taken a fancy to our Miss Lily. I know he be wantin' to look proper."

We start walking and I'm watching my feet crack through the snow and bring the mud that's underneath up and scatter it across the once-sparkling expanse that leads back to the farmhouse. I feel sad for Phil and Jazz but see nothing that I can do to change the hand that's playing out. Maybe it's almost springtime and the thought of making it back to a real city, getting loaded, and running amok is something to look forward to. Addressing anything other than Ben's last statement will be beyond futile. Once I got a pocket full of dough and am on the road, life will no doubt be grand.

We're almost back to the main house when I finally respond, "I know ya got that right, Benjamin. Red's head over heels, wants to make redheaded babies."

The main drag stretches dead as roadkill, the tar road scarred and pitted by tractors and farm trucks. The feed and grain store, an old barn once painted a bright green, has faded out to the color of dried algae over the years. The movie house, straight out of the thirties, curving marquee and everything, a Woolworth's that is just holding its own, and a pharmacy that should have a sign in the front window saying, ROB ME.

What it says is "Ethical Drugs," and as we pile out of the Cuda and I spot it my senses go into overdrive, and I can feel my heart slamming against my chest in triple time.

Federal law states that all narcotics must be kept in a locked cabinet. What that means is, once you're inside a pharmacy all you have to do is look around for a cabinet or drawer with a lock on it and rip it open. Behind that lock waits the kingdom of heaven.

It has been over a year since I've fixed and the need hits me like a magnum round, my mouth goes dry and my eyes start planning without any assistance from my brain: soft locks on the front door, a crowbar will have it open in a second, the walls are made out of thin wood that can be cut through in minutes, and, even without checking, I know that behind Ethical Drugs is a back door that will be a piece of cake and a coal chute that's the same as a private entrance for anyone small enough to slide down it.

Red's tugging at my sleeve and saying, "Come on, dog, whatcha starin' at? It's fuckin' cold out here. Phil and George are already in Woolworth's trying on clothes. Let's go."

When I look from the pharmacy to Red and raise one eyebrow and grin, he whistles between his teeth and says, "Ethical Drugs, huh? Shit howdy . . . looks good."

He frowns, shakes his head. "Can't do it, anyhow, got Lily to think about. Come on."

I get jeans, T-shirts, boxers, thermals, a double pack of socks, and a black leather jacket. Putting the new clothes on feels good. It's like shedding my old clothes, donning the stiff new jeans and a non-institution T-shirt, puts an end to the last chapter. Pulling the fluffy new socks on is almost sensual, a rush of softness. When you've been wearing threadbare, sandpaper-rough, state-issue clothes the texture of street clothes is a whole new experience.

Cross-Eyed Phil and his baby brother Big George are stirring up a fuss with the locals. These people aren't used to seeing two big dudes of different colors roughhousing and talking shit with obvious affection.

Red is profiling as hard as he can, checking and rechecking every article of clothing in the mirror, whistling at himself and keeping up a constant monologue. "Looking good, peckerwood, fine as a motherfucker. Look at ya, ya redheaded stud, gonna sweep that pretty little gal right off her motherfuckin' feet. Check it out, Bobbie, ain't I about the finest young motherfucker to ever set foot in the state of motherfuckin' Illinois? If I'm lyin' I'm dyin'. Redheaded babies on the way. Yeah, man! What choo think, dog, tell me true."

The new clothes feel great, but to tell the truth I don't care how I look. Phil and George wrestling around and loud-talking behind Red's monologue barely cuts through the fog that's surrounding my head like a cloud of gnats, buzzing out loud about how good some narcotics would feel.

The fact is that no matter how long you're off the shit it's got a call that won't quit. The brakes that had been put on what was at that time the driving force in my life by being locked down are gone. As much as I care about my road dogs, at this point they are only a distraction from casing that pharmacy and sending nirvana running up my arm like a thoroughbred running home.

Red says, louder, "Tell me true, dog, do I look cool? Will Lily get wet lookin' at me or what?"

I smile and say, "Yeah, Red, ya look like a fuckin' movie star. Poor Lily won't be able to help herself."

"Ya sure, dog?"

"Trust me on this, Red. You'll knock her socks off."

Slow-walk through the poorly lit pharmacy and the smell of liniment and medicines is thick in the air, the signs are from another era and the whole place feels misused, like it knows its time has come and gone with the fifties. The pharmacist is a dour-faced old redneck with a fake smile and a patronizing attitude. When he hands me the pack of smokes I'm buying to justify entering the store he doesn't respond to my thank-you. Maybe he thinks I'm up to no good, hard to believe, huh? I see that my first guess was right, no alarms, a soft target all the way around. Thinking about the rush of opiates hitting home rocks me so hard that I go from feeling queasy to puking from anticipation when I reach the car.

The next few days crawl. Life in the country is not my thing, Red is following Lily around drooling, Ben has adopted George and they're off and running like long-lost pals. Me and Phil kick it around the compound and do our best to stay entertained, not an easy thing to do unless you like manual labor or singing hymns.

The compound is a polyglot mix of people—failed hippies, tired outlaws hiding out, born-again dopers—and what later will be called survivalists. The binding force is the agreement that they have no use for the government and each and every person there feels a duty as a patriotic American to break the law in creative and nonviolent ways while praising the Lord.

Me, I just want to get loaded, get my dough, and get on.

Phil is fucking with the engine of the Cuda, trying to explain internal combustion to me, babbling on about manifolds and carburetors . . . and he might as well have been speaking Swahili. Not only do I not understand what the fuck he's talking about, it has no interest for me.

As he's doing something to the engine with a wrench I interrupt his mechanical monologue and say, "Listen, bub, Ben and George are running like Mutt and Jeff, the only way Red's gonna leave here is at gunpoint. Me, I'm gonna head for the East Coast quick like a hurry-up once I get my dough. Whatcha gonna do, Phil? Still plannin' on getting a job, finding a country girl, and making babies, or what?"

He keeps turning the wrench and says, "Shit, man, I been studying the way these folks make their money. I only look slow. Ben got to braggin' to George, and my little bro ran it down to me. He was goin' on about how they was makin' money hand over fist, sizzlin' insurance companies, sellin' guns, runnin' traveler's checks, shit I never heard of. Back in IYC you ran your jaws a couple of times about the big-time crooks you was runnin' with. Now, truth be told, I thought ya was lyin'."

Phil sets the wrench down and taps two smokes out of his pack, hands me one, lights mine and then his own, blows the smoke into the air above his head, and then points at me, crossed eyes locked on mine with his best psychotic stare beaming at me. He continues, "I figured you was full of shit as a Christmas goose. Looks like I figured wrong. Now, settling down does sound good, sounded just righteous when I thought I could settle down with Jazz, but Ben's stopped that, sho nuff."

He looks down, slams the wrench against his hand, maybe replacing frustration with pain, I don't know, and then he looks up with that weird, cross-eyed grin.

"But I want to see some shit and do some things while I'm still young enough to do 'em. You usta tell stories about the drugs and the rock and roll and the girls and the sacks full of money, I thought that was all jailhouse bullshit too. Well, I give it a lot of thought, and so far everything ya said was gospel true. You right about George not leavin', and any fool can see where Red's at. Me, I figure that I want to try out the rock and roll and the girls and the sacks full of money, I don't know about the dope, but the rest sounds good like a motherfucker."

I just wait as Phil takes a breath and goes on, "If you breakin' the law, a good wheelman is worth his weight in gold, and I'm a drivin' fool. You've seen me thump, I'll go knuckle and skull with any son of a bitch alive, any motherfucker breathin'. I say all that to say this: If ya want a ride to the East Coast, or wherever the hell you're goin', I figure with my good looks and your brains we should be able to kick up some dust. Whatcha think, killer?"

"Well, as these yokels say, shit howdy, why the fuck not. Rob that little drugstore, get my dough, and bright lights, big city, here we come."

Red's face matches his name, his head is hanging like his neck is broke, Ben and George are standing side by side and Phil is between them and me gritting his teeth.

We're crowded into the room that me and the fellas have been sleeping in, clothes and old furniture now distributed among the mattresses. Lily is peeping in through the door and it's pandemonium.

I had been lying on my rack, reading a collection of Poe's stuff, when Ben came crashing into the room, followed by the fellas with the lovely Lily bringing up the rear.

I had jumped up, adrenaline pumping and ready for whatever was coming, 'cause Stevie Wonder could have seen that this was not going to be an intellectual conversation.

Ben's swollen up like a gold-toothed bear, spit flying out of his mouth with every word, pointing at me and hollering, "Motherfucker, motherfuckin' dopefiend son of a bitch, I live in this goddamn town. You hit that store it's gon' bring heat down so fast and so hard that it'll make your goddamn head spin. Don't ya understand shit? Talkin' about how you ain't gonna do nothin' that ain't planned. What are you, fuckin' stupid, or did the thought of slammin' some of that goddamn shit turn your brains into crap? If Lily hadn't told me what y'all was up to the first I'da heard about it would be when the man showed up at our door with a search warrant. You gotta go, Bobbie, and take your gorilla with ya. The rest of your boys can stay and make a future here, but you as crazy as a fuckin' loon."

The onslaught has me frozen. I can't believe Red opened his mouth to Lily about what I was planning, and the mix of emotions that's kicked up leaves no simple answers. As soon as he started going off I knew Ben was right, you can't shit where you live and expect it to smell like roses. But the confrontation's got me wired. Whether he's right or not, all this bulldogging, loud-talkin', and general woofing has got my adrenaline all the way up. I'm making like I've got lockjaw so I won't say something I'll regret.

Once Ben winds down I take a deep breath and say, "Yeah, you're right, I'm wrong. Gimme the dough ya owe me and I'm outta here tonight."

He looks like he is hooked up to an air hose, swells up and explodes.

"The dough I owe ya? Fuck the dough ya think I owe. I ain't payin' shit. You're as crazy as those fools you usta run with, that bitch Syd set the whole thing up . . . you think it left me owing ya for that last contract? She thinks I'm some stupid nigger who can't figure shit out, fuck her and fuck you. Get outta here. Hitchhike to the motherfuckin' East Coast."

He hesitates for a second and then spits out, "You're burnt, motherfucker, fuck you if ya don't like it. Got it, white boy?"

The room shrinks down to a tiny, strobing corridor leading from me to Ben, the sound of rushing water fills my brain, and the wooden chair that I've been leaning on is suddenly in my hands and swinging through the air, and when it hits Ben across the midsection it's like I've smashed it into a wall, the chair doesn't even slow him down as he rushes me, driving me back and smashing me into the wall. He's got both hands around my throat and my feet are off the ground and I'm kicking as hard as I can and know I'm not doing any good as my vision starts to fade and my dogs tackle him, pulling him off, and Phil's got him in a sleeper and Big George is screaming, "Don't kill him, don't kill his black ass, you cross-eyed son of a bitch, let up on the choke, Phil."

But the whole time George is yelling at Phil he's got Ben's legs pinned so Ben can't do shit, except gasp and spit at Red, who by now is sitting on his chest growling, "Cool out, big man, ya can't be killin' my dog. Chill out."

Ben's people are pounding up the stairs, trying to crowd into the room, and Phil applies enough pressure to make Ben's neck pop like a firecracker and says, "Y'all fuckin' back off or I'm gonna snap old Ben's neck like a motherfuckin' twig. Ya with me on this, Ben?"

Ben takes a deep breath, and croaks, "I'm with ya, boy, seems like we all got a little bit crazy. If you young fools will get up offa me we can mosey downstairs and discuss this over some good whiskey . . . maybe without killing each other."

I feel stupid as a stump. Planning to hit that drugstore was inexcusable stupidity, there's no cleanup for something like that.

I don't have a clue that part of the human condition is the errors we make, the incredibly stupid things we do and later regret. We all have our share of them, but when one specific thing can short-circuit your brain you're doomed. I'm under the illusion that if I think enough and learn enough I will no longer fuck up. I think everybody else has a built-in system that is like a road map on how to live life. At this point in my young life, I am still awfully naive.

I got a smoke going and can feel the bruises on my neck where Ben had his fingers. We hit the main room downstairs where civility reigns, big soft couches, easy chairs, a pool table in a side room, and a monster stereo system. The dark hardwood floors are covered with oriental rugs and the wet bar is top-of-the-line.

Ben walks behind the bar and rubs his throat, pulls a bottle of Jack Daniel's down and fills five shot glasses, downs one, and says, "Here's mud in your eye."

As me and the fellas down ours I tell him, "Listen, Benjamin, me plannin' on hittin' that store was wrong. Fuckin' stupid. Hope there's no hard feelings. Know what I mean? I'll roll as soon as I can, but I need that dough."

Ben pours all the shot glasses full again, and as we down them he says, "Yeah, I know what ya mean. Me too, I don't need any new enemies. The U.S. government is enough. And you boys work good together, I lost it, too much pressure. I ain't the Reverend Jimbo . . . try to fill his shoes, but he had the magic touch, and me takin' over when he was killed . . . keepin' this place together, paying the bills, settling disputes, you four showin' up made it worse than ever."

He rubs his neck, trying to smooth out the ache of Phil's choke, or maybe the stress of being top dog in the craziest kennel in the country, I don't know. He says, "Here's what's up. I've worked too goddamn hard to let anyone fuck this up. I ain't real happy with Syd, but that ain't here or there. Shit happens."

I nod my head, try not to let my eyes show that I know why he's not too happy with Syd. I flash back on the whole mess, knowing that Syd was part of the only real family I ever had, and I trust her ninety percent, but the other ten percent got blown when she lost her senses after Mel bought it, and she set Ben up, and Billy Bones and Black Cloud and Al and me in the bargain. That was my second hard lesson that anytime a for-profit crime is mixed up with vengeance it isn't just the bad guys whose blood gets spilled.

Ben goes on, "I got about five, six grand in cash. I'll go to the bank tomorrow and get another fifteen in traveler's checks. You can burn those all the way to the East Coast, Jersey or Boston or wherever the hell ya end up. Tell me if I'm wrong, but the way I figure it, you and Phil are probably gonna head that way together. Am I right?"

"As fuckin' rain."

"That's what I figured, ya both got the devil workin' in ya. We settled on fifteen gees, I'll give ya five cash, fifteen in checks. Give ya two weeks to get 'em all cashed. Call 'em in stole, they'll refund my money, I'm only out five and you come up twenty. Joesy will have IDs for you two in the morning. The sooner you're out of here the better for all of us."

He points at Big George and Red and says, "You boys are welcome to stay, you know that. I don't hold that little ruckus against y'all. You did the right thing, helpin' your friend. Just one thing, y'all stay, your loyalty is to me. We can't have no confusion. What's it gonna be?"

It's probably only a minute or so but it stretches on forever. Finally Red looks at me out of the sides of his eyes and says, "Reckon I'll be stayin', Ben, long as it's all right."

No surprise to me, Red wants to make redheaded babies.

Big George and Phil are staring at each other and finally Phil says, "Do it, bro. I love ya no matter what, you'll do better here than out in the madness anyhow."

Big George says, "Yeah, you right, I'm gonna miss your ugly white ass, though. But I'm stayin'."

Ben grins ear to ear, the enamel gleaming through the star cut into the gold cap on his front tooth. He says, "Tomorrow we'll do what we gotta do, and then Bobbie and Phil are on their way."

Pouring the shot glasses full one more time, he raises his and says, "A toast to the four of you, good luck coming, good luck going."

We drink.

seven

The sun is still sleeping when Ross kicks our door open and yells, "Rise and shine, motherfuckers, appointments to keep, asses to kick. George and Carrot-Top, you boys get to hoppin' . . . Ben's got an errand for you two in Chi Town. Step on it, boys, time's a-wastin'. Gotta get gone."

The whiskey has left me half drunk, and, looking at my friends, I know they aren't feeling any better. Phil struggles into a sitting position and throws a wadded-up shirt at George, saying, "Sweet motherfuckin' Jesus, never thought I'd see the day that a half-witted cracker wannabe would call my little bro 'boy' and keep all his teeth. Sad situation, guess me and Bobbie hittin' the road just in time, they'll have ya wearin' a dress next."

George is still half asleep and slow with a comeback, so I take a shot at Red, saying, "Gotcha a new handle, dog, 'Carrot-Top,' sounds like old Ross thinks you're a vegetable. Yeah, man, you guys are gonna have it made. Me and poor Phil gonna be out there runnin' amok, you two got too-tough Ross to run your lives. 'Carrot-Top,' shee-it, if the fellas could only see you two now."

It's all becoming real, the crew is splitting up in a way none of us could have anticipated. Phil and George are blood-close, brothers, and me and Red are so tight we often don't have to talk, road dogs. The four of us are to the point where we just track each other, a tight crew. Each of us knows the pain and loss that the other three are feeling but the thing is that no matter how much you love your running partners it's never acknowledged. Any feelings that are perceived as less than manly are denied before they ever draw breath.

Big George has a catch in his voice when he says, "Don'tcha worry your cross-eyed head, before the day's out I'll beat that wannabe nigger's ass so bad he'll never think about actin' black again or callin' anybody 'boy' that's older than five. You take care, fellas."

Phil's got something wrong with his eyes and is rubbing them when he grabs George in a bear hug that would have crushed a normal guy's ribs.

Red's looking at his feet when he says, "Yo, killer, you still my dog, ain'tcha?"

I got a lock on all the shit that's trying to tear its way out of my chest, my voice is steady, and as we shake hands I tell Red, "Always, dog. Till we die."

"Yeah, peckerwood, till we die. I got somethin for that piece of shit too, Carrot-Top, my fuckin' ass. See ya."

Now it's me and Phil and if he feels the way he looks, then he's runnin' neck and neck with me. Sad like a motherfucker.

The odor of frying foods is filtering through the main house, and when you're used to eating on a regular basis you get hungry on a regular basis. Not knowing where we are headed except down the road, not knowing much of anything except that breakfast smells good, we stuff ourselves.

We have our shit packed and we're ready to go as soon as we eat and after Ben makes the bank run. Ross pokes his head in through the door and says, "Yo, zup, Ben be wantin' you two downstairs in the main room. Step it up."

We grab the burlap bags holding our few belongings, look at each other, and Phil says, "This don't seem right, hoss."

I light a smoke and say, "No shit, Sherlock. Let's roll."

In the main room Ben's standing and staring out the window, there's a fire already burning merrily in the fireplace and the couches and easy chairs are occupied by all the males on the compound except the few that had been waiting to trail in behind us.

We're boxed in, the only question in my mind is whether we're gonna get hit or get off with an ass-beating. As my brain is calling me names for not secreting a knife when I had the chance, Ben turns from the window, takes the pipe from his mouth, and says, "It's a mighty nice day out there, almost wish I was still young and dumb and full of cum my ownself, go down the highway raisin' hell with y'all. But I'm a man grown and with a grown man's responsibilities, and then some. Now I prayed on this situation, thought on it long and deep, and here's where I stand."

He stops talking and chews on his pipe for a second and then points at me with it, saying, "Puttin' all that ruckus last night aside, you ain't a bad un. Did me no wrong. BUT. The fact of the matter is your friend Sydney didn't serve anybody's purposes but her own. So my point is that while you served my cause and, of course, the good Lord's, there was a darker force behind you."

Ben's starting to preach, voice rising and diction becoming clearer as he gets into his roll, a habit he's picked up during my absence, one that is beyond disturbing because I know that whatever bullshit he comes up with he is going to feel completely justified. He's going to find a way to keep the share I'd earned when we did that job, I know it.

Ben continues enunciating each word and rolling that ministerial moan, and I am waiting for the silent jury surrounding us to start yelling hallelujah when he gets to the bottom line, saying, "So, boy, out of the goodness of my heart, and common Christian charity, I'm going to give you a thousand dollars in cash to get you on your way . . . another five thousand in traveler's checks that you'll have one week exactly to pass before I call them in stolen and get my refund. When you get to New Jersey, tell my old friend Syd that if she thought I was unaware of her scheming she was wrong. She can pay you the balance owed for your labors. Mark my words, Bobbie, anyone that uses drugs is a betrayer. Syd, you, and this gorilla you brought to my home."

Of course he is right and he is also wrong, I know this as he is talking and I want to tell him so, that there are no absolutes. But it's too late.

Cross-Eyed Phil takes two steps towards Ben and says, "Drugs, betrayer? What the fuck you talkin' about, motherfucker? I just . . ."

And that is as far as he gets before Ross raises a double-barreled sawed-off shotgun from his side and points it at us, saying, "Loud-talkin' white trash, shut yo mouf, mo'fucker."

I can sense the impulse racing through Phil to rush this idiot holding the shotgun whether it will get us both killed or not, and I grab his arm and say, "Cool out, killer. Don't let this wannabe negro call the shots."

I point at Ben and say, "What's up, boss, you gonna let this flunky talk for you? A fuckin' white boy that acts blacker than you do. Kick with the cash and the checks and we're in the wind. Let this punk waste us, and not only will ya have to live with your own betrayal, Red and George won't be real happy. Plus, I might be wrong, but I suspect that some people who know both of us might get upset if you put my lights out."

Ben smiles real easy and says, "Ross might not be very bright or diplomatic, but his loyalty is beyond question. If I ask him to he'll kill you both in a heartbeat. . . . But I don't want that. For us to part on good terms you have to know that the betrayal started almost two years ago. I don't know if you were a participant or got used in the game, it doesn't really matter. Point is, Syd put those punks up to kidnapping our women so's we'd hit 'em for revenge *and* rob the drugs 'n' shit. She got her percentage of the take, but Baby Al and Black Cloud went down unnecessarily . . . and, jus' in case you f'got, you purt' near bought the farm, too."

I try to keep my face blank. No point in letting Ben know that I *had* figured out how Syd had set it all up, but I also knew she was half out of her head from losing Mel. Shit, I was all the way out of my head from losing Rosie and Mel, both. People do some fuckin' stupid things when their brains are on hold from grief.

Ben's rolling on. "Because I choose not to participate, I've found a safe haven for me and mine. I do what I choose. My only loyalty is to me and mine. You two have a different agenda, cheap thrills and a early grave. God bless or God damn, it makes no difference to me. Go in peace. My little Jazz is safe, this isn't costing me more than I want to give away, and my conscience is clear."

And with that he raises his hand in a peace sign and laughs, saying, "If you get tired of playing with the devil, come back and visit."

Phil takes one more step forward and says, "Playin' with the devil? Shit, man, I'd be happy plowin' fuckin' fields and courtin' your niece. I ain't even a druggie. I got no problem being clean. I can even sing hymns with the best of y'all. Gimme a break."

Ben looks at Ross and says, "Show them out. If our friend Phil causes any problems, kill him."

I can't figure out what it is about Phil that makes Ben turn so nuts. Maybe he thinks crossed eyes are a sign of evil, but if so, he's wrong.

As we pick up our burlap bags and head for the door, Phil turns and says in a calm, level voice, "Fuck you. You a fuckin' hypocrite and if there's a hell you gonna be there."

Ben sticks his pipe in his mouth for a second, stares at Phil, and says, "Then we'll be burning together, boy. Get 'em outta here, Ross."

I think, This is the last time I'll ever see Ben.

One more thing to be wrong about.

A hemi engine has a noise all its own. A deep howling growl, the feeling of limitless power surging through the vehicle even when it's idling, is immense. Ferraris and other high-performance cars don't even come close. When Phil slams it into first we start fishtailing all the way down the unpaved drive; he hits second going onto the paved road outside the compound, and as he smashes it into third and we leave burning rubber behind we are already going over seventy, it crosses my mind that I really hope Cross-Eyed Phil can drive as good as he says. Downshifting around the tight turns in the country road and flying up a steep hill at 120, he speed-shifts into fourth and when we hit the top of the hill we are flying through the air. Weightless. My ass is floating above the seat, my head touching the roof, and I grab the dash just as we come back to earth, smashing into the asphalt still accelerating, both laughing and screaming like maniacs until we get to the town limits.

Phil drops the Cuda into second and cruises to a stop in front of the Woolworth's. Swinging his feet to the pavement, he says, "Tell me true, dog, did that wake ya up?"

Laughs and slaps himself in the face hard enough to leave a handprint, saying, "Gets the old heart pumpin', don't it. Hang tough, I gotta pick somethin' up. I'll be right back."

Staring at the pharmacy and smoking, figuring that as sweet as it looks, Ben would never forgive me if I were to hit it. Planning on cashing some of the traveler's checks in Chicago and scoring, waiting to get loaded like a penitent waiting on absolution.

When Phil comes sauntering out of Woolworth's I know that robbing that drugstore and committing a couple of murders would be nothing compared to what is going down now.

Hair swept back, light cocoa skin and gold eyes, suede coat over a tight knee-length skirt covering a body that is as hot as the legs it is walking on, those crazy long legs going down into medium-heel ankle boots, Jazz is arm in arm with Phil, both faces smiling ear to ear and still kissing as they walk.

I take a hit off my Camel and know that no matter what happens it is torn now. Ben is never going to forgive this one. I open my door and slide into the backseat and when she closes her door she grins back at me, saying with a soft drawl, "Why as I live and breathe it's my old friend Bad Bobbie. How you doing today, Bad?"

"Never better, Jazz. Life gets more entertaining by the minute. Never better."

The Cuda howls, rock and roll plays, they kiss and we laugh like idiots all the way to Chicago. Bright lights, big fuckin' city, here we come, here we are.

Having been locked down, you develop a good imagination, and every time they kiss I can feel what Jazz's lips must feel like. And she has a style to her that is different from the street chicks and walking female voodoo dolls that I've always run with, different enough from Rosie, with her hard-assed, straight-from-the-hip Puerto Rican charm, to make it just a little easier to think about another woman now. Jazz has an innocence and optimism that is fascinating. I rarely feel guilt, but the knowledge that I think my partner's old lady is fine spins me.

The result of this is I am on my absolutely best behavior, careful not to flirt, doing my best to act like Jazz is one of the fellas, respectful as I can be.

Phil metamorphoses in front of my eyes, the big dumb dangerous peckerwood becoming thoughtful, almost shy, introspective, motherfuckin' courtly. "Fuck," "shit," "cunt," and the other words of a four-letter variety that normally count for half our vocabulary disappear from his sentences, and the intelligence that he normally hides is brought out and exercised.

Jazz is a ball, fun to be with and probably good for both of us, but like the preacher's daughter, she is ready to fly. I wonder if Phil will be able to keep up.

*   *   *

"So, Bad Bobbie," Jazz says, "how does this check thing work?"

I'm happy to give lessons, so I tell her, "Traveler's checks are a wonderful invention, my little chickadee. You get a couple grand in traveler's checks, give them to someone you trust. They run from store to store cashing them, then you call them in stolen and get your money back. Double your money, double your fun. Loan your ID to your partner, and even if you look nothing alike, nine times out of ten they'll fly. Because nobody even checks them."

The first store specializes in pipe tobaccos and cigars. Three cigars cost ten bucks, the change from a hundred-dollar traveler's check is ninety. In and out. Passing traveler's checks is a gas; we rarely get asked for ID and every place we go into is happy to take them. We pick up all the incidentals we need, one at each store and one check at a time.

Eating lunch in a place called Three Kings Steak House gives me an opportunity to display the fact that I know about something other than theft. Among the many lessons Mel and Syd taught Rosie and me, they introduced us to high living and great food. I figure I'll do the same for Phil and Jazz, so I order steak and king crab legs all the way around, a nice red wine to go with the meal, and three double Wild Turkey Old-Fashioneds for dessert.

As we walk out into the slush and wind, Jazz is hanging on Phil, murmuring, "Baby, baby, baby, this is surely a long way from the farm."

I'm thinking that her uncle will have a gang of heavily armed motherfuckers combing Chicago looking for us, and knowing that we aren't nearly far enough away.

We pass the last of the checks at a pawnshop that's willing to sell me an old .32-caliber revolver and a box of shells without busting my balls. Before the day is out we have bailed out of Chicago and we stop in the first town we come to that has a nice hotel. Lesson number two, passed along from Mel and Syd to Rosie and me, and now from me to Phil and Jazz. There are hotels a lot nicer than the farm if you've got the cash or the card to get past the lobby.

And we have the cash. It is splashed across the king-sized bed, looking pretty. The carpet is so deep that our feet sink into it, and after spending the last year and change on concrete and dirt, pulling my boots off and walking on it is the best. And as Jazz points out, it's a lot better than walking on chickenshit at the compound, too.

Life is grand and going to keep on getting better, I can feel it coursing through my body like electricity, good times are coming.

The TV is on, we have a bottle of Cristal champagne each, and as soon as I can exit gracefully I am gonna score. If I can't connect on the street I've already spotted two pharmacies that are doable on the way to the hotel.

Phil is doing his best to drink like a gentleman, and Jazz is sipping her champagne like she's taken classes on being ladylike. We are smoking the cigars and high-signing. I drink two glasses of the champagne, and as soon as it hits, any finesse I might have had goes out the window. I chug the rest of my bottle, and the gentle fire and immediate giddiness unleash the demons that have been lying dead since I got busted. Set the bottle down, grab the dough off the bed, flip a couple hundred back, and tell them, "Have fun, kids, I'm going out and about. See ya in the morning."

Jazz just wiggles her fingers and Phil freezes for a second, sensing what's up, but one look at his new girl and he remembers he wants to be alone with her. So he just says, "Don't get busted, wood. See ya in the mornin'."

The wind is cutting into me like cold razors, the slush has turned to ice, and the first bar I hit is a blue-collar joint that has little promise but it's warm and worth stopping in for a second just to get out of the cold. The dark and smoke hit my eyes like a surprise. I've been out of circulation for too long, and all my senses are on full. The whining bubble-gum singer on the jukebox should be all the clue I need to know that this joint isn't happening. The bartender is an old broad with dyed hair like reddish hay, and when I ask her for a shot and a beer she snorts phlegm up and swallows it. Pours the shot, sets down a mug of beer, and says, "You're too clean to be coming from the plant. Ain't from around here. Passing through?"

I down the boilermaker, say, "Sure 'nough." And roll.

Flag down a cab. The driver is a clean-cut-lookin' guy of about twenty, lame as they make 'em. Wave him on.

Hail the next cab that passes and the driver is a hard-looking

Latino, Mexican, Puerto Rican, whatever. The operative term is "hard." I lean in the window with a twenty in my hand and say, "Qué pasa? I'm lookin' to score. Where do I gotta go in this town to pick up?"

He gives me a once-over and pushes his hair back off his forehead, glares, then says, "You heat? Stupid question, huh? Whadda ya lookin' for?"

"Stuff."

"Stuff?"

"Heroin, smack, stuff."

"Shee-it, man, weed, pills, speed, yeah. Heroin is a whole different thing. I don't know."

I keep the twenty in his sight, think for a second, and ask him, "Ya got a ho stroll in this burg?"

"Shee-it, commandant, you lookin' for pussy, that's no problem. I know workin' girls. How much you want to spend?"

"Only if they're junkies, pal, that's why I'm lookin' for where they stroll. Bottom of the barrel, bust-out dopefiend bitches. Got a part of town that matches that description?"

He sucks on his lip for a second, eyeing the bill extending from my fingers, and then says, "Gimme the cash, plus the fare. It's your ass. Ya wanna go down there, I'll take ya."

Trashed wooden fourplexes, liquor stores with shotguns hanging on the wall behind the counter, barrooms whose neon died long ago, human waste bundled as warmly as they can get standing around trash-can fires drinking wine, waiting for spring or death, whichever comes first.

The air is different here, the smell of dreams cheaply sold is as thick as fog, and it feels good. This is what I come from, hopefully not where I'll end up. I'm the only white dude for blocks, and if you're from Podunk, Montana, or somewhere, that might seem strange . . . but this is home to me, not because I know the rules or like the people or some kinda lame shit like that. There are no rules, there are no people, just animals surviving. If you're here you are the dregs of society, scum.

That's the great equalizer, everyone down here knows that. I'm gonna get loaded or get dead. Getting loaded is way preferable.

Walking slowly, feeling eyes evaluating me, judging the way I walk, what I weigh, how hard it would be to take me down, and the really important question. Is there a gun in the hand in my jacket pocket?

Working girls pass and none looks right. Three black kids about my age start trailing me, one of them finally calling out, "What choo need, white boy? What choo lookin' fo'?"

I turn and smile, saying the first thing that comes to mind. Telling them the absolute truth. "Salvation. Eternal fuckin' bliss. Nothin' you can help me with. Thanks."

As they start to circle, the smallest one squints against the cold wind and says, "Shit, white boy, you down here you need our help just to get down the block. I asked what ya lookin' for. What choo mean we ain't gonna help you? Maybe we gonna help you whether you want it or not. Show you salvation, stupid motherfucker. How you like that? Now whatcha got for us?"

I'm still smiling when I say, "Got nothing for ya. I'm looking for tranquillity, redemption from my sins, freedom from my own thoughts."

The sound of my thumb pulling the hammer back on the revolver in my jacket pocket echoes loudly in the tired street and punctuates the statement, then I finish talking by saying, "Thank you, anyhow."

They're temporarily frozen, the sound of a piece being cocked unmistakable, and then the spokesman screws his face and courage up and asks, "What choo got in your pocket, man?"

"Peace, pal, eternal peace."

And as I laugh the other two black guys laugh with me, the biggest grabbing their ex-spokesman by the arm, saying, "Come on, bro, dis white boy's fuckin' crazy."

And I keep on walking, looking in the faces passing me by until I find her. Her walk is as nasty as she can make it, strolling hard. A white girl that stands out down here as much as I do, dirty blond hair past her shoulders and what's left of a nice body and pretty face, dressed in as little as possible in the freezing weather. She has stoned bust-me eyes, pale blue with her pupils in her purse, so pinned that she could be carrying a sign that says, "Under the influence of good opiates."

The girl of my dreams.

I step directly into her path and hold out a cigarette. When she takes it and puts it between her lips I light hers and then light mine. She checks me out slowly, starting with my feet and working her way up to my face, letting her eyes linger on mine for a minute as she smokes and then asks me, "Why you down here, man? You ain't a cop, and you don't look like a trick. What's your scene?"

She hesitates for a second and when I don't respond continues, "I'm workin', talk fast or I'll be down the block. What's up?"

"I just got out. Gonna be here for about the next twelve hours and want to score. Trying to get decent dope on the street is an idiot move, end up buying shitty shit, getting burnt or having to kill somebody. You're the answer, darlin', your eyes are a stone bust. Pretty blue eyes with no pupils, just the way I want mine to be. Stoned."

Watching her reaction, knowing the whole scenario before it plays out, taking a drag off my smoke, I tell her, "It's too fuckin' cold out here to have a long conversation. Tell ya what's happening here, reason we're even talking. You know who's got the good drugs. You're out of dough and dope or you wouldn't be hustlin' in this weather, you're gonna be getting sick in a little while and I'm the answer. You and me go to your guy and pick up. Fix. Go our separate ways. I kick you down enough shit to keep you right for a while. Simple."

I can see the angles banging around her head like ricocheting bullets, almost hear her thinking, so when she says, "Yeah, I can get the kind. You walk to the place with me, gimme your cash. I'll go inside and bring it out. OK?" I've already got the answer.

"No. I'll go in with you. Introduce me as your long-lost cousin or brother or whatever the fuck will fly. I pay for the shit, taste it, and put it in my pocket. We leave, fix, and I kick you down."

She widens her eyes and almost pulls off lookin' hurt, saying, "What, you don't trust me? I wouldn't burn you."

I just laugh and say, "Of course you wouldn't, but . . . I don't trust my own mother, let alone pretty little dopefiend chicks. My way or no way. Whatcha wanna do?"

Silly question.

The dope comes in glassine envelopes made for holding stamps. The stuff itself is a dirty gray, white smack with so many impurities that they show clearly. The man sells twenty-four bags to a bundle, one hundred bucks per bundle, and if you wanted to go into business you could sell individual bags for from five to ten bucks apiece, depending on your clientele.

The whole time I am negotiating with the guy I keep telling myself that I will only get enough for that night, then I'm thinking only enough for a couple of days, and finally, my last thought on the subject is that I know all the pitfalls of getting hooked and it doesn't matter how much I get, I am in control. I'll only fix when I really want to, I'm telling myself, no way am I gonna get strung out again.

So I buy his last five bundles. With no habit to feed, they should last for a while.

As we go down the stairs my stomach is turning over from anticipation. I hand her five bags and say, "Thanks."

She hesitates for a second and without missing a step or turning her head, says, "I was working so I could get a room for the night, think I could stay with you?"

We're on the stoop of the wasted house that the dealer runs his store out of and I freeze up looking at her, taking in the too-thin face, once very pretty but now looking tired and aged before its time, the still-tight little body in not enough clothing, and feel myself responding to the gamin grin that she is now wearing.

I tell her, "Yeah, I think I'd like that."

My room is the same as Phil's and Jazz's, nice. As soon as we get in the door we both start our own private rituals, ending with me slamming a vein in the back of my hand, and, after countless tries and much bleeding, she gets a register and sends salvation up a vein in her leg.

When the dope hits after all that time away from it, it's like finding a loved one you thought was dead, a huge emotional release, and then that slow-motion itch starts. There is no tomorrow and life is good.

I watch her nod and scratch for a second and then she says, "Don't go away, darlin', I'm gonna take a hot, hot shower and I'll be right back."

I fix again while she is in the shower, and come out of my nod staring at the first naked woman I've seen in what seems like forever.

She smiles and says, "Stand up."

She looks so pretty standing there, probably not much older than me, a natural blonde with small round tits, who at one time must have been a gymnast or dancer, the muscle tone still apparent in her thin limbs. Tracks run down her arms and from her feet up into her calves, the self-inflicted stigmata that born-to-lose, throwaway people like us always wear in one form or another. I admire her for a minute not saying anything, just enjoying looking at a nude female human for the first time in a long time, then tell her, "Don't sweat it, darlin', you don't gotta do nothin' except get loaded and have conversation."

She places one hand on her hip and tosses her head to get her still-wet hair off her face and says, "I know that . . . if I had to I wouldn't want to. Stupid. But . . . I don't have to, so I want to. Got it? So stand the fuck up."

When I come out of the chair she unbuckles my jeans and I am already harder than penitentiary steel. Once my body's reactions get past the heroin it is a grand night. Coming on heroin is a lot of work. When she oohs and aahs I act like I believe it. When she says I was the best ever I try my hardest to keep a straight face, but it's just too much to ask. I start laughing, and for a second she looks hurt . . . and then joins in laughing until tears are running down her face.

And I come, and maybe she does too, or maybe not. Any guy that thinks he always knows what's up with women is full of shit and stupid as a fuckin' stump. And we smoke and slam and fuck again, and then just nodding and holding each other feels as good as the sex, better almost because now the crazy urgency is gone, and I have been dying inside from my need for affection.

The physical contact and soft caresses are a high of their own. Whispering about nothing and everything, telling each other selected segments of our hard-luck stories as effective as any therapy I've ever heard of.

As dawn is creeping past the windows and reality is getting ready to make its grim entrance she says, "I'm so tired of just getting fucked, it's nice to be held."

I don't say a word, just hold her and stroke her hair. I never ask her name, and there is no reason to tell her mine.

It is a real nice night. As she says, "It's been wicked good." She doesn't see the irony, but I do.

We part that morning with the best thing any of us can hope for: no new scars.

eight

The truck stop is full, bustling with activity, and the diner is jammed, the truckers uniformly giving Phil and me hard stares and looking at Jazz like she is a part of their meal that has gone to the wrong table. Aside from the sadly lacking ambience the food is great, bloody greasy burgers and thick fries dripping with saturated fat.

Jazz has been giving me strange looks all morning and I wonder if she knows I'm loaded. I've been careful to keep my fixing as undercover as I can, but one of the drawbacks of blue or gray eyes is that they are a bust, and if the girl from last night had her pupils in her purse mine were now in my back pocket, solid gone.

Phil isn't noticing anything except Jazz, so I assume that there's no sweat there. I got a mouthful of burger when she asks me, "So are you the kind of dog my uncle says you are? You slept with that girl last night and told her goodbye this morning. He said that guys like you only want to have a good time, then split. What's up with that, Bad?"

I don't know whether to laugh or cry, I'm glad she doesn't know I'm loaded but I don't want to seem like a slut with nuts. For some reason her opinion is important to me, and after I take a hit off the malt to wash the burger down I say, "I ain't a dog, she was a real nice chick, just she had stuff to take care of and so do I. That don't make either of us bad. Know what I mean?"

Phil is shoveling food in with both hands, having momentarily forgotten that he wants to act like a guy who graduated from charm school with honors, so he's bewildered when she says, "Yeah, I guess so, but . . ." And elbows poor Phil in the side as hard as she can and adds, "But Philip here better not be gettin' any funny ideas about any of these nice chicks you seem to meet so easy. Whether they bad or not."

Having missed the whole thing, Phil spends the next couple of hours giving me reproachful looks, sure that somehow whatever happened was my fault.

Between the tension at the table and the behavior of our fellow diners, lunch goes downhill fast. On the way out the door Phil treats one of the louder and more blatant redneck truckers to one of his all-the-way psychotic looks, and when the guy looks back, trying to match stares, Phil stops, leans over, and whispers to him, "Y'all keep starin' at my girl I'm gonna rip the eye right out of yer head and skull-fuck ya here and now. Got it, ace?"

The guy doesn't say another word, just studies his fingernails until we are out the door.

The room is the same chain hotel room we've all stayed in a hundred times, TV bolted to a mount on the wall, easy-clean carpet, fiberboard furniture, a little paper strip telling you that the toilet has been cleaned and sanitized and plastic cups furnished at no extra expense.

As soon as we check in I buy a paperback whodunit, go to my room, and try to read. Look from the page to the ceiling, from the ceiling to the wall, then back to the page in front of me and try to find the line I was reading, back and forth and back again. Jump up and turn on the TV and get disgusted the second time through the channels. Do a couple sets of push-ups, back to the bed and the book, stare at the ceiling and turn the TV on again. Three or four times through this exact routine and it's enough, too much even.

Fill the plastic glass with tap water, take the spoon, syringe, and glassine envelopes out of the stash I cut into my leather jacket, and dump a couple of bags into the cooker. The shit heats up clear with just a few little specks of some bonus substance floating around in the solution in the spoon. Draw it up and tap the point in. When my blood rushes up into the outfit mixing with the smack like a deep red lava lamp, the plunger sends it all home. Thick red blood and opiate-rich water rush through the needle and into me.

The anxiety is going, going, motherfucking gone.

Kicked back, legs crossed dopefiend style, one knee hooked over the other. Cleaning the .32 revolver, admiring the worn wooden grips and the pitted blueing on the barrel stamped "Made in Brazil," noticing that someone has filed the front sight off so it won't get hung up on your clothes when you pull it. Working with a rag and solvent trying to get the rust off the filed area where the sight was. Probably not accurate more than five feet away but I don't intend to do any target shooting. One thing this piece will do is stop a heart and that's all it's for.

Content, Camel burning in the ashtray next to me, TV on with the sound off. Planning my next moves in slow motion with the supreme confidence that opiates inspire, until the nightmare moment they quit working.

The knocking on the door is loud and clear, not a cop knock but not a maid either and this place doesn't have room service. I drop six rounds in the empty holes, snap old Made in Brazil's cylinder closed, and, holding it behind my back, say, "Yeah. Who's that."

"Phil, foolio. Open up."

He lurches through the door with a bottle of Jack Daniel's in hand, raises it in my direction, and falls into the easy chair, saying, "Shit, partner, women are stone fuckin' crazy. Jazz is sure I'm gonna start chasin' everything in a skirt. Know what we been talkin' about for the last few hours? No. Hell no, ya don't. I'll tell ya. Her saintly Uncle Ben, how he warned her about guys like us, and if *you* want to fuck everything walkin' how can *I* be any different? I say all that to say this: dog, can you please do me a favor and keep your tramp ways away from her? She's a nice girl, raised on a motherfuckin' farm, for Christ's sakes. Now she don't got no idea you're shootin' dope, and I hope she don't find it out 'cause she'd surely go fifty-one/fifty. So do your ace deuce, cross-eyed road dog a favor, keep a low profile with your city ways."

He takes a hit off the Jack and says, "And kick with some stuff, hoss. I might have been born in the mornin', but it wasn't this mornin', and I want to give that shit a try."

I'm frozen, you don't ever give someone their first taste of smack unless you hate them, even as a dumb eighteen-year-old I know this, and I tell him, "Chill out, dog, you don't want no motherfuckin' heroin. The shit's poison. What makes ya think I'm fuckin' with smack anyhow?"

"Shit howdy, ace, you in slow motion, your voice sounds like ya been gargling with gravel and your eyeballs look like they made outta glass. Like I said, I mighta been born in the mornin' but not this mornin'. Kick."

"Tell ya what, killer, I ain't gonna lie to ya but I ain't gonna give ya any of this shit, either. Let's go get Jazz, hit a couple of bars, and I'll get you guys some reefer. Fair 'nough, dog?"

"If the shit's so fuckin' bad for ya, why do you wanna fuck with it, my brother?"

That stops me for a minute and then . . . believing every word I say . . . I tell him, "I'm just chippin', but I been fuckin' around with this shit since I was twelve. I can control it. You try it, you'll end up hooked like a laboratory monkey. How do ya think your old lady would like that?"

It's great weed, not that I smoke the shit but the smell is sweet and sleepy, and Phil and Jazz laugh all night and eat everything they can get their hands on.

I dig watching them, wondering what it is that they have that I've misplaced somewhere that makes me feel so much older and burnt out at eighteen.

Around three A.M. we toast each other and I head back to my room pleasantly drunk.

I climb under the covers and dig how good the clean sheets and soft mattress feel. Trip on the pleasant quiet of a room with only me. Luxuriate in not being surrounded by a dorm full of snoring idiots. Feel the security of being in a strange town where no one knows me. Know that life is going to keep on getting better. Close my eyes and wait for sleep to come, twist and turn, ball my pillow up and then smooth it out, kick the covers off, pull them back over me. Finally say "Fuck it" out loud, turn the light back on, and slam.

Heaven.

I'd gotten Syd's number while we were on the compound, called, and received an open invitation. Phil is sitting on the edge of the motel bed, Jazz is curled up next to him, and I'm leaning on the wall trying to explain the game to these two country bumpkins.

"Sydney was my crimey's old lady. He ate it. She's got shit wired in this part of the country. Here's the thing, we can run around like idiots robbing everything that ain't holding a gun and end up locked down before the week's out. Or . . . we can get a bankroll and pick our shots, only do shit with a low risk factor that pays good. Sydney is willing to help us, we gotta be crazy not to take her up on it."

Phil is thinking through everything slow and careful and I don't blame him. He's gotta figure for himself, and he wants his old lady to know he's not just some rube, that he's got a brain that works and doesn't want to blow it. He says, "Listen, dog, you thought Ben was cool."

Then he rubs Jazz's leg and says, "No disrespect intended."

She grabs his hand and chews on it, mumbling, "None taken, I understand."

Phil smiles and continues, "And I said that to say this: we ended up starin' down the wrong end of a sawed-off shotgun. What makes you think that this broad is gonna be so happy to see us?"

I take a bite out of the ham and egg sandwich that is breakfast, wash it down with a can of malt liquor, watch these two play kissy-face for a second, pop the top off another can and kill half of it, finally saying, "If you two want to fuck, let me come back later, but checkout time is eleven A.M. and that only gives us an hour to get gone."

They both laugh and finally Jazz says, "That's time enough to do it three or four times. So tell us true, Bad, why is this woman going to help us out?"

"Because she's righteously my friend. Because I asked her. Because she wants to. Simple."

Jazz is doing the talking now and Phil is just watching and drinking from his can of malt. Jazz has a combination of intellect and innocence that I don't know how to react to, some of the shit she comes out with floors me, but sometimes she makes sense, like now, when she says, "Shoot, punkinhaid, my Uncle Ben was Bad's friend, too. But when *anyone* shows up drivin' into the compound— 'specially hotdoggin' in a Cuda—they *will* be met by a sawed-off shotgun until they show their true colors or get shot, one. But he helped y'all out, didn't he?"

Phil looks like she's the smartest thing on two long, long legs. "Sho, baby, you're right, he did. But 'member, I had to steal ya to get ya for mine 'cause Uncle Ben thought I was a devil . . . a cross-eyed devil . . . not exactly hospitable, sweet thang."

I say, "Sho, dog, you're both right. Ben helped us, and would again, but he thinks he's protecting him and his. Syd's a whole other story. This broad and her old man damn near took me to raise. I've known a bunch of motherfuckers of all different kinds and none of 'em are any cooler than Syd and her old man were to me. Your uncle and I know each other pretty good, but it's not the same as Syd and me. A deal went down that he didn't like with me and Syd and a few other people. Shit, Jazz, you know for all his 'praise the Lord' shit your uncle's in the game, he's pissed at Syd 'cause she outsmarted him."

I'm thinking how Syd didn't exactly shoot straight, either, and how she used Ben's urge to protect his own to get him to pull a full-out invasion and heist, one that cost all of us some people we cared about. I decide not to mention that part of it right now, seeing as how I am sure Syd will be as much of a surrogate mom for Phil and Jazz . . . and me . . . as she was for Rosie and me. Sort of a New York Jewish Ma Barker, in stiletto heels.

"Shit, man," I go on, "look what Ben did with the dough he owed me, not only shorted me but found a way to do it where he felt good about it. I ain't saying Ben's a bad guy, just that he's the same as all of us, he wants everything to go his way. Oh, well. I'm tellin' you you're going to dig Syd, and we're going to make serious money. Life is gonna be good like a motherfucker."

We tool into Short Hills, New Jersey, and the homes are gorgeous, new mansions and old Victorians, all with well-manicured yards and shrubbery still dusted with snow, an upper-middle-class pocket of prosperity in a state where pristine-looking woodlands are interspersed with urban ghettos, toxic dumps, and some really nice neighborhoods. New Jersey is a very strange place.

Pulling in front of a yellow-and-blue Victorian and double-checking the address, Phil swivels to face me in the backseat and says, "This is the address, hoss. What kinda fuckin' criminal is this woman that she lives in a place like this?"

"A smart one, bub. A real, fuckin' smart one."

Jazz isn't saying a word, just digging the pad.

When we reach the steps leading up to the porch the front door comes swinging open and Syd is there in all her glory, bleached-blond hair, tight figure, knowing face with bright red lipstick and cobalt-blue eyes all the way pinned. Dressed like a female banker, conservative gray skirt and top, sensible shoes with little tassels on them, stylin'.

When I hit the top stair she opens her arms and hugs me for a long time, then spins and grabs Jazz, shaking her hand and hugging her, and looks Phil up and down and says, "My oh my, oy. This is a big un. Come on in, all of yez. Have some tea, or somethin'."

Walking and talking at the same time, waving one hand and saying, "This is the living room, kick back. Whatcha want? Coffee, whiskey, narcotics? What? Don't be shy. Oy, Bobbie, let me look atcha. Ya got so fuckin' big, muscles on toppa muscles."

And I smile ear to ear, it's warm in here and feels safe, seeing Syd is a gas, all the bad and painful memories have taken a hike, and I'm as close to being happy as I can get when she shrieks and goes, "Mein Gott, are ya meshugenah? Lookatcha, no fuckin' front teeth. What didja do wid your teeth? Oy fuckin' vey. Leave ya alone for a little while and ya come back an ex-con with a missing grille."

She grabs my lip and lifts it, examining my mouth, saying, "Like my own flesh, this hurts me. We'll get ya a new grille quick and in a hurry-up. How's the guy that knocked 'em out? Dead, I should hope and pray? Tell me he's dead. Bobbie."

I can't stop grinning, missing teeth or not, and I assure her, "Don't know if he died or not, cut him wide open, though."

She slaps me lightly on the cheek and says, "Good boy," spins and grabs Jazz by the hand and says, "Come on, honey, help me put some stuff together for you kids to nosh on. You caught yourself a big un, didn't you? My Mel was big, huge, even, and . . ."

Syd's voice fades as she drags Jazz down the hall towards what I assume is the kitchen.

Phil's mouth is hanging open, he pivots slowly and takes in the fine antique furniture and Persian rugs, the oil paintings hanging on the walls and the sideboard full of silver trays and utensils, then says, "Ain't none of my people, either black or white, ever seen nothin' like this, hoss. Except in movies, maybe. How the sweet Jesus do you steal this kinda money?"

I'm as shell-shocked as Phil, this is one bad pad and one of the permanent variety, not just a bonarood hotel. One look at Syd's baby blues and I know she has a habit the size of Godzilla riding her back. Tell ya the truth, I'm dying to find out how she's doing it, staying that loaded and living like this. I just whistle and say, "I guess she'll tell us if she wants to. One thing about Syd, regardless of what Jazz's uncle thinks, she don't mind sharin' the action, we'll get hooked up. That's off the top dog. Emes."

Phil raises his eyebrows and asks, "Emes? What the fuck's an emes?"

Syd is washing her outfit out in a champagne glass full of water, sucking the liquid up through the needle and squirting it out onto the carpet. She's so gowed she's in slow motion, eyes below half mast and face slack. She's running one hand through her bottled-blond hair while the other is going back and forth to the glass with the syringe. The suit is gone, replaced by jeans and a flannel, she finally drops the works on the coffee table that has dope, cookers, wine bottles, and paraphernalia scattered all over it, then, voice both gravelly and slurred, says, "The big-time kid, for reals. Real estate, stocks, IPOs, limited partnerships, bust-outs. Stupid money, stealin' a million is nothin'."

My tongue's hangin' out of my mouth, I want to be part of that whole scene so bad. All the drugs you can want, fancy cars, great clothes, big-time. I'm seeing myself there.

Syd sees it, sees it all, and she says, "The thing is you got as much polish as sandpaper. Melvin usta always say you were as tactful as napalm, and God help us both it's the truth. To get inside it takes work, lotsa work and a lot of finesse. The deal we're doin' now should be good for ten or twelve mil. Cut that up eight ways, which is how many of us are workin' this one, and after expenses it's still a cool million each."

She takes a deep breath. "There just isn't any way to put ya in it. Not this one anyway. This ain't like a robbery or burglary, the setup takes months, sometimes years for the real big ones. That's why the payoff is so high. What I can do is this, stake you to some dough, get your grille fixed, and hook ya up with a paper hanger we work with, when we need bogus ID that will stand up he's our guy, set ya up with a kiting ring. Good dough and not too much risk, get ya some threads and you and your little crew can kite payroll checks and money orders all over the Eastern Seaboard."

The idea of burning checks is all right but doesn't really sound like my idea of a career, I want to learn about this high-level shit that gives you access to millions. I'm thinking that maybe I don't got the polish I'd need yet but I can sure as hell get it one way or the other; the idea of stealing millions has captured all my attention. I want to know how ya do this shit now, soonest, immediately. I scratch and nod for a second, looking inward, and then say, "Yeah, man, checks sound great for now. If you don't mind me asking how's this thing you're doing work, checks is yesterday's news, I never heard of this other shit you're talkin' about. Educate me."

"Oy, here's da deal, with real estate ya got titles, ya got a title ya can get a loan. Havin' the title don't mean ya got the property, get the loan and get gone. A real estate loan for a half mil is like nothin'. This thing we doin' now, takin' a company public, first ya get a product, cosmetics . . . you know, perfume and shit . . . is always good. Ya get invoices showing how much product you're movin' and the dough to have your bank accounts look right. Then ya get a ware-house or ten full of inventory, get bogus orders, and show all this shit flying out the door at a big profit. Ya with me?"

To have followed her conversation any more closely I would have had to have been in her mouth, I'm not missing a word. I just say, "Yeah, so far."

She lights a cigarette and takes a hit from the bottle of wine sitting by her chair and continues, "OK, so ya got all this action on paper, Number one, ya can borrow against future receipts. . . . Number two, ya insure your warehouses. . . . Number three, ya get a crooked underwriter and take the shit public, start sellin' stock. . . . Number four, ya set a warehouse or two on fire, collect on those. . . . Number five, ya drive the price on the stock as high as ya can. . . . Number six, ya get all the dough together. . . . Number seven, get the hell outta Dodge."

I whistle in serious appreciation. "So how do ya put it together? This is a long way from what we were doing a couple years ago."

"Lawyers and accountants, front men that look and act the part of business guys. And a lot of dough, it takes money to make it. Working it like a job, I go to an office for Christ's sakes, take suckers to lunch. Give it some time, Bobbie, for now just fly the kites, get some gelt."

"Sure, no sweat. Pass paper all day. Flew traveler's checks to make it out here, courtesy of Ben. I guess you two haven't kissed and made up yet, huh?"

"No, bubelah, not yet. He'll come around, or then again maybe he won't. Shvartzes got no sense of humor, a whole race with a chump complex. We'll see. . . . Anyhow I wish him the best and if he can't take a joke . . ."

Here Syd starts laughing and finally slaps herself on the knee and grinning through the heroin slurs, "Fuck him. And his current racist bullshit."

She looks at me from under her eyelids, watching for my reaction, and says, "Yeah, I know all about it, that Jazz is really a nice kid and willing to expand her horizons, we talked about all kinds of things. The girl has a brain and a half, she's a joy. And Ben's just the way he is, soon as he needs something he'll be magically returned to his sweet reasonable self."

I don't know how to respond, my last impression of Ben was not what one would call sweet and reasonable but I know he can be both of those things. I tell her, "Yeah, sweet and reasonable. So what next, boss, you and Jazz are thicker than thieves, life is lookin' better by the minute."

And I pause for a second before asking her, "So do ya ever hear from Billy Bones? It would be good to see him. What's up there?"

"Oy, Billy's still killin' 'em. Comes down from Boston once in a while on a contract for the fellas in NYC. If I was you I'd do checks and groom myself for bigger things, stay away from those Irish maniacs, but I'm sure he'll be around before too long. The I-talians like him again, so he's a busy guy."

"Oh, yeah, I'm sure of that." I'm laughing, thinking of just how busy Billy can be, eliminating inconvenient people for pay. A strange man, Bones, but a good friend who saved my ass more than once, quick with the Irish wit or the bullet to the head, whichever was appropriate at the moment.

For now, though, getting some cash comes first. "When can we put the check game together? Ben was gonna get us IDs but it slipped his mind or something. And I need to put a bankroll together. Fast."

"A couple things we gotta do first. This guy I been seeing, he's a real sweet guy, a square even. Anyway, he's an ophthalmologist. Your pal Phil should get those eyes fixed. My friend can do that for him, says it's a one-hour operation. He's gonna do it on the cuff, no charge. That little Jazz is way too pretty to have a cross-eyed boyfriend, and Phil is too sweet not to look as handsome as he can. And you, meshugenah, oy, that grille, you're going to my dentist soonest. That's that. Tomorrow we take yez to a nice hotel, check ya all in, show ya the town. Mazel tov."

I'm still running the shit through my head about real estate loans and taking companies public. Thinking, Fuck a whole bunch of passing paper, running checks is strictly small-time. But . . . I grin and say, "You the best, Sydney, shalom, mazel tov, and all that shit."

Phil takes the news like the stand-up, fearless guy that he is, coming up out of the couch so fast that it looks like he's trying to fly. Jazz is staring up at him in shock and Sydney and her friend, the good Dr. Alan Kaplan, are frozen in midsentence.

I told them he might not like the surprise they were planning. But what did I know? I just shut up and waited for the fireworks.

Alan has no idea what to do, he's a healthy-looking guy with badly thinning hair, got glasses on with gold rims and is real soft-spoken. He had outlined a part of the procedure to Phil and first the blood drained from Phil's face and then for a second fear showed through the mask that we all wear, then it transformed into rage.

Syd is not unused to dealing with maniacs and is putting a game plan together so fast I can see the wheels spinning around in her head. But the fact is that at his most easygoing, Phil is a big intimidating guy; throw a little adrenaline into his bloodstream and you got something like a cross-eyed, pale-skinned, rabid gorilla.

He's pointing at Alan, saying in that jailhouse whisper that precedes mayhem, "You plannin' on takin' a knife to my motherfuckin' eyes, you little cocksucker? You gonna do what? I'll rip your fuckin' head off, you little piece of shit. I'll pull the eyes right outta yore motherfuckin' haid and skull-fuck ya. Cut on me? Are you outta your cottonpickin' mind?"

He grabs Jazz by the hand and roars at me, "Let's get the fuck outta here, bro, these fuckin' people are nuts."

Jazz has found her voice and says, "Slow down, baby, he's a doctor, listen to him."

Phil's the one who's frozen now, he's got no idea what to do. I tell him, "Just chill for a second, dog, won't hurt ya to listen, you might like the idea."

Sydney is back on her game, stands up and points at Phil, yelling, "Listen up, peckerwood, you are in my house, loud-talkin' my friend, who out of the goodness of his heart offered to do this for ya. He makes big dough, has people lined up begging him to help them, and you act like a scared baby. You got that beautiful girl and if ya want to keep her ya should look as good as ya can. Plus if you gonna be a professional criminal instead of a professional convict, those crossed eyes have gotta go, cops could ID ya in a heartbeat with them. So you owe Alan an apology, and if you don't have the guts to better yourself, how you gonna have the courage to make it through life?"

Phil is weaving almost like he's dodging punches, trying to figure out how he's supposed to react to this crazy little broad, he's gone from rabid gorilla to whipped puppy in seconds. Moving in slow motion he turns his back on everybody except Jazz and leaning down and almost whispering, he says, "Would ya like me better, if I did it?"

When I said Jazz was smart I wasn't kidding, without hesitation she picks up where Syd had left off. She smiles up at soon-not-to-be-cross-eyed Phil and croons, "Baby, you're perfect, I couldn't like you any better 'cause I already love ya. But if you let Alan fix your eyes you'll be handsome as a movie star. Why don'tcha go ahead, you're not scared, are ya?"

And of course that does it, Phil swings around, gets his posture right, and says, "Scared? I ain't scared of nothin'. Sorry for gettin' excited, Doc. The way I was talkin', well, sometimes my mouth tends to operate without askin' my brain. When do ya wanna do it?"

Phil turns toward me and away from the rest of the room and I see terror skittering behind his eyes and across his face. Of psychotic Phil there is no trace. Then he catches himself, winks at me, and gets his grin back, saying, "Yeah, man, gonna look like a movie star."

The smell of rich leather and burnished wood fills the car, the seat I'm in feels like it was designed specifically for my body, and the hood seems to stretch on forever past the dash. A deep shining black without blemish, the shine so deep it's like looking into obsidian. The dash itself light burlwood and the sound system bad to the bone, and Syd puts an R&B station on and we're cutting in and out of traffic like a motherfucking shark.

Syd's dressed in another conservative-type dress suit, this one a pale red with matching pumps, and got her hair swept back. Me? I'm in jeans and a T-shirt topped by the black leather jacket I picked up in Illinois, my boots are spit-shined, and I feel OK, driving into motherfucking New York, New York, in a Jaguar V12, got a pistol in one pocket, money in the other, and dope in my veins.

Syd is driving with one hand and gabbing away and gesturing with the other. Life is getting better and better. Holding my new front teeth in my hand and looking at them, putting them back in and they feel uncomfortable, taking them out and holding them again, and finally Sydney stops her monologue and says, "Shove those fuckin' things in your head and leave 'em there. The clothes are bad enough, the missing teeth are too fuckin' much. Oy vey, bubelah, you'll get used to 'em. Leave 'em alone."

I shove the teeth into place, light a cigarette, and smile as wide and as big as I can and say, "Yassum."

Syd just laughs and accelerates.

The new grille still feels weird, constantly playing with it with my tongue, every time I'm by a reflective surface checking to see what I look like with my new front teeth. Gray-blue eyes, nose kinda crooked and the rest of the face not bad, not what you'd call pretty, but not a bad-lookin' kid.

The paper guy is from England, a Brit with the right accent and clothes and a dedicated thief. About as tall as me but that doesn't take a whole lot and dressed in a nice black suit and loafers, got a thick build like a powerlifter or something. When we go to shake hands I notice three different rings all holding at least two carats of diamonds except for the one on his right-hand ring finger; it has a solitaire that has to be three carats by itself. This guy's hands are a major score all by themselves.

I grab his hand to shake and he says, "Whittington, Shelton Whittington at your service." Sounding exactly like Sean Connery saying "Bond, James Bond," he grins and waits to see if I caught it and when I laugh, he continues, "The most overqualified purveyor of bogus paperwork in the free world. Once worked for Her Majesty. Sadly she has no sense of humor when it comes to freelance employment."

I grin and doing my best to mimic his James Bond impersonation, tell him, "Prine, Bobbie Prine, full-time thief, at your service too, Shelton. Pleased to meet ya."

His studio is in a plush office building in Manhattan. Past the doorman and up to the twenty-eighth floor in a high-tech elevator with reflecting two-tone brass walls that give me another opportunity to check my new teeth. Down the deeply carpeted hallway and through the thick oak doors into bunco heaven.

In the front room are wedding pictures and portrait shots set into artsy frames overseen by a demure-looking blond chick with an English accent that sounds as hot on her as it sounds silly on him. She's petite with blond, almost white hair that shines like platinum, she's wearing round glasses on a soft, pretty face and a conservative dress over a very bodacious little body, and she looks directly at me and says, "I'm Susan, not pronounced with an s, Sue *Zann* if you please, and you, of course, are Mr. Prine, Sydney's friend and business associate. I'm so pleased to meet you."

I want to sound like a class act myself and do my best but my repartee is sadly lacking, "Uh, yeah, that's me. Nice meetin' ya."

And of course I feel like an idiot for not having better social skills. The overhead lighting is reflecting from those glasses as they track me and Shelton heading into his domain. She and Syd know each other and seem to have plenty to talk about, and as the door is closing behind me I spin to check and those glasses are still on me.

Phil and Jazz are kicked back at the hotel while Phil heals up. Me? I gotta make money, and lots of it. So I'm here getting ID and setting up what is gonna be needed to run these checks, doing my best to focus on Shelton Whittington and wondering what color the eyes behind Sue Zann's round glasses are.

"Let's have a smile, old chap. There ya go, didn't hurt, did it. Yer rather a grim little bugger ya are. Now, mate, you got an accent but I can't place it, could be somewhere here on the East Coast or maybe Chicago, help me out here. What major cities do you know well enough to pass as a native? Not that anyone should interview you but you always want to have your back story ready. Say I give you paper for Detroit and you know shit about it, nothing. And the person cashing your check just happens to be from there, wants to talk about your old hometown, and do you know good old Mary Sue and Freddy Blue, then whatcha gonna do? Stand there with yer arse hangin' out? Where do ya want to be from, mate? Gimme three, four, five cities. Won'tcha now?"

The room surrounding us is full of props for the kind of photographs showing in the front. What Shelton is pulling out of concealed closets are the different backdrops used in the states he's going to be preparing licenses for, and on rollers two cameras that have been stolen from DMVs in different states.

He changes the cardboard backdrop he was using on the first set of pictures and replaces it. Sets up one of the weird cameras, saying, "This fine piece of equipment was delivered just last week. Stolen right from the motor license bureau in Los Angeles, California; anyone can pass as a native of LA, you ever been there? Lovely town. Lovely. Look at the camera. Smile. No smile? Oh, well. You say you've been there?"

I know I haven't said anything of the sort because I haven't even tried to make conversation. I'd rather listen than flap my lips, which works well most of the time because, God knows, most people love the sound of their own voices. Once he starts working, Shelton's accent changes to a harder, more street-sounding dialect of English, and when he realizes he has a willing audience his mouth starts working overtime. Instead of answering I ask a couple questions of my own: "How'd ya get into this racket, and what part of England ya from?"

"Well, mate, truth be told, I really was in the service of Her Majesty, setting up the same kinda paperwork for some of her more clandestine representatives that I'm doing for you. Well, without boring you with a tale of woe, suffice it to say that the slings and arrows of outrageous fortune hit me right in the ass. In other words, this and that happened and I found the prospect of immigrating to this fair land beyond enticing. I'm from Manchester, sort of a blue-collar town with its share of lads like yourself and yes, me ownself when I was much, much younger. If I'm photographing the mayor or a movie star I put on the old polish, talk very stiff lip, veddy, veddy proper don'tcha know. Wit da likes a' you I let me upbringing show. We know each other, don't we, mate. Thick as thieves."

Moving and changing cameras and backdrops the whole time he's babbling away, finally taking the last shot and saying, "Chicago, Illinois . . . Kansas City, Kansas . . . Denver, Colorado . . . Los Angeles, California . . . and Trenton, New fuckin' Jersey. All with the last name of Landers. So ya don't get confused, the first letter of the city matches the first letter of the first name. Chicago is Charles, Kansas is Karl with a K, Denver is Dave, LA is Larry, and Trenton is Tom, middle name on all of 'em George. Different numbers on each piece you're gonna have to memorize as you use 'em, these will stand up anywhere you go. If you get busted you just have to make sure you make bail before they run your prints. Now, what kind of checks do you fancy?"

"Whatcha got?"

He looks at me like I've suddenly grown another head and after pondering my question for a second, says, "Anything you desire, mate. Payroll, Fortune Five Hundred companies or small firms. Traveler's checks from all the major banks and suppliers. Money orders both postal and private. Bank drafts and overseas cash drafts. Name it, my friend, it's yours."

"Whatcha think, Shelton . . . paper ain't really my game. Just did a big nickel in traveler's checks and that was pretty easy. Maybe those? What's the best shot?"

"Traveler's are good, but . . . they're limited. The upside is you can cash them anywhere, the down is going for more than a hundred a shot is very difficult, and of course you must purchase something when you use them. If you're going into a bank, why go in for a lousy hundred or two? They're a bit of a nuisance, if I may say so. Let's try payroll and money orders, they can be made out for nice sums and with the ID you have there should be no problems."

He grabs a pencil and does some figuring and then says, "I'm going to fit you with a New York ID, uhhh name and town? Ah, yes, Buffalo, Bill. Why not? So you'll have a total of six, you can work Jersey and New York for a couple of weeks and then throw 'em away. Keep the stuff for the other states as backup. This will get you the working capital you need. . . . Let's see, twenty-five paychecks at six hundred and twenty or thirty each, ten money orders at fifteen hundred each times two states comes to . . . right around sixty thousand. Bust yer ass for two weeks and you should have these cashed out."

He's chewing on the pencil looking at me, waiting for a response. Finally I say, "How much is this costin' me? All this shit's gotta be expensive. Let's cut the extra IDs, except the one for LA. What's the bill?"

Once again he raises one eyebrow and looks at me like I got two heads or suddenly turned blue, then drops his voice and in a growling British accent says, "Not a farthing, mate. All taken care of by her nibs."

Looking at me and spreading his hands, says, "Sir Laurence Olivier, don'tcha know? Birds dig it."

Now it's my turn to look at him weird and finally I ask him, "What the fuck ya talkin' about? Sir Who? Birds . . . you mean chicks? Dig what?"

Shelton looks sad, saying, "Sir Laurence Olivier, an actor, a great actor. That was my impression of him. It's a rather good impression, everyone gets it. Women . . . chicks love the way he talks, don'tcha know."

"Oh, yeah, sure I got it."

Doing my best to look sincere, then asking, "So if Syd or her nibs as you call her is covering the bill, when do we get delivery?"

"Tomorrow, early evening. Let's say sixish, after the carriage trade is done for the day."

We go back into the front room, and, stopping the conversation she's having with Susan, Syd blows past me and starts her social butterfly routine discussing what is happening where and catching up on news and gossip with Shelton. Who's stealing what, who's busted, and who got dead. The regular stuff.

I walk over to the glass-and-black-chrome counter and pretend I am looking at the photographs there, finally get my nerve up to say something to Susan. "Sue Zann?" Then I spell it: "Sue Z-a-n-n? Zann? Sounds Russian or something, it's pretty cool. Christ, you're pretty cool. A righteous knee-buckler, a stone knockout." I'm feeling as lame as I sound and wishing I had just kept my mouth shut.

When she smiles and blushes it makes my day, then she says, "Knee-buckler? Stone knockout? You do have a way with words. That's what my friends call me, Mr. Prine. Sue Zann, it's spelled S-u-s-a-n, but not pronounced that way. Sue Zann. Right, love? As for stone knockout, I assume that that's a compliment. Thank you."

And then she folds her hands over each other and waits for me to say something or go away. I got no clue what to say, how do you talk to a girl who isn't a dopefiend? It's all the way beyond me, I can feel a whole encyclopedia of great things to say, wonderful conversation sticks right on the edge of my tongue but there is no way to get any of it past my new teeth. Finally I tell her, "Take your glasses off."

She does and her eyes are like the blue of a spring day, light and soft and blue, and she is so fuckin' beautiful making small talk is all the way out of the question. I say, "Yeah, man, baby blues. A stone knockout. Thank you, Susan," making sure I say it right, rolling that Zann out all by itself. Smile at her and trail out the door behind Sydney, looking back as the door swings closed and the glasses are back on her face, pinning me.

We stay at a townhouse owned by one of Syd's partners in crime on Fifth Avenue. At the front door is a uniformed flunky guarding the entrance from people like me. He is sooo glad to see Sydney again, blah-blah-blah. The way he looks at me isn't too glad at all.

In the elevator going up to the twelfth floor, Syd lectures me, "Pay attention, ya act like ya got class it's good. Ya dress like ya got class it's better. Ya do both people will line up to let ya rob 'em. That guy was dying to hold the door open instead of locking it. Because every time he sees me I'm dressed good and act like a fuckin' lady. If ya wanna hit the big time, you better go to charm school or some-thin'. Ya with me?"

The door slides open and I follow Syd into the hallway leading to a triple-bolted door. As she undoes the locks she is still talking a mile a minute. "We're going out tonight, meet my baby, Alan, and have some drinks, take in a show or somethin'. It'll be fun, ya gonna run those checks, we gotta dress ya up. Ya still look like a hood . . . hangin' out with that fuckin' Billy Bones didn't do ya any good in the deportment area and this last year in the joint has done nothin' to help your polish."

I'm laughing, some things don't change, and Syd's pushy take-charge attitude seems as implacable as Mount Rushmore. Arguing won't do any good at all and I know that to fly kites ya gotta be dressed well. I flop down on one of the sofas in the living room and look around, taking in the art on the walls and Chippendale furniture and Waterford lamps that any good burglar would recognize as the real thing, say, "Yeah, yeah, yeah, gonna clean up my act. Soonest. Promise. Nice pad, they let ya use it whenever you want?"

"Yeah, it's part of the deal. You need a really good front to pull off the big scores."

She hesitates for a second and then opens her purse and, taking out her kit, starts mixing a hit as she's talking. Syd has my undivided attention, not because of the dope but because she's talking about how the shit she's doing works, how ya actually put it together.

I follow suit and start mixing my own medicine up. Watching the off-white granules dissolve in the bottom of my cooker I ask her, "How come? Why the big front?"

She draws the shit up, catches a vein in the back of her arm and sends it home, pauses for a second and rubs her face, then continues, "We got offices in NYC, Miami, Dallas, and Chicago. I live in Jersey, but I come into the city a lot on business, fly all over the place pushing this stock. If ya gotta entertain you have to look like the last thing you need is money. First ya put enough dough together to get property. Then ya borrow against it, float the cash from account to account. It's like a shell game . . . now ya see it now ya don't. I think I went over this once before, remember? So you have your front— homes places like this and my joint in Jersey—you know, class all the way. Beautiful offices. Fat bank accounts. Cars. Get the picture? Do your IPO, that means initial public offering, float some cash back to the buyers and jack the price on the stock past the moon. Borrow against everything and cash in the insurance at the same time. Rob your own stuff, set a warehouse on fire. Like that, you know. Get all the dough liquid and that's when it's time to crash and burn it. Simple, huh?"

I slam and know that salvation is flowing through my system once more as surely as I know that someday I'll be doing my own crash and burn. Now it's my turn to scratch and nod for a second, then I ask, "How do ya get all the dough together? How do ya know *when* to get outta Dodge?"

"Lawyers and CPAs, guys that can front like Elmer. You'll be meetin' him soon. Looks like a fuckin' cowboy, slow-movin' and -talkin', wears the boots and hat, the whole schmear. He's really the brains on this one. When it's over he'll just look like another sucker. Making this kinda move, it's like gravity, the more cash you make the more comes in. The trick is to have it all hit at once, have the stock as high as it will go. Have all your tangible assets leveraged to the hilt. The insurance dough coming at the same time. Then sell everything ya can, real estate, cars, machinery, everything. Nail it all at the same time. Crash and burn it, baby. Then it's hasta la vista, darlin'."

I want in so bad I can feel it swelling in my chest. Some guys want to play in the Super Bowl, some want to be rocket scientists. This sounds beyond enchanting, robbing rich people by outsmarting them, wow.

If I knew then what I've since learned riding down the edge of the razor, I would have become a lawyer. I'd have gotten to do the same thing without getting punished. Would have made the papers for being a genius law guy instead of a regular thief. Then I could have run for public office. Become president even. But the sad fact is that I went for the illusion of easy money, constant action, and cheap thrills.

I ask, "What then, Syd? Whatcha gonna do with all the dough?"

"Then Alan and I are going to take a vacation, visit Europe for a while. Let shit cool down. Come back and I'll do it again and do it again."

The heroin is working just right, my brain is chuckling like a happy computer, I am a euphoric genius. When it's good, it's really good. The best, even. The nightmare starts when the shit stops working. Yeah, it had happened to me once but I thought it was just life getting the better of me then. I still have no idea that a crash is inevitable. I feel invincible and I tell her, "When you come back, I want in on the next one. Right?"

Syd laughs, scratches, and says, "Oy, better get your ass into that charm school pronto then, 'cause you got a long way to go, kid."

I smile as wide as I can, do my best to make my eyes twinkle, and tell her, "Piece of cake. By the time you and the esteemed Alan make your return to our fair country I will be speaking like a graduate of Yale instead of jail. And be dressed in whatever the current fashion for young executives is at that point in time."

Sydney starts laughing so hard that she has tears in her eyes and says, "Shit, kid, now you just sound like an articulate thug. You gonna need some work. You are a piece of work."

And lifting her bottle of champagne, Syd says, "Shalom."

We toast and drink from the bottles. Class all the way.

Another door, another doorman. This doorman is an easy four hundred pounds, a stone freak standing six-six or -seven and damn near as wide as he is tall, flying a spiked mohawk and covered with ink. Got on leather pants and even in the freezing weather nothing on top but a leather vest that shows off steroid-pumped muscles and tattoos. Running across his belly and chest five, count 'em, five bullet holes that have healed and left keloid scars.

The line to get in the place stretches halfway down the block and I have no idea where we are going until we've passed by the entire line and Syd cuts in and says to the doorman, "We're not late, are we?"

He just grins, showing missing teeth to complete the look that stops anyone that isn't insane from trying to rush this particular door, and he waves us in.

The music is twisted jungle shit, dance music for psychotics, blending with the flashing, strobing lights and the sweet, sleepy smell of reefer and hash, mixed with the acrid odor of poppers and sexually charged sweat. It is great.

Syd snakes her way to a table on the second floor overlooking the dance floor and orders drinks. I'm smoking Camels and just digging the whole thing. Thinking that I'm way underdressed or not dressed right or something, all I know is that everyone there has gone to a lot of trouble to look as outlandish as possible and I'm still in leather jacket and jeans. Fuck it.

Leaning over the table I yell, "So is this charm school? Who are these people?"

The waitress comes back with two green frothy drinks in tall glasses, puts them down, and checks me out, and whether it is my perception or she actually takes in my inferior wardrobe and sneers, I don't know. One thing for sure, she doesn't seem favorably impressed.

Syd's wearing a purple leather outfit that is what you would call revealing, and for a broad of her advanced age she looks hot, got her blond hair hanging down her back and plenty of makeup. She looks like she belongs here. Syd takes a hit off her drink and screams back, "Money, these motherfuckers got one thing in common, liquid cash.

Trust-fund babies, rock stars, movie mavens, and schmucks that just want to be seen here. This is the spot for this hot second, killer. Some of 'em are marks and some of 'em are fun. Have a good time, ask one of these little bimbos to dance."

I drain my green drink and it tastes like a mint milkshake, not my idea of alcohol. Call the waitress over and tell her to bring Syd another green thing and a double shot of Jack D on the rocks for me, watching the dance floor, knowing that there is no way I can do what these people are doing. Shooting heroin, stealing, and doing time doesn't leave room for dance lessons, and when I was a kid I was too busy dodging punches to think about any other kind of footwork.

The waitress comes with the drinks, and I order another. I down my double shot, finally leaning towards Sydney and yelling, "I can't dance. Don't know how. Don't wanna learn. Go ahead, I'll keep our table."

She just grins and raises her green drink in a toast.

A tall rangy guy dressed in a suit topped with a huge cowboy hat rolls in and I know he has to be Elmer. My take on this guy is not enthusiastic, he looks like he should be on late-night TV, selling used cars. Maybe he fools the marks, but I'm not sure why. He doesn't fool me.

Behind him is Shelton, with a petite blonde that looks like she is trying out for the part of Tinker Bell, elf dress and all. Shelton and Tinker say hello, and split almost immediately. The hat guy sticks his hand in my face and bellows, "I'm Elmer, how you doing, young man? Sydney has given you quite a buildup. Pleased to meet you. A whiskey drinker I see, a man after my own heart. Let me buy you another one. Your name is . . . Rob, is that right?"

I grin as nicely as I can, thinking that this guy has the warmth of a worm, the charisma of a cockroach, and if this motherfucker can engineer multimillion-dollar scams I sure as hell can. And take his hand.

He tries to grab my fingers and apply pressure, show me how strong he is. Some kind of macho bullshit that maybe hat guys think is cool. I don't know. So I slide my hand past the finger grip and lock on his knuckles, squeezing with all the power developed in the last year of pounding weights and squeezing rubber balls to build fore-arm and wrist strength for boxing. His smile fades for a second and when he pulls away he is looking at me a little bit closer. I keep grinning and say, "Bobbie, Elmer. Not Rob. Bobbie. Nice meeting you."

Once he settles in, Elmer and Syd huddle, conversing intensely, then a group of people I've never seen before surrounds us, kissing cheeks and yelling about how great they all look. The night seems to be going downhill. After pulling another table closer they all sit down and start talking stocks and bonds. I'm bored to death now, the whiskey taking the edges off but feeling like I'm trapped with people who are from planet blah.

Alan shows up dressed in a nice sharkskin suit and I realize that at least he's got some kind of style. He grins at me, then pushes in next to Syd, being polite but not impressed by anybody but Syd. Syd's holding Alan's hand and rubbing the back of it with her fingers, she leans forward and yells, "Bobbie, Alan. Alan, Bobbie."

We grin at each other and Alan yells, "You're getting senile, we already met."

Syd just hits her drink and mumbles, "Oh, yeah. When conversing with understated Phil . . . how could I forget."

As I watch Alan I can tell he's not into this scene at all but is willing to endure it. Figure he must like Syd a lot and after spending a minute wondering how a square and a hustler would do together think, Fuck it, and order another drink.

Elmer is screaming over the music about windows of opportunity and leveraged buyouts and I snap to the fact that they are working, spinning a web for the suckers, and I do my best to pay attention. Tripping on Alan's bemused expression and following Elmer's bullshit and how as the night progresses Syd is getting sloppier and sloppier. Zeroing in on Elmer, analyzing his patter and not finding him that impressive, when someone touches me and I spin, grabbing the hand that is sliding down my chest.

Where I come from and where I've been lately, no one touches you because they like you. My reflexes are a little bit too fast, getting used to the real world takes time.

I look up from the small arm and hand I'm holding, staring into blue eyes that freeze me in place, stupid. My mouth open and stuttering, looking into those eyes, soft and light, sardonic, satanic, gonna-rock-your-world blue eyes, and Sue Zann from England says,

"Jumpy are we? Perhaps if you don't want to break my arm we could have a dance. I left me glasses at home, you will escort me. Won't you?"

Never having danced in my life, the thought of getting out there and looking like an idiot terrifies me, the thought of looking stupid in front of this chick who is not only gorgeous but obviously a class act scares me worse than fighting the monster doorman would have. I mumble, "I don't really dance, can I buy you a drink?"

Susan smiles, winks, and says, "Neither do I, we'll both have to pretend we do."

And grabs my hand and gives a small tug.

I down the rest of my latest double shot while Sydney laughs and mouths the words "charm school" at me.

Susan tugs on my hand one more time, and I follow her down to the dance floor, scared to fucking death.

We're both drunk and loaded, surrounded by swirling, twirling freaks all dressed in expensive weird shit, and I feel like a lame but do my best not to look ridiculous.

Digging watching Susan because the girl can dance, move like an oiled snake, she's sex in syncopated movement, a wreck waiting to happen, heartbreak in rhythmic motion. She dances so good and so bad, so dirty, sleazy, loose, that it makes me look all right, it feels like I know what I am doing.

When the slow number comes on she fits herself into my arms like she belongs there. Yeah man, I can dance. Feeling her against me and knowing that under her sheer dress there is nothing but skin amps me better than shooting coke.

She leans her head back, her eyes at half mast and unfocused, her sultry "fuck me" look freezing me in midstep, and when she opens her lips and I kiss her the taste of the mint drinks and marijuana is strong on her lips. She takes my lower lip between her teeth and sucks on it, pulling it in and out of her mouth. Oh, Susan, oh Sue *Zann* . . .

With the mass of bodies swirling around us it could have gone on forever, mint and pot and probing tongues, sharp teeth and soft, soft lips.

When she drags her fingernails up the inside of my thigh, scratching slowly against my jeans and stopping and rubbing when she gets to my groin, I think I am gonna go full on convulsive.

Ending up against the wall with my fingers inside her and running my tongue and lips and teeth everywhere that I can find bare skin. She's got my jeans unbuttoned, working me slow one second and fast the next, and the music is part of it.

The freaks dancing and stopping to watch driving the intensity even higher, I start to lift her up against the wall when she says, "Let's go to mine, luv, don't want to give them a free floorshow now. Do we?"

My brain is screaming, Yeah we do, let these motherfuckers applaud and shout for more, show 'em porno like they dream about, but what I say is, "Yeah, let's get outta here."

The night with the dopefiend girl had been so much a part of the way I'd grown up that while it was a welcome respite from my enforced celibacy, it didn't have much emotional impact. Doing time, your body erects its own walls, freezing all reactions except aggressive or defensive, and after a while the thought of being with a woman takes on a mythic quality. Touching and feeling without overtones of fear and violence a dream.

I've always wanted to go beyond the little world that I came from where everyone I dealt with was hooked and desperate and just trying to survive.

Susan represents another level of existence, and it seems like being with her will elevate me magically from hood to prince. Like the ugly frog I want transformation, release from my bleak version of reality. And for a while I think I've found that.

Her pad is so feminine that it feels like stepping into a new world, lace and pink stuff everywhere, dainty antique furniture, and clean. No dust, no trash, no dishes in the sink. Clean.

We get through the door and suddenly I'm awkward again, don't know what to do or say. I'm in her world and feel more like the frog than ever. I shake a smoke out of my pack and she smiles at me and pulls the dress she's wearing over her head. I was right, the only thing under it is her. She's standing there in nothing except high heels and stockings, not a natural blonde, her pubic hair shaved into a motherfuckin' heart. Wow. Thin waist and nice hips, her breasts set high and small with long brown nipples, her eyes taking me in when she says, "Off with your trousers, luv."

And she twirls on her toes like a ballerina and walks into her bedroom.

I shove the cigarette back in the pack, breaking it in the process; getting my boots off seems to take forever. My fingers have their own agenda and they aren't working the way I want them to.

Wearing only my jeans, leaving everything else in a pile on the floor, I follow her and when I come through her bedroom door she murmurs, "Your trousers, then kill the lights, luv."

Candles are already burning and her big bed deep in quilts and pillows is framed in the soft golden light and in the center Susan is sitting cross-legged, watching me drop my jeans and waiting, the flickering shadows playing across her white velvet skin.

Lying beside her and running my lips up her arm and across her shoulder, down to her nipple, and she starts making a soft keening sound. Working my way down her stomach, tasting salty sweat and smelling her perfume and the odor of sex.

Then licking and sucking on her until she is spastic, feeling her twist violently, taking my cock in her mouth and attacking it like we are competing to see who can make the other come first.

Working me with her lips and teeth, taking me all the way down her throat and feeling her screaming around my dick as she grabs my hair and shoves my face into her like she wants to kill me, smother me between her legs.

Holding my head between her legs and feeling her keening like a big cat, bucking and thrusting against my face and lips and finally shuddering, smashing her hips into my face as I respond, doing the same to her, thrusting into her mouth and throat with no more mercy than I am receiving.

Knowing she is coming I thrust one finger into her ass, making her scream and buck so hard we are bouncing off the bed and then coming like it is killing me, coming so hard that everything strobes and goes black, and looking at her after and being so loaded on endorphins and adrenaline that they cut through the drugs and alcohol like they aren't even there.

And when she breathes, "Oh, darlin', that was so good," I believe her, and when I say, "Un-believable. Fan-fucking-tastic," I mean every syllable.

There's a lot of watching going on. Shelton is back at work in square clothes, watching me. Susan is behind her specs and wearing a dress, watching the counter. Syd is sitting on one of the trendy little couches watching her nails.

I'm looking at two handfuls of paper, IDs, checks already made out, money orders.

Shelton is saying, in his crisp, professional Brit voice, "There are four different major companies represented there. Burn the banks the checks are drawn on in the appropriate cities. The money orders you can cash anywhere. Figure you have about two days from the day you fly the first kite or money order from any one company. Work five days a week and in two weeks you'll have flown all these lovely kites. Turned them into coin of the realm. When you get done with one ID, throw it away immediately."

Shelton is looking at me askance, I figure he's not liking the fact that I spent the night with his counter girl and crime partner. As me and Syd roll out the door, Susan waves at us with her fingers and Shelton smiles halfheartedly.

In the elevator going down, Syd says, "I didn't mean that particular bimbo. Ya shouldn't get your pussy and your paycheck in the same place. Oy, bubelah, what am I gonna do widja?"

I grin, then laugh, saying, "Shee-it, you like the pot calling the fuckin' kettle. First Mel, now Alan. They both your crimeys. Why is it different for me? I like that one. Like you said, charm school baby. The girl's got class and we both agree that's what I need. Gonna get it by osmosis. Right?"

Syd shakes her head and laughs. "Meshugenah, what a mishegoss this is gonna be. First off, Alan is my sweet baby, not my crimey. Alan just puts up with my shit, he knows it's part of the package, he's as square as they come. Wants to marry me. He's one of the nicest guys I've ever met, maybe I will end up marrying him. But first I want a couple mil of my own sitting in a Swiss bank. And Mel, well, we both know what happened there. . . . How'd ya say ya gonna get this class, schmuck?"

I laugh at her and repeat, "Osmosis?"

"Oy, osmosis yet. An articulate thug you are. Osmosis he says."

As I'm walking out to the street to meet the newly un-cross-eyed Phil
and Jazz, who is doing the driving on this particular adventure, Syd
yells at me, "Hey, schmuck. Prosper, come back with lots of gelt, I
think you're gonna need it."

I flash her a peace sign and yell back, "Mazel tov. It'll be a mitz-
vah. See ya."

She is still shaking her head when I hit the sidewalk and climb
in the Cuda.

At least I look classy. The slacks are black linen, the sweater
gray cashmere, my boots have been replaced by loafers made from a
soft, dull leather that the shoe guy swore were the kind.

Clothes may make the man, but this man is scared anyway,
smoking and watching the streets and trash of Newark, New Jersey,
pass the window as the Cuda approaches our first bank. The rumbling engine and the rock and roll blasting out of the speakers combine with the low-level panic I'm feeling to make it a driving
physical sensation like way too much coffee or too little shitty speed.

The main things required for cashing checks are good paper,
looking good, and the ability to act normal. Whatever the hell
normal is.

My hands are sweaty and every time I rub them on the pants
legs they leave marks, my whole body is sweating like I just got done
working out, and I can smell my own fear. I don't know if I can pull
it off. After carefully cultivating a mad-dog look to terrorize all potential enemies for most of my young life, now I have to look some
lame in the face and make him believe that I'm a regular guy who
gets money orders for whatever the hell people get money orders for.
That thought kicks the sense of panic through the roof. What do
people get money orders for? I have no idea. What if they ask why I
have it, where'd I get it?

I don't even know the difference between a money order and a
check. All I know for sure is that it's Wednesday and I am gonna
start on the payroll checks Thursday, when they are dated. That
means that today is money order day. End of inner dialogue.

Screaming inside for my mind to shut up.

Jazz is driving and Phil is crunched up into the backseat. Not a happy guy. The swelling around his eyes is almost gone and the red that rimmed them is fading to pink. He's got strict orders to rest his eyes, in other words he ain't allowed to drive.

We cruise into the bank's lot and do a couple of circuits and it's a normal workday. People coming in and out, no special heat or obvious surveillance, and my mind is going a mile a second, all the way on overdrive.

During one point in my life . . . at Syd's suggestion . . . I was determined to read as many literary greats, philosophers, and spiritual tomes as possible, doing this with the mistaken belief that it would work some miraculous change in the way I perceived the world. One of the guys I'd read was named Goethe and a line from one of his pieces now keeps bouncing around in my head.

As I climb out of the car my heart is trying to tear its way through my rib cage and all my senses are on high. I can hear the rustle of people's clothes all the way across the parking lot, smell the exhaust from cars and the odors from restaurants down the street, and suddenly I got the magic. I'm loose and free as thought. Everything is connected. All my limbs and body parts working together, brain clear and clicking like a machine and I'm part of everything around me, knowing what's coming a split second before it happens. All the way on.

Phil surges out of the backseat, saying, "Anyone comes after ya I'm takin 'em down. You and Jazz skedaddle, just make sure I make bail. Ya up for this, dog?"

I smile and say, "Goethe said, 'In the beginning was the deed.' Now I just gotta get the deed done. Stay loose, dog. This is gonna be a slice a' pie, a motherfuckin' cakewalk."

Phil does a double take, uncrossed eyes rimmed in pink and red, charcoal smudges under them like a monster raccoon, spits, and says, "You is a strange motherfucker. Who the fuck is Goethe? If they come after ya, ya gonna want to Go-ethe sure as God made little green apples."

The loafers float across the blacktop, the slacks hang perfectly, and the cashmere sweater feels a whole lot better than any piece of clothing I've ever worn. The one-hundred-dollar bills are fresh and crisp, with that new-money smell, better than baking cookies, sweeter than any flower, the smell of good times.

I grin at Phil and when he holds the front seat forward, sticking me into the backseat, I just grin some more. After Phil closes his door behind him, Jazz looks over the seat and asks me, "How'd it go? Were you scared?"

I just fan the bills back and forth and say, "Scared? Hell no. Step on the gas. Go-ethe."

And Phil repeats, "Go-ethe." And starts the laughing that soon hits us all.

Go-ethe is the word for that run, like an omen. We do all the money orders by that evening, every time I get out of the car Phil and Jazz call in unison, "Go-ethe."

Every time I climb back in I tell them, "Go-ethe."

The cash is piled on the table in the hotel suite, Phil is sitting across from me, Jazz on his lap, playing with his hair. They look pretty happy.

I've spent some dough on clothes for all three of us and the hotel room for the night. Room service is on the way with three lobster dinners and booze. All the Jersey money orders are gone, turned into fifteen thousand bucks in hundred- and fifty-dollar bills. All that's left until we hit New York is the payroll checks.

I should have been happy, too. Wrong. I count out five grand and slide it across the table to Phil and Jazz, saying, "That's your end. You guys get one third of everything I take down, as long as we're working. This is a business like any other, expenses come off the top. Any questions?"

As I lay it out, I keep hearing those same words spoken to me, floating up from my memory and bringing with them a feeling of loss that rocks me like a baseball bat. The life expectancy for junkies and fools like us is short, and Mel, who taught me the game and said those same words to me, died way too early. Now I'm being Mel for Jazz and Phil, all of us being mother-henned by Syd, but no more Mel, no more Rosie . . . both gone . . . fulfilled their life expectancy . . . except I guess neither Syd nor I expected to lose our lovers. Now, here we are again, and I'm playing Mel. I have kept going like a bad dream, and now the sense of déjà vu that hits me when I finish that sentence is terrifying.

The next two days are a grind, in and out of banks and check-cashing places, so many so fast that they blend together. It starts to feel like work. Cramped in the backseat of Phil's Cuda, eating and drinking on the run. Stopping from five in the afternoon till eight in the morning and then speeding from target to target.

Friday afternoon at a little after two I cash the last payroll check for New Jersey. We go back to the hotel and cut the dough into two piles. Twenty gees my end, ten to Phil and Jazz, the total for the week. Good money, but nowhere near what I want.

Phil is speechless, counting their ten grand over and over, fanning the dough and smelling it. Looking at me occasionally and shaking his head.

Jazz seems to take it in stride. Her Uncle Ben is one of the most competent thieves working and stacks of cash don't impress her a bit. It is obvious what makes her happy is Phil, and his eyes, crossed or uncrossed, are as focused on her as they are on the dough.

I am envious of the obvious joy they take in each other and I want that for myself. But picking a chick up for the night doesn't seem like it would fix me, and I'm on my best behavior for Jazz anyhow.

I take my cash and lock up in my room, with a paperback book, needle, and spoon.

Phil's wearing some of his new clothes, camel-hair sport coat, white turtleneck, black slacks, dress boots, and it's obvious he feels uncomfortable dressed like this.

He comes to my room early, waking me up. When I ask him what's up he just gestures at himself and looks at me with a question on his face. I light a smoke, take a couple of hits, and say, "Make sure the door is locked."

And start my morning ritual. Getting a glass of water, pulling my kit out of its hiding place, setting the cooker down, placing a small cotton ball next to the cooker, emptying my wakeup into the cooker. Apply three burning matches to the mix and swirl it until it all goes into solution. Draw it up, and slam it home.

Three weeks before, one bag buckled my knees, had me on the edge of a drooling nod. To get out of bed now I'm doing five papers and not getting real loaded. I jack the hit a couple times in the hope that it will give it a boost, take the rig out of my arm, and say, "Top of the morning, dog. What's up? You look perplexed, confused, bewildered even. Talk to me."

Phil's smoking and watching me put my shit away, finally he says, "These clothes . . . I feel funny being dressed nice. Shit, killer, you and Syd . . . y'all know what you doing. Dress, talk, act like all this shit is old news. I feel like a fish outta water. Last night you was just throwing that dough around like it was nothin'. I had to keep my jaw clamped not to holler and scream . . . I never saw that kinda cash in my life. And I didn't really do nothin' to earn it, just taggin' along like a big old lop. Shit, dog, I just . . ." And he lets the sentence die.

I sit there, not knowing how to express anything other than certainty and confidence. Because: Don'tcha know, anything else makes you look weak. And guys like us can't appear weak. What if anyone finds out you're not Superman and Jesse James rolled into one? What then?

Maybe the heroin gives me the confidence to be honest, maybe I really trust Phil so much I am able to tell the truth. Who knows? I take a hit off my Camel and tell him, "Anything but jeans and stuff makes me feel fuckin' weird. I got no idea what I'm doing, I'm driving blind. If I act like I know what I'm doing, that's just what it is, an act. Tell ya the truth, I figured out how to bust these checks by doing it, hands-on job training so to speak. Syd's ex–old man and her took me under their wings and gave me a lot of game, showed me how to make dough doing burgs and like that. This paper shit is all new to me, tell ya the truth I don't like it that much. Syd put this together, so we could get a bankroll, I didn't even do that. But the deal works the same. You're driving and running backup, if someone comes after me I know you got my back. You're earning your dough, my brother, let's hope ya never have to bust a grape. Think about it, Philip, if you or Jazz righteously have to drive getaway or you gotta tackle some security asshole you're earnin' every penny. I say all that to say this: I know I can trust ya. I know if the shit comes down you'll be there. Don't sweat the small things."

He sits down and grins, saying, "Last person called me Philip was my pops when he was mad at me. And the last time I heard ya say not to sweat the small things we had a fuckin' M16 pointin' at us. The thing is . . . maybe I look all right in these duds but I don't feel that way. Maybe I'm earnin' my end of this dough but it don't feel that way, either. This Jazz girl touches my fuckin' soul, and I want to let her know I'm about somethin' other than muscle."

I'm not sure where he's going with this, so I just nod and wait. "I've had regular jobs bustin' my ass," Phil says. "Construction and working on an assembly line one time hanging tires on Chevies in Detroit Michigan, but never nothin' where I called the shots. I feel like a big old redneck wearing nice clothes, like an impostor. Know what I mean?"

I laugh. "Sho nuff, bro, I feel the same way when I go in with these checks. But truth be told they don't know how I feel, only how I look and act. You may feel like a redneck but ya look like a junior executive or lawyer or somethin'. For real. A fuckin' movie star. You don't look like the backwoods maniac you really are, lose that drawl and you could pass for one of the Kennedys. Go get your old lady and let's get back to New York. I gotta go to charm school my ownself."

Thinking maybe a little Brit chick . . . pardon me, "bird" . . . would be just the teacher.

.

ten

This is before answering machines, practically the stone age, the ringing is driving me nuts, let it ring six times hang up and say fuck it. Slam the phone down. Who cares anyhow? Won't call again. Pace my room, read, do a few push-ups, look at the phone, pace, turn the tube on and turn it back off and then dial that same fucking number and let it ring six times. Start over. Two A.M. comes and I decide absolutely, positively, that calling again is out. Fix enough stuff to bring on a good nod, kill most of a quart of bourbon and lie down to pass out, when my phone rings. Get it to my ear and that soft English accent comes across the line. "Did I wake you, luv? I was out dancing with some of me mates and ran into your friend Syd, she said you were back in town. Thought I'd give you a ring. . . . You're not busy, are you?"

The whiskey is doing its job, I'm hanging on to reality by a thread, my vision is narrowed down to keyhole size. I tell her, "Yeah, went to sleep early, let's hook up tomorrow, I'll take ya to lunch. Whatcha think?"

"Sounds lovely, Sunday brunch around one then?"

"Sure, sounds OK. See ya then."

"G'night, luv."

"Yeah."

And when I hang up give a rebel yell that would have made Phil proud. Eeee-haaah! Passing out with a grin plastered on my face.

Brunch is at a class joint on Madison Avenue, a brownstone turned into a bar and restaurant, waiters in monkey suits hovering with champagne and coffee.

The buffet is outrageous. Crab legs, shelled lobster, caviar, omelets made to order while you watch, prime rib and pork chops, bacon and different kinds of sausage, Belgian waffles and French toast, mountains of fresh fruit. It is boss.

Susan is a trip to watch, taking little bites, sipping at her Mimosa, talking with that accent, and I'm all the way enchanted. Really believing that maybe some of her polish will rub off, and maybe it does. Instead of loading my plate and stuffing food into my mouth with both hands I'm aping her moves, watching to see what fork she uses for what, how she holds her knife.

Studying the people around me and taking small bites and little teeny drinks instead of chugging. Charm school.

Leaving the restaurant, going straight to my hotel and getting naked, this time I'm ready for the competition, and what we do isn't making love in any sense. But it is entertaining. I dig adrenaline as much as I like drugs, and violent sex provides that. Hurt me a little bit and I'll do my best to cripple you. That's the deal and she seems to like it. To like it? Little did I know.

We're lying in bed in my suite. I'm studying Susan's face and discover a small scar going through one eyebrow. Ask her how she got it and instead of the horror story I expect, she says, "Slipped when I was a tyke, fell down the stairs. Me mum and dad were panic-stricken, don'tcha know. Didn't really hurt, just scared the bejesus out of us all. It's not very noticeable, is it?"

"Only to someone studying your face."

"You do stare, don'tcha."

"Yeah."

The day's spent running from bank to bank, from one check-cashing place to the next. Burning it up, tellers and clerks blurring together. Working.

At a club the next night, Susan and me dancing and drinking with Phil and Jazz, the two of them billing and cooing and loving each other, the two of us calling it quits early and rushing back to the Ritz.

Showering together and making it. I'm watching the candlelights reflect off the fine gold down on her arms, running my tongue across her belly and seeing the same almost invisible golden hairs climbing toward her belly button and following them down with my lips and teeth until she is moaning and we start again. Nothing like Jazz and Phil have, but it'll do.

The next night Alan and Syd take the four of us out for lobster and to hear a symphony at Carnegie Hall. A symphony . . . another new concept. All dressed and on our best behavior and I'm tripping on Phil, who's developing a Southern gentleman sort of routine. A long way from Cross-Eyed Phil the Psychotic Peckerwood.

Jazz really digs the symphony, actually seems to understand it, carries on an impressive conversation with Alan about the orchestra and the relative merits of this one versus others she's heard. Heard where? Where the hell did Jazz learn all that stuff, I wonder, watching Phil watching her in a kind of awestruck haze. Fuck, I think, this guy doesn't even do hard stuff and he can just trip on her. Syd sees it, too, leans over to me and whispers, "Such a deal, huh, bubelah?"

Now we're at Thursday, after a day's labors me passing bad paper and Susan making bad paper, meeting at her little pad, and she tells me that there's a club she wants to check out, got something new happening, something called punk rock. I am not enthused. I know about rock and roll, blues and jazz, now after the other night I know about classical music. I never heard of this shit, punk rock.

Where I come from a punk is the lowest of the low. Inside the walls a punk is someone who has no self-respect, who would rather get buttfucked than fight. I say all that to say this: The idea of listening to punk rock doesn't sound too exciting.

But I go. To hear . . . hear? . . . the Ramones and some other band. Cooking, loud angry music without sense or sensibility. And I love it. Some people think rock and roll is about good times, and maybe it is. For me it has always been about anger and outrage, sex and violence. Chantilly lace and a pretty face; motherfucker.

Now it's called moshing, once it was slam dancing, and that may have evolved from pogoing. Who the fuck knows? This night the music is a freak occurrence with no label to apply to it, the floor is alive with pure sensory overload and adrenaline. Everyone there smashing into and hurting anyone within range of elbows and shoulders, feeding time at the shark exhibit. Lust and lightweight violence and crazy, no-melody rock and roll mixing together.

Susan is wearing jeans and a pullover, and for once I fit right in with my almost grown-out jailhouse haircut, blue jeans, and steel-toe boots kicking anybody that slams me or Susan too hard, feeling all right.

We stumble out of there at four A.M., bruised and overamped on adrenaline. And from the time we reach the Ritz until well into the light of day we do our best to damage each other. We climb into bed and wage war. Pulling her hair so hard that she screams, while she rips gashes into my back and shoulders with her fingernails. Biting me in the chest so hard that blood is flowing all the way down to my groin and I reciprocate, leaving my own teeth marks everywhere that no one will see them, grinding my teeth into her, and screaming around her flesh as she does the same.

Coming together like ships of war, and when peace is declared, holding each other. Unable to speak, unable to do anything except breathe in each other's sweat, sex, and spent passion. Holding each other so close we are bleeding in each other's wounds. We like/hate each other pretty well.

Weird. I don't quite get what this is. There was a time with Rosie, when our violence was all wound up with loving each other, when we were no more than continuing the tradition we both had learned at the tender mercies of our parents . . . the inner conviction that we were basically bad, that pain is redemptive, that nobody could love us unless they hurt us, that fucking is better when it hurts. Whatever this is with Susan, it's different from with Rosie. It's a lot like addiction. But it ain't love.

Phil's behind the wheel again. With or without doctor's permission he's going to drive. I'm riding shotgun and Jazz is off doing whatever. Shopping, getting her hair done, female stuff. Phil is determined he's going to be the breadwinner. End of that particular story.

I have no urge to argue. I'm as cheerful as a guy can be, wearing an outfit that Susan picked out for me, continental-cut gray wool suit with a light pinstripe, navy-blue dress shirt, dress boots. I'm stylin'.

Phil is dressed good, we got this shit down.

Two checks to go and this little run will be over, almost sixty grand up and life looks grand.

Waiting for the teller to get the OK on this next-to-last check and it's dragging. I look at him and he kinda grins and holds up a hand with one finger raised indicating it's only going to be a minute more.

Check my new watch and try to look like a business guy with important stuff to do. The manager gives me a look and a half-assed, tight little smile and adrenaline hits my gut and I know something is all the way wrong. The teller's still standing at the manager's desk and the manager walks over to one of the other people behind the counter and has a little whispered conference. They both surreptitiously check me out. Goes back and says something to my teller, who then comes and tells me, "Sorry for the inconvenience, if you don't mind just have a seat for a second while we get this paperwork straightened out. Should only be a sec and you'll have your money."

I grin and say, "Only a sec, huh? Thanks."

Start walking towards the chairs and couches in the bank lobby and veer towards the door, moving slowly and purposefully. Walking like a guy with no worries, maybe going out for a smoke or to use a pay phone. Casual.

When I hit the doors the manager yells and it is on, I'm moving as fast as I can, hurtling over benches and headed across the street to Phil and the wheels, when some John Wayne motherfucker clotheslines me. I see my feet flying above my head and then I smash into the sidewalk and all I can think about is trying to breathe. Feel a knee on my chest and look up into the eyes of John Q. Citizen aka Johnny Justice.

Check to see what's taking my backup so long and see Phil and the Cuda disappear from across the street with squealing tires and know that I'm on my own one more time.

The guy crushing my chest is so excited at having helped apprehend a fleeing felon that he's talking all crazy. Maybe he's a Clint Eastwood fan, maybe just a very verbose vigilante, but through trying to get air into my lungs I hear him yelling, "Run now, motherfucker. What didja do? Huh? Caught your ass, though, didn't I. Gonna put up a fight, here I am. Go ahead, try and kick my ass."

Catching my breath and telling this moron, "Put up a fight? Kick your ass? You got a hundred pounds on me and are sitting on my chest and crushing my rib cage, dickhead. What do ya think, I'm Bruce Lee? You're confused, get offa me and I'll explain the whole sad situation to you."

Johnny Justice grabs the lapels of my new suit and I feel it ripping across my shoulders, and he spits out, "Confused? Tell that to the police."

He looks over his shoulder at the manager and teller, who are now on the sidewalk watching, and asks, "What did this scumbag do? We got him, don't we?"

I know trying to talk my way out of this isn't going to work. Hoping I make bail fast, right this second just tripping on the righteous indignation this football-player-built idiot is displaying.

He suddenly levitates off my chest and from my vantage point lying half on the sidewalk and half in the gutter I get to watch the look on his face when he is abruptly suspended in midair and looking into Phil's uncrossed but thoroughly psychotic eyes.

Phil sets the guy down and growls, "Why don'tcha skedaddle before I put a beating on your fat ass that'll last so long your children will feel it? Hmmm?"

I get to my feet with as much dignity as possible, still trying to play it like I am an aggrieved citizen, and the bank manager says, "Hey, just you wait a sec—."

And like John Q. Fucking Citizen, he cuts the word off on the first syllable. Not because he wants to sound cool or something but because Phil takes a step towards the three-man-deep posse and roars, "Git!"

And git they do, three cheap suits running back into the bank in tight formation. Courageous trio. Phil says, "The car's around the corner, that's what took so long. Can't let 'em get the plates, I love that vehicle almost as much as I love that little Jazz."

As we walk briskly down the block and around the aforementioned corner I can't help myself and whoop, "You about a corny motherfucker." Throwing my voice into a whine and repeating his words, "Almost as much as that little Jazz."

Phil growls and throws a punch at my head, pulling it at the last second, then chases me to the Cuda, laughing and threatening mayhem when he catches me.

The drive back to Manhattan is uneventful, quiet even. At about the halfway point Phil looks over, whistles, and says, "Sure did fuck that pretty suit up. Folks just hate it when ya look too good."

I laugh . . . and remain silent for the rest of the ride.

And as we pull into the Ritz know what the answer has to be and I spit out, "Shelton."

Phil gives the keys to the valet and as we are crossing the lobby he asks, "Shelton? What's a Shelton?"

Elmer's drinking a scotch on the rocks and smoking a pipe, got on a tweed jacket and tan slacks, light brown snakeskin cowboy boots, and I'm trying to figure out why Syd is so enthused with this lame. He's doing his best to sound intelligent and sincere, reason with me. Patronizing motherfucker. The fact is I'm driven all the way to the nutsack, got visions of dead Englishmen filling my head. Feeling self-righteous like a motherfucker and this Elmer is not going with the program.

As a matter of fact he's laughing at me, saying, "Well, son, Sydney said you were a piece of work. Let's try this another way, Shelton is a smart, capable professional. Whatever his relationship is to Ms. Susan is a moot point, it makes no difference. Women lie, Susan lies more than most. If his perception is that your presence will damage his operation, what choice does he have except to try and remove you? Hmmm? Really, son, tell me what options he had?"

I want to sound like something other than a hood, trying to sort through the words in my head for a way to express my rage without using a sackful of "motherfuckers." Take a deep breath and feel the scream in the back of my throat. Down the rest of the scotch rocks that Elmer had given me and remember that I don't like scotch at all. Light and smoke part of a Camel while he's watching me.

Elmer's smoking his pipe and sipping his drink, smiling slightly and wearing a look of pleased anticipation that is driving me crazy, and finally I say, "He could have talked to me, told me what was up. If Susan's his old lady I'da backed off. For Christ's sake if he hates me that much he should have had me hit. He tried to get me busted. That's not part of the game, it's chickenshit. It's not fair. I want to move on him and Syd says you gotta OK it. All right, what do I gotta do to get a green light on this guy?"

There: Didn't say "fuck" once. Very proud of myself. Charm school. Self-taught. Rule one: Drop the word "fuck." Gonna learn the rest of the rules as I go.

Elmer laughs, rolls his eyes up, and says, "Why me, Lord? Why me? Here are the facts, my young friend. The game we're playing has no rules. If you survive and stay free you win, otherwise you are indeed the loser. The only fair you'll find is the kind with Ferris wheels, don't look for it in real life. As you suggested, he could have had you hit, or done it himself. Don't think for a minute that our British friend is not capable of killing. Believe me when I tell you he is. The easier and safer course was the one he chose. Sadly for him and happily for you it didn't work. Sooo, that leaves us with determining what the appropriate course of action is, and in this case the appropriate action is none."

Elmer stops speaking and looks at me, still smiling, waiting for the wisdom of his words to hit home and for me to agree with him.

This is when charm school goes out the window. I can feel my voice rising and have no control over it as I'm saying, "The cocksucker tried to get me busted. Dropped a dime on me. What the fuck am I supposed to do, kiss the son of a bitch? I want a piece of his ass, with your green light or without it. I don't care how good he is for your operation."

Syd comes in, wearing jeans and a flannel and muddy sneakers, taking her coat off as she's walking at me, saying, "Wake the fuck up, Bobbie, this is the real world—not a fairy tale, not a movie. People do what they think they gotta, there ain't no rules. Wanna know what the rule is, without Shelton's expertise we got a hole in our organization that'll cripple us. The rule is we ain't gettin' crippled. I told ya not to fuck around, but didja listen? No, hell no. Hadda go and bone Susan. You're lucky Shelton didn't ice your silly ass. Well, I hope it's good and I hope it lasts forever."

She shakes her head in disgust. "Here's the deal, Bobbie. Billy Bones is going to be in New York next week. You wanted to see him anyhow, now's a good time for catchin' up on old times. Do some serious Irish idiot male bonding, rob some armored cars or something, but you guys head for Boston. Do whatever the fuck you want. Leave our people alone, you wanna fuck around with Susan do it on your own time. Not burning paper we set ya up with. That's the deal. Shelton will chill, he knows you know. Now you know he knows. Everybody is even, you get the broad. If you can keep her, you're in for a ride with that one, let me tell ya. Visit her between robberies or whatever, give Shelton time to find a replacement, and move her in with ya and make babies. Who gives a shit, as long as you don't fuck with this operation."

I feel like I've been hit by a Mack truck. This is anything but motherly Syd, more like a viper, fangs dripping.

Her face softens, a little, and she says, "Work on your manners and grammar and next time around if you're willing to squash this thing with his lordship we'll put you in. Big-time scores, big-time money. Your decision. Whatcha wanna do?"

A guy with deep moral principles would have left plotting revenge. Me?

Greed and ambition have always been as much a part of my makeup as the red, white, and blue in our flag. The American nightmare in person. Syd's last sentence gets all my attention. I don't know what I feel about Susan, except it's intense. Got no clue what she feels about me. Don't know much of anything except Syd has never lied to me and the thought of learning how to bag millions without breaking a lock or pulling a gun has me enchanted.

I finish my Camel, weighing all the possibilities out, and then say, "I freeze on this and you'll put me in the next one? For reals?"

Syd smiles, then nods and gestures to Elmer, who plays with his pipe for a second, then says, "I've met Mr. Bones, and I must say his social skills are lacking. If I were you I'd attempt to associate with people with a little more polish. Refine your act enough to pass as a civilized member of society and I see no reason you wouldn't be a strong candidate for our next little endeavor."

I look at Syd, catch her eyes to make sure she's with me, and she gives me a little nod. I take a breath and say, "Don't patronize me, ace. I decide to I'll be able to pass as a Harvard fuckin' professor. Am I a candidate? Or am I in? What I do depends on your answer. What I do will determine what my socially lacking friend Billy does, as well as my other equally uncultured friends. Are you with me on this, cowboy?"

Elmer laughs and says, "Cowboy, huh? Aside from the nicknames you seem so fond of . . . well put, young man. Your position was clearly stated and acceptable. Indeed you're in. Has Sydney explained the time frame we're talking about before we start our next little venture?"

"Nope."

Syd laughs and tells me, "If you can make it for a year without getting busted or dead, we'll be in business again. Like I said, whatcha wanna do?"

I've always tried to be a reasonable human being. I smile and say, "Perhaps Shelton and I should meet for cocktails so that I can personally express my admiration of his abilities. Furthermore, I would sincerely enjoy buying him a drink and letting him know that not only are there no hard feelings but that I look forward to working with him in the future."

Syd grins and Elmer starts clapping.

I feel proud as I can be. Not one "motherfucker" in the whole paragraph, and I'm pretty sure it was all grammatically correct. All right.

But I still trust Elmer not at all.

The backyard at Syd's starts with a glassed-in patio furnished with wooden furniture that still has the bark on it. Outside the patio is an area covered in cobblestones with a fountain topped by a marble cherub who, in warmer weather, would be peeing into the basin below him. As it is he just looks like a small winged pervert holding his dick. Beyond Cupid is a vast lawn broken by shrubs and sleeping rosebushes. The grounds end in woods that eventually lead into another piece of prime real estate.

The deal is that we're going to talk, have conversation. Become buddies, shake hands, and promise to be good boys. Me and old Shelton are gonna cut it up like the gentlemen we are. I have the .32 stuck down the front of my jeans, not because I don't trust Shelton, but you never know when you might get attacked by lions or tigers or bears, for that matter.

Shelton's got one foot resting on the fountain, leaning on the raised knee with both arms, biceps bulging through the sleeves, his body so tense you can see the knotted muscles under the sweatshirt he's wearing.

Once he's out of his normal business attire it's obvious that this guy is a healthy motherfucker, his shoulders look like bowling balls rolling into his neck, hood blown all the way out. A look you only get from powerlifting, no body builder or pretty boy here, Shelton is solid efficient muscle and not real fond of me.

He's squinting into my eyes. I keep a direct gaze and do my best to smile like there's no hard feelings, and he's not buying it. He spits into the empty fountain and says, "Shit, mate, I know you would like to stop me clock. Don't blame ya, really. Where I fucked up was not just killin' ya. Let me conscience get the better of me. Thought it would be better just to send ya down the road for a bit, rather than end your days. Stupid. The story of my native land, let our sensitivity rule us, lost an empire because we're too goddamn civilized. So what do we do? Kiss and make up?"

I stare back with my face slack, let all the bullshit go, no facial expression, just look into his eyes and say, "No. I'm outta here for a while. I'm going to be seeing Susan eventually. I don't know what's what with her, but if ya wanted me outta the picture ya shoulda told me before this shit started. If that's a problem we should discuss it now. Otherwise I look forward to working with you in the future. Do we have any problems here?"

Shelton's right shoulder drops and his eyes tighten and I know he's gonna try and take my head off, then he grimaces and sighs and suddenly I flash that this cat is in serious pain, the rage he's holding in is as much at himself as it is at me. He rubs viciously at his forehead, growls, and says, "Susan's a piece of work, as you'll no doubt find out. I let me little head do the thinking again. She and I have been on-again-off-again for a couple years now. My mistake is in thinking that any one bloke is the problem. Tellin' ya I'm sorry would be the act of a coward and a hypocrite. I'm neither. Fuck with me and we'll have problems, otherwise let's try and treat each other with professional respect."

He stops and looks inward, eyes blank, then laughs and continues, "After all, we're both men of the world. Right, mate?"

"Right."

"The operation we got going is too sweet to let anything fuck it off. Syd is inordinately fond of you, so we have to be able to work together. Susan will make her own choices, and let me tell ya, youngster, some of 'em will amaze you. Enough on that. The question is, can we work together, do I have to watch me back with ya?"

I clap him on the shoulder and grin, saying, "Hey, shit happens. Like Syd says, grab the gelt. Get the fuckin' money. Susan will do whatever the fuck she wants anyhow. Right?"

As Shelton smiles and mutters, "Right," I can still see the tension holding him like a gun holds a bullet. Waiting for the hammer to drop.

I hope it won't come to a showdown, because now that we've talked I know that old stiff-upper-lip Shelton would be a vicious enemy, and wouldn't make the same mistake twice. I wonder if it would be smarter just to kill him. And from the brightness and obvious sincerity of his response I know he's wondering the same thing.

The next few days are strained. Susan is withdrawn, and for the first time we start arguing. I say it's a nice day. She disagrees. I want to go out. She wants to watch TV. I dress up and she says I look better in jeans, getting louder and more aggressive every time. I have no clue what to do. One day I tell her she's gorgeous and she goes 51/50, screaming at me, "You're a liar, I'm a fuckin' cow! Bobbie, you're a simple-minded fool, only an idiot like you would find me attractive."

I just stare at her. How the hell do you respond to shit like that?

It makes me crazy, doubting my own actions and perceptions. One minute everything is grand, then those eyes turn from angelic to straight-up demonic, and I don't know if it's me who is nuts or if Susan has suddenly lost her motherfuckin' mind.

The crazier our situation gets the more dope I shoot. Until one day I come out of a nod with her hitting me with an uppercut and screaming, "Ya bloody dopefiend degenerate, I'm trying to talk to ya and you can't even keep your bloody eyes open. Well, fuck you, then. Fuck you."

And she storms out.

Here's the thing that perplexes me: I was in my hotel room alone when I fixed. Sure that I was by myself with the door locked before I started that particular little voyage into dreamland.

I sit there feeling the shock of the punch, listening to the echo of the slamming door, wondering what the hell happened. I get up and look in the mirror and after wiping the blood from my dripping nose I see a confused pair of blue-gray eyes staring back at me. Walk around in circles, go into the bathroom and splash cold water on my face. And still my mind is full of milling, fragmented thoughts. Stick my head under the shower and let the freezing water pound against my scalp until I feel my mind start to clear.

Towel my face and hands, and with water still dripping from my hair light a cigarette, which is soon as soggy and misshapen as my emotions. Take a hit of wet tobacco and paper and throw it away. Do a better job of toweling off and light another smoke. Then, second by second, I go through the events of the day and know I am not out of my mind or hallucinating.

She had to have let herself into my room, walked in, found me nodding, and then wound up and punched me with everything she had. Started screaming at me and then split, slamming the door behind her.

Back in the mirror staring at my thick as a brick, stupid, Irish-Scottish, completely bewildered face, wondering what happened.

A bar full of business types, smoky and upscale, the booths packed with groups of young wannabe tycoons and their secretaries.

I am nursing a beer and Syd is sipping at her martini, she's dressed for work, conservative. Staring at me over the rim of the glass and finally saying, "Kidling, what a mishegoss. I tried to tell ya. Shelton is top of the line, but he's got one weak spot, Susan. 'Scuse me, that's Sue *Zann*. And she's got one weak spot, she's out of her fuckin' mind. I been watching this over and over like a bad commercial. One day she loves him and only him. It stays like that for a while, and then she takes some poor idiot hostage, sweeps him off his feet. Then she goes nuts on him, beats him up until he runs for his life. Unless Shelton goes crazy first, and puts him in the hospital. Shot one guy. As soon as Shelton even looks like he's found someone he really likes, Sue *Zann* works her voodoo and it's on again. She's what my dear old ma would have called a shiksa bitch. She deserves credit—whatever she does she must do it good. Now this thing with you, it's too close to home. The girl needs help, what you need is to stay the fuck away from her. Emes. Pay attention. She's trouble."

I drink some of my beer and shaking my head, say, "No problem.

If I never see her again it'll be too soon. She's nuts, man."

Syd smiles, glad that I've come to my senses.

When I say it I believe every word. I don't have any idea that I have as much control over Susan—or myself—as Shelton has. Like heroin the habit is now there, the ride has only started. You don't kick drugs until they quit working, and I won't be through with this until she is done working me.

Susan isn't through with me yet, so of course she's with me when I go to hook up with Billy Bones.

It's a little after one A.M. at CBGB's, the air full of smoke and discordant noise, Lou Reed is playing with his backup band, and the joint is packed, a who's who of the New York scene. Phil and Jazz are in one side of the booth, hoodlum down. Leather jackets and Levi's, Phil's got some steel toes and has been trying them out on different surfaces, waiting for someone to get obnoxious to really test them. It might be a while, not many people are rude to Phil.

Jazz, who continually blows my mind by what she seems to know that a yokel from an Illinois commune shouldn't know, points out Andy Warhol and his crew, who are high-signing, amped on speed and if not impressive, impressed with themselves. The band kicks off another song and the Jack D rocks I'm drinking is mixing with the smack and coke I've been shooting. Life seems all right.

I'm scanning the crowd and finally spot a tall, emaciated character wearing black shades, black T-shirt, bike-chain belt, and black jeans stuffed into engineer boots, his face pitted and scarred and grinning ear to ear, showing off his chipped yellow teeth.

Billy Bones, beloved crime partner and a certified psychopath from Ireland by way of South Boston. Genuinely a nice human being as long as he's your friend. We acknowledge each other and as he saunters to our table, I jump up to greet him because this is a blast from the past of the best sort.

I'm all the way up, happy to see Billy and ready to get the hell out of NYC and into something more profitable and entertaining than flying kites.

We shake hands and I do introductions, telling Billy, "This is my partner, Phil, and his old lady, Jazz. This is Billy Bones. Killer extraordinaire."

Point into the booth at the drop-dead-beautiful girl I'm sitting with and say, "And this is my friend Susan."

And she gives Billy the full-wattage British china doll charm. Who would think? When she's good she's real good. And when she's bad . . . oh, well.

Susan is downright demure. She chats for a while and then she coos, "M'luv, I've got to work in the morning, and I'm going to have to call it an early night. Wouldja mind escorting me home?"

So I make a date to meet Billy Bones later and I escort the lady home, where we once again tear each other apart, blurring the distinction between violence and sex until it's all one thrusting, screaming, shuddering, bloody climax and I don't know when she's good or when she's bad or who she is at all.

And then, when I think we'll hold each other close like before, her pretty blue eyes turn into fractured ice, splintering in all directions, and, once again, she's screaming at me, "Get the fuck out, go back to your fuckin' crazy dogs, as you call them, you asshole—that's all you want to do, anyway, once you've fucked me, right?"

And I'm stumbling out the door, pulling my pants on, dodging the bottle she's thrown straight at my head, wondering why I went and did it again. Like slamming after the habit gets you, the good times are smooth fucking gone.

Our meeting place is a good Irish pub on the West Side where the smells of bad cigars and cheap booze are battling the odors of frying food for primacy. There's rock and roll on the jukebox and the patrons are Billy's partners of Irish descent. All of them got thick East Coast/Mick accents and dress the same way me and Billy do, jeans and leather jackets, engineer boots and steel-toe combat boots being the uniform.

Billy is drinking beer from the bottle, empty shot glasses lined up in front of him, got his back to the wall in the booth in the back of the bar.

I'm stuck with my back to the door and hate it; some people

think I'm paranoid but it seems like common sense. Highly refined survival skills if you will. It bothers me immensely when anyone can come up behind me, and I guess it shows because Billy grins and says, "Lookin' like a whore in church, lad. You're among friends. Ain't no one coming up behind ye, and I got your back anyhow." He belches and screams at the bartender, "Another round for me and the boys, Seamus. We're dying of thirst, sir, more alcohol, ya sod."

The guys crammed into and around the booth laugh and scream and swear and spit. Downing shots and chugging beers, taking turns buying rounds and cutting up rails of coke and speed, snorting the shit and fucking with me until I participate.

And right in my face is this cat who goes back with Billy eons. Since the dawn of fuckin' time, he says. Two manic green eyes glaring at me from under brows that have more scar tissue than skin, set over a nose with no bridge and spitting through lips covering no teeth, "What, are y' too good to take our fuckin' drugs then? Who the fuck are y' anyhow? Who is this fuck, Billy?"

And Billy smiles and says, "Why bless your heart for askin', Mental. He's t' lad with a pistol aimed at your wee little dick. Show him your gun, lad."

I smile into the drunken maniac's eyes and raise my piece from beneath the table to much laughter and shouting. The ex-boxer or crash test dummy or whatever the hell he is downs a shot, grins with his empty gums, and says, "Eh, I might fightcha later, but for now have some of these fine drugs, my friend. And put your gun away, with Billy Bones backin' ye you need nothin' else. I'm Mental by the way, Mental Moore."

I grin, say, "Cheers." Praying that this guy will forget about anything other than getting high, fighting Mental Moore is not a pleasing thought. Grab a straw and do a fair imitation of a vacuum cleaner. The coke numbing my face and the meth burning like acid through the freeze from the coke. Whether I want to be awake or not it's on the way, heart picking up its beat, rolling from a walk into a sprint that won't stop, the soft blur that heroin imparts to the world changing into a crystal-clear luminous blaze.

Billy's holding court, all these dudes are friends of his and when we walked in it was like a fucking reunion. The cold stares I initially received have melted now and been replaced by friendly, crazy, full-on fool behavior, once I have passed Mental's little test.

Billy lifts his Bud longneck, saying, "Boys, I want yez to meet young Bob Prine, an Irish-Scottish lad I've had many profitable and bloody fuckin' adventures with."

He points out Mick or Paddy, or who the fuck knows who, because I get introduced to so many dudes, so fast, names mean nothing. Everybody's brother, ace, pal, or killer.

Billy waxes eloquent. "Like the good Lord himself," he says, "Bobbie here came back from da dead. Of course he crucified himself with that shit that's killin' so many of us. Motherfuckin' heroin. And gentlemen, I. Meself. Billy fuckin' Bones was t' angel t' good Lord sent t' save his unrepentant, constantly sinning Celtic ass."

Stopping to cross himself and then continuing, "Living to do t' Lord's work, Father Bones at your service, boys. Sometimes saving souls . . . and often dispatching them."

Then making the sign of the cross over me like a priest, he says, "Bless ye, my son. A toast to me friend, lads."

And with much laughter and blasphemy a monumental drunk begins. Staggering from one pub to the next, downing whiskey and beers, stopping in one place that has a kitchen and eating corned beef and cabbage. Billy's mad Irish eyes staring across the table at me while he's talking and eating at the same time, saying, "Eat up, lad, your heritage is on that fuckin' plate. Potatoes and porridge five days a week if yer lucky. Corn beef fer one, then t' hash, then back to t' fuckin' porridge. Tomorrow or the next day it'll be lobster for the likes of us, but here we eat the food of our homeland."

I know nothing about the people and land my ancestors came from but I find the whole thing fascinating. I'm thinking someday I'll go there and actually see what Ireland and Scotland are like, that's if the good old US of A will ever let me have a passport.

Right now, I'm just proud to have Billy as my friend and proud of my heritage . . . whatever it is.

The drunk ends at sunup a couple of days later when me and Billy fall out of a cab in front of the Ritz and stagger through the lobby and take the elevator to my room. Billy's singing "When Irish Eyes Are Smiling" in a fair tenor all the way through the lobby and in the elevator. Once I lock the door he passes out across the bed and I don't have the energy to wake him or the desire to crash in the bed and listen close up to the snores and fragmented sentences that are already coming from Billy Bones's sprawled form.

I kick back in one of the chairs and start nodding if not sleeping. The phone ringing cuts into my skull and that soft voice crawls into my head saying, "Hey, lovey, just wanted to give you a ring and let you know I was up all night playing with meself and thinking about you. Maybe I can see you tonight? Can you fit me in, luv?"

She slices right through the booze and drugs like a sensual straight razor, just hearing Susan's voice makes my guts roll and breathing increase, and I say, "Yeah. Hell yeah. Abso-fuckin'-lutely I can fit you in. I'd cancel a meeting with the president. What time?"

"You have such a way with words. Perhaps nine, perhaps ten. Which is better?"

"I'll pick you up for dinner at nine. Why wait an extra hour? Right?"

"Right you are, luv, you do sound all in. Other women? Or just bad companions to go with your bad habits? Hmmm?"

I laugh to stop my own questions, knowing she'd probably spent the nights I wasn't around with Shelton or my new replacement and was grilling me anyway. Once I trust my mouth to speak without betraying me I say, "No women, just the best of bad companions."

She is silent for a second, then says, "See ya then."

"Bye."

Just talking to her makes me hard, why that particular girl makes me so nuts I have no idea. But common sense, not to mention any small measure of sanity I may possess, dies when she acts right.

I yank pillows off the chairs and throw them on the floor, fall out on my makeshift bed, then pull my jacket over me. Drifting on the edge of sleep, knowing that I am making a bad move getting more involved with Susan. Wondering why I have no control, and contemplating the awful thought that perhaps Shelton and I have more in common than the same taste in women. Could I end up in the place where I want her more than I want self-respect? Naw, no way. Finally saying, Fuck it. Never had control of the way life works, why should that change now?

Thinking about Susan's lips and hips, eyes and thighs, and that soft voice with the high-class accent. Listening to Billy snoring like a grizzly bear and conversing with his ghosts. Then drifting off into the nightmares that have always ruled my sleep.

eleven

Time to move. Billy has filled his contract and is ready to leave, and I know I'm going but Phil and Jazz don't seem to know what to do. The twenty grand they made from the checks seems like a fortune to them and Jazz is talking about maybe going back to Illinois, trying to start a small business, maybe get married and have a baby.

Jazz looks worried a lot lately, and I don't get it. We're doin' fine, far as I can see. But I hear her say to Phil, "But honey, yo not a badass; Bobbie is, and he's good at it. But you jus' a great big lamb chop."

Phil puffs up, looking bad and affronted, and Jazz just laughs.

"My man, I know you big and tough and I've heard all that talk you make to scare people about how you'll rip yo eye out of yo haid and skull-fuck you . . ."

Phil, I swear to God, blushes. He obviously hasn't done so well in disguising his native language from the beautiful Jazz.

"That's OK, honey, but I know you ain't really a badass criminal, tha's all. You gonna get in real trouble if we keep on with this stuff. We could get somethin' goin' with this money, and be honest folk, go to church, have a family. You'd be a righteous good daddy."

"Jazz, baby," Phil's pleading now, "yo Uncle Ben don't want us back, Bobbie's my dog, and we're on a roll, baby. I do cotton to the idea of having babies and doing real work . . . I can do that . . . but . . ."

I'm still underestimating Jazz's brain, think I know better, like Mel knew better than me once upon a time. So I try to explain that twenty thousand is not really a lot of money, that maybe it might be a good idea to expand their bankroll a taste before becoming venture capitalists.

We're still knocking it around without a decision when Billy shows. We take a cab to Max's. Iggy Pop is playing and we want to catch his act. The show is great, smoke fills the room and the crowd is beyond eclectic, rock stars and hoods, junkies and speed freaks, faggots and dykes, and beaucoup fine little rock-and-roll broads vamping.

I am doing great until I see Susan and Shelton, he's wearing a badass suit made out of washed silk, she's in a dress that's made out of little squares of silver reflecting material and she's snuggled into his side. I don't know if he feels my eyes or has spotted me earlier and knows I am now tracking him. Shelton swings towards me and raises his glass in a half-assed toast, his eyes sad and ashamed and homicidal all at the same time.

I almost puke, rage and a mix of emotions I can't name tear through me and as I raise my beer back in a silent toast I realize that my face feels like a mirror of his.

I work my way to the door and split, taking a cab back to the Ritz and diving into the cooker.

The morning is crystal-clear, soft cumulus clouds with gentle tangerine hues from the beaming sun are floating past the window in my suite. Spring is almost here. Room service has come and gone, leaving plates scattered all over the room.

Start the day talking to Phil and Jazz, trying to make a decision on what they're going to do. Jazz is homesick, Phil misses George, and I'm worn out. This thing I got for Sue *Zann* makes no sense, at my tender age I still think things should make sense. I am very confused.

Billy walks in on the tail end of the conversation, and knows that it would make me a happier guy if Phil and Jazz come to Boston and keep me company. Like I said, I am worn out and so unsure of anything I feel incapable of telling anyone that I want them around. To tell the truth I feel as useless as flyshit, and I am sure that Susan is only the first to discover the sad truth about Bobbie Prine. My brain is working on me overtime, screaming that Jazz, Phil, and Billy all have arrived at the same conclusion.

Phil's smoking and looking at the ceiling, keeping his face blank. Jazz is slumped against the wall, knees akilter, sipping coffee, watching us, not saying a word.

I got my shit packed and am ready to go, this Susan has taken up full-time residence in my head. Maybe going on a crime spree in

Boston will evict her. All I know is that I'm starting to feel sorry for Shelton, which means I'm vulnerable in too many ways.

Billy's staring out the window smoking a joint. Turns back into the room and extends his absurdly long pipe-cleaner arm to Phil, waving it in front of his face, saying, "It's up t' you, lad. Come or stay as you will. What I'm tellin' ye is that once we get to Beantown there's plenty of work. Green to be made. I got me own line of endeavor, but if you and Bobbie want to steal there's a good crew y' can work with. There's a good crew here, but for me friend here . . ."

Billy stops and points at me with the hand still holding the joint, takes another toke, and this time when he extends it, Phil grabs it and takes a deep hit. As Phil's holding the smoke down and fighting to keep it in, Billy continues, "For young Bobbie, New York is not a good place to be. He's got woman troubles brewing that could get very messy. This fuckin' Brit is a bad motherfucker, not that Bobbie ain't of course. But killin' or gettin killed over pussy would be a sad and terrible thing. To add to the problem, although I'm not crazy about the English empire, I've done a piece of work here and there with Shelton and have become fond of his decadent Limey ass. So, Philip, what will it be? Twenty gees ain't shit. Call it, lad. Are ya comin', goin' somewhere else, or stayin' in New York?"

Jazz has been so quiet that it's almost as if she wasn't there, but she's been studying Phil's face, and Phil's face is a picture of hangdog woe. You can tell he's torn by looking at him. Suddenly Jazz stands up and walks to where Phil is perched on the edge of a chair. Starts rubbing his neck and back and says, "They right, honey. Twenty won't get us nowhere."

She's still massaging Phil when she turns her head to me and says, "Besides, Bad's going to be awfully lonely in a new town all by hisself. How long would it take us to raise fifty, Bad? Fifty large in cash, and then me and Phil are going back home."

I shrug and grin, saying, "Tell ya the truth, I don't know. One big score would do it, three or four little ones, we gotta see what's happening. Figure at least a month, maybe two. Are you guys up for that?"

Jazz doesn't miss a stroke in her massage, just smiles and replies, "Yeah, Bad, maybe George and my uncle can come visit. . . . I think Uncle Ben's ready to forgive us. . . . But we'll hang with y'all till we get fifty clear, then Phil and his baby brother are gonna open a business and I'm gonna keep the books."

I'm suddenly in a much better mood, spring is right here right now, it's a beautiful day and I got friends. I say, "Cool. I'm glad, I woulda missed you guys."

Phil smiles up at me, hangdog no more, and Jazz leans down and whispers in his ear loud enough for it to carry, "And then maybe we'll make a cotton-topped baby with praline-colored skin, to play with Lily and Red's red-haired baby, whatcha think, my beautiful dude? Now, you gonna smoke that whole joint or can I have some?"

Billy wraps that no-muscle arm of his around my shoulders and sings, "Home of muggers, fuckers, and thieves . . . mmm-mmm, Boston, you're my home."

The Boston Common is full of hippies, dopefiends, and deadbeats. Negro burn artists looking for victims from the local colleges. Kids from the colleges looking for dope. Townies looking for college girls. College girls looking for adventure. Cops looking for all the above, and we're sprawled on the grass digging it.

Phil, Jazz, and Billy Bones sharing a joint and I'm half high, just right, feeling the sun trying out its muscles as it warms my skin.

We got a pad today, a big two-bedroom on Beacon Hill right by the Common. Paid cash. Three months up front and we have a place to live, hardwood floors, huge windows, old-fashioned wallpaper, furnished with nice if not expensive furniture. Home sweet home, the first one I've ever lived in other than shooting galleries, hotels, institutions, and, of course, the ancestral palace that I escaped at age twelve.

The grass just starting to come back after winter's onslaught feels good against my hands, the pot smells great, and the sun is tingling against my eyelids and creating red and orange dots swimming across my closed eyes.

There's a band playing at the other end of the park and the conversation around me is droning back and forth from Billy's brogue to Jazz's soft feminine drawl to Phil's redneck proclamations.

A new voice cuts in soft, strident and way female with that slurred Boston "r," saying, "William Bones, you're back, huh. Take me to the bahhh, get some beeaahs. Who're your friends? Come on, Billy, they got pitchas for two bucks, I got some 'ludes. . . . Come on, Billy."

I hear Billy getting up and saying, "See yez all later. Duty calls."

Their feet whispering against the new grass, the sun still creating the red-running-into-orange globes against the back of my eyes, and moving or talking is way too much work as I lie there wondering what Susan is doing and when I will stop thinking about her.

The office is in Somerville. A lower-class blue-collar town, home to Italian, Irish, and Jewish families, infused with swarms of college students from nearby Tufts and Harvard and MIT, and smattered with aging, spaced-out flower children.

From the ceiling hangs a hundred-watt bulb on a frayed piece of wire, putting out too much light for the small room that contains it. Showing every detail in the rusted-out filing cabinets and banged-up metal desks. On the walls hang foldouts from *Playboy* and *Penthouse*. Behind one desk is a wizened little character wearing a faded and stained aloha shirt under a sport coat with leather patches on the elbows. His beady brown eyes are surrounded by yellow orbs and the bags under them could hold a week's worth of groceries.

I walk in, followed by Phil, and look around, lock eyes with this character, Abe, and he grunts, "Sit, take d'load off. So you two friends of Syd, friends of Irish Billy Bones. That's nice. So what the fuck yez do?"

He stops and takes a cigar from his ashtray, sniffs at it, and re-lights it. Sticks it in the corner of his mouth and continues pointing at Phil. "You, beefcake . . . whatcha, a legbreaker? Dime a dozen. Getcha work, but beatin' on people don't pay much."

He chews on the cigar for a second and stares at me, I light a Camel and stare back, cross my legs and wait him out. Finally he says, "Whatcha? A burglar or some fuckin' thing? You steal shit, I'll buy it. Whatcha want?"

Looking into this old man's wrinkled and crafty face and figuring if he's a friend of Syd's and Billy's maybe this is a test. Say, "Whatcha want? What kind of question is that? Legbreakers and burglars are a dime a dozen, like you said. So are fences. I'm a pro, good as they get, otherwise I wouldn't have been recommended to you. If all you can do is fence, we don't need ya. If we were amateurs, you wouldn't need us. The question is, what do you want and what can ya pay?"

Abe smiles around his cigar and says, "Yeah, they said you was a wise guy. Good as they get, huh? At your age? More likely you're a cocky kid don't know his ass from his elbow. . . . Well, we'll see about that."

He takes a couple puffs of his recycled cigar, blows the smoke at the ceiling, and hollers, "Ernie, get in here."

Ernie's got bad shop tattoos on his weight-lifter arms, Mickey Mouse and Yosemite Sam on one, a sick-looking tiger and the Tasmanian Devil on the other. Ernie is about six-two, or -three, got big guns and a big gut. Moves awkwardly like his feet hurt. Obviously someone has told him he's tough and he believed it. He sneers at me and Phil and I want to laugh. I know his weight advantage has got to be considerable, but this guy don't scare me. Phil just grins through closed lips, letting his expression do his talking.

Abe points vaguely between me and Phil saying, "Give these two somethin', try 'em out. What we got on soonest?"

Ernie plumbs the depths of his intellect and enumerates, "That fuckin' PR from Watertown needs his legs broke, uhhh, got a jewelry store in Worcester but that's gonna take a crew, how 'bout the furs?"

Abe looks at me and raises one eyebrow, and pursing his lips without removing the clump of tobacco in the corner of his mouth, makes a "hmmmmm?" noise, waiting for me to respond.

I look at Ernie, look back at Abe, and say, "Tell us about the furs."

Ernie reaches down and scratches his nuts, then shares his thoughts with us. "Nuttin' to it, straight hijack. Run da van off the road, pistol-whip the shit outta the driver. You know, knock all his teeth out and shit. Make sure he knows better than to testify or say shit about Shinola. Take all the fur coats and shit and drop 'em with our guy in Waltham. We give you two a couple grand each. Nuttin' to it, right, Abe?"

Abe tries to hit the cigar and discovers it's died, removes it and puts it in the ashtray, then pulls a strip of tobacco off his lip, flips it over his shoulder, and tells Ernie, "Thanks. I think that's all for now."

Looks at me through those yellow eyes and asks, "How's it sound?"

"Fuckin' stupid, pistol-whipping citizens. Stupid. What's the score worth?"

"None a' your fuckin' business. Whatcha, writin' a book? I can pay ten K, total. Yez want it or not?"

I look over at Phil and he shrugs, pin Abe for a second, and say, "Twenty on delivery. We do it our way, you get the goods, we get the dough."

"Fifteen on delivery. Yes or no?"

"Fifteen's good for the first one, once you check our style you'll know we're worth top dollar."

Abe closes his eyes and leans back in his chair, looking like a lizard sunning itself, gets a little half grin at the sides of his mouth, says, "Oy, style yet. We'll see."

The roar of traffic speeding by comes in waves almost like the ocean, glaring headlights rushing at us and soft red taillights running away. The night crisp and clear, the moon shining down so strongly that the trees surrounding us cast shadows, the stars tiny chunks of diamond all through the sky and country-western music playing real soft.

Phil's profiled against the driver's window staring straight ahead nodding his head in time with Johnny Cash, smoking and humming along. The crossbow lying on the front seat between us is a precision piece of equipment, tungsten-alloy bolt gleaming against the dark wood.

Shudderingly beautiful weapon. Haven't shot one of these things in years, not since dear old Dad decided to share some quality time with me, taught me to shoot by hitting me upside the head every time I missed. Got a minor concussion, but the pain of that was nothing compared to the sick feeling I got watching him smirk when the weapon hit a deer in the haunch, sending it off into the woods in agony, dying slowly from infection. I was grateful when he pushed the bows into the closet with his guns, letting them grow dust while he added the delights of prescription drugs to his other enthusiasms.

But I did learn to shoot one of these things, and I hope I still can because here one is. It's ready.

As the van we've been waiting for flashes by, Phil drops our van into drive and fishtails out of the woods onto the highway. Accelerating smoothly and still humming along with Johnny.

I'm pulling on a pair of thin black cotton gloves and then grabbing the crossbow. The window behind Phil has been modified so it can be lifted out of the way and then dropped into place. It's already locked up against the roof and the wind is roaring through the van and Phil looks at me for a second and asks, "Ya ready, hoss?" Then starts to pull even with the other van's rear wheel.

Holding the bolt in place with my thumb as I jump from shotgun to driver's side behind Phil and still hear him humming and smell the woods around us and see the moon and stars shining down. Snuggle the crossbow into my shoulder and line it up slowly with the rear tire. I'm so on, so fucking aware, the tires on the road make a distinct sound—wishhhhh—and the crossbow sings—whanggg— and the impact when it sinks into the tire plays counterpoint— pthunk. I tap Phil and he slows and we take up position about a half mile behind the other van.

Listening to country-western, feeling the wind slice through the wide-open window, smoking and waiting as Phil hums along with the steel guitars, banjos, and fiddles.

It takes a few miles for the tire to go flat. We pull off behind the other van, and when our tires leave the road and dig into the dirt I'm already moving, got a flesh-colored stocking over my face and my new .380 Colt Mustang in my right hand, my feet are on the ground and moving as soon as the van stops.

Phil's got the high beams on and I'm crouched, crabwalking along the edge of the woods and coming up behind the driver as Phil is approaching him from the front. By the time Phil is close enough for the guy to tell that his face doesn't look right, I've grabbed his coat between the shoulder blades and put the .380 in his ear, leaning around to his other ear and saying, "You don't want to die. We don't want to kill ya. Hand my partner your keys to the van."

The dude's eyes are wide open and he's babbling, saying, "Man, please, don't kill me. I got kids. Got two girls and a boy. I'm only a fuckin' bonded courier man, I don't make enough money to die for."

I flash on how this guy must feel and decide that after this score if at all possible I am going to stick to things that don't involve holding guns on citizens. One of the first things Mel ever taught me . . . don't hurt citizens. I hope that the modifications I've made in the original plan work.

I gather the back of his coat a little bit tighter in my left hand and increase the pressure of the gun barrel against his ear, saying, "Just get behind the wheel," walking him to his driver door, where I push him into the seat and handcuff him to the steering wheel, telling him, "Gimme your wallet."

The poor guy is shaking, he thinks I'm going to rob him personally, and when he hands me his wallet I grin at him through the stocking and take his driver's license, putting it in my top pocket, and extract the five one-hundred-dollar bills I've got folded in there and count them out for him. Then put them where his license was, saying, "Listen, pal, we wish you no harm. All we want is the fuckin' furs. When the cops come, describe anybody but us. Anybody. Got it? We have a guy on the cops. Soon as they question you and I know you're down with the program we mail another five of these brand-new hundred-dollar bills to the address on your license. If you describe us . . . well, what you'll be getting won't be nice. Are you with me on this?"

I'm holding his wallet with one hand and my gun with the other, staring into his eyes through the fine mesh of the stocking. I'm so close I can smell the garlic on his breath and see the pores on his skin. He takes his wallet back, moving slowly, and I keep my voice flat, real matter-of-fact, wanting him to know that while I have no desire to fuck him up I'm as serious as a guy can be.

He opens the wallet with his free hand and looks at the five cees staring at him and says, "Shit, man, I couldn't describe you two if I wanted to. What if I fuck up and give 'em what you look like by mistake?"

I pull his license from my shirt pocket and see his first name is Maurice and tell him, "Listen, Moe, don't make a mistake. Please. Two broads, two midgets, anything you want. Except anything that resembles us. OK, Moe?"

He lifts up off the seat and shoves the wallet into his back pocket, saying, "You got it, man. Anything but you. Sure."

"Take it easy, Moe. You'll get the other nickel as soon as we get the police report. See ya."

I help Phil with the last two armfuls of fur coats and we're driving back towards Boston. Smoking, listening to steel guitars, banjos, and fiddles while me and Phil harmonize as best we can.

Jazz is stylin' around the pad in her new sable coat. Running her hands down it and stopping to admire herself in every window and mirror she passes. She looks good, great even. Phil's proud of himself and I don't have the heart to tell him he fucked up. If you want to stay in the game for any length of time you should never keep stolen goods. Never. No ifs, no ands, and no buts. Never.

Finally I get it together to tell Phil not to let Jazz wear the coat around town for a while. Just in case, you know.

We've found a small article about the heist in that morning's *Globe* and discovered that we've stolen over $200,000 worth of mink and sable coats. Fifteen gees doesn't seem like enough money, but from now on our price will be much higher. Either that or we just go solo. But the benefit to having a hookup like Abe is that scoping and planning scores takes a lot of time; when you can have stuff preordered and set up you can get a lot more done.

Phil's reading the paper and admiring Jazz at the same time. As he gets to the end of the article he growls, "Brothers? Why'd he think we was black? Now this shithead in Somerville is gonna think we farmed the job out. What's up with this motherfucker? It says three six-foot black guys. You five-seven, -eight, I'm six-three with no shoes, we both stone peckerwoods. Whiter than rice. What's up?"

I explain about the five hundred and tellin' the guy to describe anybody but us and Phil keeps on grumbling, "Blamin' it on brothers. George would be wantin' to kick my ass if he knew this. Shit."

I shrug and put the other five hundred along with his driver's license in the envelope for Moe. Always keep your promises.

* * *

Ernie is glowering at me, upset that no pistol-whipping took place. Everyone has their own theories, and mine and Ernie's are diametrically opposed. He's sitting on one of the steel desks in Abe's office smoking Kool after Kool, lighting each from the butt of the last and then throwing the burning butt on the concrete floor and grinding it out. This guy wants to intimidate me, some big guys are conditioned to use that size to end arguments. Poundage counts for a lot, but the thing about cats like this Ernie is that getting hurt themselves is an alien idea. They never throw their chest out with anyone they think could hurt them. Consequently if you can damage them real good and real fast, usually all the fight goes out of them. That's my theory anyhow.

Bolstered by that and knowing that Ernie's actions are going to be dependent on his master's desires, I have no problem glowering back at him.

He finally sneers at me, saying, "So ya was scared to fuck the dude up, huh? Or did you and pretty boy just hire some niggers? I toldja how to do it. You gonna work for us ya gotta take orders. Get it?"

This moron sounds like a bad imitation of James Cagney. I keep staring at the wall above his head, concentrating on Miss December and wishing that Abe would hurry up, wondering if I should have brought Phil to keep this idiot in check, and finally, growing bored, ask him, "You always put a hurtin' on your targets? Why not get in and out clean? Ya get less heat and less aggravation. What's up with that?"

Ernie lights another Kool, spits on the floor and rubs the spit and his last butt into brown paste with the sole of his boot, and stares at me from under his eyelids, finally responding, "I like it. It gets my shit hard, fuckin' people up. What I really like is kidnaps. Dope dealers and bookies with no protection. Snatch their old ladies and sell 'em back. Not that they're good for much when I get through with 'em. If you ain't hard ya can't make it in this business. I kill puppies for fun, get it? Your big friend, I eat punks like him for breakfast. You, shorty, cross me again I'll cripple ya. Got it?"

Tough guy 101 in action. What am I supposed to say to this moron? One thing I know is not to make threats, someone talks shit you just smile and wait. I smile and ask, "So, killer, how long till your boss gets here?"

He growls and stomps out of the office.

I'm sitting in Abe's chair, got my feet on his desk, and am on my way back to bored when Abe finally makes his entrance. The mangled remains of a cigar protrude from the corner of his mouth and he glares at me for a second, then laughs, says, "Outta my chair, schmuck. Out."

I stand, then sit on the other desk, and Abe flips an envelope at me, says, "Count it."

One hundred and fifty one-hundred-dollar bills. I stick them in the inside pocket of my jacket and watch Abe as he gets settled in behind his desk. He pulls a bottle of peppermint schnapps out of a drawer and fills two dirty-looking tumblers, pushing one to me, says, "Tell me about it."

And I do, in detail. Occasionally he laughs or asks a question. When I get done with the story he asks, "So didja send him the other nickel?"

"This morning. First thing."

Abe pulls out a new cigar, lights it, and refills both the tumblers with schnapps. Says, "Here's da deal. I like your MO. Ya made the guy an accomplice, now he can't incriminate yez if he wants to. I don't know how ya did it, but from seein' Ernie twice ya made him hate ya. From here on if I got work I call ya, we meet. You like it you do it. Two things to remember, naw, make that three. One I'm half Irish and half Jew, two ya fuck with me I'm a hundred percent murderous mick, three ya fuck wid my money I'm a hundred percent homicidal hebe. That was a good piece a' work. Stay away from Ernie. He's a fuckin' psycho, but he's my psycho. I'll call ya in a few days with somethin'. Any questions?"

"No questions, just a couple of things ya should know. The first is we're lookin' to make serious dough. Anything under twenty apiece ain't worth it to us. The second is we don't hurt citizens, it ain't worth the heat. The third is that Ernie might be your psycho, but if that's the case ya better pull his chain. Ask Billy or Syd for my pedigree, I don't like being pushed."

Abe grins, looking more like a lizard than ever, and says, "Tough

guys all of yez, gonna wear an old man out. I'll speak to him, youngster, you just behave your ownself."

Back at the pad, pizza and beer, Phil and Jazz are watching TV
and I'm bored out of my head. The book I'm reading is about im-
proving your vocabulary and social skills. It's a drag.

This particular tome suggests that you mix a little bit of French
in with your everyday speech, it will make you seem much more
sophisticated. Like a world motherfuckin' traveler, even. Found one
word I like: "outré." It's French for outrageous, sort of all the way
out.

As I'm going out the front door, Jazz yells, "Where ya goin',
Bad?"

Wondering if I sound like a world traveler I say, "Down da road,
Jazz. Gonna get all the way outré."

Jazz giggles. "Oh, Bad, you're outrecuidant, mon ami." And as
far as I know, she sounds like a mademoiselle from the Left Bank.

Close the door on Phil's rebel yell.

Outrecuidant? What the fuck does that mean? I find out later it
means insolent, arrogant. I guess that's me, Bad Bobbie. And Jazz
speaks French. Once again, the chick amazes me.

Walking through the door is the same as it always is, smoke and
noise, the smell of beer and booze, but what I find beyond that is a
different scene than I've ever experienced. A college bar on Charles
Street, rock and roll playing and full of people my age who seem to
be from a whole different planet. The clothes they're wearing are
casual and the language they use is semi-hip. Not gangsterese, or
street slang, but not square either, talking about grass and acid, 'ludes
and poppers, exams and tests, parents and siblings. Politics and rev-
olution with a left-wing slant.

I'm people-watching and eavesdropping, trying to assimilate
enough of their moves to be able to pass as one of them. Feeling
inside like this is the last place in the world that I belong, like these
people are so much further ahead of me that I could never have a
frame of reference. College? I never finished seventh grade. But the
feeling I get is that I'd like to experience something other than flims

and flams, robberies and scams. Realizing that I've stumbled into another class for charm school, I down my shot and sip the beer I got backing it up and absorb the conversations flowing around me.

Noticing one girl in particular, our eyes touching for a second but she's in animated conversation with some guy. She's flirtatious like a motherfucker, eyes all the way alive, smiling and vamping, babbling away with this obvious lame.

Find myself cutting this guy to ribbons in my head. Thinking that not only does he look like a spoiled brat who grew up, he talks like one. College my ass, this cocksucker could never survive the kinda shit I cut my teeth on. Watching the girl's little muscles bunch along her arms, while her soft breasts are trying to escape from her top. Eyes, I'm trying to determine what color they are and can't pin it down. Amber? Hazel? Green? I just know they're pretty and way spirited, her amber-hazel flashing eyes twinkle at this motherfucker and I'm tripping on how stupid he looks with his pigeon chest stuck out and wishing that I could say something intelligent about politics, which is what they're talking about.

She's saying, "America is a nation dedicated to the oppression of the masses, waging a constant war on the third world to keep them in the place of vassal states. That's how we maintain our standard of living, and soon it's all going to fall apart. We, too, will have only two classes: the very rich and the very poor."

I'm fixated on how white and even her teeth are, she's got big soft lips that the good Lord sure as hell designed for kissing. I can tell, just watching her mouth move. And she looks right into my eyes and asks, "Don't you think so?"

I'm frozen, knowing I got busted staring, but she doesn't seem to mind, got a cocky grin and now those amber-hazel dancing eyeballs are dancing with mine and I say, "Yeah, man, rich and poor. I'd rather be rich. Sure, you're right. My name's Bobbie. You're . . . ?"

"Michelle. You go to school?"

I hesitate and come up with what I hope is a good answer, "Dropped out of UCLA back in California to concentrate on writing. Got some stuff published in Europe. How about you?"

"Go to Emerson. What do you write?"

At this point her friend Pigeon Chest cuts in and tries to bust me: "Who published you?"

I pause and take a hit of my beer to have a minute to think, then the attempt I'd made earlier to augment my social skills pays off as I say casually, "Do a column for *Outré* magazine. You know, kinda artsy underground stuff."

I step away from the bar and step back in, so now I am standing next to Michelle and edging Pigeon Chest out, saying, "This place is awful noisy, maybe we could find some place with more pleasant ambience. Whatcha think?"

Pigeon Chest is looking at me like he wants to kill me, and Michelle tilts her head to one side, studying me from a different angle, then says, "I'd like that, but I have to be in early. So what do you write about?"

We wave at her classmate as we walk out.

Stroll down Charles Street, the wind soft from the Charles River blowing and in my head I'm hearing Billy's tenor singing, "Yeah, man, love that dirty water, home of . . ."

She's talking away. This girl thinks. She's talking about the poor and downtrodden; about have and have-not societies; about how people get alienated from everything because of neglect or abuse. She talks about books she's read for classes, ideas, theories. She's excited about just about everything.

Me? Just listening and nodding occasionally, coming up with the appropriate noises, you know, yeahing and uh-huhing, with an occasional "Know whatcha mean." But thanking Syd in my mind because she's the one who put me on to reading philosophy, so I at least know something about some of it.

So when Michelle mentions Marx, I can say, "Yeah, he nailed it for what people were going through at that time and that place. But don'tcha think that an economic philosophy of dialectical materialism is unrealistic for here and now? The world has changed, it's no longer agrarian . . ."

Michelle stops and studies me with those amber-hazel eyes and I'm swimming in them, my mind intrigued by her college-girl ideas and my body intrigued by everything else about her. She says, "You're right, you're right! And my professor in Economic

Philosophy just doesn't get that . . . he still thinks communism will save the world. He's just so unrealistic. . . ."

She stops cold, locking eyes with me, switching from mind to body in an electric flash. Out of nowhere she says, "I usually go with women."

I'm looking at her and asking, "As in . . . ?"

She's grinning and answering, "Yeah. As in."

Laughing and saying, "Guess I'm a little bit butch, huh?"

Grabbing my hand like we were kids and our hands swinging together as we walk, not talking until she says, "But you're so butch it might be a nice change. We'll see."

Holding hands, her still talking, me back to nodding and uh-huhing.

She says she'd love to read some of my stuff. We make a date for that Friday night. I'm thinking that I'll wine her and dine her and she'll forget all about reading, plus it's already been established she likes chicks. Why sweat it? Right?

Ride the subway with her to her dorm and when she repeats that she'd love to read something I've written when I meet her on Friday I say, "Sure, why not?"

Stand out front with her for a minute and as she's going in I kiss her. No tongue, no hot embrace. My lips touching hers. Simple.

Get home, fix, and think about her until sleep comes.

I buy a typewriter the next morning.

Tuesday morning I have a short story, eight pages single-spaced, typed using my index fingers and the hunt-and-peck method, looking for the letter I want and hitting it. I write about doing juvenile time from the point of view of the guy doing the time. Create a character and interview him, finally get it where I feel like it reads all right and show it to Jazz, explaining my motivation and asking for her thoughts on the story.

Phil's in the kitchen cooking breakfast, the smell of burning bacon is thick in the air, I'm drinking a beer and smoking, completely focused on Jazz as she reads, trying to tell from her expression how she's reacting.

Phil lumbers into the living room carrying plates and grinning, mimicking the PA system at Plainfield, yelling, "Chow time, chow time. All inmates report for chow. Chow time."

Jazz keeps reading, taking the plate from Phil and picking at it with her fingers until she finishes all eight pages. Hands them to Phil and says, "Read this, baby."

And putting her plate in her lap, directs her eyes at me, then says, "Good, Bad Bobbie, really good . . . but you got the worst spelling and punctuation I ever did see. We'll fix that up for ya. Who's this girl, anyhow? She must really be somethin', Bad. Where didja meet her?"

I'm grinning so hard it feels like my face is going to break and I ask, "You really like it? It reads OK?"

Jazz laughs around a mouthful of bacon and eggs, then says, "You ain't Hemingway, but I liked reading it. I'll retype it for ya and fix up all your mistakes. Ya oughta go to school, learn how to spell and shit. Aside from that it's real good. You done any writing before?"

I shrug. "Yeah, teachers always said I had 'potential,' but school was a drag."

Jazz says, "Hmmm. Well, you do got potential, Bad. So tell me about the chick that inspired this."

"She's nice, goes to college. Real pretty, was with some punk that thought I was lying when I said I was a writer. Well, fuck him, know what I mean? Can't have her think I was bullshittin'. Right?"

Jazz is looking at me askance, then says, "Told her you was a writer? Like a job? You too much, Bad. I guess you a writer now. So didja bone her, or what?"

"Naw, kissed her good night, like a gentleman. Gonna see her Friday, she's got tests or some kinda shit she's studying for."

Phil finishes reading, rolls up the pages, and lights a cigarette. Then points at me with the tube of paper and says, "Shitfire, hoss, this made-up guy was Joe Moppa, wasn't it? Tell me true, dog, you wrote a story about Moppa. You got the way he talked and the way he acted. Am I right or not?"

I don't think I've ever felt as proud of anything I'd ever done, no score, no nothing has ever made me feel as good as I do right this second, and I say, "Yeah, man, Moppa Immortalized."

twelve

The Naked Eye is a strip bar in the Combat Zone, Boston's old skin-and-sin section. It's full of tobacco smoke. On the runway behind the bar is a girl bumping and grinding for all she's worth, she's down to her panties and boots and she shoots one leg straight into the air, balancing perfectly like a Tibetan yogi in pink panties, and she removes one of the boots. Abe nudges me and asks, "So whatcha think, kid? She can put both her legs behind her head and fuck ya blind. Got muscles where ya'd never think muscles could be. That's what keeps me motivated, got her and a couple others for personal stock. Keeps lead in the old pencil, know what I mean, pal?"

"Yeah, sure, Abe. Lead in the pencil. Right. Whatcha got?"

"Hijack, razors. A tractor trailer full, worth a buck a pack, sell 'em for fifty cents, give you twenty cents per. Two hundred thousand packs in the load. Forty gees for you and your partner. Ya want it or not?"

Across the bar Ernie is paying more attention to me than the dancer, he's got a mug of beer and peers at me over the top. When he hits it I gesture at him and ask Abe, "What about your boy? Why not give it to him?"

Abe's concentration is fixed on the dancer, he looks just like a lizard contemplating an incredibly tasty insect, finally he tears his eyes away from the current love of his life and says, "Too much heat. Ernie's good for some stuff, but every time I send him on a piece of work, someone gets hurt or dead. You want it or not?"

"Yeah."

I'm counting out ten brand-new one-hundred-dollar bills, paper-clipping them to a note saying "Good Luck."

Phil laughing at me and asking, "What's next, dog? Gonna start sendin' 'em wrapped gifts?"

I consider it for a minute and say, "Maybe, who knows. Makes me feel like a cross between Santa Claus and Robin Hood. I dig it."

Then folding the cash and note around the driver's license we'd got from the razor blade guy and putting it all in the envelope.

Walking down to the mailbox and just digging the day, clear blue sky, no clouds anywhere, sun beating down and Charles Street is full of foot traffic. Stopping at a liquor store and buying a quart of malt liquor, leaning against the brick side of a building and drinking, smoking, and watching the passing samples of humanity.

A wino asks me for a smoke and I hand him one, then offer him the bottle. He's not much older than me, wearing rags, has grime and dirt all over his face. I take the bottle back and watch more people go by, take a long hit and am passing it back to my new friend when I hear Michelle's little-girl whiskey voice: "Bobbie. Hi. Whatcha doin'?"

"Having breakfast, kicking it. Where ya goin'?"

"School."

I take one more hit from the bottle and hand it to Wino Boy, saying, "It's yours. See ya."

Then grabbing Michelle's hand and walking with her towards the old brownstone on Beacon Street that's been butchered up for college classrooms.

Breeze blowing on our backs, pocket full of money, and entranced by this girl I haven't even really kissed let alone fucked. Listening to her talk about her classes and cramming and takin' speed to study.

"You haven't asked me what my major is," she says.

I think quickly. "I guess I just assumed it was politics," I lie, never having thought in terms of college majors before.

"No, silly," she breathes. "I'm interested in politics and philosophy and stuff . . . but I'm going to be an actress. I'm majoring in drama. I'm on my way to my Shakespearean Language class now."

Seems reasonable to me.

As we get to the mahogany door of the brownstone, I'm holding her hand and rubbing the back of it with my other hand's fingers, marveling at how soft her skin feels. I'm all the way gone, Jack. Lost. I'm living in a universe made not of planets and stars but the way she looks and talks and smells when she says, "You sure have strange friends. But it was nice, the way you gave that poor guy your bottle. Very compassionate."

And I kiss her. Sometimes a first kiss is awkward, sloppy. You know immediately that it needs practice. Kissing this Michelle is like poetry. When our lips part she stares at me like a deer caught in headlights and I feel my knees ready to buckle, then I smile and reply to her last question or statement or whatever it was, "Yeah, strange friends . . . you don't know the half of it."

She dashes through the big doors into the mysteries of college classrooms, whirls, and yells, "Friday night."

And whoosh, she's gone, along with my mind.

Stroll back to my new home whistling, not than I can carry a tune but whistling nonetheless. As I come through the door, Jazz is watching TV and Phil is pacing, dressed in a button-down shirt, slacks, and brand-new cowboy boots. "Get some decent duds on, dog. Syd called ya, wants us to get dressed up and meet some hot-shit criminal at Abe's place."

I'm headed toward the refrigerator to investigate our grocery status when I yell out, "Who's the criminal? What did she say? When?"

The fridge holds all kinds of stuff, beer, wine, cold cuts, eggs, too much shit to make a fast decision. Jazz hollers in a good imitation of Sydney, "She said for you two schmucks ta put on ya best clothes and make a good impression. She said for ya not to talk or act like a fuckin' hood. Ya got it? Act like a fuckin' preacher who steals as a sideline."

Then, laughing at her own imitation, Jazz adds in her own voice, "I took the call and if that's not word for word it's awful close."

I grab a beer and throw a bunch of salami between two pieces of bread. Get dressed, mohair, slacks, blah, blah. Dress to impress. Right?

Phil's driving and not at all happy about the road conditions. The Cuda is not designed for heavy city traffic, every time we catch a red light or traffic stops the car feels like it's going to shake apart. I'm watching Boston crawl by in fits and starts and listening to Phil swear at the traffic, at the other drivers, and at his pride and joy, this high-performance, made-in-America Hemi Barracuda. He's so amped that it seems like everyone on the road should be able to see psychic danger signs flashing. I consider telling him to calm down, and then decide to keep my own counsel. Smoke Camels and stare out the window and as we cross the bridge into Cambridge the traffic clears, and we're flying, got the pedal to the metal all the way to Somerville.

Stroll into Abe's operation, and before we get to his office, Ernie scopes us, makes sure he has established eye contact, and spits on the floor. Some people have no finesse. Phil looks at me as I keep moving, he's got that close-lipped smile, and I know that after experiencing city traffic and his vehicle acting like it was having a heart attack or whatever the automotive equivalent is, it won't take much for him to go smooth off. I throw my arm up and over his shoulders, saying, "Don't sweat it, bro. We here to make dough. Fuck that lame."

Phil is walking with me but mutters, "Maybe fuck that lame up. Go up in his ass if he ain't careful."

I grin and go, "Shhh. Fuck it."

Abe's at his desk, in his normal splendor, a bright red sweater under a checkered sport coat, cigar in place. Sitting across from him is what looks like might be a college professor, the guy's got a good haircut, beard trimmed tight to go with the hair, glasses and wearing a tweed coat, white shirt, tan slacks, and loafers. He does not look like he belongs in Abe's domain. Abe gestures and says, "These are them, they workin' in my territory. Bring the contract, we'll fill it for ya. Ya said ya had to meet the fellas doin' the work. Outta respect for Sydney we'll do it dis way, once. Under normal circumstances that ain't gonna fly, but for what we talkin' here I'll broker the deals."

The professor stands up and appraises me and Phil, finally saying, "I'm Mr. Smith. My clients sometimes have special items that must be obtained by other than the normal channels. If you agree to the proposition, when your services are needed, I will place the order. It's up to you to fill it without using violence or any other actions that will generate undue attention. Once I receive the articles I've requested I will make payment to you. For his service as a broker

Abe receives twenty percent of the total on all our transactions. My concern is that you can conduct yourselves in a professional manner."

He's staring into my eyes, trying to weigh or judge me or something the way cops and parole boards do. I don't know what he's looking for, and I glance at Abe and then at Phil to see what their reaction is. I'm getting a double blank. Finally Smith whistles silently, pursing his lips and blowing air through them, then says, "Speak to me. This could be the most important interview of your life."

My pulse is picking up fast, I have no idea what I'm getting into, but this guy's opening sounds real good. I pause again and glance at Phil, who nods, and I say, "Since we don't know what these articles are or what we will be required to do to locate and obtain them, our response can only be one of qualified interest. We're professionals, we always work clean. If we hadn't impressed Abe and come with one hell of a pedigree you wouldn't be talking to us. So . . . what can we do for you and what does it pay?"

Mr. Smith pulls an envelope from his inside jacket pocket, opening it and handing it to me, and says, "Those are the items we desire. They currently are being held by one of the large art wholesale companies to clear debts that my client's family incurred at the hands of some rather shady individuals."

He then mentions the company name and explains why it is supposed to be so hard to extract these things. Alarms, armed guards, and the things he wants extracted weigh close to a ton each. Marble fuckin' statues. Two of 'em.

I'm looking at the photographs, thinking that it can't be too much different from a regular burg. I ask him, "What's the time frame? Do you have floor plans?" And of course the most important question: "What's it pay?"

The time frame is two weeks, not much time even if you have the floor plans, and of course the answer to question number two is "No." He has no floor plans, no information except what he wants and where it is. The answer to number three makes me smile and Phil whistle through his teeth. One hundred thousand dollars.

Even Abe reacts, rubbing his hands together, making a dry rustling sound, rubbing them like a cricket rubs its legs. When I say,

"Nothin' to it," Phil manages to keep his face straight, but knowing him I feel his reaction.

Abe pulls out his dirty tumblers and schnapps.

Smith just says, "We'll see. Won't we?"

Red brick building with a recessed entryway, white marble steps leading up to the highly polished wood-and-glass front doors, behind the doors a reception area guarded by an efficient secretary, wearing horn-rimmed glasses, gray skirt suit, blondish hair swept off her face.

My initial approach is anything but promising. The front doors are wired, as are the windows; next to the woman running the desk is a black guy wearing a security guard uniform; along with the uniform is a holstered sidearm.

My ploy is I am looking for a job. The woman hands me a stack of application forms that are so thorough they could be for top-secret government shit. I spend as long as possible filling them out and sizing the place up.

From the few people coming in and gaining admittance to the back while I am sitting waiting for my job interview it is obvious that in order to get past the reception area they have to clear you and buzz you in.

The good part is that there is no sign of motion detectors or sonic alarms. The bad is I have no clue where the goddamn statues are. One of the essential ingredients for a successful burglary is getting in and out without wasting time and energy. This is a three-story building. Finding the exact location is essential.

The interview itself lasts less than five minutes.

A very flamboyant gay guy comes out, takes my paper work, says, "Lovely, this looks wonderful. Don't call us, we'll call you if we need you." And he sashays out. Motherfucker doesn't even try to flirt with me. Back to the drawing board.

Sitting home and going through the different possibilities with Phil. Armed robbery is out. Not just because it could get messy, but because this is going to be a major moving job. I wonder what's involved in examining the art. People must be able to look at the goods before they bid on them, right? I look at Phil, who's still wearing his shitkickers and slacks, got his feet up on the table and drinking beer, and ask him, "Think you could pass as an oilman?"

He blows into the top of the bottle, making a whistling sound, and says, "I don't know, whatcha reckon?"

"I gotta think if that lop Elmer can convince all them people in New York he's an oil tycoon you sure as hell can. Just gotta get ya some more country-fried hot-shit oil-tycoon-lookin' clothes."

I catch Jazz's eye and ask her, "Whatcha think, could he do it?"

"Hell, yeah. We goin' shoppin, huh?"

Jazz is looking way too mean, wearing a skin-tight black dress that hugs her all the way to her knees, got on some bright red spike heels and a new hairdo that's got her hair hanging down in ringlets. A strand of real pearls gleaming against her café-au-lait skin.

Phil's acting dumber than a rock, so knocked out by how pretty Jazz is he's walking into doors. Aside from that he looks like a goddamn young oil tycoon, tailored soft black suit, gleaming ostrich-skin cowboy boots, and the biggest cowboy hat I've ever seen anywhere, looks like he's wearing a birdbath on his head. I'd picked up a hot Rolex as soon as my bank was right and my fuckin' watch looks almost as good on Phil's wrist as it did on mine. Jethro Clampett with class.

This is one expensive recon job. If nothing else, watching these two preen and dig each other makes it worthwhile. They're very happy individuals.

And listening to Jazz coaching Phil is a trip in itself. "No, darlin', you gotta have class. You can't say 'I got me a fuckin' big bunch of oil wells so I wanna buy me some motherfuckin' art.' You gotta say somep'n like 'We've just built a three-million-dollar home on our Texas ranch, and I want to fill it with really fine art. You know, make the little woman proud.' "

She grins at Phil and me and I wonder, How can she do that?

Thursday, and we've traced the floor plans, got the alarms all listed and marked in red. Forty-eight hours into surveilling the place and we have the guard schedule pretty well wired. The statues are on the second floor, the best way in is to cut directly into the second floor from the building next door. If we can't do that, then it's got to be through the roof. Either way cut into the building, put the pieces on dollies, wheel them to the freight elevator, and take it to the ground floor. Throw down on anybody there and wheel the statues into a truck.

Not the best plan in the world, and the three of us are discussing different options. Phil is saying, "How's this, we get the statues to the elevator, have Billy or somebody set a fire in front, we wheel 'em out the back while everybody's running around crazy."

I'm so frantic I'm rubbing the skin off of my face, knowing that there's so many holes in every idea we've come up with, and I feel like screaming at him that ya can't be setting shit on fire because it might go out of control, restrain myself and explain that as calmly as possible when the phone rings.

Jazz catches it and says, "Hello. . . . Yeah. . . . Uh-huh. . . . Hang on." And hands me the phone.

I grab it and say, "Yeah."

And the soft British accent says, "Not interruptin', am I, lovey? Had a spat with Shelton, he seems to be tiring of me. I'll be in Boston until tomorrow at noon. Whatcha doin' later?"

Jazz has her hands on her hips watching me with a tight-lipped expression, Phil's shaking his head *no-no-no-no*, and my mouth says, "Hangin' out with you. Meet me at the Rathskeller in Kenmore Square at ten."

"See ya then."

"Yeah."

Click, buzz, and I know that meeting her is stupid, a dump truck move if there ever was one.

Looking at Phil and Jazz I can feel myself blushing when Jazz says, "I declare that girl must have good pussy. You out of your mind? That Ms. Sue *Zann*"—and she puts enough acid into the *Zann* to etch a metal plate—"is nothin' but trouble, a great big balloon full of trouble all ready to break all over you. I'm tellin' you true, Bad, she is not for you. Don't go and forget about this nice one you met and be likin' so much you writin' books for her. Don'tchoo do it."

She stares at Phil for a second and says to him, "May as well lay it out now. He's gonna be fuckin' the bitch anyhow."

Jazz stares at me and then says, "We was tryin' to avoid having you talk to that tramp, but since she chose now to call I may as well tell ya. . . . They'll take a certified check for those statues. You two don't gotta burgle nothin'. Buy the paper from Shelton, then me and Phil will fly it. Give 'em the check and have them carry the statues down and load 'em into the truck for ya."

It takes a minute to sink in, then I ask, "They'll take a check?"

Phil drawls out, "Yep, Jazz asked 'em. As long as it's a certified kite, drawn on their bank and made out right, there ain't no problem at all. Y'all think squares pay cash?"

Then I start laughing. Jazz is way sharper than most. I gasp out, "You're a fuckin' criminal mastermind."

Jazz forgets she's mad at me for a second and smiles ear to ear, saying, "It's a family tradition."

The subway into Kenmore Square is as trashed as the people riding it on this spring night. Garbage and graffiti line the sidewalks and walls. The car itself is half full with an assortment of humanity, winos and junkies, Puerto Rican kids wearing hard looks and senior citizens huddled into their clothes staring out of hostile and frightened eyes. Jazz and Phil are playing around, Jazz pretending she's surfing, balancing while the train rockets under Boston, Phil egging her on.

I'm inside my head, not as excited about seeing Susan as I think I should be. Watching the smoke from my Camel drift past the No Smoking sign and way conflicted. I don't want to mess with another guy's girl even if they both agree there is no relationship between them. Susan is looney tunes, no doubt about it. And even though nothing has happened yet, this Michelle has really got my attention.

Reaching Kenmore and cutting through the crowd, dressed for the Rathskeller, aka the Rat, Boston's top punk rock joint. All three of us in jeans and leather jackets, three pairs of steel-toe boots. Moving through the people-jammed streets and halfway down the block we hear the first discordant notes burning through the air.

By the time we're in front we know it's going to be a rowdy night. The volume is so high that it's blaring through the walls like they don't exist. As we roll into the entrance a fight is going on between a dude in polyester disco shit and one of the punkers. Both slinging with everything they got and the growing circle around them is screaming for blood and death. Phil grins and screams, "Kill da motherfucker! Eeeehaw!" Somehow the rebel yell doesn't sound out of place.

Pushing into the dark mutant-packed environs of the Rat and the noise level is deafening, no melody, violent trash music, and Phil screams, "These motherfuckers are good. Who are they?"

Squinting to see through the smoke-filled air I can make out the name on the drum set and tell him, "Thrill."

"Thrill what?"

Jazz yells, "Anybody that gets in our way, baby. Let's get up front, trash and thrash."

Like a good attack dog, Phil bulldozes all the way to the front of the pit and we're in there, slamming. Elbows flying, chins tucked into our chests, and knees high to protect the groin and do damage to fellow dance enthusiasts. Waltzing it is not.

The band breaks and we stagger to a table, adrenaline still rushing so hard everything has a surreal edge or maybe everything is surreal, adrenaline or no. Rage and fear still amp me, the thing that's disturbing is that the drugs aren't working right anymore. No matter how much stuff I do I don't feel loaded, nothing will shut my brain down, and I don't understand it. What the hell is wrong?

Susan staggers to the table around eleven and I respond, but there's no sense of impending magic, no passion. Now I'm wondering if there's any way to get out of spending the night with her, and as soon as the thought comes I'm pushing it down because real men always want to get laid. Right? If I'd rather just hang out with my friends and go home and pass out by myself there's got to be something wrong with me, and I smile at her as hard as I can and tell her, "Long time no see, Sue Zann, whatcha been doin?"

"This and that. Shelton's tired of me, but work is good. Showing a handsome profit, might cash it in and go back to Britain."

She leans forward and the weak light catches her eyes and I know they're way pretty, set in a nice face on a knockout body. I feel nothing.

Nothing.

Susan's studying me and my lack of response scares the shit out of me. I do my best to twinkle at her, bring some life to my expression, and hope it will fool my heart. She remarks, "Your nose is bleeding a little. That slamming thing is too violent for my taste."

I find that a touch ironic coming from her, but she doesn't look like she recognizes the joke.

She says, "Not to be pushy, but wouldja like to go elsewhere? Like yours, maybe?"

I wipe my nose and study the blood on the back of my hand and with my stomach plunging in free fall, I say, "Sure. Sounds good. Yeah. You, me. Let's go."

Phil and Jazz decide to split early too, and they leave with us, both of them giving me warning looks every time Susan looks in a different direction. On the way out the door, Ernie from Somerville and a crew of his guys are coming in. People pushing by and I'm watching Ernie as he leans into Phil while pointing at Susan and Jazz and yells, "So these are you two's old ladies?"

Phil mutters, "Yeah. See ya later."

And Ernie puts his hand on Phil's chest, holding him in place. Whiskey courage and having five, six guys as backup often make a motherfucker brave, and Ernie is feeling all the way courageous, I'd spell that s-t-u-p-i-d, when he asks Phil, "So tell me, pretty boy, does your old lady fuck as good as she looks?"

Phil does a double take and responds, talking so quietly Ernie leans in to hear what he's saying and I'm already moving because I recognize the whisper that's saying, "Never thought I'd be called pretty boy by a bucket-ass punk like y'all. But I gotta thank ya for the compliment. And for y'all's information she fucks even better than she looks. Kinda like yo mama, Ernie."

Dropping his voice even lower, but still whispering loud enough to carry, he continues, "Except your poor mother is awful ugly, who'd ever guess she sucks two, three hundred dicks a day."

And he brings an uppercut all the way from the pavement into Ernie's chin, ripping his head back like it's on a spring, then grabbing the back of his neck with the same hand as it's coming down and pulling Ernie's face as hard as he can into his forehead, breaking Ernie's nose to match the jaw the first shot shattered. Dropping to one knee and grabbing Ernie around both legs and holding on and shooting into the air like a basketball player going for a jump shot, using Ernie as the ball, Phil's flinging him into the air, and for a few seconds he keeps going up and up, defying gravity before he arches back to earth and smashes into the sidewalk.

No one says a word, I don't have to do anything, Phil takes Jazz by the arm and says, "Let's go, darlin', somethin' don't smell too good around here."

I grab Susan and give Ernie's guys my most pleasant grin as we step over his twitching form.

This night is an error in judgment in many ways, one of which being we sure as hell have made enemies. When we get back to the apartment, Phil is up and excited and Jazz is suitably impressed and I am trying to figure out how to get rid of Susan before we get in the door. But no way. I don't know if it's the drugs or lack of interest but this night is a real drag. Embarrassing even. Not a good evening.

Looking at Susan's sleeping form sprawled in my bed and dreading her waking up, starting the day with my regular ritual, needle and spoon, and the feeling of being trapped. It hits me as soon as I start mixing my wake-up; at eighteen I've been fixing since I was twelve and my veins are already giving out.

Digging in my hands and arms and finally saying, "Fuck it." My insides screaming from the terror of breathing in and out and eight hours with no opiates. I walk into the bathroom, flick the light on, look in the mirror, and see scared blue-gray eyes looking back at me. The muscles that had come from pounding iron day in and day out are getting soft and my jeans are hanging off my hips from the weight I've lost.

Looking back in the mirror I shake my head and grimace at the fear on my face and roiling through my insides. Trying a smile on myself, then turning my head to the side and blowing my cheeks up like a blowfish. Yeah, good fucking morning. I get the vein running up the side of my neck to stand up and catch it.

Deep-red blood swirling up into my rig mixing with the temporary salvation, waiting for it in the clear tube and then emptying back into my neck. The bubbles making a distinct noise and tickling as they rush with my breakfast to my brain.

Praying for a few moments of relief, and as my knees buckle and

I hold on to the sink to keep from falling, I know I'll be all right. Just have to eat more and get some exercise.

Push myself into full standing position and clean my rig, using the water running from the cold tap. Look at me again and the fear is not evident, face calm and confident. Muscles just need a little work. The jeans falling off my hips? I am lean. So what?

As I walk back into the room, Susan's propped up in bed staring at me and I grin and shrug. All's right with the world. She says, "Better wipe your neck, luv, rather conspicuous, that."

I make the first call from the room, dial the number, and when a female voice answers, "Crown Photos," I ask for Shelton, who gives me a pay phone number to call him back on in a half hour.

Foot traffic is flowing past me, and as the second hand hits the half-hour mark I punch in the last number and on the first ring it's picked up and a British accent says, "That you, mate?"

"Yeah, man, need a certified check and ID to go with it."

"For you?"

"Naw, my partner. The big one."

"So we gotta shoot new flicks, you're payin' top dollar now, mate. Twenty percent on the paper, a nickel for the ID. Ya still want it?"

I freeze for a second, knowing that the price on the statues has got to be high, otherwise they wouldn't be paying a hundred gees to steal them. I say, "We talkin' big numbers, twenty percent is outta line."

"How big, old sod?"

"Not sure, somewhere around a half mil."

"Well, that's a whole different kettle of fish. Isn't it now? Under a hundred is twenty. Up to a quarter mil is twelve. From there to a half is six. Over that we negotiate. Come in with the figures, the bank you want to use, and the bloke to be photoed."

He pauses, then laughs, asking, "Seen Susan, mate?"

"Uh, yeah. Uhhh."

"Better you than me. Ya got my blessings on that, Yank. She's a lovely girl. When will I see ya?"

"Monday, Monday morning we'll be there."

"Rightcha are."

Click, buzz, and I'm thinking that Shelton is a lot smarter than

I am, the motherfucker has stuck me with baggage I do not want.

Susan is not a woman to sit around idly, and as I roll back into the pad she's on her way out the door, waggling her fingers at me and saying, "Later, luv, don't want to overstay me welcome."

I breathe a sigh of relief and wonder at my own thought processes, because as her feet echo down the hallway I have an urge to call her back. Crazy.

Sitting and reading and rereading the eight pages I've written, going back and forth from thinking it's genius shit to knowing it is unreadable crap. So excited about seeing this Michelle that I can't sit still, having Jazz proofread the stuff one more time and she tells me it's spelled right and the punctuation is now correct. Looking at me from the sides of her eyes and saying, "You bad, Bad. One girl leavin', another one comin'. You about as flighty as my uncle. He be marryin' 'em, though. Why y'all like that?"

Think about trying the truth, and decide that she wouldn't believe me. How the hell do you tell someone that things aren't what they seem? Don't bother because they'll never believe you. I just shrug and ask, "Ya sure that it reads good?"

The knock is soft and I yell out, "Who's there?"

That little-girl, whiskey-raspy voice answers, "Michelle."

The door opens and I'm stuck on stupid. Can't think of any chit-chat, bullshit, or drag to run. Trying to figure out if she's beautiful or almost. Grab her hand and kiss her closed-lipped, soft. Thinking, Thank God she's a talker, as she takes up the slack, dashing in and doing hellos with Jazz and Phil, rapping on about music and school, parents and friends, and I'm nodding and making appropriate noises and Phil is all the way quiet, afraid of giving away his noncollege roots.

Jazz fills in for both of us and lights a joint while babbling away now about clothes, now about college, and it soon becomes evident that she's not lying. Jazz has gone to school. College.

"When didja graduate?" Michelle asks.

"Just last year, religion major . . . my Uncle Ben made me do that. . . ."

"Too bad," goes Michelle. "I'm in drama . . . only a sophomore . . . hafta spend a lot of time on shows. . . ."

"You lucky, girl. That's what I wanted. I did do a lot of theater on the side."

"Nah . . . for real? This is too weird. . . . Whadja play?"

"My favorite was Lady Macbeth. . . ." Jazz unfolds her slinky self from the chair, stretches out her hand, stares at it mournfully, intones desperately, "Out, out, damned spot. . . . All the sweet gums of Araby will ne'er cleanse this little hand. . . ."

Michelle applauds, and off they go on Shakespeare.

I look at Phil in amazement and he just gives a sheepish shrug. He knew about this. I guess I should have.

Phil hits the joint and I hit my beer and turn the stereo up.

Call out for pizza and spend the evening smoking and drinking, eating, being thunderstruck by Jazz and Michelle. An evening of being kicked back, doing wholesome, healthy All-American Shit.

Around midnight I'm in the kitchen getting beers for everybody and Jazz corners me, whispering, "She's sweet as pie, Bad. Tell the girl the truth. If ya don't ya gonna have to trade her in before ya even get to know her. Tell the truth. Try it. Y'know, 'The truth shall set you free,' John, eight thirty-two."

I got two bottles of beer in each hand, extend one to Jazz, and laugh, saying, "Yeah, uh-huh, sit down and say, 'Oh, by the way, not only am I completely uneducated but I'm a junkie and a full-time thief.' I don't think so. Tell her I wrote that shit just to impress her and you had to fix all the spellin' and shit? Naw. Not this lifetime."

Jazz focuses on me like a cat on a mouse and hisses, "Do it, Bad. Tell that girl the truth. Do it."

Michelle's telling silly jokes and it's going back and forth from her to Jazz. Me and Phil laughing but not bothering with the joke-telling part because we both know our jokes would be considered way sick by any normal person.

When I'm least ready for it, Michelle takes a swig of beer and says, "So, Bobbie, y'got something for me to read?"

Jazz pins me with her eyes, but I shrug, pick the story up off the table, and hand it to Michelle, stuttering, "Uh . . . this is a story I'm working on for . . . *Outré* magazine."

Phil and Jazz exchange looks, Michelle immediately starts to read, my heart is hammering, I'm feeling queasy, adrenaline coming up as if I was criming. She's so intent on the story, those amber-hazel eyes glued to the page, hardly breathing until she comes to the end.

I can't even ask. I'm barely breathin' myself.

She looks up at me misty-eyed, whispering, "Oh, Bobbie, this is really good. Wicked good. I feel like I know this poor guy. See, he's a victim of this society, jus' like we were talkin' about before. How could he be anything else when they threw him away? How could parents give their kid to the state to raise? What a life he's had! Where did you meet him? How do you get an interview like that?"

I'm twenty feet tall, head touchin' the ceiling, so fuckin' proud that this little college girl likes my story I could bust, wondering how the hell I'm gonna answer all her questions because it is obvious she's gonna have a lot more for me.

Jazz looks at me pointedly and takes Phil off to bed. So now it's just me and Michelle and I tell her, "Come on, I'll escort ya home."

She's getting into her coat and we walk to the door and as I'm holding it open for her she pauses and looks up at me, saying, "Don't want me to stay, huh?"

This time when I kiss her it is electric, sucking on her lips and she on mine. She tastes like beer and pot and smells like flowers and smoke.

Before there's time to wonder if the drugs are going to fuck this up I am responding to Michelle from all the way inside me. Picking her up and kicking the front door closed and carrying her into my bedroom and watching her undress, large breasts covered with small freckles, tiny waist and fuck-me hips. Kicking my way outta my jeans, coming together, not like enemy ships but like motherfuckin' poetry in motion. Those brown, orange-amber, gold eyes locked on mine as we draw apart and come together, making something bigger and better than either of the halves.

Rolling from one position to the next like we are choreographed, finally with her on top riding me like a cat on a dog, both arching and screaming and collapsing into a tangled pile of sweat-covered flesh. Holding each other. Breathing hard and shaking. Maybe fifteen minutes, maybe an hour later stroking her hair and saying, "I gotta tell ya somethin'."

For a guy eighteen years old who knows everything, I guess I got a lot to learn. If Michelle is moved by my Joe Moppa story . . . she's even more moved by mine. She's blown away. And if the truth shall set you free, it ain't a bad aphrodisiac, too.

thirteen

A four-hour drive back to New York, and Shelton's got Phil posed in front of the State Seal of Texas shooting head shots. Clicking away and running his mouth, saying, "Look spoiled." Click. "Come on, mate, lose the tough guy look. Smile." Click. "Picture it, mate, your mum and dad are stinkin' rich." Click. "Ya had nannies and butlers and ya just found out your thousandth oil well came in." Click. "Ya been accepted to Yale and your bleedin' fuckin' dick just fell off." Click. "That's right, laugh, ya bloody thug." Click. "That's right." Click. "Lovely." Click. "That should do it. I'm a fuckin' artist if I do say so. So it's gotta be the First Bank of Boston, eh? I'll have it all for ya in the mornin'. Check for six hundred and twelve thousand, ID for Philip in the name of Jonathan E. Hoover, aka J. Edgar himself but they'll never catch it. My price is twenty-five large, all in hundreds. Right, mate?"

Watching this guy work, it is easy to see how good he is. And the way he comes out with figures, they sound reasonable. Twenty-five thousand and the check is guaranteed to fly. A bargain. Shake hands, say, "Right."

And roll out past the new receptionist. Down the elevator and head for our hotel. Phil still dressed in oil-tycoon attire.

I hail a cab and it pulls over, the cabbie jumping out and holding the door for Phil like he's motherfuckin' royalty. I grin and Phil lights downtown Manhattan with his patented "Eeeee-haw."

Jazz has a new outfit; she insists that a class act wouldn't be seen twice in the same pumps. These are bright yellow, matching her new spring dress and the gold-and-topaz necklace she's wearing. Knock-out. And our young oil tycoon is back in his suit and ostrich-skin boots, same ridiculous hat and wearing my Rolex. The beautiful people will arrive at the front door in a chauffeured Cad limo.

I'm driving a lovely four-speed, dirty-gray, banged-up box truck, wearing a stylish light blue workshirt with the name Chuck embroidered over the pocket. Got it tucked into clean jeans, work boots polished, and yeah, they are steel-toed.

Pistol in my back pocket under my wallet because at this point I feel naked without it.

Wheel into the loading dock and back into the slot indicated by the armed guard. Get down and walk up to him carrying a clipboard in one hand and a cup of coffee in the other, saying, "Hey, boss. Got a pickup. Statues or somethin'."

I look down at the clipboard and say, "Hired by Hoover Oil, out of Texas. . . . Where is this shit I'm loading?"

He's Italian or Greek or something, got greasy black hair falling across his forehead from under his cap. Big arms and no chest or shoulders, a weight lifter who's only discovered his arms, wearing aviator shades like the cops do and looks through them down his nose at me, steps into the door on the dock and calls someone on the phone. Stands there talking quietly into the mouthpiece, finally hanging up and saying, "Hang tight, ace. Soon as they give me the release we'll get ya loaded and back on the road. Where ya headed for?"

I'm ready and say, "Texas. Rich motherfuckers got me drivin' all the way from Chicago, through the Midwest, all over New England and New York pickin' up weird shit that catches their eye. This is my last stop, leavin' for Texas tonight with a full load. Transfer these two boxes to my Peterbilt and that's it. Dump the trailer and contents with the owner and head on back to Chicago. Home sweet home. I'm workin' this one job for 'em. Pays better than workin' a regular route. Know what I mean?"

Lighting another Camel off the butt of the last one, taking a hit off my now-cold coffee, and asking him, "How is it workin' here? What's this place do?"

And he's off, it seems like if you're genuinely interested and pay attention people will talk your ear off. I'm making mental notes, you never know when art might be appreciated . . . and paid for.

Smoking and listening to the guard expound on the various treasures he's been entrusted with over the years and enjoying watching their warehouse guys wheel out two big wooden boxes and load them into the truck. Signing the receipt Chuck Landers of Chicago and waving as I drive off and battle Boston traffic into Somerville.

Pulling into the rear lot of Abe's ramshackle building and opening the back of the truck, watching the pristine Mr. Smith vault into the back of the truck and go to work on the crates with a wrecking bar.

Splinters and packing material cover the front of his sport coat and slacks. Face completely blank and wrecking bar dangling from his hand, Smith is now looking down on me from the back of the truck. Dark clouds are streaking across the fading blue sky above him and the smell of old oil and industrial solvents is strong in the cracked concrete yard around us.

All my senses are sharp as the razor-wire fence framing this scene. Thinking that something has got to be wrong, like it's double-cross time like a motherfucker. One or two bullets is a whole lot cheaper than a hundred grand. Studying Smith's face for some play of emotion, aware of Abe and one of his cronies behind me and to my left.

Now I'm circling right so I can watch Abe and his goon without taking my eyes from Smith, moving slow, casual. Resting my hand on my hip. Casual. Fingers touching the handle of my .380 and asking, "So. What's up? That's what you ordered. Right? Where's the dough?"

Voice sounding casual. Giving myself points for sounding good when it sure looks like things might get real bad.

Smith smiles and says, "Good job. Merchandise as ordered. Let's go inside and count out your money."

I smile back and once we reach Abe's office keep my back to the wall. Still smiling pleasantly all the time as the one thousand hundred-dollar bills are counted and divided. Abe has his twenty and I have my eighty. I'm ready to roll, but Abe says, "A toast to capitalism and free enterprise."

Licking his lips and looking exactly like a lizard wearing glasses and a tacky sport coat, he pours those same greasy tumblers full of his favorite embalming fluid. Raises his tumbler and says, "L'chaim." And we all respond.

Feeling the sweet burn of the schnapps and listening to the building around us, hearing every creak and sigh. Leaning against the wall and drinking Abe's peppermint schnapps with my left hand; thinking that you could get a whole lot of guys killed for eighty grand. Wondering if I'm worth more than that alive.

Setting my glass down and calling for a cab, still using my left hand to dial and shoulder to hold the headset. Fingers of my right hand caressing the butt of the .380.

Talking sports until the horn sounds, announcing the arrival of the taxi.

Finally letting the grin drop as Smith is escorting me to the cab. Just before we reach the vehicle he claps me on the shoulder and says, "Nice piece of work. Got something big coming up. You're young but I think I'm going to recommend you. Nice job, sir."

I got a shopping bag full of hundreds and feel pretty good but as I'm climbing into the backseat of the cab I can't help asking, "How big?"

Smith is back to looking like he's chewing on a lemon, puckers his lips and says, "Five times what you made today. Big."

I whistle and say, "Whenever. We're ready."

A pile of hundreds on the coffee table, the aroma of ink and new paper is heavy and the smell of that pile of greenbacks is sweeter than the best perfume. We're playing catch with the banded bills, Phil demonstrating his passing ability. Celebrating. Cutting the pile into three stacks, one for expenses, one for Phil and Jazz, and one for me. Comes out sixty K split down the middle when everything is said and done.

Phil takes one bundle from their stack and folds it, sticking it in his front pocket. Shoves the rest of their end to Jazz, saying, "Stash it or somethin'. How far do we got to go till we get our fifty?"

Jazz chews on her little finger for a second, figuring, and says, "We almost there, maybe need another ten."

Phil puts some country-western on and, singing along, walks into the kitchen and comes out with three beers, lights a joint and gives it and one of the beers to Jazz, hands me a beer and chugs his, asks, "What next, killer? We almost there. I want to call George and let him know when he can expect us."

I have no urge to visit the wilds of rural Illinois. Boston, New

York, LA, yeah. Anywhere with horticulture and barnyard animals, no. I take a hit off my beer and say, "Smith, remember Smith? Says he got something lined up that will pay around a half mil. Didn't say what or when. I say we give it a couple of weeks, do some partying. See if it comes through. Let's not bust our crew up before we know what he's got."

Jazz passes the joint back to Phil, who takes a deep toke, holding the smoke down, and talking without exhaling asks, "A half mil? Five hundred thousand motherfuckin' dollars? For reals?"

Before I can answer, Jazz cuts in, pointing at me with one finger, voice rising a little, says, "Bad! Have you gone crazy, Bad? That kind of money is for dying, that's gettin'-dead money. This won't be no easy deal. They gonna pay that much? For what? For gettin' your fool heads blown off. Or gettin' busted. My oh my, it is a lot of money. Thinkin' about it makes me scared. Just you and Phil do some more checks or somethin'. Fuck that noise."

I know Phil well enough to read his face, the idea of taking down that kind of cash is too tempting. I grin and say, "Yeah, maybe you right, Jazz. Let's see what it is anyhow, that won't hurt. Right?"

Jazz makes a noise like steam coming from a kettle, shaking her head, says, "You so full of shit, Bad. Already got your mind made up. Don'tcha? We'll see."

I wink at Phil and he grins like a dog waiting to bite, saying through his smile, "That's a quarter million each. That's a double-deep pile of dough, my brother. Double-deep."

Jazz shakes her head, shrugs, asks, "So if we be partyin' tonight ya gonna call your Michelle, or do ya want me to do it for ya?"

Morning sun filters through the curtains, softly filling my room, and for the first time I notice how empty it looks. Mattress on the floor, color TV sitting against the wall unplugged, books scattered all over the place, bare hardwood floors, and piles of jeans and T-shirts everywhere.

Michelle is dressing as silently as possible. I sleep lightly, come fully awake at the smallest unusual noise. Otherwise coming back to consciousness is a slow, painful process. As soon as her feet hit the floor my eyes open and I lie without moving.

I'm watching her run her fingers through her hair, then tiptoe to her clothes and get dressed, lower lip caught between her teeth. Soft sun creating planes and shadows across the curves and hollows of her. Once she pulls her top on and has her shoes in hand she slides by the bed and looks down on me as I fake sleep. When she bends and places her lips on my face my arms go around her waist like they are fitted to her and those topaz-amber eyes go from surprise to soft enjoyment like magic. Pulling away for a second, whispering, "I should be in class . . ." and then kissing me, running her lips down my chest, and now I'm watching the sun reflect like gold and black velvet from her hair as her head goes up and down. When I pull at her trying to take her clothes off so I can respond she growls, imitating James Cagney, "No. Don't fuckin' move. Got it, wise guy?"

And she laughs, taking me back into her mouth and not stopping until I am full-on convulsive.

Watching her check her face in the mirror, and wave her fingers at me. I like this chick more every time I'm with her and I'm still stuck on stupid. Not knowing what to say when she says it for me, or asks it for me, or whatever, she's holding the door and leaning forward, hair hanging down almost to the ground, face hidden by the hair and pointed towards the floor as she mumbles, "Whatcha doin' later?"

I say, "Any fuckin' thing you want to."

Now she looks up grinning, and says, "Ballet, tonight. You, me. I'll get the tickets. Bye."

For a few seconds I feel confused, elated, scared.

Then I start my catechism: Fire, needle, spoon.

Jazz says, "Ya look nice, Bad. Real nice."

I ask her, "Are ya sure?"

And Phil cuts in, "Shit, hoss, look like a ballet-goin' motherfucker if I ever saw one. You a class act, old wood."

Jazz smiles and says, "Couldn't of said it better."

Michelle is drop-dead gorgeous, motherfuckin' beautiful, so pretty that every time I look at her I get confused. No track marks. No psychosis. Smart, going on brilliant, and she seems to like me as much as I like her.

I'm scared to death and doing my best not to show it. If Susan looked and acted like class, Michelle is class personified, inside and out. Like a real human being with the gift of life. All the way out of my league.

Deep down I know that I am as doomed as a guy can get. Born behind the motherfuckin' eight ball with no way out. Prayin' that my born-to-lose status isn't contagious, that I won't hurt this girl, won't bring her down.

Fix just enough stuff to chill, got my best suit on and hair combed, shaved, and my .380 doesn't show through the wallet pocket in my jacket.

She's wearing a black dress that hugs her body like a perfect tattoo. Nice everything, thick brown hair with a couple of red highlights, not much makeup, and every time she looks at me her eyes light up like I'm some kinda superstar instead of a hood with a habit.

Filing into the auditorium with stone squares, dressed to kill, enough gold and diamonds evident to make a mass armed robbery worthwhile.

Sitting and listening to her tell me, "They study for years and years, unbelievable. Sacrifice everything to perfect their art. I hope you like it."

And the lights dim and the curtain raises and the music floats and roars and these motherfuckers soar. Muscle-bound dudes in tights flying through the air, stop-your-breath-beautiful girls dancing on their toes like they weigh nothing. Floating. Suspended, immune to the laws of gravity. It is a gas.

As we walk out, Michelle fits into my side like she belongs there; and we float, too. Because for that minute in time the laws of gravity are lifted for us as well. And I flash that maybe the eight ball might just miss me on its way to the pocket.

The sun falls into night like an orange into swirling oil, the smell of barbecue and pot are heavy and sweet in the air. Thrill is playing, hard-core punk shit blaring.

The entire park is full of leather-jacketed, drunk, and loaded fools. Billy Bones is with a Latina chick with off-blond hair, and his buddy from New York, Mental Moore, is there, out of his mind on acid, downs, and booze. Punk show, party a good time for all, drugs and sex and alcohol.

Mental as scarred up and scary as ever, sporting a black eye that is fading to purple-yellow, his boxer's body in shape, washboard stomach complete with old stab wounds showing because there's no shirt under his leather. He's with a girl with green hair and safety pins rammed through her cheeks. The chick's so skinny that you can see the ribs showing under her halter top. Mental's grinning his no-tooth smile and saying, "Punk-rock Matilda, my very own blood-thirsty babygirl."

She grins and her dental work is almost the same as his front grille. Gone. I let my front teeth slide down and grin back, all three of us saying, "Look, Ma, no teeth." And laughing.

I'm drunk and loaded and got my arm around Michelle, who's tripping on the animals. Phil has wandered off with some guy from Dorchester who is in love with robbing banks, guy can't hold a conversation without bringing it around to what a rock-and-roll bank-robbin' motherfucker he is. I ain't interested.

I'm just paying attention to my new girl and shooting the shit with Billy and Mental. As the sun leaves and the streetlights take over I start getting sick, excuse myself like a gentleman, and go to the nearest public rest room to slam.

The odor of piss and vomit is pleasantly combined with industrial disinfectant, the light is poor at best, and my veins are shot out. After digging around, being my own voodoo doll, I finally say fuck it and muscle the shit. No rush, no relief. Muscling takes about fifteen, twenty minutes to hit home. Eternity.

When I get back, Phil is standing with his new dog the bank robber, saying to Billy, "Shit, hoss, Gary here robs banks all the time, we do one and I got the money to hook up with my baby brother and start a legitimate business. Huh, Gary?"

Gary is wearing the mandatory leather jacket and jeans, got a weight lifter's body and a weak-looking face topped by sandy blond hair styled perfectly, maybe the first punk bouffant. He hits his beer, belches, and says, "Sure thing, made ten gees last week. Do another one as soon as I run short. It's like havin' your own printin' press.

Soon as I get another good partner I'm gonna knock down a few and kick it for a while."

Billy takes a hit off a joint, and then rips a piece of meat from a beef rib with his teeth, leaving a clown's smile of barbecue sauce around his mouth, says, "So what happened to your last partner? Hmmm, stickup man?"

Gary does his best to give Billy a tough look but backs down. Billy is the top of the criminal hierarchy here. Contract killings are as serious as you can get, and skinny Irish Billy Bones is known to be the best there is. Gary drops his eyes and mumbles, "He got busted, doing a quarter up in Walpole. Went off on his own. Idiot should of stuck with me. I know how to plan 'em."

Billy wipes his mouth on his sleeve and laughs, saying, "The average bank job will get y' two, three gees. Your partner's gotta flatten a quarter for chump change."

Billy stops and asks, "I got all the sauce off my mug?" Then continues before he gets an answer. "Philip, if I were you I'd stick with young Bobbie. Leave robbin' banks to Gorgeous Gary here with his lovely groomed hair."

Throwing the stripped rib bone on the ground, then lifting his shades for a second and pinning the bank robber, Billy continues, "And from what I hear, y' have the courage of a hamster, the mouth of a dragon, and the balls of a hummingbird. Gary Haircut y' are from now on. Twenty-five years. Holy fuckin' Christ. Forgive me, Father, for takin' your name in vain, but the situation calls for it."

Mental laughs and says, "Takin' the Lord's name in vain ain't the least or the worst of your sins, is it now, William?"

Billy's face grows as serious as a loaded M16, his mad brown eyes focused on Mental, and he says, "Who knows, lad, if I send a fella t' meet his maker is't my will or t' Lord's? When we killed those last lads for the I-talians, was it a sin or an act of mercy? We killed 'em quick, now didn't we? I always work clean, I always work fast, no torture, just instant peace descends upon them. Ahhh, sure, now, Mental, once again y've earned your motherfuckin' name. Of course using the good Lord's name in vain is the worst of my sins, and perhaps a little fornication now and again. But dyin' and killin' is just a part of life. Y' understand, don'tcha, Mental?"

Mental got his name because he is all the way nuts, if he isn't your friend he is one of the most vicious motherfuckers walking. But the force of Billy's gaze and the beer-slurred sincerity he utters these words with cuts right through any insanity that makes Mental mental. His grin fades and he responds, "Of course you're right, Bones. The alcohol is loosening my tongue; a foolish question it was."

Billy smiles.

Gary, keeping his eyes on the ground, shambles away, telling Phil, "Call me, or I'll call ya later this week."

Mental looks from Gary's back to Billy's face and grins at what he sees there.

Michelle is leaning into my back, got her arms around my waist, kisses me on the back of the neck and whispers, "You do have strange friends."

I reach back over my shoulder and run my finger down her face and whisper back, "Toldja. Whatcha think so far?"

She's got her mouth right against my ear, I can feel the exhalation with every whispered word as she says, "I like them, Billy and Mental are real scary, but real nice. They really like you, so I like them . . . except for Gary."

Billy is watching Gary's retreating back with no expression and turns, saying, "She's a smart one, lad. Don't let her go."

I tell him, "Not unless someone kills me. Gonna try and keep her."

Michelle hugs me a little bit tighter and whispers, "You better. . . . How'd Billy hear what I said?"

Me and Billy both know but it's up to him to say it and he hesitates for a second, then responds to her whisper, "Why, I read minds sometimes, lass, only good ones, and only people I like and who like me. Nobody else matters."

I think, Right ya are, Billy, and he grins and nods. They say the Irish are fey, have some fuckin' sixth sense, are in touch with spirits and ghosts. Knowing Billy, I believe it.

fourteen

Abe's sipping his schnapps, burning the foulest cigar ever created, talkin' about the good old days, Prohibition and numbers, Jew fighters and killers, when you could buy a cop and he'd stay bought. Back before the whole country went to hell. I'm agreeing. Not that I got any idea what the hell is wrong with things the way they are.

Abe gestures with his tumbler of high-proof mouthwash, says, "Think it's tough now? Shit, kids don't even make their bones anymore. Fuckin' social organizations. Worry has rotted my kefockdida stomach. The shvartzes on one side, spics on the other, not to mention the goddamn I-talians, fuckin' wops. And youse, ya fuckin' micks are runnin' all over like rabid dogs. Makes me ashamed of the mick in me. Oye, the gas is enough to kill a man. Useta be clear-cut, ya break the rules ya get dead. Ya step on toes ya get yours cut off. Now it's a mishegoss, rob this one and every motherfucker in town wants action. That's why I need thirty percent from here in. When Smith pays I need thirty offa the top. Ya with me, boys?"

Abe gestures behind him in a vague motion towards Ernie and another of their crew, who are standing behind Abe looking as big as they can.

The splint holding Ernie's nose in place doesn't help the image he's trying to project. His opposite bookend has a good psychotic look, one drooping eye and a perpetual sneer. Has it so perfected you know that this guy must stand in front of a mirror practicing looking scary. Abe isn't getting the reaction he was hoping for, he's paid way too many dues to let doubt or hesitation show on his face but his voice falters a little when he says, "Plus I gotta pay my boys, anything goes wrong they help protect ya. Right, fellas?"

Before either of the goons backing Abe can respond, Phil sucks a huge glob of snot into his mouth and spits it on the floor, saying, "Fuck with our money and we'll fix it so your stomach don't bother you no more."

Abe looks over the rim of his glass at me, waiting to see which way I'm going to go with this.

I shake my head and say, "Shit, pal, we made a deal. Maybe in the good old days a deal didn't count for nothin'. According to Smith or whatever his name is, he's got a big score coming up. Not that I think you would let greed cloud your judgment, but we bail, ya gonna have to make do with psycho boy and his pals. Smith don't want sloppy."

Abe chews on his cigar, says, "Twenty-five percent?"

Phil laughs, spits on the floor again, much to the dismay of Abe, Ernie, and their pal, then says, "Keep it up, old man, maybe after I get done buttfuckin' your boys you'll find out about protection. Maybe we ace your ass out right here and now."

Phil pauses, rage swimming behind his eyes like piranhas in brown pools, exhales, then asks, "Whatcha wanna do, Bobbie? We'd be taxin' these motherfuckers in the joint. Call the shot."

I tell Abe, "We'll kick ya an extra two points. Is there anything else, or was this what we came here for?"

Phil's all the way 51/50, so mad his hands are shaking as he turns the key in his Barracuda, flips the radio on full, and we rocket out of Abe's yard, Phil focusing all his adrenaline on driving like a maniac. We hit the street with the tires smokin'.

Rock and roll blaring in counterpoint to the hemi's howling, Phil's eyes glued to the road, taking corners on two wheels, tearing through the smallest hole in traffic. See a cop car going the other way, they spot us doing 120 in a forty and they hit their lights and start to flip a U. We're gone.

Phil slamming through the gears and tearing across the bridge from Cambridge into Boston, gliding into the side streets on the hill and parking.

Phil lights a smoke and starts tapping on the wheel, accelerating the tempo until he's smashing the heels of his hands into the steering wheel hard enough to shake the whole car.

I'm staring out the side window, watching pedestrians and pigeons and smoking. Eventually the shaking and pounding stops and Phil grates out, "What's up, dog? Lettin' those punks pressure us?

Fuck givin' up any of our action, that weasel just shook us down for two points. Why'dja fold, what's up?"

I flip my smoke out the window and look at Phil, turn the radio off, and tell him what's up. "They gonna try and burn us no matter what we do. For a half mil any one of those cocksuckers would hit his own mother. If they think we'll negotiate they won't expect us to get off first. Think about it. We gotta get around Smith to whoever the buyer is, we still don't know what the score is, maybe we won't want to do it. Who the fuck knows? One thing for sure, they think they got us in a position where they can leverage us. We gotta change the position. Ace them out, right now they got an extra two percent of nothin'. When the shoutin' is over they gonna have nothin' at all. Ya with me, dog?"

"Half a mil, shit, I might kill my mama for that. Those guys are dead meat walkin', they think they gonna fuck us around. You one treacherous little motherfucker, aren'tcha. Plannin' on blindsidin' 'em from the jump."

I just grin. This deal is going to unfold in its own way. Once I'd decided they were going to try and fuck us, all rules were off. Fuck them. I turn the radio back on and say, "I wasn't plannin' it till just now, when I saw how it was shakin' out. But they started the dance. We'll finish it. Let's roll."

We pull sedately into traffic.

That night creeps by, the lights from passing cars splashing across the walls of my room. I'm lying on my mattress and smelling the odor of my own body and stale cigarette smoke.

Shooting heroin is all about not feeling. Good, bad, happy, scared, none of it. The purpose of the opiates is to block it all out, leave you floating euphorically numb. It's not working.

Smoking and watching the gray-blue mist twist and trail towards the ceiling, then disperse into nothing when caught by the weak wind blowing in from the street. Craving the illusion of safety, knowing that there is no such thing this side of the grave. But wanting it anyhow. Beginning to feel the fear of blowing it, getting killed, busted, seeing more friends die. Brain hammering at itself, not knowing if I am making the right choices.

If things go the way I have them analyzed, if I'm able to pull the hat trick off. End up with all the dough, double-cross everybody except Phil, and then head for the coast with him and Jazz, Big George in tow. Maybe take Red and Lily. And when I get really weak, feeling my own need, seeing Michelle's face float in front of my eyes, the fear of trashing whatever is starting to happen with her like chewing on broken glass.

Going over all the angles and coming back to the same place every time. There is too much cash involved for Abe and his guys not to try and take it. A professional contract goes for around ten grand. Half a million would equal fifty deaths. Doing me and Phil was the only thing that made sense. Was Sydney aware of what was going down, or not? Billy is as close to a friend as I've ever had, but with this kinda money involved, would he turn? How do we get around Smith?

What I want is to run, fuck the whole thing, but I know I'm not going to. Half a million dollars means Easy Street for a long time. Fragmented thoughts rising from the bottom of my psyche, pictures of what I think a good life is, and it's all linked to making a huge score. Enough money and you can purchase college degrees, enough dough you can buy anything. Maybe kick, see what life's like clean. Take Michelle and put together a little square life, not that I have any idea what that is.

All I know is that this is the shot of a lifetime, no balls, no blue chips, no guts, no fuckin' glory. I'm ready to start screaming, actually do a couple sets of push-ups in the hope that it will lessen the anxiety. Not tonight. If anything, struggling through the last set makes me realize what bad shape I'm in, muscles fading fast.

Praying to find a vein, praying for the dope to work the way it's supposed to, and it's time to try to shut the babble in my head down.

Empty envelope after envelope into my cooker until there's a mound of off-gray heroin almost reaching the top. Squirt in almost a full syringe of water and heat it. For the first time in what seems like forever catch a vein on my first try. And know when the blood rushes into the outfit that for a little while I'll have peace.

Send it home and clean my rig, light another Camel, scratch and nod. And while I observe my pinned pupils in the mirror and feel the slow-motion quality of my thoughts, nothing is any better at all.

The voices won't stop screaming. "Whatcha gonna do, Bobbie? What the fuck you gonna do?"

The next morning trolling down Charles Street watching the toes of my boots, hands in the pockets of my jeans, the sun working hot and humid.

Cars honking and I hear two drivers screaming a bunch of "motherfuckers" at each other. Pause and look up in the hope that they're going to actually start fighting. No such luck. "Motherfucker" and "Suck my dick" and "Ya better watch your ass" and they drive off with their frustrations relieved.

Walking across the bridge into Cambridge digging the way the sun dances and flies sending purple and red highlights up off the dirty, muddy water of the River Charles. Watching crews of guys in little skinny boats, paddling like they are being chased by sharks, cutting through the water, and wondering what the hell they are doing.

Kicking an old Coke can ahead of me, walking and kicking that can until two black drunks stumble out of a neighborhood bar and I give my can one last kick and turn, pushing into the dark smoky joint.

My throat is parched and the sweat is rolling down my face and sides from the day's heat and the long walk. I just want a beer or maybe fifty, seeking to quench my thirst and hopefully drown the conflicting thoughts and feelings bouncing in me like the old can bounced and hopped with each kick.

Inside is soft red lights and a smoked mirror, R&B playing, Otis singing about that famous dock, and the odor of barbecue is rich over the booze and tobacco. Let my eyes adjust for a second and saunter up to and lean against the bar.

The bartender is an old black cat, got a skinny mustache and prison eyes, wearing a red shirt and a leather vest, lean like a tall welterweight. He pulls up in front of my stool and looks at me from one side of his head, tips his neck the other way and checks to see if I look any different from that angle. Leans forward and stares into my eyes, finally saying, "Why ya here, boy? Lookin' for black pussy? Wrong place. Don't take to white boys cruisin' sisters in here. Drugs?

Not here. Not for you. Look around. Ain't no other paddies here. Whatcha lookin' for?"

I tell him peace and quiet, a few drinks and maybe some barbecue. He shakes his head, wondering what the fuck I want to be in his bar for, but asks what I'll have. I order a Jack with beer behind it. The AC on real good, the sweat drying on my arms and shoulders and the whiskey burning inside me, mixing with the beer chaser and sending tendrils of peace and warmth wafting through my body simultaneously. The third or fourth boilermaker and the peace has settled in. I'm comfortable. The other patrons have decided that while they may not like white folks I'm minding my own business and all my attention is on getting drunk.

Loading the jukebox with quarters and hitting all the numbers that match with the blues. Listening to Willie Dixon, Sonny Boy Williamson, Jimmy Wood and Chucky Weise, Howling Wolf and Muddy Waters.

Ordering a plate of barbecue, and when it comes, realizing I am starving. Thick chunks of beef swimming in the sweet hot sauce, sausages that light up your mouth and make the beer chasing the fire down your throat feel like cold heaven, red beans full of salt pork and rice, corn bread that is as sweet as motherfuckin' cake.

Staring into the mirror downing boilermakers until I feel my head resting all by itself on the bar. Pushing myself up and trying to look dignified, saying, "Later."

The bartender smiles and says, "Oughta call yo'sef a cab. Gonna get arrested for drunk-walkin'."

Falling out the front door and climbing back to my feet, bouncing down the sidewalk, so drunk that I'm using walls to keep myself upright. Pedestrians avoiding me with looks of concern or disgust, depending on their outlook, or maybe depending on my behavior. Who knows?

Staggering across the bridge, back to Boston. The moon has replaced the sun in dancing off the river, the smell of water and chemical waste rising up to the bridge and the headlights of passing cars splashing me and throwing the iron railing into stark relief.

Knees and feet still have a will of their own, my attention is all on walking as straight as possible, not staggering, not falling off the walkway, occasionally having to lean against the cold and rusty side of the bridge. Stopping and lighting a smoke, staring into the black-and-silver water rushing underneath me, and the smoke is hitting my chest like bricks, tasting good, and the spinning of the world around me is slowing and I look up and for a second or so, the yellow-orange moon is shining as hard as it can. A perfect half-moon, a topaz half-circle, and then it's covered by clouds so quickly that it looks like a cat's eye winking. I wink back and when I start walking again my stagger is almost gone.

I'm across from the old Charles Street Jail, looming above the subway like a gray granite nightmare brought forward from another time. Glad I'm not on the other side of the wall.

Still watching my boots make progress. Walking real good now, one foot going right in front of the other and feeling a sort of pride in walking in almost a straight line. Look, Ma, no hands, able to stay on the sidewalk without falling off . . . when I hear, "Hey, pal, can ya spare some change? I ain't eat in about a week."

Looking up from the sidewalk and I see Wino Boy leaning against the wall under the steel bridge going up to the train. I have rarely been so glad to see anybody in my life. Whether it's because he is doing so bad and I feel so bad, or if it is just seeing someone I've met before, kinda know, but who has no expectations of me, I don't know. I grin and say, "Sure, man. You actually want food or ya trying to get a bottle?"

He's wearing what looks like the same clothes from a week ago, face dirty and one eye blackened from falling down or getting beat up. He does his best to grin and the shakes are so bad that the muscles of his face are dancing like insects are running under the skin. He says, "Mainly a bottle. Can ya spare enough for a quart of Wild Irish?"

I've never heard of Wild Irish, I got my hand in my pocket and am ready to give this guy whatever he needs, when I ask him, "What the fuck's Wild Irish?"

"Wild Irish Rose, man. Two bucks a quart. Wine. Full of embalming fluid. Chemicals. Fuck you all up. Drink one quart, you're nuts. Drink two, and you're on your way to jail. Drink three, and they bury ya. Can ya spare a deuce?"

Thinking that this shit sounds too good to be true, I tell him, "Do better than that. We'll go get a couple quarts and a pizza."

He pushes himself off of the wall, all bones and rags, looks like he is dying and I know he can't be any older than me, saying, "God bless you, man. Wild Irish and food. Wow. Let's go."

As we walk towards the nearest package store I ask my new drinking partner what his name is. He spits and keeps walking, saying, "Wino. What else?"

The alley that is Wino's home feels comfortable, whether I am running from me or from failure or success or if plain old-fashioned fear has taken root and is driving me makes no difference. Kicking back against the brick wall, sitting on cardboard piled deep as an armchair, illumination provided by the dim glow of streetlights and the few windows lit in the buildings above us, drinking Wild Irish Rose, is just fine with me.

The thick, chemical-tasting stuff fills all of Wino's claims. By the midpoint of the second bottle my drunk is back on with a vengeance, vision doubling and tripling, words so slurred that as I speak them they are incomprehensible.

Staggering arm and arm out of the alley and back into the liquor store and loading up, we buy a case of Wild Irish and the party is on.

Before too much time has passed every street bum and wet brain in the making has showed, all with stories and sad ones they were and sad ones they are. Because while the winos die the stories live on and get sadder and sadder with each small death.

Sometime around four, five in the morning the cops show, flashlights and billy clubs shining and swinging. Me and Wino accompanied by six, seven, eight new friends exit as fast as possible, leaving the slower and more feeble members of the party to revel with Boston's official representatives.

We take up residence in one of Wino's alternative homes, the basement of a condemned building, and keep drinking until snakes start crawling behind my eyes and under my skin and I come out of being stone passed out, annihilated, to dead-ass drunk and full-on screaming, want to die or get well now, dope-sick. Run falling and careening off walls back to the hill.

Fall into my pad, past Jazz and Phil, who look at me like I am what I look like: a retching, puking, booze-soaked maniac. They try to talk and I can't hear them, just see their mouths moving. Crawl and stumble into my room, slam enough stuff to take my sick off.

Put my works and the rest of my stash in my sock, and while Jazz yells for Phil and tries to stop me, I roll back out the door covered in blood and vomit from the night's entertainment, and for a while there I believe I have found my true vocation.

The day becomes night and Wild Irish is all I consume except for exactly enough heroin to keep well. The alcohol is doing what it's intended for, it provides walking anesthesia.

Eventually I come to, wake up, regain consciousness staring up at Phil and Irish Billy Bones, trying to tell them that I'm OK, that they should have a drink and kick back, that crashing in an alley is really what's happening, man. Reaching for my rig and stuff and finding it gone.

Feeling Phil on one arm and Billy on the other telling me, "Everything is gonna be OK. Just walk, bro, put one foot in front of the other."

And seeing Wino sprawled with the rig still sticking out of his arm and foam caked on his lips, flies crawling across his still-open eyes, and knowing who had grabbed my stash, and I want to make time go back, to tell him that it was good shit. That the definition of good shit is that it will kill you. That he shouldn't fuck around with it if he isn't a junkie, tell him to stick with his Wild Irish. Tell him I am sorry for lettin' him get close enough to roll me, but I put one foot in front of the other, and Billy and Phil carry me with the love and concern that only guys that are doomed and waiting for it to arrive know for each other, and I was sad they'd never meet Wino.

Hands shaking like an old man's with terminal palsy, the mystery aches hurting much worse than the cuts and bruises that cover my face and body.

In a state of total panic, dope-sick and getting sicker, hungover like I'd been drinking antifreeze. Tore up from the floor up, beat up from the feet up, and messed up from the chest up. It didn't look like it was gonna be a good day. Nope.

Scoring on the street is for idiots, ya get sick enough you will volunteer for idiot status quick. Phil and Billy escort me into the South End, not to be confused with Southie.

The South End is mainly Puerto Rican, the bar we enter playing Afro-Cuban music. A Santería altar over the door, a statue of the Virgin, flowers, food, wine, and burning candles.

At one table a group of dark-skinned guys dressed in raggedy jeans and polyester coats with two cages holding fighting cocks. A couple of heavily made-up and seriously underdressed Latinas working the bar and behind the bar the biggest Puerto Rican in the world. Receding black hair worn in a pigtail, face scarred to the bone from acne and cocaine abuse, shoulders like motherfuckin' boulders, arms like fire hydrants covered with tattooed words, not just a couple of words. I'm talkin' full letters, articles, short motherfuckin' books scrolling down his arms and onto his hands. A walking five-hundred-pound library, with a bad attitude and not much apparent grasp of English. This is Gordo.

My usual routine is to pick up a half ounce at a time from NYC, no muss no fuss. Send Syd the dough, get the drugs FedExed back. Simple. Not this time.

Gordo is the guy, you want weight in Boston he is the jefe, the host with the most.

We lean against the bar and all conversation stops, the Spanish and English slang that was flowing as we walked in dries up like a dammed river. The screaming silence is broken only by the noises made by the roosters clucking homicidally at each other.

I'm hoping that Billy's assurance that we'd be welcomed was right as Gordo lumbers over to us and asks, "What choo paddie want here, mang?"

I'm shaking so hard it feels like I'm going to fall apart, the toxins coming out of my body smell so strong that they're gagging me, and my guts are a ball of acid-soaked rope. I say, "Stuff, man."

Gordo leans forward and almost whispering says, "Oyay, what choo talkin' about, white boy? What's this stuff? I'm a friendly Puerto Rican, don't make me unfriendly. Buy a drink, then get lost."

I'm so sick I don't know whether to cry or pull my piece and try and force this huge motherfucker to do business. Then Billy leans towards Gordo and laughs. Loud. Keeps laughing until he's got tears running down his face, slapping his hand on the bar, laughing so loudly and genuinely that Gordo starts smiling and then chuckling, finally asking, "Shee-it, mang, wot's so fockin' funny?"

Billy stops laughing like his throat is cut, leans real close to Gordo, and whispers, "I'm Irish Billy Bones, y' know of me. As I know of you, jefe. Now, y' fuckin' sod, let us quit the malarkey and get down to business. This lad is feeling poorly. You got the medicine he needs. We got the money for the medicine. After all, my friend, this is the US of A. The land of free enterprise, capitalism. Do you not want to do business with me, then? Don't hurt me feelings, sir, I'm a sensitive man and can't be held responsible for what will take place if I'm treated poorly."

Then Billy smiles at Gordo like he is his oldest and dearest friend, waiting for an answer, and looking as angelic as possible for a certified madman. Gordo smiles back with an equal level of warmth and goodwill, saying, "So, Billy Bones, huh? Welcome. Mi casa es su casa. Come into the back."

Yelling to one of the rooster guys, "Pancho, watch the bar."

Walks to the back and unlocks the four deadbolts on the door leading into his office/storeroom. Cases of booze and stereos and TVs are piled ceiling-high with cartons of cigarettes and racks of clothes.

Pushing a pile of women's clothes, still holding the price tags from the stores they were stolen from, onto the floor and setting his immense weight on the space this creates on the desk, Gordo asks, "So, cabrón, what we talkin' about? A piece? A half? Couple bundles? What?"

Billy sweeps his arm at me to speak, and I ask, "How much for a half piece?"

Gordo grins. Sucks air through his teeth, looks at me from head to toe, and says, "Normally, about twenty-five hundred. Pure as you gonna get it. Times are hard, there's a panic on. Thirty-five hundred."

The same thing would go for about fifteen in New York and be of better quality. I know he knows I'm sick and he's going to charge as much as possible. His casa might be our casa but one thing for sure, this cat knows all about free enterprise and capitalism. Doing my best to keep my voice level, I say, "Two gees cash money, here and now. And that's too fuckin' much."

All five hundred pounds of the motherfucker start shaking with mirth, belly laughing, and he's slapping his knees with amazing dexterity for a mountain of flesh this size and he gasps out, "Oye, I like you, little gringo. So much I'll let ya have it for three."

He pushes behind the desk, opens one of the drawers and pulls out a hundred-pack of insulin syringes and pulls one out, extends it halfway to me and adds the words that end all negotiations here and now: "And you can take care of business right here."

I am counting hundred-dollar bills before he finishes the sentence.

As we walk back onto the street I am in slow motion. The screaming of my nerves and body's pain have stopped. But the feeling of an explosion building in my chest and the sound of shorting neon lights buzzing behind my eyes is as loud and as strong as ever.

Showering forever, letting the hot water beat on the bruises and abrasions I've picked up on the drunk. Pulling clean jeans and socks on. Checking to see if my hands are still visibly shaking, and they look steady. Throwing some grease in my hair and walking into the living room.

Jazz is watching me from lowered eyes, not sure if I've gone permanently nuts or if this is a freak occurrence. I'm not sure if she looks worried or scared or mad or maybe all three. She just mutters, "Bad moves, Bobbie. Real bad."

Phil is drinking a beer, got his feet up, and as I walk towards him he tosses a closed can to me, saying, "Hair of the dog, dog. Ya thinkin' straight? Ya ready for this shit or what?"

I pop the top and chug the can, feeling my belly clench and my throat close, fighting to hold it down, and then say, "I'm ready, but I don't know what shit ya talkin' about. What's up?"

"Abe says we meet him and Smith today or he'll bring someone else in. It's root hog or die, hoss. Whatcha think we should do?"

Lighting a Camel and watching the slight tremor in the fingers holding the match, I say, "He ain't gonna call nobody else in, my brother. They want us to do the score. We're better than anybody else he's got. Gimme another beer, we'll head over there in a minute or ten. Ain't no rush, dog. They don't want to kill any of their regular guys, anyhow."

Ernie's sitting behind the normally vacant desk, Smith leaning on the desk by Ernie, Abe already drinking from his tumbler, and he looks about like I feel, shaky and unfocused.

Phil and me have our backs to the wall, and Smith says, "My client has decided to go ahead with this project. As you may or may not know, the largest collection of ancient Greek coins in the world is in Cambridge, Massachusetts. It is currently in the Fogg Museum at Harvard University. These coins are literally priceless, some have no existing counterparts, many are as close to perfect condition as possible. The individual who wants this collection will pay more than you could normally make in a very active year of felonies. One big one. Half a million. U.S. hundred-dollar bills."

Smith pauses for effect, goes on, "My client requires the entire collection. No bloodshed. The security is no doubt the best money can buy. Yes or no?"

Ernie is literally licking his lips, little pig eyes as masked as he can make them . . . but I know he's planning on killing me and Phil. Now, if I say no. As soon as the score goes down, if I say yes.

Abe is sipping his schnapps, watching Ernie as closely as he's watching me, and Phil and I think that Abe's in a bad position himself. Ernie is not the kind of right-hand man a guy can count on.

Smith is standing with his lips pursed, probably knows that me and Phil have already been counted out. Part of doing business.

I work at my best grin, crinkle my eyes, and say, "Best offer we've had all week. Tell your guy it's gonna take some time to put it together."

Smith gives a little smile and says, "Excellent decision. I'll relay the message."

Ernie is grinning like a crocodile, and I want to shoot him then and there as he says, "Man, wish I was in on this one. What the fuck, right, fellas? Everybody has their specialty, I just ain't the right man for the job."

Abe almost loses it, coughing into his tumbler and looking at

Ernie from the sides of his eyes, then shoots them at me to see if I caught the gloat in Ernie's voice. I'm smiling like an imbecile and ask Abe, "How about some of that schnapps . . . let's seal the deal."

Smiles and laughter all the way around and Phil, who is grinning like a big old dumb country boy, still has hand in his jacket pocket wrapped around my old .32, and mine is on my hip, my fingers touching the handle of the .380 under my wallet.

The most cheering thing about the whole situation is that if we start shooting each other Smith will be right in the middle.

Cheers!

fifteen

I've reached a decision. Cutting through everything I do, every thought and feeling, is how much I like this Michelle.

My brain is what you'd call real active. Figuring angles, planning the score and how to survive. And mixed in with all of that, every moment, is Michelle. No matter how I add it up I can't find a way to offer her much of a life. Wondering if it's possible to live without shooting dope, knowing it's not. And knowing as sure as I know that my eyes are blue that she's righteously a nice chick. Educated. Sweet.

Way too cool for a fuckup like me.

Way too fascinated by me, by what I do. Once ran her fingers across the tracks on my arms, my neck. "Does it hurt a lot, baby? What does it feel like? Is it wicked good? Better than pot?"

I had said, "Nah, doll, y' don't wanna go there. It's only good for a little while, and then it's all the way stone-cold bad."

So I reach a rock-solid decision.

No matter what . . . I'm not going to call her. If I run into her I'm going to ignore her. If she calls or comes by I'm gonna say, "See ya," and get away from her. The heartache and loser status that is inevitable being with a junkie is nothin' to offer someone you really like.

And I really, really like this Michelle. This one time I'm going to do the right thing. End of story.

Reading a book titled *How to Win Friends and Influence People*, going from it to a Louie L'Amour shitkicker. Read a couple pages of self-improvement and then a couple chapters of outlaws and cowboys.

The situation swirling from the front of my mind to the back, reading and figuring angles at the same time. How to play Abe, how to get around Smith, and who the hell can you trust when there's this kinda dough involved?

Got empty quarts of beer surrounding my little island in the middle of the floor. A couple of full quarts next to my hand and ashtray, chain-smoking Camels and downing suds.

Getting up and staring at the phone and thinking about that night at the ballet, motherfuckers flying through the air. Shit.

Lying back down and chugging at the beer, hitting my smoke so hard that it crackles as it burns down. The day has faded into a sticky night, summer is not official yet and I'm prayin' for this hot spell to break. Pouring some beer across my chest and letting it cool me as it dries in the weak breeze.

Thinking that to utilize any of the information in the self-help book I'm gonna have to be the equal of any of the tough guys in Louie's shitkicker just to survive, and not knowing if I can hang.

One thing I'm not is without fear, getting up in the morning is tough enough, the events I've involved myself in scare the shit out of me.

Brain feeling like it's going to short out, and under it all or over it all or through it all, what I really want is for the heroin to do what it used to and I want to curl into a ball with Michelle—who I'm never going to see again—and feel safe for a while. To lose myself in her the way I know I could if only I was a different guy.

I pass out on my side, the beer and heat and heroin finally combining to shut my head down.

Wino Boy is holding a rig as big as a baseball bat, blood dripping from the end, dead eyes covered with flies and howling at the purple shimmering fog surrounding us as shapes like huge insects dance just beyond the shining purple veil that is closing upon us as surely as death itself.

The scream stuck in my throat is bringing me back to the edge of consciousness, that feeling of being stuck in your body and paralyzed. Trapped, feeling your arms and legs, but cut off from them.

Knowing that if I can force the scream past my lips I'll wake. Survive at least for a while.

And the dream changes, soft arms are holding me, a hand stroking my face and now lips kissing the back of my neck, soft, so fucking soft that it's way better than the real thing could ever be and I'm responding.

The terror of the first dream gone like your last fix, not even a clear memory, and feeling those impossibly soft lips kissing, then sucking on my ear, then running down my neck and back and up again.

The breath gentle against my ear as a raspy, throaty, little-girl voice is saying, "Hey, baby, hey, it's OK. It's really OK."

And rolling onto my other side and kissing and holding that dream and not ever wanting to wake. Coming all the way back to the world and so full of need and consumed by my own weakness that as my eyes open and stare into Michelle's all I can say is, "Man, I fuckin' missed you."

Hating myself as I kiss her and run my hands down her body, feeling her respond, lifting the skirt she's wearing and feeling her grow wet as my fingers go inside her.

Pulling her panties off and thinking that even her underclothes are nice. Plain cotton like a kid might wear, not a G-string, not fancy lace fuck-me-quick regular bimbo shit. White cotton.

As she tries to unbutton my jeans, putting my hand in the middle of her chest, pushing her down on my mattress and working my way down her belly, licking and kissing, and her saying, "No. I want you inside me."

Telling her, "No. This is all for you."

And in some way seeking redemption and maybe a form of absolution for sins not yet committed, I do my best to return the joy and pleasure that I'd felt just waking up to her.

Digging her salty, musky taste and first softly and gently licking and sucking at her clit and lips and then when she starts shaking and gasping increasing the pressure of my lips and tongue and teeth until she is full on convulsive and screaming, "Stop. Ya gotta stop. It's like electricity."

Kissing each of her thighs and climbing up her body and holding her as tightly as I can, trying to pull her into my chest. And kissing the tears from her eyes and wondering what I've done to make her cry.

*   *   *

The night cools and goes by like the dream of waking up to her had never ended. A thing of motherfuckin' wonder. Her telling me how scared she was when I disappeared, how much she dug hanging out. How she understands that I am in the game and not gonna get out and it is OK with her.

Doing my best to level all the way, explaining that I've never heard of a hope-to-die junkie getting clean and staying that way.

That in my line of work there are no happy endings, and her pinning me with those orange-brown-yellow eyes, lit like a candle flickering behind smoky topaz, lookin' at me like I am the prettiest, smartest, baddest motherfucker ever to walk on two legs, and I break. Tellin' her all about the shit you never, ever talk about.

How confused and scared I am, how I don't know who I can trust. Babbling on about Syd and how I think she is OK, but she set us up with Abe, who put us together with Smith, and how I know as soon as the score goes down they are going to do their best to hit us. And does Syd know or not?

Actually stuttering when I say that I love Billy like a brother but don't know if he'd cosign them movin' on me and Phil if the price is right.

Because in the world I've been living in, loyalty is always suspect.

And what the fuck should I do?

And she is holding me the way I'd been holding her earlier and she asks me, "You're going to go ahead with this, no matter what?"

Thinking about it and feeling like this is the one big shot I am ever going to get. An awareness that I am as hooked on the adrenaline as I am on the drugs surfacing for a second and then fading. Like contemplating your own death, it is there for a second and then gone, replaced by a more palatable thought.

Not knowing that the trick is to survive, that living small is better than dying big. Or that learning how to really think and plan and having the courage to dream is what makes those dreams possible. Or that big balls and blazing guns aren't worth shit unless you want something bigger than you are. So I tell her, "Yeah. No guts no glory."

Substituting a tough-guy line for what I can't express, the desperation that consumes me and still drives me.

She pulls away and her eyes cloud as she pulls inside herself and then clear and she grins like an elemental force: fine, fiery, fe-line, and female, saying, "Ask them. I saw Billy Bones when he and Phil were tearing the town apart looking for you. He was scared. He loves you. If Syd is what you say, try trusting her. She might know what to do. If she crosses you, if Billy doesn't kill her . . . I will. I think I love you, Bobbie, I'm with you."

That pretty face staring at me so serious I don't know whether to laugh or cry. Knowing that I want to possess this chick like a guy falling into hell wants salvation I say, "Okay."

And kiss her, feeling her writhe against me, and moving like one animal with two parts we make love. This time we come together.

Waking that afternoon still holding her. Creeping into the head and checking my face in the mirror: no fear. Looking inside me and feeling ready for whatever might come. Time to get busy or get dead. Fuck it. Putting just enough in the cooker to keep me right and start-ing the day.

Billy is in O'Malley's, a pub in Southie. South Boston, South Boston aka Southie . . . the largest Irish ghetto in the United States. Tene-ments stretching to the sky, filled with rats as big as cats, garbage piled as deep as my head on the sidewalks. Old fourplexes rotting in the springtime humidity have their stoops covered with poorly dressed, howling, rock-and-rolling Irish kids, all hoping for a miracle or to go out in a blaze of glory.

If one thing stands out about Southie it's the lack of hope. White faces, pale and showing the signs of malnutrition and the despera-tion that being poor gives you. No one to blame, no weak excuses and almost no way out.

Strolling into O' Malley's and spotting Billy holding court im-mediately, with Mental shooting pool in the back of the room. He waves, then sinks the eight. Grinning and coming towards me and Phil, saying as he gets within shouting distance, "House champion. Either of you boys wanna try the champ on for size?"

Phil checks me out of the corner of his eyes, and when I nod he grins and says, "Kick your Irish ass, pal. Pure redneck peckerwood here, representing the greatest pool players in the world. Homicidal fuckin' honkies, ya thick mick. Let's do it, Mental."

Mental throws a textbook-perfect left hook at Phil's head and pulls it, laughing and throwing the same left around Phil's shoulder and staggering with him to the pool table.

I down shots and beers and when the bullshit slows at Billy's table for a second ask him for a minute of his time. Stroll into the back, past the pool tables, and run the whole situation down. Looking up into Billy's ever-present black shades, ask him, "So what do ya think, my brother? Are ya with me? Or not?"

Billy kills the pitcher of beer he brought with him, holding the pitcher to his lips and chugging, Adam's apple working up and down with the disappearing suds, and when it's empty sets it down. Burps so long and so loud that it carries over the blaring jukebox and hollered conversations, and then he takes off his shades, pinning me with brown eyes that have gone from stark raving mad to motherfuckin' sad, says, "Laddie, o ye of little faith. I'd turn me back on y' never. I'm a killer of men. Not a betrayer of faith. This once I'll forgive y' not coming to me right away. We'll go see Syd tonight, drop in at Max's and catch the show. But for my money it's Ernie. Abe was once a power, he's like an old lion now just tryin' t' survive the jackals. . . . Bobbie, yer me friend. Do whatcha gotta."

He puts his shades back on and sweeps his arm in a gesture encompassing the barroom and Southie beyond, then continues, "Abe has some good boys. Ernie is the son of a famous Anglican wise guy here in Boston. A killer himself. That is the real power to worry about, because he can kill with immunity. But here, lad, here you have the motherfuckin' Murphy-oso. The Irish Mob in all its glory and grand fuckin' madness. If Ernie or his people kill ya they'll pay the price in their own fuckin' blood."

Wrapping that pipe-cleaner arm around my head and escorting me back to his booth. Hammering Irish whiskey and Guinness until Mental falls into the booth and passes out. Phil falling in next to him and mumbling drunkenly, "Fuckinmick took every game, first a hundred a game, then two, five on the last one. Two thousand fuckin' dollars playin' pool. Two thousand off our goin'-into-business fund. Jazz ain't gonna like it. Shit."

Billy comes out of his drunken stupor for a second and laughs and says, "Aye, been hustled you have, lad. Mental does two things well. The first I'm sure y' can guess. The second is he shoots pool like a motherfuckin' demon."

A while later me and Billy stumble and roll out the door and into a cab to the airport, New York bound.

Syd is looking at me like I got a dick growing out of my forehead. Shakes her head and says, "Oy, din'cha learn nuttin' wid me and Melvin? I can't stick around for this one 'cause me and Alan are leaving for Cape Cod in da mornin', then for Europe in a couple a' weeks. It's time for us to get outta Dodge. . . . Elmer wasn't quite as good as he thought. I got mine. Fuck him. Anyhow, kiddling, here's what I'd do: Abe's got a daughter, a junkie whore, works the Combat Zone. Soooo . . . do the score. Snatch the bitch, get your dough, head for the coast. Meet me here this time next year if you're still alive and outta the joint and I'll show ya how to steal like a congressman. Use a pen instead of a crowbar."

I flash on the past, remembering that neither Syd nor Mel would have cosigned on grabbing some poor junkie whore. One of their first lesson plans had been "Don't hurt no citizens." People change, I guess.

"What if it ain't Abe? Ernie's trying to move up. What then?"

Syd gives me that same look, like I was a retarded child, then sighs and says, "Kill him. What else?"

Steaks as thick as planks, burnt black with grill marks on the outside, bloody red on the inside, baked potatoes loaded with butter and sour cream. Coffee and slabs of chocolate cake so rich it hits your mouth like a drug for dessert.

Billy lights a smoke and blows out a thick gray plume, sips his coffee, and asks, "So, y' gonna snatch the broad?"

I light my cigarette, and our waiter comes to clear the table, sip at my coffee and wait till he's done and out of earshot. Thinking about the whole thing, pretty sure I know how to do this without adding kidnapping some shot-out junkie chick to my sins, and say, "Naw. Ain't my style."

Billy nods and says, "Good man. No women, no children."

Catch Muddy Waters at some joint in Manhattan. He cooks, wails, puts on a show that could raise the motherfuckin' dead.

Spot Shelton and he is with a stone knockout, a natural redhead with screaming green eyes who directs those eyes only at him, and I feel good for him and raise my glass in a salute.

Shelton grins, winks, and responds with a toast across the room.

Susan is there, trolling with some tall, gangly geek with artistic pretensions. He is playing the sensitive artist role for all he's worth and me and Billy both laugh. Billy leaning down, looking at me over his shades and yelling, "Now that lass is a killer of men, without a doubt. I think my way's kinder, whatcha think, lad?"

And seeing her does nothing to me. Zip. Nada. I flash that it would be awful nice if kickin' heroin was that painless and say, "Yeah, man."

And the band plays on.

All evening there, the whole flight back to Boston, thinking about Michelle, dreaming about a real life. Now the deal is about more than me. Something bigger. Us. Now I'm on a motherfuckin' mission.

Phil is holding the .32, asking, "Whatcha mean, I need a better piece? This won't kill a motherfucker?"

Billy lifts his shades for a half second, resets them on his nose, and sneers. "Sure. If he holds still while y' put it against his head. Come on, hillbilly."

Waltham is a suburban town, lies outside of Boston and has a sleepy, angry feel to it. Blue-collar with aspirations to white. No way it's gonna happen, a mill town with no real mills, plenty of kids lookin' for a way out. Army, Navy, Marine Corps, drugs, alcohol, and crime. A place where people bowl and talk about it, Elks Clubs and bad Chinese restaurants.

A town where Billy Bones has more than one friend, and that's why we're here. Billy's driving a vintage '39 Lincoln, black on black, gangster down, whitewalls. Stylin'. Stereo blastin'. I'm shotgun,

Phil's riding in the back with Mental, they're talkin' football loud enough for it to carry into the front over the speakers.

Billy and me smoking and ignoring the chatter about this guy and that guy winning this game and losing that game. We pull into a tiny driveway leading into a tiny house, like a dollhouse almost, a guest house with no real house to belong to.

Pile out and Phil and Mental are still cutting up old ballgames. Billy is silent and I'm edgy. Get inside and are greeted by a fat balding guy with long sideburns and myopic green eyes, skittering around behind Coke-bottle glasses, wearing a white slingshot with sweat stains under the armpits. A class act.

The furniture, what there is of it, is trashed, empty beer cans lying all over and overflowing ashtrays. Cats loitering, swishing their tails and rubbing against each of us trying to get patted. Early American Squalor, it's making me homesick.

The guy says, "Ya sure these two are OK, Bones?"

Billy makes a disgusted face and replies, "Naw, one's state police, the other's a Fed. Whatcha think, Specs? They been workin' with the Brit, doin' paper. They wanna expand. Get the merchandise out. Let's see what y' got."

Specs fusses around, finally dragging a clanking burlap bag from beneath his cat-covered and trashed couch, emptying it on the floor. A pile of pistols in various states of disrepair. Two sawed-off shotguns, a couple of hand grenades. Squatting on the floor and looking up at me he asks, "So you know Susan and Shelton? They stop by to visit sometimes when they have business in Boston. I get things besides guns, you know. Paper and things, you know. . . . Susan loves my cats."

Then licking his lips and looking like an embarrassed child he asks, "She didn't mention me, did she?"

Understanding Susan's spell and feeling bad for the guy I say, "Yeah, man, said you were too cool for school. And said your cats were motherfuckin' lovely."

Smiling so hard his glasses are riding up to the middle of his forehead, he reaches back under the couch, pulls out an AK47 with a box of extra clips, saying, "Saved the best for last. Made in Czechoslovakia, full rock and roll, folding stock. This one's the shit, man. Check 'em out, fellas. Then we can talk price."

I got my .380 in my back pocket, feel like that's all I need, kick back smelling cats and old beer and watch Phil sort through the handguns. After a few minutes he says, "Don't really know shit about artillery." Then holds up two revolvers and asks, "What about these?"

Billy talks before Specs can start his sales pitch.

"Smith & Wessons, thirty-eights, one's a four-inch, one's a six. Both'll kill a motherfucker quick and in a hurry-up. Check 'em for rust, make sure they dry-fire okay. Check the hammers."

Billy picks the AK up and looks into the breech, folds the stock back and forth, and throws it to me, saying, "Get it. That three-eighty y' pack ain't enough if we end up doing serious killing."

I look at Phil and for just a second see fear show through his normal hard-guy scowl, and then his grin is there and he says, "Shit howdy, guess we ready like a motherfucker. Gotchoo a machine gun, ace."

I smell the grease on the AK and feel the cold power that will flow from it to me or whoever holds it, and I am as scared as I've ever been. It is all becoming real.

We pay Specs for the guns and ammo to go with them. Billy buys the hand grenades because they are there. And tosses one to Mental, going, "Bang." Then he starts laughing, saying, "Only in horseshoes and hand grenades."

The drive back into Boston is quiet, the only noise Mental cracking his knuckles.

Wearing my best clothes; cruisin' slow, in one room and out and into the next, digging all the weird stuff. Wondering about it all and not having to fake interest.

Marble floors, paintings from all over the world and sculpture to match. Oriental rugs that are fuckin' gorgeous, old silver sets. Weapons from the Middle Ages. All kinds of neat shit.

The coins are in one room upstairs, the ones we want filling three glass cases. Felt-lined boxes holding some, some displayed lined up in plastic envelopes. A gang of 'em. All kinds of ancient coins from Greece. In glass cases. With chickenshit locks. Without alarm one on the cases. Lord have mercy.

In a building made to show stuff off and not protect it. Contact alarms on the doors and windows. That's it. Amateur hour. Your grandma could take this down. Yeah, man.

Spending as much of the daylight hours with my new girl as possible. Watching her study. Making love. Babbling at each other like half-wits. I'm all the way nuts about her, she looks at me like I'm Elvis reincarnated. Bigger than life. Yeah. Together we're more than the sum of the halves. Nothin' is going to stop me. Nothin'.

The sun is sinking in a ball of scarlet and orange, clouds dispersing the dying rays like water disperses blood, soft red hues cut with smoke, and the pay phone is pressed into my ear so hard it hurts.

Traffic going by so loud that I got my other finger pressed into my free ear to block the noise. Ring, ring, and I get a voice I don't know on the other end saying, "May I help you?"

"Yeah, gimme Red."

"Who's calling?"

"A friend of his. Lemme talk to him."

Light a Camel and watch the rush-hour traffic crawling by, tapping my foot to an inner rhythm, bap-a-bap-a . . .

"Yo, who's this?"

"Recognize the voice, Red?"

"Hey, dog, zat you? What's up? Ya killin' 'em or what? Drivin' that Rolls yet? Fill me in, Jim."

"You lookin' to work?"

A hesitation, seems like hours . . . the phone line crackling . . . then, "What kinda dough?"

"A large cee, your end."

"You're shittin' me."

"Nope, serious like brain cancer. It will probably be kinda messy before it's over though, dog."

"Ohhh, I'm so scared," said in a whiny exaggerated falsetto voice.

Then dropping back into his normal redneck rasp, Red asks, "What's up, dog? Think I got puddin' in my pants since the last time ya saw me? I'm down. Messy is OK when you talkin' that kinda dough. One condition: I wanna bring my old lady. She ain't gonna dig me skyin' outta here and leavin' her. Yes or no?"

"No sweat, you can meet mine. We'll go to the ballet and shit. It'll be a gas."

"Shee-it, the ballet. Uh-huh, right. Ya kill me, dog."

"What's the chances of the other guy that stayed there with ya comin'?"

"Slim, pretty slim, but I'll ask him. Have his lighter half talk to him."

"Yeah, I'll have him call."

"When do ya want us there?"

"Next week. Hey, Red, I ain't kiddin' about the ballet."

"Lost your fuckin' mind on me, dog. Ballet my ass. See ya in a week."

"Later."

The tempo of the music pounding behind my eyes goes up a notch. Bop . . . a-bop-a . . . bahh-boppp!

Nighttime and I'm sitting across from the museum, dressed just like Wino Boy, smeared dirt on my face and haven't shaved for three days for authenticity. Drinking Wild Irish out of a bag and tracking the security. One guard inside. Two rovers outside. Two cars on regular sweeps.

Spend the next night on a roof overlooking the museum with binoculars. Same exact thing.

Another angle the following night. In bushes on campus, binoculars and a stopwatch. Wild Irish in a bag and dressed like a wino just in case. No problems except a big stray dog that comes to visit. That bush must be his home, and he's pretty reasonable about sharing it.

The dog follows me out of the bushes in the morning. I buy two bacon and egg sandwiches, feed him one and I eat one. He keeps following me.

Now we got a dog. Big mangy motherfucker, one ear half chewed off.

Jazz names him Spike.

He's a happy guy, eatin' steaks and pizza, bacon and eggs. Whatever we get he gets.

Phil buys him a collar.

Spike's stylin' now.

Back on the roof. No variations. Like taking candy from a baby, this is gonna be sweeter than a young girl's kiss. A piece of cake.

Taking a break for one night, we start out headed for a private club on Salem Street in the North End. Boston's safest neighborhood, it's all Italian and no street crime is allowed. I like it, friendly people, clean streets, and the odor of garlic and home cooking is strong even just driving down the street.

Park and stroll past the two monster doormen and into the club. Dark wood and oil paintings, violin music alternating with Sinatra. The smell of Parodi cigars and red wine blending with clinking glasses and the noises of a small casino. The ball dancing around a roulette wheel, cards being dealt, dice rolling and tumbling. Nice.

Phil's in his oil tycoon getup, I'm in slacks and a button shirt. Jazz and Michelle dressed to kill, tight little skirts and low tops. Michelle in black, Jazz in white. Every swinging dick in the place is drooling when they walk by, they catch me and Phil bringing up the rear and stop droolin' till we go by. We're stylin'.

Play some blackjack and a little roulette, win a little and lose it back plus some. Roll for dinner with a couple of Northender I-talian kids and their girls, Tony and Angelica, Massimo and Maria.

Massimo is the guy driving the Cad the North End crew is ridin' in. They pull out and we follow in the Cuda listening to R&B and digging the night.

Hitting Anthony's Pier 4, one of the nicest restaurants in Boston. Class all the way. Got a banquet table with eight of us. Oysters on the half shell and shrimp cocktails with monster shrimps in them. Anthony's famous hot popovers, and Caesar salads. Drinking Tanqueray gin and tonics all around. Nice. The lobsters are set down, they're as big as lobsters get, huge fuckin' lobsters with bowls of liquefied butter and nutcrackers to bust 'em up.

Start on the claws, and as I'm cracking my lobster's right claw,

Phil says, "Talked to George. He ain't comin' unless it's an emergency. He's got it goin' on. He says good luck but he's makin' too much dough with Ben. Ya can't blame him."

Muttering, "Shit," and putting so much force into the cracker I'm using pieces of shell and lobster go flying across the table. Gotta find a replacement. Who? All the way back inside my head, the conversation droning around me and feeling Michelle rubbing my leg under the table. Grin at her and hold her hand. Wondering about Mental. Maybe. Gotta ask Billy.

Tune back into the world around me, hit my gin and tonic and catch Massimo saying, "Reason I ain't eatin' much? Desbutol. It's Desoxyn on one side, a blue bird on the other. You know, Methedrine and Amytal in one pill. Speed half is yellow, down half is blue. Wafers stuck together. Makes ya fly on a soft cloud, like a racecar with good suspension. Goin' to the dog races tomorrow, my uncle got a dog runnin'. Goin' to give that hound so much speed his heart will explode after, but guaranteed the fuckin' mutt will win. Eight dogs, we cuttin' eight Desis in two, give the other seven mutts in his race the down half, give Rover the eight speed halves. Parlay him with every dog in the next race. Perfecta guaranteed. Ya want some action?"

The women are all glaring at him, looking like he's a monster to be drugging innocent dogs.

I say, "Poor mutts . . . wha'd they do to deserve bein' fucked up?"

"Yeah," Massimo says, "but that's the way it is. Money-makers, paisan . . . know what I mean?"

Not having an interest in dog racing, but thinking that some speed might be a good idea, you know, get the rhythm all the way up, I say, "Yo, Massimo, let's talk."

Go to the head to talk, and I put a grand on a perfecta with his dog boxed with the next race, and next day I win $3,200. And I buy five hundred Desbutols. Crank up the music.

One more week of this. Billy sitting on our couch sipping at a Guinness, wearing his uniform black-on-black-on-black, I'm wired for sound. Doing stuff to stay well, speed to stay fast, drinking like a fish to keep even, and have so much adrenaline flowing I'm on full, 24/7. Hit my cigarette and ask Billy, "How about Mental? Can I use him on this score?"

Billy grimaces and says, "Now y'd be stupid not to, wouldn't y', lad? Just try not to let him get killed."

Downing my Guinness and saying, "Thanks," and watching Billy do a stage wink behind his shades.

Buy a van and two police scanners, one for the Cambridge PD, one for the Harvard Rent-a-Cops. Phil installs the scanners and hotrods the van in twenty-four hours. He's helped by a couple of Desbutol.

The next morning he's crashing so hard his hands are shaking and tells me, "That shit's poison, feel like I'm going to die, dog."

I hand him a quart of Jack Daniel's and tell him, "Drink till ya pass out. Then you'll only have a hangover."

See no reason to tell him if he takes a couple more Desis when he wakes up the hangover will disappear like magic. That's how ya get hooked. I wouldn't wish that on anybody.

sixteen

The sun is shimmering off the grass carpeting the Common, business types are passing through on their way to or from work at the State House or Courts. Winos are passing bottles and there's a scattering of college kids and townies smoking weed.

Billy is looking off into the distance and Mental is sprawled on the lawn facing me, wearing jeans and engineer boots and no shirt. One hand shading his eyes and he says, "Billy Bones says it might be a nice piece of work. Billy's a specialist, I'm a general fuckup. If the money's right, I'm in. Whatcha got?"

"A burg. You ain't in that part. The cat set it up calls himself Smith. The day we goin' in, me and Phil meet him and tell him it'll be on in a week. Abe and Ernie and that crew are plannin' on whackin' us and takin' the dough. Smith is in on it. We're meetin' at Abe's joint. They'll think they got a week. When he leaves, you follow him. One of our partners is comin' in from outta state. He drives and you guys grab Smith. We find out who the buyer is. Sell the shit we're stealin' direct. You baby-sit Smith till we get the dough. Simple. Ya in?"

"You forgot to mention what it pays."

"One hundred large, all cash."

"Think he's just gonna tell us who the buyer is?"

"Probably not. You might have to convince him. Think ya can handle it?"

Now Mental is lookin' at me like I'm a drooling imbecile, spits and says, "For a hundred gees I could make the Pope turn Jewish. Might take a little while, but believe me, boss, he'll tell us. What about Abe and Ernie and them?"

"That's why it pays so good. They probably won't like getting fucked instead of doing the fucking. You still in?"

"Never liked those guys anyhow. Fuck 'em. Shit, just pay Billy to kill 'em all."

"That's a possibility, Mental."

Billy turns from staring into the horizon and focuses on us, grinning with his whole face.

It's coming together. And the music goes up another notch. Beee-boppp . . . a-bapa-bopp . . . boom!

Phil now stays in the van from eight P.M. to eight A.M., parked up the street from Harvard monitoring all their radio traffic. He falls into bed in the mornin'. Jazz is becoming very quiet, glaring at me a lot. I'm guessing she wants the money but doesn't like the way we're gettin' it.

I don't need sleep. Better living through chemistry.

Spending every day with Michelle, she's cutting classes, says she can make them up later.

Get some Preludin from Massimo. A weird speed with a wax base and the fiercest rush there is, so strong that as the shit enters your vein your hair stands on end and your eyes cross, and it's like falling into a bottomless pit; falling and falling and falling with no fear.

As good as it is, Preludin is a fuckin' nightmare getting it into solution. First you gotta peel the pill, then carefully cook the insides till the chemical and the wax separate. Not worth it except for one small fact. It has one interesting side effect. It gives you a raging hard-on and if you're twisted anyway, kicks it into overdrive.

I love the daytime now.

Me and Michelle dripping sweat and doing things that would have driven her parents insane.

I change my hiding place every night and track the heat.

It's getting close. Michelle filling my head, Michelle and stacks of hundreds stretching to the moon. Gonna do the score, get the dough, and get the hell outta Dodge. Go to Costa Rica, California, somewhere.

Because one thing for sure, the way I got this put together we're going to have to leave Boston. Probably with bullets flying.

Two days left. We take Spike to a dog groomer. He howls like a wolf. Comes out strutting, fuckin' dog knows he's looking good. Filling out, gone from skin and bones with hair falling out to all muscles, shiny, glossy coat, bonarood collar. He's top dog and knows it. Everybody loves him.

*   *   *

Waiting at Logan Airport. The plane's late. Jittery from the speed and didn't calculate my last shot of stuff right. Needing more bad and didn't bring any, running back and forth to the bar downing boilermakers to try and stay somewhere near level.

Red is coming off the plane and walking toward us, grinning so hard his face is one big freckle, all compressed. Holding hands with Lily, who is hanging back, smiling shyly at me and Phil, and catching sight of Billy and Mental she does a double take. Scary guys.

Red yells, "Yo, dog. Zup?"

All the lames are checking our weird little group out and giving us plenty of room. Go figure.

It's coming together.

Jumping up, grabbing Red in a headlock and losing my balance because of the booze. Red saying, "Smell like a brewery, ace. Where's mine?"

Laughing and the beat goes up just a taste. Bap . . . a-bap . . . a-blam.

Red and Mental checking each other out and me going over the whole plan, grab Smith, get his buyer, do the score, sell the goods. Get the fuck outta town.

We walk outta the bedroom and Lily is looking worried, but kicking it with Jazz and recovering fast. Both of them jabbering about their plans for the money, telling each other Phil and Red'll be all right.

Michelle showing with a bag full of clothes and lighting a joint and the party is on.

Billy with a crazy-looking punk-rock girl who wants to play with his gun. No deal.

Spike having a ball, begging food from everybody and getting beaucoup pats. Happy dog.

Phil and Mental sloppy drunk, wrestling around with Spike barking and jumping on them.

Playing catch-up with Red. Me telling him about ballet. Him telling me how glad he is to be off the compound.

Michelle resting her head on my lap and me playing with her hair.

The pounding beat playing in my skull slowing from rock, to jazz, to a fuckin' waltz.

All of us talking shit and listening to tunes, getting loaded. Ready for tomorrow.

Jazz and Lily go over to the college and help Michelle paint a set for a play she's crewin' for. "It's a blast," she giggles like a little kid with girlfriends. "We just smoke dope and paint . . . wicked cool." Good. We can do what we gotta do without worrying about them. The less they know about the gig, the less they'll worry.

Renting a Ford four-door as Dave Landers from Denver. Me and Phil in the Cuda, following Mental and Red in the Ford into Billy Bones's territory.

Meeting Billy and paying cash for a basement room in Southie, no windows. A sink and toilet part of the room. No neighbors. Steel door.

Watching Mental spread plastic sheeting over the floor. We carry in two easy chairs rescued from a Salvation Army drop-off site. Mental plugs in a radio and we got music.

Red is visibly nervous, looking at the plastic sheeting askance when Mental laughs, lips fluttering like a horse's when it whinnies because there's no teeth to stop them. Letting his face go all the way psychotic, and slipping classic brass knuckles on, ridges coming out where they cover the knuckles, slipping another pair on his other hand and throwing a series of roundhouse punches with enough force to kill an elephant.

Focusing his deranged green eyes on Red and then dropping the mad-dog routine and laughing, Mental's saying, "Don't look so worried, seeing the plastic will scare the shit out of him. Once I do that little routine he'll tell us whatever we need to know. Probably won't even have to hurt him."

Red doesn't look convinced, asks, "What if he don't scare easy?"

Mental shrugs and says, "Then the plastic will already be down. Won't it, now?"

Red and Mental follow us to Abe's and park up the street. Waiting for Mr. Smith.

Abe is huddled into himself, shoulders hunched, hands clenched between his legs, sitting like he's frozen behind his desk. A tumbler and the bottle of schnapps in front of him, and that's where his eyes stay focused. Occasionally he lifts the plastic glass to his lips and takes a long pull.

Smith is seated at the other desk with Ernie beside him. There's four other dudes I've never seen before coming in and out and a couple more in the back. These guys are not real subtle.

Smith is doing the talking, asks, "When can I tell my purchaser that he can take delivery? This is dragging on longer than we wanted. What's a realistic date to get this wrapped up?"

I do my best to grin like a brain-dead baboon and it must work because he goes for it when I say, "Seven days from today. Need one more week of tracking the guards . . . and the security system is pretty sophisticated . . . I got wiring diagrams coming in this Monday. We'll do it after that. OK?"

He shoots his eyes at Ernie, then back to me, saying, "Good enough. I'll tell my client. We'll take delivery the next day."

Playing into the charade, Phil asks, "We get paid then, right?"

Smith gives one of his chickenshit little grins and says, "Cash on the barrelhead. Of course."

And pigs can fly, motherfucker.

Killing time, waiting for Smith to split. Ernie babbling about beating some chick up and me and Phil nodding our heads like we think he's too cool for school.

Abe drinking and not moving or talking. Frozen except for his right arm and mouth.

Smith finally saying, "It's been a pleasure. But I really must run. Next week then. Cheers."

And he does his best to pimp-stroll out the door. The lower-scale companionship must be rubbing off. He looks pretty fuckin' stupid.

Give it ten minutes and say our goodbyes. Phil turns the motor over in the Cuda, leans towards me, and says from the side of his mouth, "Gotta tell ya, dog, I'm hopin' we get to kill that woman-beating piece of shit."

"Probably gonna have to. It's nice of Ernie to make it so easy. Don'tcha think?"

"Yeah, man."

And the sound system in my head goes to full-on rock and fuckin' roll. Bopppp-apa-bop . . . yapa-bebop, yeah!

Smith is handcuffed to an overhead pipe. Managing to sneer at us while standing on tiptoes with one hand stretched above his head. I close the door behind me and Phil and Smith says, "Better tell them. Hurt me and Joey the Hook will have you all hit."

Joey the Hook is called that because one of his Mob front businesses is a meat-packing plant containing a lot of meat hooks convenient for hanging meat of all kinds, including human.

Mental looks at me and shrugs, saying, "He says he's a made guy. Dropping names like a phone book. He ain't Italian. Whatcha think?"

I tell Mental, "Chill for a second, let me make a call."

Run to the nearest pay phone, call Massimo, ask him if these guys are connected. Smoking and waiting for a call back and the phone rings. Massimo says, "They ain't with us. Fuck 'em all in the ass. Got it, paisan? Mr. The Hook is very upset that people would try to use his name in vain. Give them a lesson. Ciao."

Mental swings an uppercut from the floor, the first punch ripping chunks of skin and muscle away from Smith's rib cage. The second is a roundhouse that caves his ribs all the way in, cracking like branches in an ice storm.

Smith is puking and screaming, words falling all over each other, Mental standing back and shaking his head when what Smith is screaming becomes understandable. "Onassis, Aristotle Onassis. Wants the coins to go back to Greece. Onassis, you assholes. He's the buyer."

Stomach churning, not positive that Smith is dirty, holding his face, smashing my fingers into his cheeks, asking him, "Who's the contact? How much they paying?"

Sobbing and spitting strings of puke and blood, he tells us, "Spiros, that's the go-between's name. You can call him at the Hilton, Room 348. Seven big cees. Call him. Just don't hurt me anymore."

Grabbing his face again and looking into his eyes, feeling his brain squirming like a sack of snakes, holding his eyes with mine, and as they are filling with tears, saying to him, "I KNOW. Tell the truth . . . and you'll be all right. Lie and my friend with the knuckles is going to . . . beat you to death."

Dropping my voice, whispering like I am making love instead of committing mayhem, I ask, "How are they gonna whack us?"

Eyes rolling around, looking for help that isn't there, he opens his mouth and I can feel the lie coming and I squeeze his cheeks so he can't talk, tell him, "I KNOW. You're getting ready to lie. Don't do it. Don't make us kill you."

Dropping my voice into a whisper again, saying, "Tell the truth."

Holding his eyes, willing him to tell the real story and feeling him settle in. Accepting that he has lost the game, he sniffs, shakes his head, says in close to his normal voice, "Soon as you two come in the shop with the coins, Ernie and his crew are set up to shotgun you. Six of them. Six twelve-gauges set up in a crossfire. Get you from the back and the side. Blow you to pieces."

He doesn't drop his eyes, no more bullshit. No excuses.

I think about shooting him for a second and then tell Mental, "Baby-sittin' time. I don't want to kill him if we don't gotta. I'm gonna call this Greek. If it checks out . . . once we dump the swag we cut him loose."

If I could have seen into the future I would have killed him twice.

The room at the Hilton is plush, thick carpeting, full wet bar, nice. Spiros is a huge guy, one of those big cats that looks fat but moves real easy, deceptive. Eyes slow and veiled, trying for a soft look but barely concealing the man's predatory nature. Nice clothes. His bare feet look weird sticking out of his slacks. Diamond rings on three fingers. Two girls there when we first come in. He waves his hand and they glide into another room. Both moving like dancers, way pretty.

This is a powerful cat. Be cool. He asks, "Have you killed the original contractor yet?"

Keep my face cold, let him know he can get dead as easy as anybody, ask him, "Why? Who cares? Ya wanna do business or not?"

He smiles and quits trying to look like a nice guy, says, "No. Live, dead; his people or you people, all I care about is results. Let's talk business."

Thinking that this guy has to know he's vulnerable, that he's as twisted as anybody in the game, I tell him, "Killing isn't how we make our living, but we don't mind it. Your employee tried to fuck us. Don't think you can, or you'll be going back to Greece in a box. Ya with me, Spiros?"

He checks Phil, glances at Red and then back to me, saying, "Any friend of Irish Billy's is going to get a certain amount of respect."

Watching to see how I react to him knowing we run with Billy, then saying, "My information is the best. The late Mr. Smith was stupid. I never underestimate a situation. You three smell like killers. Your friend Billy is a legend, so to speak. Che sarà sarà. Whatever will be will be. No worries. When can you deliver?"

Let him assume the professor is dead, I figure. Won't hurt.

"Tomorrow morning. Cash on delivery. Seven large. In a public place."

He puffs out his cheeks, says, "It will take a week or so to get that much cash in one place. You're ahead of schedule. Intentionally, no doubt. Eight days from today, assuming you get away with it. We complete this transaction then, cash for coins."

Thinking, Motherfucker, eight days of slippin' and slidin', trippin' and glidin', dodging Abe and Ernie and their fuckin' ring of back-stabbin' fools and dings. Smiling with my lips showing no teeth, knowing that any indication of desperation would blow our negotiating position. Wondering if this eight-day tie-off has signed Smith's death certificate or if there is some way to avoid killing him. As long as they think Smith is dead, Spiros, Abe, all of them will proceed with a certain amount of caution.

Spiros is walking to the wet bar and filling four big cut-crystal glasses with a thick, clear liquid, saying, "Ouzo, a fine drink."

Handing each of us a glass and raising his, he says, "To success."

"Yeah."

The shit tastes like licorice and goes down like smooth, sweet fire.

The beat in my head accelerates to full-on punk rock, no melody, violent noise. Turn it up. Bam . . . a-bapppa-bebob . . . now!

Red's all the way on fire, so wired he can't sit still, Phil's kicked back drinking a beer, and we're going over everything step by step.

Jazz, Michelle, and Lily are on their way to Cape Cod with a stack of hundreds to rent a beach house for us to lay up in until we can get our dough and get gone.

Wiping all our tools for prints, making sure that if we have to leave them they'll be clean, finally ready as we can get.

Van full of gas, scanners functioning, tools loaded and clean of prints, fake IDs in pocket and bondsman on retainer, along with a lawyer. Racking my brain to see what we missed and can't come up with anything.

Waiting for the dance to start. By far the hardest thing of all for me. Waiting.

The music in my head speeding up and slowing down without any controls, chest feeling like it's going to explode and palms sweaty.

Going all the way big-time. No safety net, fuck a whole buncha gravity, we're going to fly. Ba-baa-boom.

Praying that we can.

A light drizzle has turned Harvard Square into a place of shining wet neon and soft reds and grays. As empty as an abandoned movie set, a stage waiting for action. The traffic and hustle and bustle of the day and early evening are absent.

Phil's driving the van, I'm shotgun, and Red is kicked back in the back. Phil is wearing work clothes and me and Red are both in dark Harvard sweatshirts, jeans, and black sneakers and already wearing thin leather gloves.

The police scanners crackling and popping, calls coming through: Domestic disturbance 181 Harvard Street. . . . Black males involved in fight 652 Mass Ave. . . . The hand on my watch hits three A.M. and the call we're waiting for comes in . . . officer down on MIT campus . . . officer needs assistance . . . officer down MIT campus . . . guaranteeing that every cop awake, whether he's on duty or not, is going to be headed for the other end of Cambridge quick and in a hurry-up. And be really mad when he finds out the call is a hoax. Oh, well.

Jazz and Michelle made the call from a pay phone. They dug participating. OK. Why not? They'll be back at the safe house on the Cape before the police get done scouring MIT.

Me and Red are out of the van and Phil is driving away, headed for his normal listening post, anything goes wrong he hollers into his walkie-talkie and we're flying before the heat is.

We're carrying book bags and figure we could pass for a couple of student types if no one gets a close look at our faces. They don't look studious for some reason. The contents of the bags are a bust, the contents look like what they are: burglary tools.

The mist is increasing to a gentle, warm rain and the mud and grass behind the museum squish softly with each footstep. Light from a couple of windows provides a little illumination and we check the window I chose to gain entry.

Magnetic strips on the glass, silver tape that if it's broken will trigger the alarm. At the spot where the upper and lower windows meet is a standard contact alarm, two contacts: one on the upper window, one on the lower. Open the window and they separate. Once they separate your whole night is fucked up.

Reaching into my book bag and taking out a roll of duct tape, tearing a strip off and matching it to the alarm tape on the other side of the window. Laying it on the glass to reinforce the contact alarm tape from the other side.

Taking a wrist rocket from the bag, a high-powered slingshot, with high-velocity rubber tubing acting as the sling part, steel tubing encased in plastic for your hand and wrist. Put a stainless-steel roller bearing in the sling part. Step back from the window; line it up so the bearing will hit right below the main window contacts, pull the sling past my ear, and let it go.

Ka-wap . . . the sound of the rubber cutting through the air and a soft tinkle as the chunk of glass by the alarm sensors disappears. No cracks in the window, just a perfect round hole to work through.

This is a lot quieter than a glass cutter, and a whole lot faster.

Grabbing the wire and clips from my bag and softly and carefully reaching in and rewiring the alarm. The first clip goes on with no problem but the angle is wrong for the second. . . . I use modified needle-nose pliers to open the clip and attach it. Wa-lahm, motherfucker.

Put another bearing into the wrist rocket and blow a chunk of glass out by the lock. Push it open and slide the window up as slowly and carefully as a brain surgeon opens a head.

Diving through the window and the music in my head goes all the way fuckin' insane, vicious white noise slammin' through me like I'm a walking speaker for the fastest thrash music in the universe . . . *rock-bama . . . boom-baba-booya, yeah, motherfucker!*

Gliding to the edge of the doorway and checking my watch. In somewhere between five and ten minutes the one guard inside this place is going to be walking past this door and down the hallway leading to the front.

Pulling ski masks over our faces. Putting a golf ball into the wrist rocket. Squatting by the door and all the way aware. So on I can hear Red breathing shallowly, hear his hair as it brushes against his collar, hear the infrequent cars passing in the street on the other side of the campus, hear the guard's fuckin' heartbeat as he approaches, then his thundering echoing footsteps and him muttering to himself.

Lining the rocket up with the back of his head, pulling and releasing and we're already moving before the golf ball hits and makes a ka-thwack noise and bounces down the hall and he's falling and we're on him, catching him before he hits the ground.

Red's got the guard's arms in a full nelson and I'm shoving a rag into his mouth and duct-taping it. Duct-taping his wrists to his ankles. Fast. Before he starts to come to. He's snoring.

Red grins under his ski mask, stretching the fabric upward, and holds his hand out, whispering, "Slicker than snake snot, dog. Gimme five."

And I do, so soft that our palms making contact is a whisper in itself.

Running down the hall and up the back stairs, hitting our coin cases with the flashlight beam just to make sure they haven't added alarms since my last tour.

Pull a wrecking bar from my bag and with a small ripping noise and a slightly louder pop the first case is open. Working our asses off, moving fast and careful.

Loading the last of the coins and both of the bags are full and motherfuckin' heavy, we're talkin' a lot of ancient Greek coins. Aristotle and all his fellow Greek patriots are getting their money's worth, if this stuff is priceless one coin at a time, and we got so many of 'em that it's like carrying hundred-pound weights . . . well, that's a whole lot of priceless. The seven hundred gees is a bargain.

Red hits our walkie-talkie and says, "Rollin', dog. Ya there?"

Phil's drawl cackles back at us, "Do it." And we do.

Red does a soft-shoe routine going down the stairs and as we're going into the now-heavy rain and the coming dawn he says, "Betcha none a' them ballet motherfuckers can dance like that. Whatcha think, dog?"

My eyes are coming out of my head, I feel as strong and fast as Superman, so aware that I'm not just part of the universe, it's part of me and Red is right. Dancing down a staircase while carrying a hundred pounds of smokin' fuckin' hot, brand-new stolen Ancient Priceless Anything is definitely way beyond any ballet dancin'.

I get a firmer grip on my bag and say, "Betcha right, dog. Betcha right. Let's move it."

Casual but fast, through the campus and out to the street, the van right there, motor idling and the door sliding open as soon as we hit the sidewalk.

Climbing in and we're off, driving nice and slow, police scanners still crackling, buzzing and reporting normal everyday mayhem and heartbreak.

The *Boston Globe* carries a banner headline covering the burglary. Full TV coverage. Eating breakfast muffins at the Copper Kettle, we listen to all the tables around us buzzing with theories and conjecture.

The music in my head slowing.

*   *   *

Digging a hole in Specs's backyard, deeper than Phil's six-two. Taking turns jumping down and shoveling, finally placing the canvas bags in the bottom and filling it up.

Tamping the dirt flat and replacing the sod that covered it. Smoking and looking at the ground. Like mourners at a grave, circled and staring down.

Specs saying, "It'll be okay here, fellas. Trust me."

And Billy, the only one not covered with dirt, smiling behind his shades and saying, "We do, lad. After all, y' want your family to keep on livin'; don't y' now? Not to mention y've probably grown quite fond of breathin' y' self. Of course we trust ye, Specs. How could y' think otherwise?"

Specs swallowing so hard we can all hear it and Phil slappin' him on the back, saying, "It'll be Easy Street soon. Don't have a coronary worryin'."

Billy folding his emaciated and too-tall frame into his antique Lincoln, and glass packs rumbling, heads back for Southie.

We're piling into the Cuda, rolling off to meet Mental and Smith and then heading for the Cape.

Relaxed.

The only music the country-western Phil has got playing.

The pounding beat in my head stilled.

For a while.

The water rolling up the soft dunes of Cape Cod is dark gray, sparkling with subdued green and gold highlights, the wind stiff and cold, the sun a pewter-colored disk sinking into thin forest behind us and the gray of the ocean melting upwards into the pink and orange of the horizon, and the smell of salt and burning wood thick in the air.

Laughter and conversation mix with the sound of R&B and Michelle's hand is in mine, skin as soft as velvet, softer even. Pulling her into my side and feeling her rub her face into the side of my neck, feeling all the way good.

Phil bellowing, "Chow's on." And turning from the ocean to the bonfire behind us and walking through the softly clinging sand hand in hand, getting close enough to feel the warmth from the fire and smell the hot dogs and burgers cooking. Spike dashing up to us and jumping from Michelle to me and back, tongue lolling, and whining, knowing that we're both suckers and chow time is here for him, too.

Eating and staring into the fire, throwing food to Spike and watching him twist and catch it out of the air. Feeling Michelle's fingers in my hair and the burnt food awash in catsup and mustard tastes like freedom and forever, chasing it with ice-cold beer, and finally, coffee and Irish whiskey, with roasted marshmallows. A solid group, together, staring into the fire, happy and as content as people and one big dog can be. With one small exception.

Ten of us, Spike the dog, Phil and Jazz, Mental and punk-rock Matilda, Red and Lily, me and Michelle. So who was gloomy? Mr. Smith and his bandages.

The huge house we've rented for two weeks overlooks our own private beach. As the stars and moon take over the sky we drift back to the pad, fire roaring in the huge fireplace, thick covers on the beds. We handcuff Smith as comfortably as possible in the cellar for the night, leaving him blankets and whiskey and Spike for company.

A vacation, waiting for the eighth day, when we'll get our dough and roll for California. All gonna live happily ever after. Yeah, man.

Day seven and strolling into town for breakfast. It's a little after noon and the restaurant is filled with citizens eating lunch. We're finishing our bacon and eggs. Looking forward to tomorrow. Payday.

The waiter is a little fat dude, got blond hair and perfect mustache, refilling our coffee and taking our breakfast dishes away when I notice the front page of the paper being read by one of our fellow diners, look closer to make sure I read it right.

It feels like I got kicked in the chest, my lungs won't work and my head has a band of steel tightening until my eyes feel like they're going to pop out and I watch my feet and legs make the journey to the newspaper machine on the street.

Feel fingers that have the nerves cut dig in my pocket for change and feed it into the machine and pull four papers out, walk back to our table and drop a paper in front of Michelle, one in front of Red, and one for Lily, all lying front page up, and hear Red's strangled "Motherfucker, motherfucker. What now?"

Staring at the front page and the picture of the little old man with his arm around our former first lady and the headline that reads, "Aristotle Onassis Dead."

Hitting my still-hot coffee and mumbling, "Damned if I know, dog. Damned if I know."

The day slides by without anything but tension increasing, our crew body-punched. Spiros answers the first call and says it is all a dead issue. No pun intended. Try again and he's gone, Greece-bound.

Collectively trying to catch our wind. Had it all and it's disappeared with the morning news.

Ya want fair, find a Ferris wheel.

Phil and Red hanging together mumbling to each other about robbing banks.

Mental staring at Smith, wondering if his next duty is going to be killing him.

Smith silent, probably praying.

Michelle rubbing my leg, and my mind is dashing around in my head like a trapped squirrel, Syd nowhere around for advice. Thinking that there must be a way to pull out of this.

Wondering about flying kites, wondering if I could convince Red and Phil that bank robbery is not a good idea.

Slamming enough dope to slow my brain and watching Michelle watch me and dying inside from the look of fear and sadness on her face. Wanting to fix it and not knowing how.

Spike looking as sad as a dog can, not knowing what's wrong but knowing that his humans have the blues.

The beer I'm drinking warm and flat like the day outside, sweat making my T-shirt stick to my skin, the bills I'm counting sticking to each other like my shirt to my skin. Looking at Phil and Red, Mental sitting with punk-rock Matilda and holding his .45 on Smith.

Twelve thousand and change. That's it. Cut it into four piles and keep one, hand the others to the fellas, saying, "That's it, all she wrote. Gimme a little time to put something together."

Red and Phil exchanging glances, taking the dough and looking at Smith. Mental keeping his face blank, Matilda saying, "Let's kill him. Fuck it. Billy would. Let's do it, Mental."

Mental grimacing and looking at me, then saying, "I ain't Billy, wish I was. Do we gotta?"

And looking at Smith and knowing that no matter what kinda scumbag he is, maybe we don't have to kill him. Figuring the odds and saying, "Fuck it, let's do a good deed. Let him go. He might find a buyer."

Mental audibly exhaling and Matilda pouting.

And Smith babbling, "God bless you. You won't be sorry."

Backing towards the door, lips still flapping, and as the door slams behind him I'm remembering that old jailhouse expression "No good deed goes unpunished."

Telling myself I've just earned good karma and wondering why I feel so uneasy.

Back to New York, looking for a plan. We're in Max's Kansas City, talking to Shelton between sets, telling him I need a front on checks and him laughing, saying, "Closing up shop for a while, mate. Syd and her mates generated so much heat with me paper it's time for me and Susan to move on. Besides, as our own Will Shakespeare said, 'Never a borrower nor a lender be.' Bad business, mate, no credit. Not for you, not for nobody."

Watching Michelle walk across the floor to the bar and as she comes up, he starts laughing, saying, "Maybe we could do somethin' after all. Fair Susan is driving me daft. Take her to Boston, she and your girl will no doubt be grand friends. I'll set ya up with enough paper for her to open a shop. Enough to put some serious ducats in your pocket. I'll charge thirty percent, on credit. Just get Susan outta my hair."

Michelle smiling at me quizzically as Shelton goes into hysterics, laughing until he has tears in his eyes. Finally gasping out, "There it is, mate, take it or leave it."

Michelle, lifting one eyebrow and saying, "Sounds good, baby . . . is this girl nice?"

I shrug, then say, "Guess it depends on your point of view."

When we shake hands, Shelton is still shaking with suppressed mirth.

seventeen

The Charles is flowing by swiftly, silver and blue, the grass on the banks so fresh it looks like green fire. The sky is a soft turquoise, as clear as a madman's eyes, not a cloud to be seen.

Red is skimming pennies on the surface of the river, watching them hop against the current and then disappear. Phil smoking and staring at me as I run it down. Doing everything I can to sell the idea, telling them, "It'll be a piece of cake. Susan is coming down before Shelton. She sets up a shop, we get paper fronted, pay thirty percent, and keep the rest. It'll take a couple, three weeks to get it rolling. Burn a couple hundred grand, then head for the coast. Get George and set up that business. Shit, Red, with your end, you and Lily can make as many redheaded babies as you guys want. Whatcha think?"

Red is still skimming change, emptying his pockets, running out of coins to flick into the river. He turns and looking at Phil and then me, says, "Here's what's up, dog. Gary has a couple banks already lined up, scoped out. Says they'll be like takin' candy from a baby. Easier. We gonna go that way. You and Shelton go ahead, put the paper together, and if it flies that's real cool but . . . we gotta make some cash quick and in a hurry-up. Sorry."

Staring at my friends and not knowing how to tell them that Gary is full of shit. How do you explain that you know a guy's no good based on nothing more tangible than his attention to his personal grooming and a gut feeling? Shrugging and saying, "I don't think it's a good idea, banks mean guns and citizens, usually big sentences for not much cash." Hesitating and then adding, "It's not just my hunch. Remember how Billy Bones reacted to Gary Haircut. It's a bad move, fellas. Tie off for a while."

They exchange a glance and then Phil drawls, "Doin' shit your way has got us broke. We gonna try this out, the paper will still be there. No balls, no blue chips. Right, dog?"

"Your ass, ace, better watch your new crimey."

"Twenty-four seven. Didn't say I liked him, or trusted him. Just gonna give this a try."

"Fuckin' maroons." Pinning these two and feeling as sad and mad as one human is capable of feeling, knowing that there's nothing I can do and then continuing, "You two know what a maroon is, right?"

They shrug and I tell them, "Double fuckin' morons, in the immortal words of Bugs Bunny, 'you two is maroons.' "

They laugh. I laugh. And we walk down the bank of the River Charles.

The candles are throwing dancing golden light across Michelle's face, the soft freckles across her face accentuating the glow in her eyes as she pulls the meat out of a king crab leg, dipping it in butter and biting into it, grinning around the meat and asking, "Remember when Shelton said he'd set up a shop in Boston? Why was he laughing? What's with you and Susan? 'Scuse me, Sue *Zann*." Concentrating on my food, spearing a piece of asparagus and chewing on it slowly, not knowing what to say when she continues, "Didja use to fuck her? I don't care, 'cause I know you want to be with me. Right?"

Wondering if she can read minds better than Billy or if my face is just clear as glass to her, I swallow my vegetable, take a hit off my Old-Fashioned, and tell her, "Yeah. You're right on both counts. Shelton has a funny sense of humor."

She grins and says, "Very dry. The British are known for that."

We order dessert and I think about her statement, finally saying, "Yeah, that's what Billy says. Very dry."

There's a long silence. And then she broadsides me, a shock out of nowhere, when she says, "Listen, Bobbie, I wanna tell you somethin'. You don't have to say anything, just listen. First, if you ever want to stop drugs and crimin', it's okay with me. I'll be right with ya. I don't need a lot of lobster for dinner. Long as I'm with you, I like pasta, okay?"

I sit there staring at her, fuckin' blown out of my mind, wondering where this came from.

Her eyebrows are drawn together over her freckled nose, those amber-brown-whatever-they-are eyes glowing with something, maybe a mist. She says, "And the other thing I hafta tell ya, Bobbie . . . Please don't be upset . . . I showed your story to my creative writing prof at school. He said it's really good, suggested you send it in to *Story* magazine."

I manage to gulp, "Yeah?" At my most articulate.

She grins. "Yeah! So I did."

Michelle reaches into her purse, hands me an envelope. Inside is a check for three hundred dollars and a letter that says,

> *Dear Mr. Prine:*
>
> *Thank you for submitting your story to us. We would like to print it in the June issue. We are enclosing a check for $300.00 to cover first publishing rights. Will you please send us a short bio to include with your piece?*
>
> *Looking forward to receiving future submissions from you.*

And it's signed, "Sincerely, John Augustus, Story Editor."

Michelle is smiling so hard she's about to bust her little face. Her eyes are all the way lit up. Me, I'm gaping, chuckling, flabbergasted.

"See, Bobbie, see? You can be a writer, you can be the next Stephen King or . . ."

I'm laughing, choking, "Baby, this is wonderful. You're wonderful. This is fuckin' great . . . But three hundred dollars just about buys lunch. I can't make a livin' on it."

And, I'm thinking, crimin' is what I do, that's what I am, a fuckin' crimey and junkie . . . and I know there just isn't enough adrenaline in writing to fix me.

"Just think about it, okay, Bobbie? You could be a wicked fantastic writer. But no matter what I'm with ya, okay?"

Gary has his chest stuck out so far he looks like he's been pumped up with air, swaggering and drinking beer, pistol stuck in the front of his pants. Mouth flapping endlessly, "I'm down like a mother-fucker, robbing banks is my game. Runnin' with me you'll be fartin' through silk in no time."

And so on and so on. He robbed this bank, he robbed that bank, scored this much . . . sounds like bullshit.

Red and Lily laughing like kids. Phil roughhousing with Spike, and Jazz looking at him with veiled disapproval. Or is it worry? I can't tell for sure.

I know I'm worried. Something isn't sitting right. Even at eigh-teen, I've had more experience than any of them, but I don't know whether the bile in my throat is because Gary's in my territory cut-ting it up with my friends, or if the warning sirens that go off every time I see him are telling me the truth.

Jazz doesn't seem to think much of Gary, either. But she wants out anyway and thinks one last score is gonna get her there.

"You're a genius, Bad," she says, "but you think too big for your britches. Phil isn't a big, smooth con man. He's just a big, sweet, basically honest clunk. If he keeps doin' crime, he'll be doin' time. Let him get the money, get out, make a life with me."

I snort beer out my nose. "Honest?"

"Sure, honey." Jazz smiles. "Killin' a man 'cause he's killin' your ma, that's honest. Even robbin' a bank is honest, straightforward, no con. Always there, always backin' you up, always savin' your ass when you're way deep in shit, that's honest. Phil's not cut out for big crime, and I want him out of it. I like the money we get, but I'd like to know my man's not goin' to be in jail when I need him."

What can I say? Phil is as straight as you can get. And Red and Lily, what do they know? They just signed on, and they think Gary is way cool.

Jonathan Richmond and the Modern Lovers are headlining at the Rat, the stage covered with empty beer bottles and garbage. Rich-mond wearing a ripped up T-shirt and jeans screaming, "Roadrunner once, roadrunner twice. Gonna drive my roadrunner alllll fucking night." The song has more melody than most and the crowd has more college kids than normal. Michelle sipping on a beer, eyes sprung from eating speed.

Around us the human tide ebbs back and forth. The smell of sweat and adrenaline as thick as the smoke and booze it combines with and under it all I can smell me and Michelle and the hours of rolling tumbling lovemaking that preceded our leaving the pad.

Some of the kids Michelle knows from college cruise by with "How ya doin's," then talking exams and professors and shit and the room is filling up as the whiskey goes down. Eavesdropping lightweight on Michelle and company while scanning the crowd and realize I'm the subject of the conversation. Flashing on how young they look although they are all a few years older than me.

It's something about the eyes, a lack of feral wariness that is the norm in some worlds. Instead of a sunken look to the cheeks, a softness that makes you understand why some old ladies pinch cheek. Bodies not buff or malnourished but just kinda soft and generally healthy. Knowing that any buff I had, had gone the way of the dinosaurs. But even with most of the meat gone from my body and no education, still feeling like I was cooler than they could ever be. At the same time feeling like they knew things and had a grasp of the world I'd never have in a million years.

Michelle's fine pale fingers rubbing the leather of my jacket. Her face happy and proud. The speed and her natural motormouth combing into a torrent of words and she's pulling at my jacket, saying, "Tell them about your new career. Where you get ideas. Your stuff is so rad they'd dig it. I know they would. Tell them about it, Bobbie."

"I just write. Put words down. Got lucky. Know what I mean? The luck of the Irish." Blank-faced as this poem played behind my eyes.

> *You talk of the luck of the Irish.*
> *Women raped.*
> *Children starved.*
> *Fields burned.*
> *If ya had the luck of the Irish,*
> *Ya might wish an Irish wish.*
> *We lost many a soul to hunger,*
> *The Brits chopped many a head.*

If ya had the luck of the Irish,
Ya'd wish that ya were dead.

Jazz pushes through the crowd followed by Phil. I kick out a chair, the debris underfoot making it tilt and flop towards the floor. The heroin and booze slowing my grab at it and an engineer boot covering Gary Haircut's foot kicks it back upright. Phil grabbing a chair from the other table and ignoring the "Hey, somebody is sitting there!" that results as the three of them push in.

Gary pinning me for a second and then yelling, "Yo. Service. Waitress, ovah heah." Getting a look from the barmaid that would have frozen nitrogen . . . until he fans a roll of hundreds at her.

Her smiling hard, cutting through the crowd and bending over the table towards Gary, showing off her attributes. Asking, "Whatcha want, ace?"

Gary hitting his smoke, holding his breath for a second, then blowing a stream of smoke rings at her, saying, "Shots and beers all around." Gesturing at me and adding "Jameson's and Guinness in honor of my mick friend here."

The waitress still working hard, bending further into his face, saying, "No Guinness. Howabout a Bud?"

"Bud then, baby. All around. Hurry back."

Gary grinning at Phil, saying, "She wants me. Don'tcha think so, stud?"

Jazz looking askance when Phil says, "Yeah. Boy howdy. Thought she was gonna flop her tits right in yer face. Nice set too."

Michelle looking from Haircut to me, measuring, and more than ever I don't like having this guy in my space. As the waitress is setting our drinks down, wondering if I could take this motherfucker in a head-up fight, and telling him, "Thanks. Next round's on me."

Watching Michelle's eyes go from her friends who have drifted away from the table to Haircut and back to me. Then telling the waitress, "One more all around. On me."

Smiling at Haircut as I say it, thinking I'd have to hit him first and hard and make up for his weight advantage. Then asking him, "So how's it hanging, pal?"

Gary winks and says, "About nine inches and to the right." Then stopping in mid-motion, standing and yelling, "Yo, Ernie. C'mere."

Ernie now standing at our table extending his hand towards me and saying, "I was fucked up the other night. No hard feelings?"

"Right."

He gets done shaking my hand, swings to Phil, slapping him on the shoulder and asking "We're okay, right?"

Electric eels are swimming through my brain and the whiskey won't take the bitter taste of fear and jealousy out of my mouth.

Phil's hair is in his face. Wearing jeans, cowboy boots and no shirt, he's got his feet kicked up on the coffee table, the ashtray in front of him holding an assortment of half-smoked joints. Pointing around vaguely and saying, "Jazz wants to get out of this scene. Shit, hoss, look atcha. You weigh about ninety pounds. That shit has you so light in the ass ya couldn't fight your way outta a paper bag. We all had a good time last night. Gary's all right, knows people, hardly even drinks, not compared to you anyhow. You always want to call the shots. But half the time you're so loaded on smack your eyes are crossed. Other half of the time you're drunk. Now here's the fact, Bobbie. Maybe your Irish friends don't like Gary, but my take on that is it's 'cause he ain't a paddy. They probably ain't too crazy about this motherfuckin' redneck either."

Looking half homicidal, half sad, giving me the look reserved for friends that are fucking up, he points at me. I think he's wrong about Gary, but I know I'm out of control. Having no idea that that is part of what using is for me, that it takes over, not knowing what to say, shrugging, and saying nothing. Phil goes, "I say all that to say this: Ya think ya gonna call shots, ya gotta leave that shit alone. We're your crimeys. The only one that thinks you're all right is Michelle and we both know she don't know what time it is on the real side. We're gonna do some banks. I know I ain't John Dillinger. Gonna do a couple and quit. Quit everything, dog, leave all this criminal shit to you, you like it so fucking much."

Lighting a Camel, buying some time, saying, "I'm trying to tell ya. You're better off not fucking around with anything that has a bunch of citizens involved. Banks, supermarkets, all that kinda shit can blow up in your face. One fucking idiot decides he wants to be a hero and ya got a situation that can get ya life without. Maybe

Haircut is all right. Maybe he's not. I know Jazz wants outta the game. I'm cool if you wanna be square. But if you're going to square up, why go out in a way that's so high-risk?"

"You're tripping, dog. You got a hard-on for Haircut and we all know it. Back the fuck offa me. You're hating not callin' the shots. But why should we listen to you? Last time we tried doin' shit your way, we got burnt. We keep doin' shit your way, me and Jazz would be starvin'. I don't give a good fuck, pal. Me and Red are rollin' on this. Got it?"

"Fuck you, pal. Ya think you're so sharp, go ahead. Rock and roll."

Phil glaring, me glaring back, and everything I wanted to say to him about how he was my friend and how whatever he did was okay with me and how I wished him the best—all those things left unsaid. And we both did what we knew best. Acted like we didn't care.

The breeze is soft and humid. Gnats buzzing in the air and around us are saplings going into bloom as the pond in front of us shimmers like quicksilver reflecting the clouds passing overhead. Michelle's hands hold mine like that was what those particular hands were designed for, squeezing, saying, "Walden Pond. Henry David Thoreau stayed here, wrote about it. I love it. Away from the city and all the bullshit . . . Something you might want to trip on while we're on the subject: Thoreau said, 'Dwell as near as possible to the channel from which your life forces flow.' But you—it's almost like you try and stay as far away as possible from that natural channel that can fill you. Like you hate it or something."

Knowing that she's right, that I'm happiest when comatose, that all feelings were my enemy, I reply, " 'What does not destroy me makes me stronger.' Nietzsche, darlin'. Thoreau is a little light for my taste." And the channel from which my life forces flowed was a motherfucking sewer.

She looks away, topaz eyes cloaked. "Nietzsche died in a nuthouse, you know. Stark raving mad."

"Was he happy?"

"I don't think so. Anyway I was thinking about your friends today. . . . This guy in class is hilarious. Comes from Lowell and was in the school play once. Thinks for sure he's the best thing walking. Every time I see him I want to laugh he thinks he's oh so fine."

Watching her eyes and knowing there's some reason for mentioning this dude. My paranoia is strong and well and it's kept me alive so far and I go, "Uh-huh?" and wait for whatever is next.

"Kinda like your friend Gary. Always looks sharp, always watching to make sure you're watching him. Know what I mean?"

"Yeah, man." Knowing more than I wanted to. If Michelle is aware enough of Gary to know that's he's always well-groomed, she's too aware of him.

Wondering if I'm being stupid. Flashing that maybe this chick sees me as entertainment, a walk on the wild side. Wanting to explain that her world was basically alien to me. Unable to tell her that I tried to read Thoreau and was bored to fucking tears. Thinking it was because I was somehow damaged. Feeling like I should be able to take care of her and knowing that she doesn't need anyone to take care of her amplified everything I saw as wrong in me.

Scared she'll leave me for suburbia and I'll continue my little tour of hell. Hoping there's a way out for both of us.

Hating my jealousy and fear. Not trusting in love. Scared.

Then, fuck analysis. Fuck wondering. When I'm with her, it feels good, eases somehow the ever-present empty pit in my gut. Her hand in mine and we're more than two people.

The Hillbilly Ranch is on the edge of the Combat Zone, featuring live country music, strippers who work lames for fake champagne at fifty bucks a bottle, and sawdust on the floor to make it easier to clean up spilled booze and blood.

The Ranch has the dubious honor of being the most dangerous joint in the whole zone. A group of wannabe rednecks are dressed in overalls and playing country-western Boston-style: they're behind a chicken wire screen that protects them from the thrown beer bottles and mugs, sounding like Waylon Jennings, but all the r's are slurred as the singer whines about working in a factory.

Trashed broads are bumping and grinding to the tunes, and in the booth next to us some lame in a business suit is getting blown by a bar girl who has more tattoos and less teeth than me.

Haircut is holding court, Polaroids of a suburban bank spread over the table. Pointing at one, saying, "Front entrance? Double glass doors. Put a chain lock on in case someone triggers the alarm or one of the customers tries to run. Only way in or out is the back, which is what you use. Police station is eight minutes away, two rovers working the area and we call in false alarm to get 'em outta there."

The pool of sludge in the center of the table, beer and cigarette ash with peanuts sticking out like islands in a mildly toxic sea, is slowly soaking into the flicks. Phil and Red smoking and drinking with Haircut.

For once I'm not drinking, determined to be as cognizant as possible and in spite of myself starting to feel like maybe this guy knows what he's talking about.

Haircut hitting his beer and gargling, holding up, then dropping another picture in the pool of sludge. It's a picture of an old man, big belly, big red nose. His eyes obscured by thick glasses and little pipe-cleaner arms coming out of his security guard's uniform. Haircut taps the picture, saying, "This clown is the only obstacle. The piece he's got in that huge fucking holster is a forty-four mag. Ya can't see it but the holster has a snap top. We go in and take him outta the box from the jump. Shoot him in the head. Simple. The squares see this motherfucker's brains covering the walls, they ain't gonna bust a grape.

"We leave the tellers alone. Fuck those cash drawers, Only got a couple grand each. Hit the merchant teller. In and out fast. As soon as we shoot Pops, everyone freezes. You're screaming at them to freeze and guaranteed no one's gonna go for the silent alarms 'cause they know their brains will be on the walls with this puke's. Two shotguns. Red and Phil covering the joint with the gauges. Bobbie, you got the pistol. You pop the guard and hit the merchant window. In and out with around 100K, maybe 150. Easy. Fast. Whatcha think?"

Hitting my Camel, asking, "Where you gonna be, Ace?"

Haircut smiling. Easy, confident. "Outside. I chain the front doors. Listen to the police scanner. Do the driving. I supply the plans, the car, the weapons. You three go inside."

Red and Phil have their game faces on, not showing anything, eyes as empty as the pit of my stomach feels. Knowing I don't have what it takes to whack some square no matter how much dough is involved, and asking, "Why not just grab the guy and take his piece? Ya kill him the Feds and cops are gonna be on ya like stink on shit."

Still smiling, knowing he's looking good and I'm looking scared, saying, "OK, killer. We can do that. But it's riskier. Doin' a bank or supermarket you want everyone terrorized as soon as you start. Kill this guy and guaranteed ya get that. You in? Or out?"

Hesitating, then telling him, "I'm out. You guys want to do this, go in clean. But I'm not fucking with it."

Haircut not smiling anymore. Phil and Red still wearing skin masks over their skulls, nothing showing. Haircut shaking his head and asking, "Chickenshit?"

I'm staring at him, feeling the .380 in my back pocket and the urge to shove it against his forehead just so I can enjoy the look of terror he'll get right before I pull the trigger is almost overwhelming when he says, "Come on, fellas. Let's head over to the Eye. We'll get one of Ernie's guys. Bobbie don't need no money. He's fuckin' rich. Ain'tcha, pal?"

Alarm bells are going off in my head, but I'm too mad to understand what they mean as I watch my partners follow Gary Haircut into the sunlight.

Like an empty gun, useless. All the shit that was beaten into me by dear old dad running through my head. Useless, cowardly piece of shit. The mirror showing flaccid arms, no shoulders, no nothing. Shot caller, my ass. Fuck all. In free fall knowing that the concrete is waiting. Self-pity does no good. Looking at my haggard face and washed-out gray eyes and laughing at the thought that I'm taking anything seriously, because we all know that no one gets out alive.

Spike sitting at the end of my bed, head cocked to one side, ears flopping over, looking quizzically at me like he knows something's amiss. Then sliding onto his belly, legs stretched out in front and behind, yawning and growling at an invisible enemy as I cook my communion.

God's eyes and dog's eyes watching as I draw it up and send absolution, redemption, and eternal damnation into a vein running up the top of my foot. As the heroin starts to do its job, wondering if I'm losing my nerve. Or if I ever really had anything except driving terror pushing me.

I'm sliding into an abyss with no way to slow my descent.

So why not speed it up? Emptying five more bags into my cooker and mainlining another prayer and for a minute it is answered. Inner peace.

Coming out of my technicolor nod and wondering if I could ever kick.

Asking Spike, who is now lying next to me snoring dog snores, "Watcha think, pal? Is it possible?" When he doesn't answer, checking the magazine in my .380 and slipping it into the back pocket of my jeans. Putting the steel-toe boot back on my right foot and taking Spike out to pee.

I have a little chat with Billy.

"So what do the Irish in Southie say about Gary Haircut?" I ask.

"M'lad," he says, laying on the brogue, " 'tis right y'are, right as rain. The wee people tell me our gorgeous Gary set his partner up and that's why th'puir sod is now doing twenty-five . . . and we both know he's lyin' about how much money he gets from one bank. . . . Sure, n' I wouldn't troost him f'r loove n'r money, boy-o."

I'm laughing at Billy's exaggerated brogue but I know the "wee people" are Billy's informers, who know the score. And if the street says Gary's a motherfuckin', partner-betraying scumbag, my instincts are fuckin' close to the mark.

But are Phil and Jazz and Red and Lily gonna pay attention? Nah. Like all good marks for a con, they want to believe Gary Haircut can bring 'em the fuckin' bucks.

Michelle is visiting her folks. I'd passed on going with her, using the excuse that I should be around in case bail was needed. Her looking at me and knowing that I'm scared to meet them, knowing that they won't like me. And without me saying a word, her saying, "They're nice, you'll like them. And they'll like you, you treat me like gold. That's all they care about."

Grinning and not believing her. If I was her parents, I wouldn't like me. Told her I'd meet them later.

Now I'm staring at three piles of cash on our dining room table, one for Phil, one for Red, one for Gary, the take from the bank robbery they just pulled despite my sage advice. I'm wondering if I'm as stupid as I feel. Looking at all this dough and not owning any of it. Gary nudging me and smirking, "Takes heart to make money, ace."

Grinning with my lips closed and shaking my head. Knowing that as attractive as the cash is, robbing banks ain't my scene. And feeling in my gut that even if it worked this time, it won't the next.

Thinking "fuck you" at him and sipping my beer, wishing that this dude would take his dough and get out of my pad.

Making my excuses, Spike acting like a fool barking and jumping when I hit the door and taking him with me.

Heading down to the river with Spike running ahead and back.

Trolling along the shore, and hoping and praying that there is some way out of the hole I've dug for myself along with the one we buried all those ancient Greek coins in. No market for them now.

Missing the adrenaline and constant insane beat that has ruled my life for the last couple of weeks. Putting a plan together, pass enough paper to take Michelle out west. Maybe go to school, or start a business, maybe write. Maybe just help Michelle go to school and lay low until Syd gets back and I can learn how to steal millions at a time.

Knowing two things: One, robbing banks and waving guns at squares is not for me. Two, I need a sack full of cash, soonest.

Watching the river roll towards the sea, roughhousing with Spike, and wondering what normal people do.

It's almost like the old days. All that's missing is Moppa and his crazy catsup. Red's squatting, arms outstretched on his legs, one fist holding a bottle, and cigarette in the other hand. Phil chugging malt liquor, standing and weaving simultaneously. Me leaning on the wall of the footbridge.

Around us citizens and two-legged scum scurry, lurch, and walk through the Boston Common, the little stream flowing under the bridge is carrying an assortment of garbage to the Atlantic Ocean.

For the moment there's no conflict between us. Just the sun doing its work and easy conversation. The affection we feel for each other is almost as strong as back in Plainfield, and I'm wishing I could shake the feeling that something is missing, that I'd lost track of something indefinable.

What we were all losing was our youth, and none of us knew it. Friendship being replaced by living life and the hard decisions that go with it.

I'm waiting on paper from Shelton, wondering if it's possible for a street guy and a suburban college girl to make it. The fellas are rolling, pockets full of hundreds, girlfriends who come from the life and know what's up.

Phil takes the bottle he's emptied and drops it into the stream. It splashes in the dirty water and starts its journey out to the harbor. He tries to explain, "Got our old ladies to care of, shit to do. Can't follow your lead when it don't set right. Know what I mean, dog?"

"Yeah, man. I know."

Red flipping his now-long hair out of his face and asking, "We know your bankroll's gotta be getting low. We're doin' one more bank with Gary and one of Ernie's guys. Last one went slicker than snake snot and, like ya wanted, no one got hurt, let alone shot. Ya wanna come along?"

They look at each other and shrug when I say, "No. No thanks. Ain't my scene."

Phil looking at me sadly like he thinks I'm washed up. Telling me, "If ya need some cash, we can kick ya a few grand."

Hitting my beer and shaking my head "no," as I watch the humans and scum scurry, lurch, and walk by.

Two days later on a pay phone, pressuring Shelton, "I gotta make a move, man. Put some dough together. Get your shit together. When can ya have Susan down here with paper?"

"A week or so, mate. Give it a week."

Panic growing fast, I'm running out of cash and have nothing lined up. Got a nightmare feeling about the way things are going.

Walking into my pad, and Gary is kicking it with Red and Phil.

There's a moment of silence and Phil says, "Gary might have a buyer for the coins."

I can feel my heart starting to pound and ask, "How much?"

Gary says, "About ten grand. It's better than nothin', right?"

I say, "No."

He opens his mouth and that's all it takes. The words are out of my mouth before I can stop them. "I don't trust your over-groomed ass. Take your too-hip self outta my house before I go smooth fuckin' off. Now."

He's coming out of the chair he's in, eyes focused on mine and fists closing, and there's no way I'm going to let him get his feet planted. The frustration and rage of the last week all coming to a head and Gary Haircut is the recipient as I find myself kicking him in the chest and knocking him back in the chair, toppling it, and I'm jumping as high as I can, coming down on his chest with both knees nailing him while he's trapped in the overturned chair. The air slams out of his chest and I'm throwing shots down into his face with both hands, closing his windpipe with my left and concentrating on sending my right all the way through his face, and feeling his nose break when Phil lifts me off and sits me down, not exactly gentle.

Gary holding his face and bolting through the door, and Red saying, "Shit, dog. Chill. We doin' one more bank with him. That's it. Then kill him if ya want. Just don't do it here, or before we take this score down. OK?"

Shaking my head, trying to clear the madness I can feel swirling through my brain like burrowing worms through meat, I say, "I don't trust the motherfucker dog. Ten gees? Ain't right. No locals will touch him except Ernie and his crew, why do ya think he needs you guys? That last score will hold ya for a while. Tie off."

Phil releases his grip on my arm and steps back, saying, "Gary says this one is going to be big. Brinks is dropping delivery bags, full of brand-new twenties, fifties, and hundreds. We go in right behind them and take the cash. Easy. He drives and has the setup. We'll be rollin', gotta go for it, Bobbie. We gotta."

Not able to identify what's bothering me or, at least, knowing I can't sell it to Phil, just saying, "If it was that easy, everybody would be doin' it."

Going into my room and reading an old sci-fi anthology. Aliens and ray guns, stand-up guys saving humanity, blah, blah, blah.

The shapes chasing me are huge, pulsing and amoeba-like, the ringing of the phone pulling me from my normal nightmares and starting a new one that will last a lot longer than one night.

Stumbling through the piles of clothes and ashtrays in my room, hearing Michelle's gentle, questioning voice, and falling into the easy chair that had trapped Gary Haircut for me. Grabbing the phone and knowing that this is going to be a bad news call before it reaches my ear, I say, "Yeah," and light a Camel simultaneously.

Hearing Red's voice saying, "Hey, dog. That you?"

"Yeah."

"Our bail's a half million. You was right. Walked into a setup like a motherfucker. We'll be in Billerica House of Correction. Come down for visitin' and I'll run it down to ya. Tell Lily I love her and—shit, just tell her I love her. OK?"

"Half million each?"

"Yeah, with collateral. Forget it. We're gone. You see Gary, you introduce him to Moppa. Got it?"

"Yeah, dog. He'll be meetin' Moppa soonest."

"Stay down, old wood."

"Yeah."

And I'm staring at the receiver, feeling my guts fall into the center of the earth and a scream sticking in my throat.

Michelle tells me that when she came out to see what happened, I was rocking back and forth staring into space and growling deep in my chest; with Spike sitting on the floor, staring at me, looking confused and growling right along with me, ready to attack whatever it was that was making me growl.

Tough guy bullshit aside, I hold onto my girl that night like she is a life preserver keeping me afloat above my nightmares, both waking and sleeping.

The bar is small, air-conditioned to frigid, with a fireplace full of wood burning in the back. The clientele is exclusively old Irish guys, white hair and nice suits framing solid builds getting soft with advancing age, eyes uniformly glassy and slightly bloodshot, working-class accents carrying over Frank Sinatra on the sound system.

Pinkie rings on every pinkie glinting like white fire with every shot downed and every beer raised to chase it. The subdued conversation about public contracts for construction and road work, the things left out of the conversations more important than those said, and I know this is a whole different realm of criminal enterprise.

Billy has his arm draped around my shoulders, and we approach one of the leather-covered booths, and for the first time since I've known Billy he takes his shades off and looks uncomfortable, young, less than invincible.

Standing and waiting for the guys in the booth to acknowledge us for only a second, but sensing Billy's unprecedented nervousness, it seems like a lot longer until the smallest and oldest guy in the booth looks up and says softly, "Why, as I live and breathe, it's Billy Bones himself. What can I do for you, my friend?"

Billy scuffs his engineer boots on the dark gleaming hardwood floor and says, "Perhaps a moment of your time, Mr. Quinn. In private if that's possible."

The old man sips from his glass of whiskey and says, "If you'll excuse me, gentlemen."

Stands up, limping with a rolling motion towards the back, stops in front of the men's room and says, "Step into my office, gentlemen."

We walk into the bathroom, and as the door closes behind us there's a guy standing at one of the urinals. Quinn glances under the doors of the toilets and says to the guy peeing, "Hurry it up, friend. We got business."

The dude breaks in midstream and walks out still zipping his pants.

Checking his thinning white hair in the mirror, looking at his teeth, and then looking at us through the mirror, Quinn asks, "So what'll it be, William? Who's your friend? You're vouchin' for him, are ya? Whatcha need that takes an old man away from the comfort of a fine glass of Irish whiskey? Hmmm?"

Billy clears his throat and looking into the old guy's eyes through the mirror, says, "This is me friend, Bobbie. We have a small problem y' may be able to help us with. I'd rather let Robert here tell it to y', sir."

Wondering who the hell this old man is that he intimidates Billy, looking at the back of his head and the shoulders that are still thick under his sport jacket and, still facing the mirror, his eyes catch mine in the reflection. Merry, happy, friendly blue eyes with a light shading of pink in the whites, and he grins into the mirror and says, "So what's the problem, young man? I'm Jack Quinn, and if it can be fixed in our fair town, I can fix it. Tell me."

And I do. Run it down about Gary Haircut, Abe and Ernie, Mr. Smith, the coins and Spiros. Finish with the phone call from Red and Phil that woke me. And ask, "So what do you think, Mr. Quinn? Can you help my friends?"

For a second the eyes stop twinkling and look like two blue portals into hell, and then the twinkle is back as he says, "Come back this time tomorrow. I'll have an answer for yez."

And as he starts washing his hands, he says, "See y' then."

In clear dismissal. His eyes still on us in the mirror, but as we turn, I notice that the twinkle is gone.

We go back into the bar and walk through continuing soft conversations with more words unsaid than said.

Once we're in Billy's old Lincoln and down the street, I ask, "So who is that guy?"

Billy stares at me through his shades for a second and says, "Why, he's t' Boss himself, lad. Mad Jack Quinn, none other. In t' old days he was known for using a fire ax on his enemies, chopping them into hamburger starting at their toes, talkin' t' them all the while. Developed into a fixer and an all-around political power. Got our Italian friends to forgive a couple of small transgressions I made. Ones that normally would have been terminal. Got some of the boys pardons for crimes that would usually require death or life without.

Yeah, he's t' Boss himself. Mad Jack Quinn. You'll do well to call him 'Mister.' Keep that in mind, lad. Not Jack, and especially don't imply anything to do with madness. *Mister* Quinn. Right?"

"Right ya are. Mister Quinn it is."

Smoking and thinking on this and finally asking, "What'll this cost us, Billy?"

He grins and answers, "Nothin' more than our already damned souls. Nothin' more than the fires of hell . . . which we'll both be sampling anyway."

Watching Thrill at the Rat, Billy with punk-rock Matilda, who seems to go from Mental to Billy with no confusion and no jealousy on anybody's part.

Michelle flying on Preludins and I'm drinking, already too wired from anxiety and adrenaline to fuck with anything that speeds me up. Downing shots and beers until I'm headed toward the tabletop.

Staggering home and falling into bed, feeling Michelle's hands on me and not able to respond, it's like I'm dead from the neck down and she's tripping, asking me, "Is it me? Are you tired of me? What's wrong?"

And trying to explain that the drugs are killing me off, that sometimes doing nothing is the best you can do, and watching the confusion on her face and grabbing ten Preludin, peeling and melting them down and catching the vein in my neck and as the shit burns like gasoline into my brain and my lungs fill with chemical fumes and my body goes into overdrive I pull her to me and kiss her, grinding my teeth into her lip and reaching down and finding her already dripping wet.

Fit myself into her and we tear at each other until we're both gasping and screaming. Falling into each other's dilated and scared eyes and bodies. And deep inside me a voice is whispering that I'm like poison for this girl and me screaming inside me at the voice to SHUT UP.

Praying for absolution, as we start over, lightly and gently touching and accelerating into a shared violent union. Spiraling together into temporary madness. Wondering if I've lost my soul.

* * *

The smell of unwashed bodies and baby shit is as heavy as fog in the small brick room, groups of people bunched around each phone outlet, staring into the thick glass separating them from the person they're visiting. Heated conversations echo through the visiting area as wives and girlfriends, crime partners and relatives try and get as much into a ten-minute conversation as possible.

Leaning on the wall glimpsing Red and Phil through the thick glass as they talk to Jazz and Lily, watching them put their hands against the glass to try and touch through it. Jazz turning and saying, "Talk to Phil, Bobbie."

As I slide onto the round steel stool that comes out of the wall, Red leans over into Phil's phone cubicle and grabs the phone, yelling, "Love your guts, dog."

Smiling through the glass I yell, "Back at ya."

As Phil grabs the phone and Red goes back to Lily I've got the receiver jammed into my ear and Phil drawls, "Guess you was right. Check it out. . . ." Then he points at his lips and mouths, *We was set up.* Puts his mouth back on the receiver and asks, "Ya got that?"

"Yeah. How?"

"Gary Haircut." He mouths, *"The cops were waiting . . . we got outside and he was gone . . . no getaway car . . . he fucked us good. . . ."* Says out loud, "Got all that?"

"Yeah. He'll be meetin' Moppa. Me and that tall skinny dude are workin' on somethin' to get you two out."

Phil shakes his head and says, "Not much chance of that, my brother." Pointing to his mouth again, he mouths, *"He knows about Specs . . . where the coins are."*

I'm holding his eyes with mine and ask him, "Are ya sure? How do ya know?"

Phil drops his eyes, and his face turns pale and then bright red with shame and embarrassment, and he says, "I thought the dude was OK . . . I was braggin' a little. I fucked up, bro."

I take a deep breath so I won't start yelling and then say, "Shit, dog, we all make mistakes. I'll take care of it. Take it easy, old wood. Anything ya need?"

"Naw . . . let me talk to my old lady. Take care, bro."

"Yeah. You, too."

Mad Jack Quinn is in the same booth. This time as me and Billy approach, his cronies get up and go to the bar, leaving us alone with Mad Jack himself. He's wearing a different tweed sport coat with a white carnation in the buttonhole. I'm watching him lift the glass of dark beer to his lips and noticing that the rock in his pinkie is over two carats.

The barman comes over, wearing a white shirt, his shoulders and arms so pumped it looks like they're trying to rip through the fabric, his eyes shadowed by scar tissue, and he says, "What'll you gentlemen be having?"

Before we can respond, Mad Jack says, "Two tall Jameson's and two pints of Guinness for my friends. Thank you, Paddy."

And Paddy glides back to the bar with the belly-forward walk of an old-time martial artist, centered with every step.

Jack hits his beer one more time and says, "It's going to take a little while to work out the fine print, but the long and short is this: We can trade the coins for your boys. Nobody got hurt on the bank job, so once we get the details finalized, you give up the coins, all charges are dropped. Simple, huh?"

Paddy sets our drinks in front of us and I down a shot of the Irish whiskey and sip the dark brew to chase it and ask, "What's it gonna cost us?"

The blue eyes are shining with a warm and friendly light, twinkling like he thinks we're the nicest guys in the world as he says, "Din't y' tell him, Billy? A little of this and a little of that. It'll come to me. Now can you fill your end of the bargain?"

I hesitate and look at Billy, who shrugs, and I tell Mad Jack, "I want my partners out. What's my end of the bargain?"

He laughs and says, "Killing those that got 'em busted, Abe, Ernie, Smith, every mother's son in that crew. Can y' do it?"

Billy leans forward and says, "I'll hit every one of . . ."

Mad Jack holds up a hand and says, "Shhh."

Billy freezes like he has a gun pointed at him.

Mad Jack extends two fingers and points at me and says, "You, son. Not Billy. *You.* Can you do it? Or not?"

I drain the glass of whiskey, light a Camel, and look inside me, feeling the music starting, and say, "Yeah, Mr. Quinn, I can do whatever I got to."

The friendly look never changes as he regards me for a long moment, then says, "Why, I believe you can, son. I believe you can."

Pats my hand and yells, "Paddy, another round for me and my boys."

Billy sighs and says, "So be it, lad."

eighteen

Muddy Waters is playing on the stereo when Jazz hands me the phone, and Ben's rich baritone comes through the line like friendly smoke, saying, "How's it hangin', son? Jazz says y'all been real good to her. Guess that's all I can ask for. Anyhow, George and me goin' be flying in to help y'all party when Philip and your boy Red get out. I look forward to seeing y'all, Bobbie."

I'm trying to change gears and ask him, "Shit, boss, last time we talked to ya you weren't exactly overflowing with love. What happened?"

"Times change and people change, son. I miss Jazz, and George misses Phil. Quiet as it's kept I grew right fond of your boy Red, and you and me had too many adventures to part enemies. We gonna be all right. Right?"

And I get a feeling in my chest like I want to cry. Ben was a good friend who I'd figured was X'd out of my life. I grin into the receiver and say, "Better than all right, motherfucker. I can't wait to see your big black ass."

"That's my boy. Stay down, young peckerwood. Me and George'll be there in the mornin'. Party and take y'all back to Illinois. Figure out whatcha wanna do from here."

"Take Phil and Red anyhow, don't know about me, Ben . . . I ain't too big on country livin'. See ya's tomorrow."

"Let me talk to my niece, son. See ya."

"Yeah."

And I hand the phone back to Jazz, feeling the smile splitting my face.

Susan walks through the door like she owns the joint, the cabbie following with bags piled on his shoulder like a Chinese coolie. Looks around and says, "Nice flat. If it's not too much bother I'll be stayin' for a day or two. Got to get settled in. Find a shop and set up business."

My mouth is hanging open and before I can say a word, Michelle is looking Susan up and down and saying, "Sure, we'll put something together for you. Let me help with your bags."

I'm looking at Jazz, hoping for some opposition to having Susan here, but Jazz smiles at my discomfort, then shrugs and says, "Yeah, make yourself to home. I'll make ya some tea or coffee or something. Come on."

Susan is dressed to kill, tight long dress, high heels, and a hat with feathers and fake jewels on it. Flamboyant.

Jazz takes Susan into the kitchen and Michelle puts her arm around my waist and says, "HUH! I'll be sleepin' here till she leaves. If I wasn't with you I'd think seriously about her. You do have good taste."

I scratch my head and say, "Thanks."

The stereo is blasting, pizza boxes and empty bottles all over, people coming and going and bodies all over the place, passed out on the floors, in the tub . . . every bed's got three or four people in it, some naked and busy, some barely breathing.

Ben's sprawled on the couch drinking whiskey from a water glass, George all the way gone on the floor, Susan and Jazz fast buddies, smoking reefer and planning a shopping expedition, Billy and Mental bookending Matilda, passing joints and booze.

Michelle has fallen out with her head in my lap and I'm fading fast.

The trade for the fellas is going down in three days. The party started early. Lily watching it all with an expression of disbelief, and Spike so full he's lying on his back with his paws in the air.

Dragging myself out of bed still dressed, staring down at Michelle and Jazz, who are snuggled together wearing the clothes they passed out in. Laughing at what I could remember of the night and cooking my breakfast, heroin and tap water.

Limping into Phil and Jazz's room and kicking the bed and Billy,

Matilda, and Mental all grumbling at me about disturbing their slumbers. The covers all kicked on the floor and Billy's skeleton-like frame on one side; Matilda, covered with tattoos from her knees to her neck, in the middle; and on the other side, Mental's heavily muscled and badly scarred body; all three bare-ass naked, and I gotta tell ya it was one scary fuckin' sandwich.

Michelle staggering in behind me and laughing at them, and Billy saying, "Can't y' fuckin' perverts not be starin' at three people in love, then?"

Michelle laughing even harder and asking, "We're perverts for staring? How about you lyin' there like that?"

Billy sitting up and placing his hand on his hollow chest, announcing, "If me and me friend Mental was touchin' each other we'd be headed for hell . . . with the lovely Matilda here between us the only perversion is when Mental talks fuckin' dirty. She likes us both, we both like her. We just do it at the same time, sometimes. What's wrong with that, lassie? Hmmm?"

Michelle elbowing me and asking, "Whatcha think of that?"

Grinning at her and saying, "Two girls, yeah. Two guys . . . hell-fuckin'-no."

And she laughs and says, "Thought so. Hmmm."

Hearing a gasp behind me and turning, I see Jazz holding her mouth and giggling like a little kid, her pretty café-au-lait skin flushing up with pink. Looking every way except at the bed, mumbling to the three, "Come on, we gotta check on store space in Southie."

Jazz turns away, saying, "Bless my soul, you folks are awful strange."

I'm not near ready for what hits me when I get home that night. Coming back from Southie and keying the front door lock, treading up the stairs to my pad, and my heart starts to pound from the rush of adrenaline as I see that the door is kicked off the hinges. The place is trashed, shit thrown all over, and Jazz is slumped in the easy chair with the .32 in her hand, silent tears running down her face. As I come in she looks up and makes a visible effort to pull it together. She says, "I made it out the back, they took Susan. Smith and Ernie and a couple of other goons. Spike was wagging his tail when they knocked. He thought . . . I thought it was a friend. I told Susan to open the door and they kicked it off the chain. She started screaming and Spike went off . . . they shot him."

And then her resolve melts and Jazz starts sobbing, saying, "They're going after the coins, Susan will tell 'em where Specs lives, she'll have to. Phil's gone . . . I'll never get him back." Then screaming, "The cocksuckers killed Spike." And I'm holding her and shaking with rage and the need to return the pain I'm feeling.

Michelle's standing in the door, eyes wide and scared, coming in slowly, and then when I release Jazz, Michelle holds her and they cry together. And I wish I knew how.

Reaching inside myself for calm, figuring fast and can't make any mistakes. If there's a buyer it's gotta be the same Greek. He'll be at a nice hotel. Find him and we get the dough, get out to Specs and make sure he's got plenty of backup, start a reign of terror until we find Susan and . . . Thoughts running fast, past fast, and I dial Billy, miss him at the pad and track him to O'Malley's. His brogue comes across the wire and I say, "Billy, need ya here. Now, partner."

"On my way, lad." And I'm listening to the phone hum.

Waiting for George and Ben to show, they're running late and I'm wondering if something else happened. Cleaning and checking the magazine in my .380, loading, and putting all four of my extra clips in my pockets. Checking on my AK, clean it and load three thirty-round banana clips and tape two of 'em together for a fast load, disengage the magazine, flip it upside down and ram the other side home, sixty rounds good to go, smelling the gun oil and watching the marks my fingers leave on the freshly oiled barrel.

Starting over, unloading the magazines and wiping every bullet for prints, reoiling the piece and wiping it, setting it down touching it only with the rag, and wrapping it in a beach towel. Doing the same with the shells in my .380 and putting it back in my pocket. Ready as I can be and the feeling in my chest is like electricity.

Bringing Jazz and Michelle a glass of wine and telling them everything is going to be all right. Ben and George show and don't say a word, one glance tells the story.

Wrapping Spike in a blanket and Ben grabs my shoulder and

George says, "We gonna waste 'em, dog. We kill these motherfuck-ers."

And I say, "Yeah, man."

Carrying Spike's stiffening form into the alley, laying him down and playing with his now-cold ears and feeling tears and pain that I can't describe burning in my head and in my soul and screaming, and it all turns into rage that's so strong that I feel nothing now except burning hate. Pure like a pharmaceutical product, uncut, un-diluted, burning, fucking hate.

Mental comes in the door first, green eyes all the way psychotic, Billy sliding in behind him, cool, unruffled. Ben has his arm around Jazz and George is staring out the window, shuffling his feet like a fighter between rounds.

It's on me and my brain is working fast, get to Susan before it's too late, protect the coins, hit Smith and Ernie, get the dough. If we grab the dough, anything they got planned will be fucked off.

I say, "Ben, here's the deal. The guy that wants these coins is a Greek named Spiros . . . track him and we got the dough. You and George hit every nice hotel in Boston till ya find the motherfucker. Me, Billy, and Mental will roll out to Specs, make sure he's ready. And then start hunting these cocksuckers. OK?"

Ben grins, light beaming off the gold tooth with a star cut out showing the enamel underneath, stretches, and asks, "How much dough dis Greek supposed to have?"

"Over half a mil."

Ben and George exchange looks, and Ben says, " 'Stead of watchin' him, why not just rob his ass? If he broke he ain't gonna buy nothin' nohow. Am I right?"

"You're right, you rob him. But we split the dough. Right?"

"How many ways?"

"Down the middle, half and half. You and George get half for takin' it down. Me, Billy, and Mental split the rest."

Jazz cuts in, "Whoa . . . how about Phil and Red?"

I say, "Let's get 'em out first, then each side can kick 'em fifty grand. Sound good?"

Jazz and George both nod their heads, George saying, "Let's do it."

I'm kissing Michelle and telling her, "Call a cab, take Jazz with ya to your folks. I'll call ya when this is over."

Escorting Michelle and Jazz downstairs, and this time knowing why my girl is crying, and still not able to do anything about it. Staring at the cab as it leaves.

Ben and George heading downstairs, going to work.

Calling Specs again and again and no answer. Me and Billy and Mental loading up and going down the stairs, headed for Billy's car and the drive to Waltham.

The evening traffic is light, day sliding into night, and the smell of cut grass and running water coming off the river mixes with the odor of baking pizza.

The streetlights just coming on and I'm feeling the concrete under my feet and then it's like I got punched in the hip, the city is spinning around me and gunfire is tearing through the quiet, the towel-wrapped AK is flying out of my grasp and I'm tumbling and ripping at my back pocket for my .380 and Billy has his hands thrown in the air and is bringing one down, spouting fire back at the car holding Ernie and Smith, who are emptying M16s at us.

Lying prone and bracing my right wrist with my left hand and emptying the first clip and slamming another one in. Billy on one knee, pulling another revolver out and getting knocked back by more rounds and Mental screaming and rushing in front of Billy, throwing his chest out like he is greeting the bullets ripping into him instead of Billy Bones, and emptying his .45 even as two streams of full rock-and-roll .223 bullets tear him to pieces.

The odor of blood and cordite as thick as soup as I track the now-fleeing car, pulling the trigger on my now-empty .380.

Not a noise can be heard except brass shell casings rolling into the gutter and Mental slowly sitting down in the street, staring up into the gathering twilight and falling onto his side with a thump as his skull impacts the curb, surrounded by a growing pool of blood.

Feeling the concrete under my palms, pushing myself up and limping towards Mental, and Billy is crawling toward him, crying and screaming. Helping Billy up onto my shoulder and looking down at Mental and knowing that the line of holes across his chest is as permanent as a bad tattoo. Mental's mad green eyes peaceful now.

Billy sobbing, "You was a good auld sod, Mental."

And reaching down and closing his eyes.

Limping with Billy to his Lincoln and him saying through the blood bubbling on his lips, "Y'll be the first to drive this beast other than meself. Get us to Southie, lad . . . I got a croaker . . . who'll fix us up."

He grins and adds, "If we can be fixed, that is. I got a doubt or two about me repairability."

And I drive like I know how, like fearless Roy the stock car boy, flying.

My right leg soaked with blood and my hip starting to hurt, feeling like it's on fire, every time I use my foot on the brake feeling blood slosh around in my boot but still flying; leaving the conversing sirens and Mental's peaceful green eyes behind us.

Billy bleeding all over my shoulder, so much blood that my jacket and shirt are soaked, the hole in my hip making me limp and slowing progress even more.

Stumbling down a dark and refuse-filled alley to a steel door with a hundred-watt bulb in a wire cage illuminating it, Billy beating on the door with the butt of his revolver and it opening, revealing a skinny Latin cat with white hair ringing the bald top of his head, thick glasses, and a paunch.

Without a word he takes Billy's other arm and we walk him in, letting him collapse on a beat-up couch.

The guy asks, "Habla español?"

I say, "Naw. Poquito . . . no bueno."

And he goes into the back, returning in a minute with another guy who says, "He don't look too good. The doc will be here in a few minutes, he's just getting off duty at the dog track now."

Flipping a butterfly knife out and cutting Billy's shirt off him, he looks at the holes running from belt level up to his collarbone on the right side of his chest, says, "Missed his heart and spine, that's the good news . . . the bad news is that if we don't stop the bleedin' he'll be dead within a few minutes."

Then he goes to work. Slapping pressure bandages over gauze packing to slow the bleeding and hooking up an IV drip. Looking at me and saying, "Drop yer pants, let's see the damage."

And checking the chunk missing from my right hip, starts laying gauze and a compress bandage on it. Says, "Chipped the bone, it'll hurt like a motherfucker, but if it don't infect you gonna be okay."

The front door slams and shuffling footsteps come into the back where we are, a small round gnomelike man with bags under his eyes that could hold a wardrobe for ten comes into the room walking sideways, a half pint of gin in his hand, takes a sip and lights a small cigar, saying, "Billy-oh-Billy, ya fuckin' idiot. Let's take a look at ya."

Billy opens his eyes, grins with one side of his mouth, and says, "How ya doin', Doc? Will I live?"

The Gnome says, "Shit, lad, only the good die young. Your right lung won't be good for much. But the rest of ya will continue with your wicked ways."

Looking at his coworkers or whatever they are he snaps, "Wash up, ya fuckin' assholes, we got work to do."

Billy lifts his head up and points at me, saying, "Call the Brit. Tell him the story, tell him I'll trade him two for one on dead men. There's killing ya must do, and at that he excels. Call him."

I'm looking down at Billy's torn and bloody form and think maybe he's confused, because I can think of only one Brit we both know, and I ask him, "Shelton?"

He nods his head and whispers with the little strength he has left, "None other, lad. He loves death more than I do. Call him."

Dialing Shelton from the doc's, ten rings, no luck. I'm rolling.

Headed toward Waltham pedal to the metal, flying. AK in the trunk, .380 reloaded and stuck in my jeans. Throbbing pain spreading from my hip into my midsection and down my leg. Billy's Lincoln handles like a high-powered tank, and I'm muscling it around corners and sliding to a stop at Specs's.

Limping at full speed to the trunk, grabbing the AK, seeing the front door hanging open, dashing inside and no Specs, cats lying around and the TV blaring.

The back door is open, go through it with the AK ready and see the hole where the coins were and Specs now rests, legs akimbo, sticking half in and half out of the hole.

Light my Zippo and see that a shotgun was used to finish Specs. His chest and lower face are hamburger, flies buzzing and walking across the raw meat. Poor Specs.

Walk back to the Lincoln and roll to the nearest pay phone. Digging for change and feeding it into the phone . . . dialing, *ringing . . . ringing . . . ringing,* and "Hello, Shelton here. May I help you?"

Talking fast, doing my best to code it, but hurrying too much and I know it. "Shit went all the way off-wire. Billy says he'll do ya a two-for-one on stiffs. That broad we both know got snatched. Need ya down here, like right now. All our little problems aside . . . this is serious shit."

The line crackling, the sound of breathing coming from New York right into my ear, and then, "The broad you refer to . . . my coworker?"

"Sorry, man. Yeah, her."

"I'm on my way, mate. I assume equipment will be needed?"

"Yeah."

"I'll be on the first direct flight. Meet me at yours. Yes?"

"*No,* got big heat there, it got *real* messy. Meet me in front of the Rat in Kenmore Square. Tomorrow morning."

"See ya there at nine A.M., mate. Is that it, then?"

"Yeah. Thanks, man."

"The pleasure will be all mine. Cheerio."

And I'm tripping on the calm and cheery tone Shelton maintains through the whole conversation. Obviously there are dimensions to Shelton I never suspected.

Driving and listening to the glass packs growl and my brain howl. Feeling the rage and fear taking turns, making me shake like I am in a 10.0 earthquake.

Checking into a flophouse as Joe Jones, a room like a cell, toilet down the hall, the smell of bad food and bad lives thick in the air.

Placing the AK by the head of the bed and blocking the flimsy door with the foot of the bed, going to sleep holding my pistol.

Dreaming of Mental and Spike wrestling and playing and rotting as they move. And Michelle disappearing into the clouds of pain that envelop us all.

A light rain is falling, softening the look and sound of Kenmore Square, the foot traffic heavy, people dashing to try and stay dry, and I'm standing and smoking, got my cigarette cupped and the rain is running down my face under my leather jacket and pooling in my boots, my brain is all the way in slow motion. Between me and the world is a veil and it seems like I can't break through it.

Staring at the subway entrance and spotting Shelton's broad form coming up the stairs, opening an umbrella. He's dressed in nice clothes, leather jacket that comes past his knees, slacks and dress boots, got a suede cap on, and looks me up and down and holds the umbrella so it covers both of us, saying, "Lovely invention, umbrellas. You look all in, mate. Where do we start?"

"Somerville."

Parking a block down from Abe's place, got the AK in a guitar case I picked up on the way, and Shelton is carrying a pump shotgun under his jacket.

As we near the entrance I tell him, "One in front, one in back, I'll take the back . . . give me one minute to get inside and get the drop on 'em. You come in the front and we got 'em in a crossfire. They see me first we gonna have to start poppin' caps from the jump. Ya with me?"

He nods and says, "Let's get it done."

Fire spreading up my side, my hip audibly clicking with every step, dashing down the driveway to the loading dock in back, rolling up onto the dock and flipping the guitar case open, checking to make sure that the safety is off and the fire selector is on full auto, keeping my head below the level of the window in the door and trying the knob . . . and it's locked. Using the gravity knife I'm carrying, I pop the lock and slide inside, heart trying to claw its way out of my chest. Face feeling like it's made out of concrete and spotting one of Abe's guys spotting me and him screaming, "Motherfucker."

And pulling a piece from his waistband he's pointing it at me and popping a cap and it whangs off the security door behind me.

Lining the AK up with his chest and just touching the trigger, and the rifle makes a short ripping sound, traveling upwards, and like black magic his chest and belly explode with geysers shooting blood as he leaves his feet and flies backwards like he's been thrown by a giant.

Running full speed and the pain in my hip and side are a distant sensation as I approach the door, and Gary Haircut and another dude come through it with shotguns already blazing . . . as I feel something impact my chest I'm knocked back a step, hitting the trigger and sweeping the AK across them, sending chunks of flesh and bone flying, screaming like a madman, screaming with such intensity I can feel it ripping my throat . . . keeping the trigger down, full rock and roll, a stream of bullets tearing into them until the AK47 clicks empty.

The incoherent howling noise dying in my throat as I flip the magazine and reengage the bolt. Ready.

Flying over the bodies into Abe's office. Shelton is already there, shotgun at waist level, and Abe is duct-taped to his chair and Smith is kneeling on the floor.

The office has been trashed and reeks of gasoline, one desk tipped over and files emptied into piles, cans of gasoline sitting on the floor and the desk that is still upright. Abe's face is covered with bruises, some old, some new.

He gives a weak snort, and says, "Took you fuckin' schmucks long enough. Never thought I'd welcome getting shot, but these cocksuckers were gonna torch me along with the place, let me burn to death. Ernie snatched my kid. My flesh. Think I wouldn't kill ya to save my baby? Think again. Hit me. I got it comin', I crossed ya sure as shit. Two things I ask. . . . Number one, make it clean, put one in my head. Number two, make *sure* ya get . . ."

And Smith lunges for Abe's throat, yelling, "Shut your goddamn mouth! Shut . . ."

And Shelton takes one step, completely unhurried, casually grabs Smith's arm and seems to pull lightly, and Smith screams and convulses. The sound of the arm breaking is like dry wood snapping.

Shelton looks down at Abe and asks, "So where is Ernie? Where is Susan, Susan of whom you were so fond? Hmmm, Abe?"

One double-ought buckshot had gone through the leather of my jacket and buried itself in my right pec. As they're talking I lift my T-shirt up and check out the damage, the hole in my chest outlined in cloth and dribbling blood. I touch it and can feel the buckshot deep in the muscle. It feels like a solid punch was landed, sore but not too bad yet.

Abe spits and says, "I don't know. Shit-for-brains here can tell ya, though. Hey, Limey, do me a favor?"

"What would that be?"

"Cut the tape offa one of my hands, let me have a last glass of schnapps before ya kill me."

"In a minute, mate, in a minute."

Turning to the crying, pewling thing that just a second before had been one hundred percent tough guy, Shelton asks, "So where are they, Smith?"

Using his good arm to wipe his face and taking a couple of deep breaths, Smith looks up, and suddenly a look of confidence spreads across his face. He sneers and says, "Your bitch is dead meat if you mess with me. I'm not telling you anything. Here's the deal: First we burn this filthy old man, then I make a call telling Ernie I'm all right. I leave and we'll send your whore home to you when we're finished with her. Otherwise Ernie will kill her and Abe's daughter before the next hour is past. Got it, you Limey faggot?"

Shelton smiles and sets the barrel of the shotgun gently on Smith's foot and says, "You're wrong, Smitty."

And he pulls the trigger. The explosion seems like a bomb in the confines of the office and the blast separates the foot from the ankle, blood pumping in red jets, and Shelton says in the same reasonable tone, "Tell me exactly where she is and you get a tourniquet. Otherwise I count to ten and blow your fuckin' balls off."

Raises the shotgun and racks one into the chamber and rests it on Smith's groin, saying, "One, two, three, four. . . ."

"I'll tell you, I'll tell *anything* . . . don't do it . . ."

Shelton grabs the duct tape off the desk that Smith had used on Abe and holds it above Smith's head with his left hand while pressing the barrel of the twelve-gauge into his crotch with his right, saying, "So talk then. Give us what we need and you get this tape. You can wrap your leg tight enough with it so you won't bleed to death.

Otherwise I finish counting and you get to feel your balls vaporize before you die. Talk, mate. Five, six, seven . . ."

Smith's eyes are darting from his trashed ankle—and what is left of the foot and shoe that were once connected to it—to the barrel of the shotgun pushing into his genitals with an expression of disbelief and horror. He gasps, "Watertown, 4356 Elm Street. Right off Watertown Square. It's a house, they have Susan and Abe's daughter. Ernie snatched her from a dope dealer. Both of them tied up and locked in the basement. Anything happened to them wasn't my fault. None of it."

He's whining now, sniveling, whimpering, "None of this was my idea, for Christ's sake, I'm an art dealer, I'm not a thug. I swear to God, Ernie and Elmer made me do it. You have to let me go. Please, I didn't want to do it. They made me . . . they made me . . ."

I'm thinking that the skin on his face looks like he's already dead; knowing that he'll bleed out before we get all the information we need, I tell Shelton, "Give him the tape."

Shelton drops the tape into Smith's hands while keeping the shotgun stuck into him like a pin holding a bug. Smith frantically wraps the duct tape around his lower leg like a tourniquet, wrapping it so tight it cuts into the flesh and stops the flow of blood.

I ask, "How about the back door, what kind of lock? They got a dog? How many guys inside? How many guns?"

"Yes, yes, there's a back door. Old Yale slide lock. Three men, Elmer, Ernie, and Tommy Costello. They're all carrying guns. That's it."

Feeling like the world is spinning around me, looking from Abe to Shelton and back to Smith, thinking about Phil and Red looking at twenty years each and what had to have happened to Susan. I focus on thinking only about what has to be done and tell him, "Talk fast and ya might get to a hospital in time to save your life. Who put it all together?"

"Elmer, Elmer. That fake cowboy. He knew about Abe's daughter and told Ernie to use her to muscle Abe out. Knew all about your crew. He put it together, I had nothing to do with it. I had to help them or they would have killed me."

"How about the coins, Smith? Are they at the pad?"

"Yes, yes, Elmer won't let 'em out of his sight. For God's sake . . ."

I stare into his eyes, searching for any sign of deceit, and ask him, "Did Syd know about this?"

Smith is getting paler by the second as shock sets in, but he answers, "No, hell no. She and that doctor took all the cash from the swindle they were working with Elmer, got away clean. Elmer knew about this score and figured we could take it all."

I say, "Let's make sure I'm clear on this and then we're outta here. Susan and Abe's daughter are locked up in the basement, Elmer's there and got all the coins, Yale lock on the back door, no dog. Three guys all packing. Syd had nothin' to do with it. Does that cover it?"

"Yes, man, yes. You know I always liked all of you . . . I'd never have done this if they hadn't made me. I told you everything. That's all of it, I swear on everything that's holy."

Shelton raises an eyebrow and asks, "Are you sure?"

When Smith nods yes, Shelton smiles and says, "I lied about you living through this." Then pulls the trigger, the buckshot lifting Smith off the floor, doubling him over in midair, blood, bone, and meat flying everywhere, a piece the size of a bowling ball blown from his groin. Smith falls back onto the concrete howling and twitching while trying to push his insides back inside.

Shelton smiles, racks the pump and places it against Smith's head, and blows half of his face off.

I turn to the desk and ask Abe, "How well do you know Watertown?"

"Like I know my own face."

"Good. Would you still be wanting that schnapps?"

Abe grins and says, "More than ever, pal. More than ever."

nineteen

Abe's behind the wheel, dark is falling, and on the first pass the flickering light from a TV illuminates the front downstairs window in the small suburban house. One upstairs window has a light on and the neighborhood is quiet, no foot traffic. The only car cruising it is ours.

On the second pass nothing has changed.

On the third round, we park and Shelton slides out of the Lincoln and I follow him, lugging the guitar case. I lean back in and tell Abe, "Just cover the front door, anyone tries to get away stop 'em."

He grimaces and says, "They snatched my kid. I'll stop 'em all right."

He's patting the pump shotgun on the seat beside him, the bruises on his face making him look more lizardlike than ever. The smile he summons is worthy of *T. rex*, an ancient homicidal reptile.

The grass on the side of the house squeaking and the mud squishing under my boots, the flickering from the TV coming out a side window and lighting Shelton's pleasantly smiling face, as I open the wooden gate, creep up the stairs to the back porch and flip my gravity knife open, push gently on the door to get a little working room, and hit the slide lock with the blade, a little wiggling of the shank . . . and the door pops open.

Creeping softly into the living room, there's one dude I've never seen before watching TV, and I'm lifting the AK to use it like a club on the back of the guy's head when Shelton pirouettes like one of the ballet guys, spinning in front of me, grabbing the guy's skull, one hand over his face, one covering the crown of his head, and twists with his whole body, pulling so hard that with a loud snapping noise the guy's face is now staring over his shoulder, eyes still open but already dead.

Creeping up the stairs to the room with the light, I'm all the way aware. Focused on getting this done and nothing else, checking the other rooms and then opening the door with the light on.

Seeing Elmer lying on a single bed reading a magazine, jazz playing on a small radio, and suddenly feeling completely stupid, knowing that my conversation with Syd with Elmer present was how these guys had stayed one step ahead of us all the way, knowing that I should have figured it out before it happened.

Elmer looks up and his eyes widen and his mouth opens. Making a grating noise down in his throat, he swings his feet to the floor while jamming his hand under his pillow . . . and I smash the butt of the AK into his face, knocking him back, and jam the barrel into his mouth, feeling teeth snap and break off as it hits the back of his throat, and I say, "Nod your head yes or no. Are the coins here?"

Frantic nodding in assent.

"Susan. Is she alive?"

More frantic nodding.

"In the basement?"

Grunting, "Uh-huh," around the barrel.

"Where's Ernie?"

Head shaking back and forth in an I-don't-know.

"Anybody except the dude downstairs and Ernie stayin' here?"

Head shaking, no, no, no.

Asking him, "Where are the coins?"

And he points at the closet.

Shelton opens the door and the dirt-encrusted bags are sitting right there.

Walking Elmer at gunpoint down to the basement, looking at the steel fire door with the security bars across it, having him remove the bars and go down the stairs first.

Smelling urine, rot and mildew, sex and blood, the stairs ending in a cracked concrete floor, seeing Susan tied with nylon rope, eyes swollen and black, and that cute pug nose broken, smashed under her left eye, lips split, another girl sprawled next to her in the same shape.

Shelton saying, "Let me use your knife, mate."

And when I flip it open and hand it to him he cuts Susan's ropes and does the same for the other chick, asking Susan, "So did our old friend Elmer hurt you, love?

She coughs and spits, clearing her throat, saying, "Only a little. After all, what fun is getting raped without getting beaten?"

And she takes the knife from Shelton's hand and buries it to the hilt in Elmer's chest, a look of total concentration on her face, no rage or hate showing, just total focused concentration, like a child doing a very difficult task.

She looks into Elmer's bulging eyes, bites her lip, pulls the blade out, and rams it in him again and again, rage beginning to erupt, following his sinking body to the floor and screaming with each thrust, "Do you like it? Beg me to stick it in like I had to. DO YOU LIKE IT?"

Until Shelton and I pull her off Elmer's corpse.

Shelton wrapping his arms around her, murmuring softly, "There, there, lovey. Do ya feel better now? We must go."

Once we get back to the Lincoln the small brunette dives in and is holding on to Abe and crying, he's rubbing her back and saying, "I'm sorry, baby. You gonna be okay . . ."

And she's holding on to him tighter . . . and seeing tears stream down the face of Abe, the lizard man, is beyond belief. I slide behind the wheel and we're outta there.

Dropping Abe and his kid in Somerville and wheeling into the Hertz car rental in Cambridge, Shelton going in and Susan sitting and rocking back and forth, holding her hands between her legs and humming to herself.

Me smoking and staring out the window, not having any idea what to say.

A brand-new bright-red Chrysler pulling up and Shelton getting out, walking up to my driver's window and telling me, "Tell that skinny fuckin' mick we're even, he don't owe nothin'. Tell him I said maybe this will square some of my activities in his homeland."

Then Shelton smiles, winks, and says, "Cheers, then."

And he walks around to help Susan out of the Lincoln and into the rental car they are taking back to NYC. Gone.

The tenements and shabby fourplexes of Southie glide past the windows of the car as I enter Billy Bones's territory, rolling to a stop in front of Mad Jack Quinn's hangout, and park the Lincoln.

A torn-up dog looking like a reincarnation of Spike when I first met him chases a cat past the car and into an alley. Watch them disappear and feel something stuck in my chest. Something that hurts a lot more than the piece of buckshot.

Kicking an old beer can till I reach the door of the bar and walk through, got my chest and shoulders as firm as I can make 'em, put a saunter into my step and come to a stop at Mad Jack's booth, saying, "Excuse me. Have a second of your time, Mr. Quinn?"

He looks at the guys sitting with him and jerks his head toward the bar and like they've rehearsed the booth empties of everyone but Quinn, he twinkles his baby blues, grins showing all his teeth, and gestures at the seat opposite him, saying, "Sit, my boy, tell me how goes the battle."

And I do, running it down about Billy and leaving him with the Gnome, bringing Shelton down as backup, all the events leading up to me sitting there with him.

He smiles, looking like the sweetest old man in the universe, and says, "I don't know about your judgment, lad. Must be the Scot in ye. Letting that fuckin' Brit do your killin', workin' with niggers, Billy gettin' himself shot to doll rags by cretins like Ernie and them. S-oooo, are ya tellin' me ya didn't kill the Jew?"

Lighting a Camel, remembering the tears running down Abe's beaten and bruised face and his daughter's shaking hysterics, feeling rage start to build and then killing it. I need this motherfucker and will not cop an attitude. Taking a deep drag, focusing on his happy, happy, happy, mad, motherfuckin' blue eyes, and saying, "Yeah. That's what I'm tellin' ya. They used his kid to pressure him. The rest of 'em are dead and Ernie has gone missing. As a threat, those guys are history. Now, will ya help me get my friends out?"

He keeps smiling, then starts whistling a soft tune, maybe a poor rendition of "Danny Boy," maybe "Amazing Grace," something like that, slow and sad. Sips his Jameson's and says, "We can let old Abe go, he ain't a bad sort and is half Irish anyhow. But Ernie has to quit flappin' his lips, motormouth motherfucker has been killin' me verbally for two, three years now. He's gotta quit flappin' his lips. Got it? Shut him up for me and it's done. The fix is in, we surrender the coins and your boys are released. Charges dropped. Of course, they better haul ass out of the Commonwealth of Massachusetts as soon as they hit the bricks, or they'll be busted immediately for anything the lads in blue can dream up. So, son, how do ya wanna do it?"

Can't trust anyone, but gotta trust someone, what the fuck do I do? And now I got it, saying, "Find Ernie for me, I'll take care of him. One of the black dudes—a solid motherfucker, believe it or not—is named George. As soon as I do Ernie, we're square. George will swap the coins. Once Phil and Red are released, they walk out the gate, he'll put the coins in your hands."

Mr. Quinn's white eyebrows shoot up. "Not my hands, we have lawyers for things like that. And unlike you kids, I don't work with niggers. What makes ya think ya can trust this fuckin' bug, anyhow?"

I think of the old line . . . so-and-so ain't prejudiced, he hates everybody equally. It's a long-standing Boston tradition.

He writes a name and phone number on his napkin, slides it to me, and says, "Have the porch monkey call this guy. Come back this time tomorrow with a handful of these fuckin' coins so we can prove we got 'em. I'll tell ya where to find our friend Ernie. Once ya shut him up, it's on. Fair enough?"

I squash the Camel out, think about a dozen or two snappy rejoinders about callin' George a porch monkey, decide against it, and say, "Fair enough. See ya tomorrow."

Fever setting in hard, the shotgun pellet in my chest is surrounded by a bright-red saucer-sized area and the hole itself is leaking pus and starting to stink, the chunk missing from my hip is just as bad, the red inflamed area spreading almost to my knee. Fuck it.

I want to go home, I want to curl up with Michelle and wake up someone else. On autopilot, knowing it's a stupid move, but going back to my trashed pad, anyhow. Cleaning Spike's blood off the floor, looking around at the upended drawers, empty bottles and refuse, and I cook my dinner. Get the vein in my neck and send it home.

Call Michelle's folks' house. When her dad answers I talk as properly as I can, and when she gets on the phone I want to scream that I miss her, that I am losing my fucking mind. Her raspy, little-girl voice hits my ear, saying, "How are you, baby? Are you okay? What happened? When can I see you?"

Nodding with my brain running around like a trapped squirrel, the heroin only working on my body now, hearing the gravel in my voice as I say, "Everything's cool . . . gimme a couple days to get it all straightened out. I'll call ya. Just wanted to say hi. Make sure you're okay."

She's saying, "I want to see you. This is all crazy, I'm going to come down to Boston. It'll only take me two hours. . . . Bobbie, I don't need to be protected. . . . I'll do anything you want to make you happy, Bobbie. . . ."

And that kicks my heart into overdrive, not knowing much but knowing I want to keep Michelle as far away from this madness as possible. I growl at her, sounding mean on purpose and hating it, "*No, you are not coming here*. Stay the fuck away from here till I tell ya to come over. *Got it?*"

Hearing her start to cry through miles and miles of phone lines, disconnect the call, pushing the button down with my finger and dropping the phone onto the floor. Listening to the shrill beeping coming from the receiver, telling me it's off the hook. When it stops beeping I make dessert, back to the neck.

Coming to as the sun is coming up, the rig lying on my lap, dried blood thick and cracking with every movement, all over my neck and shoulder, and burning with fever and mind racing, all the way redlined.

Limping into the bathroom and grabbing what medical supplies we have.

Putting the phone back in its cradle, dragging it next to my bed. Waiting for Ben and George to call.

Looking at a bottle of penicillin pills with ten or twelve tabs left in it. Pop a beer and take them all.

Lying on my mattress, pouring peroxide over my chest and hip, it's foaming, pink and yellow foam pouring from me, smelling like rotten meat. I'm gagging when the phone rings . . . picking it up and George saying, "Done deal, dog. We comin' over."

Telling him, "Cool."

Hanging up and pouring more peroxide, pink-yellow stinking foam, and I'm puking, hanging my head into the waste can, praying to die.

Squeezing Neosporin ointment into the hole in my chest and the chunk missing from my hip. Bandaging them as tightly as possible.

Washing my face and pulling on clean clothes, throwing more grease in my hair and pushing it back.

Now waiting in the living room.

Listening to the voices filling my head.

Ben is reenacting the score, seems to have missed his calling; motherfucker should have been an actor instead of a thief. George is leaning on the wall arms crossed, taking it all in and occasionally laughing.

Draping a white towel over his arm and turning his normally military posture into a slumping question mark, Ben's saying, "Room service, sir, jes' ole niggah Ben and yo' vic'tals, suh." Grinning and pretending to push a cart in front of him, enacting lifting a lid off a plate and saying, "Rack of lamb, suh." Then pantomiming pulling a piece from the bottom of the cart, straightening his posture, and yelling, "With lead for dessert. Hit the floor, motherfucker. Hit the floor or we buttfuckin' y'all right now, which you Greek cocksuckers is famous for anyhow. Where's the money, fat man? Oh . . . don't got no money? Guess me and my boy just gonna kill you greasy fat ass for fun. Wha's that?" Putting his hand by his ear acting out listening, smiling to make sure me and George are digging his act, then saying, "Oh . . . yo do have some money after all . . . well, now, shoulda said so, saved us all some time and aggravation."

George breaking in and saying, "Show him, Ben."

And Ben opens a suitcase full of banded hundred-dollar bills.

I'm cutting it into two stacks, thirty banded stacks of a hundred per side, $600,000. Taking my end and dumping it into the guitar case with the AK. Then running it all down to George as lucidly and quickly as I can.

He's saying, "So all I gotta do is call this man, give him the coins when they release Phil and Red, and get the fuck outta Dodge?"

"Yeah, man. That's it."

"What choo be doin', Bobbie?"

"Takin' care of our end, my brother. Made a deal, gotta keep it."

Giving him Michelle's number so they can get Jazz when they split.

Freezing for a second and adding, "Tell Michelle I'm nuts about her, let her know . . ."

And I run out of words, the pressure in my head past the bursting point, the sound of shorting neon lights buzzing behind my eyes, making conversation impossible, trying to smile and act normal and it's like my face is frozen, it won't do what I tell it.

Ben is looking at me with obvious concern on his face, a fact I register but that has no impact, and he says, "You comin' apart, son, let us hep out. What's up?"

I grab the guitar case and say, "See ya."

The door slamming behind me and watching my feet run down the steps, like watching a movie of someone running taken from the top of their head. No sensation, no control, past autopilot, my demons have taken over, I'm just along for the ride.

Cruising into Southie, pulling into a block of projects that eat the sun and spit out misery. Limping into Billy's pad, a tenement apartment that, once you get inside, looks like a rock star's crib. Zebra-skin rugs, weird motherfuckin' art, oil paintings showing nuns fucking each other with dildos, children crying in what has to be Ireland, tears running down their faces as they carve a roast human against a beautiful green landscape. Weird. Guns lying all over, shotguns in the corners, pistols on the tables, fucking real battle axes and swords hanging on the walls punctuating the oil paintings.

Billy's on an antique couch made out of hand-carved wood and some kind of tapestry fabric, his long legs hanging off the end, bandages from his shoulders down to his groin, an IV drip at the end of the couch going into his arm, and a huge color TV going with no sound, Sex Pistols playing backup to the two girls hovering around Billy's sickbed.

Punk-rock Matilda in her normal tattered regalia and some tiny broad that looks like a gymnast, blond hair cut short and spiky; a muscular female elf in cutoffs and a tank top. Even through the fever haze and pain that's become my universe my eyes tell my mind that she's fine as wine. I slide the guitar case under Billy's feet; do my best to grin, and tell him, "You my hero, motherfucker, shot to shit and still got fine fuckin' women hoverin' around ya."

Billy coughs and spits a mouthful of blood into a beer can he's got resting on his stomach, puts a cigarette in his mouth, and asks, "Got a light, lad?"

I light his smoke and tell him, "Ben and George hit the Greek, our end is in the case. So's the AK, it's been used. Get rid of it. I'm going to have a talk with Ernie. Once that's done, Phil and Red are out. Anything goes wrong, tell Michelle I liked her a lot."

The fever has the whole room pulsing, the paintings and swords seeming to float off the walls, words echoing and twisting in my head, and it feels like I'm on fire. Billy tries to sit up and falls back coughing like he's trying to get rid of his lungs, managing to gasp out, "Hang on, laddie, wait . . ."

Then he's losing it in a fit of coughing as I feel my feet hit the floor and take me through the door and back across the street to the Lincoln.

I'm heading for Somerville, not knowing much but clear that it's my ultimate destination, stopping outside of Harvard Square and calling Mad Jack at his bar. Paddy answers and says he'll get him, hold on. . . . Waiting, watching the square swirl around me and wondering if I'm dying, laughing, and when he comes to the phone asking through the insane giggling that has overcome me, "What's the scoop, dad? Where's our boy Ernie?"

Jack gives me an address on Mass Ave and the name of the bar the address matches. I'm moving, got nothing more to say, leaving the phone hanging, his voice still coming from the earpiece as I get back in the Lincoln. Rock and roll, turn it up.

So fuckin' weak and hot, just driving takes everything I got. Checking addresses and can't keep numbers straight in my head . . . the letters over the shops and bars make no sense. The third time going back and forth on the same stretch of Mass Ave, I decide I've found the right place, match the letters and numbers I wrote down against the sign and numbers on the door.

Show time.

Breathing deep and doing my best to summon some rage,

adrenaline, the hatred that has fueled me as long as I can remember. No luck. All gone, burnt out by the fever or maybe just lost for a little while.

Breathe deep and move, move, move.

Having the sense to close my eyes for a few seconds before I walk through the door, swinging to the side and taking in a big dude behind the bar, a couple of blue-collar guys drinking beers.

Eyes now all the way adjusted, and in the back I see a pool table under a hanging light, Ernie's back is to me, he's lining up a shot, and I'm so spaced it feels like I'm floating. He's playing pool with a fat, balding dude that looks enough like Ernie that maybe he's related.

As I get close he says something and Ernie is spinning and the .380 is in my hand, lining up on his chest, and he's holding his pool cue and screaming, "NONONOPLEASEPLEASEPLEASENO . . ."

And I freeze, my mind screaming, *Do it,* but my finger is stuck, I can't drop the hammer on this motherfucker, and the pool cue is swinging up from the floor, smashing into my arm, gun flying, and Ernie is on top of me using the pool cue, smashing it across my face and head, feeling my hands grab at it when his kick to my chest lifts me off my feet and I'm watching myself fly in slow motion in the mirror behind the bar, and wondering why I can't make my body act right as the floor knocks the wind from my lungs, Ernie rushing like a pit bull, charging.

I'm getting up as fast as I can, trying to move smooth and quick but all the way in slow motion, all my speed, fast moves, hand-eye coordination have left. Catching his boot over my right eye and hearing it echo through my head as I feel the skin split from my eye to my temple. The next kick knocking my false teeth out and sending them flying, broken just like the originals. Curling into a ball so he can't kick my head all the way off, then, *boo-ya,* my spine is almost driven through my chest . . . knowing that he's using a bar stool to beat my back and kidneys into pulp, hearing him screaming and it sounds like my head's in an echo chamber, "Gonna kill ya, motherfucker, gonna kill your fuckin' bitch, gonna kill your motherfuckin' momma." Punctuating each statement with a blow from the bar stool and a kick, "Killed your dog, you piece of shit, gonna beat you to death like the fuckin' dog you are."

The whole universe narrows down to a Budweiser longneck beer bottle lying on the floor, and whether I grab it or it teleports into my hand I'll never know, but the next second I am in overdrive, the fever, pain, slow motion, confusion all the way gone, Jack. I'm beyond fast, flying, bulletproof, like motherfuckin' Kid Flash the superhero.

Looking up into Ernie's screaming face and bloodshot psychotic green eyes and my left hand grabbing his shirt as my right comes down on his forehead with the bottle. His knees sagging a little, bringing his face into better range, and this time when I club him the longneck breaks, leaving jagged, razor-sharp shards of brown glass protruding from my fist.

Hearing myself say in a calm and measured voice, "Yeah, man. You did. *You. Killed. My. Dog.*" Feeling a scream come out of my throat as my hand and the broken bottle go to work, stabbing and slashing. Moving so fast that it is a bloody blur of broken glass and bleeding meat as his lips fall away from his teeth, and his cheeks open in gushing wounds, permanent furrows that reveal the skull hiding beneath the skin appearing in his forehead.

Until the glass is gone, used up, and all that remains is my hand pistoning into his trashed face and the sound of my screaming mixing with his, and the police sirens whooping all around us, coming together like an a cappella group of rabid wolves all howling at the moon.

My eyes recording the cops loading both of us on stretchers, brain-dead, gone. Limbs hanging, feeling like rubber, the fever back so high that I can feel it burning all the sin out of me. Knowing that real soon the fever will stop along with everything else, welcoming death. Beyond tired.

Strapped to the hospital bed, the IV running into my chest. The veins in my arms and legs are long gone. The doctors and nurses talking and the sounds that were words morphing into gibberish. Phantoms and demons playing behind my eyes, now withdrawal starting and I'm so far gone it's just one more aggravation. Twitching against the restraints and convulsing till my shoulders dislocate. Satan telling me he owns my ass and me praying for one more chance.

Time going by, maybe days maybe weeks, I'm hobbling in front of a judge and having no idea what's up, who I am, blank as paper.

Bridgewater State Hospital for the Criminally Insane was built in the 1800s, granite and steel, bars as thick as your wrist. The howls of the mad a constant melody. My first few days there are a blur, shuffling around with my fellow nuts.

A couple weeks in I start to come back, old survival skills die hard, and without thinking about it, my back is always against a wall, eyes watching.

In the dayroom, TV going, cards being played, chess games proceeding, when I notice one of my peers with a football helmet tied to his head rocking back and forth and mumbling while trying to remove the helmet.

With a howl of glee he finally rips the helmet from his head, spikes it into the floor, bends over from the waist, then runs full tilt into the brick wall opposite him. *Boo-ya!* Blood and brains all over the wall and the floor.

Chesspieces are moved, cards played, conversations continued.

I keep my back to the wall and watch the body twitch.

This is when I realize that my mind is coming back from wherever it had gone.

The people around me are not just dopefiends and killers and crooks. They are motherfuckin' nuts.

Hmmmm.

My awareness increasing, digging my fellow nuts talking to nonexistent people, screaming at God and the Virgin Mother, mutilating themselves in fits of rage.

Shining it on with psychiatrists, taking their tests, learning that I'm a fuckin' sociopath due to childhood abuse . . . showing remorse, eagerness to grow beyond where I am, desire to quit drugs. I may be young and sociopathic, but I ain't stupid.

I know what they want to hear.

They get me a new grille . . . the view in the mirror is a little less scary than it was.

One morning at chow, watching a skinny old man with bulging eyes pour his oatmeal into his jacket pocket, then look across the table at me and say, "Savin' it for a rainy day. Uh-huh, a rainy day. Are you understanding what I'm telling you? You fucking fascist swine!"

I grin and tell him, "I'm with ya, bud, can't ever have enough oatmeal saved."

He glares and grabs mine, pouring it into his other pocket.

In the joint this would have called for immediate retaliation. There are no survival rules here and I have no desire to fuck the old man up. None.

I hand him my toast.

Drifting, feeling nothing, except relief that I am done running.

Starting a push-up/sit-up/pull-up routine and my body is starting to work the way it used to.

Content.

Until loneliness hits like bad, bad acid. Missing Michelle like an amputee misses the absent limb. Telling myself that she's so much better off without me this is the best thing that could have happened. Knowing she may have learned too much about drugs and crime already, that I could ruin her life, maybe already have.

Remembering that she'd been into girls before me, I think, Let her find some fine young broad and live happily ever after.

I hear the bull screaming my name this burning hot and humid afternoon, heart rate picking up, wondering why . . . report to the guard's cage. Tell him, "Prine here. What?"

I get manacled hand and foot and taken down to the administration area, chains clinking with every step.

Passing through a series of solid steel doors and two security cages to where the pale green concrete walls become pressed-board paneling, and the clack of typewriters and the sound of a radio playing swing music are an unsettling change from the screams and yelling I've grown used to.

At the desk I'm led to is a woman dressed in migraine-bright polyester. She's the first female I've seen since my mind took its vacation. She's bigger than I am, hair a bright dyed yellow, lipstick so thick you can see globs of it on her lips, multiple chins running all the way to her overinflated chest. Her voice is an East Coast shriek: "Prine, a lawyaar is here fer ya."

Pointing into a room to the side of the main administration office, she continues, "In dere, getcha ass in wid him. Da man's waitin'."

I shuffle through the door, pull one of the steel chairs away from the beat-up steel table in the middle of the room, and see staring at me from the other side a guy in a gray pinstriped suit, perfectly groomed hair, clear nail polish gleaming on his nails. He shoots his cuffs and flashes a Rolex Presidential, and says, "Close the door."

Watching my eyes, pinning me to see if I'm dangerous, he's poised on the edge of his chair ready to bolt if I make any fast moves.

I grin, shuffle and clank, close the door, sit back down, and ask him, "What's up? Who sent ya?"

"Your friend Billy's payin'. I work for Mr. Quinn, this is not my usual bailiwick. So tell me: Are you really insane?"

Get real, pal. Who knows? I do know I should be trying to get out. I feel too comfortable in here, before long I won't be able to leave. There is no confusion here, no decisions to make. Just keep your back to the wall, want nothing, be nothing, do nothing. Simple.

What I say is, "No, I'm not nuts, man. Back to my first question: What's up?"

"What's up is this: You're charged with Mayhem, Attempted Murder, etc., etc. The list goes on. Mr. Quinn feels that cutting your opponent's lips off fulfilled your obligation to him. He considers the other damages a . . . uhhh . . . an exercise in thoroughness. In other words, he's very pleased with you."

Cut his lips off? Is that what happened? Think about telling him that that was just the way it worked out. That if I hadn't frozen, punked out on the homicide, I woulda just shot Ernie. Then realize that the guy wouldn't believe me and if he did he'd really think I was nuts. I remain silent, the scene in the barroom replaying behind my eyes, feeling my body start to shake and my mind going away.

Pulling it back like pulling a load of concrete from quicksand. Forcing myself to stay there, stay aware.

Wondering if my face is betraying the battle being waged behind it.

The attorney sets a briefcase on the table and pulls a pile of court papers from it. Holding them in front of him and putting gold-framed spectacles on, he starts reading, then says, "Your opponent had three existing rape convictions. A pending White Slavery and Pimping and Pandering case. Two assault convictions. Multiple other arrests that are still on his jacket even though he beat the cases. Your priors were all juvenile. Nonadmissible. Our position is he attacked you, you defended yourself, possibly a little too enthusiastically . . . but given his record and my relationship with the judge, it's going to fly. Here's the deal. You're here for another thirty days for psychiatric observation. I appear for you, plead temporary insanity. You're back on the bricks in thirty-one days."

I manage to ask, "Phil and Red?"

The lawyer says, "Your friends . . . ah, yes. Out and gone. Back to Illinois, I believe."

I nod. I can't feel much yet, but I do feel relief.

My contact with reality fading in and out, the room strobing and warping, a sound like rushing water filling my head. Managing to keep my face blank enough that he doesn't seem too disturbed when I say, "Cool."

Incapable of further speech, rising with as much dignity as possible, shuffling back through administration to the comfort of the insane asylum.

Waiting, thinking again, restless. I steal a ballpoint pen and a stack of lined writing paper from the guard's office. A major score, in here anything with a point is considered a weapon and strictly prohibited. Paper can be wet and rolled into a club, making a decent weapon, or easily set on fire, a favorite pastime of our resident arsonists.

Why do I want them? I'm writing my ass off, scribbling my hopes and fears, daydreaming in ink, writing poems about Michelle and heartbreak and love. And somewhere around the hundredth page of jotted madness I have an epiphany of sorts. The drugs and my own self-destructive behavior have put me where I am, there is no one to blame but me.

Page 150 or so brings a righteous revelation. All I have to do is stop using, learn a trade other than theft, get a job.

Simple.

I run out of paper. Now I'm as hooked on the escape I achieve while writing as I ever was on drugs and adrenaline.

For two, three, four days I walk the small yard, do push-ups, full-out wind sprints from granite wall to granite wall till my lungs are burning and I'm ready to puke.

If I'm going to change I gotta go all the way, no more drugs, no more stealing. Not even the paper I need. Right?

Pressure building, head swirling, find myself yelling back at the nuts, starting to burn with a constant rage, on the edge of hurting one of these motherfuckers.

Scoping the guard's cage, loitering, watching. For a few seconds the door is open and the bull is outside his cage, jamming a tongue depressor into the mouth of a guy convulsing, the ding is flopping like a fish out of water, foam running from his mouth in a torrent, and I got a full stack of blank paper stuck inside my shirt and am strolling away, no thought, no hesitation.

My demons flow from my fingers through the pen and are trapped on the paper. Leaving me in peace.

I've found the answer. Counting the days, anxiety increasing by the second. Can I stay clean? Is it possible? What the hell can I do except steal? Over and over around and around a mantra playing 24/7.

Sometimes I feel rock-solid. Maybe I'll get the miracle, a fresh start, the girl, telling myself that. . . . No matter what happens I can do it. Whatever it is.

Time to take the reins, make a change.

Ready.

The whispers and groans, screams and whimpers recede with the night, the sun is turning the blue-black horizon to a soft silver as the morning whistle blows, and the guard yells into the dorm, "Prine. Roll it up for release."

Stripping my mattress and rolling the sheets and army surplus blanket into a package, dropping it at the front of the dorm, watching the blank faces and crazy eyes watch me walk by.

Fear running through me like a river in full flood, torrential, overwhelming.

Here comes the real world.

One foot in front of the other all the way to the release area.

Getting fingerprinted before release so that they know I'm me. Signing for my possessions, asking, "What's the date?"

The guy says, "August 25th."

It registers that it's my birthday. Nineteen years old, today. What's that cliché . . . the first day of my life. Hmmm.

Watching the steel now shining through the ripped toes of my boots, the last couple of months of hard use and neglect have trashed them. They shine up at me and lead me into the parking lot.

The air smelling different, piss and vomit replaced by cut grass, the shadows cast by the walls gone, morning sun just starting to work, feeling sweat bead my face.

Lighting a Camel, spotting Billy Bones standing in front of his Lincoln, gleaming in the sun like a candy-apple hearse.

He straightens his frame, adjusts the black shades over his eyes, and limps towards me using a cane, moving like a tired old man, the dangerous edge still there, but subdued now.

The sun haloing his head and the grease in his hair glistening as he says, "Welcome back to t' auld world, lad. A fine job of work."

Looking at me over his shades, he laughs and adds, "Ye shoulda just shot the cocksucker. Murder's easier t' beat than mayhem. Come on, then. 'Tis time to leave the Commonwealth."

Not able to talk, not sure what I feel, but strong in my resolve to change my evil ways. Holding Billy's door for him as he painfully folds his body behind the wheel. Rolling. R&B playing on the radio, glass packs rumbling, and I ask him, "What now, Bones?"

"Stoppin' in Lexington to see a couple of your admirers. Then off for the coast. Got the dough in the trunk, we're outta here come tonight."

Glancing at him, I see he has his black leather jacket on even in the hot weather, driving with one hand and smoking with the other, and I ask him, "Michelle?"

"Maybe, lad, then again maybe not. 'Tis a surprise that I'd not ruin for ye."

Hoping for a second and turning away from my thoughts as they form, like if I don't let a complete thought form I'm not responsible.

Knowing that it's got to be Michelle and that I'm bad news. That I should just roll for Cal. Maybe mail her some dough and leave her a pleasant memory. Do no more damage.

Pulling into a motel that looks like somebody's bad rendition of a Swiss chalet on the Lexington-Bedford line, and Billy saying, "I'll be back after dark. Room 112. Have fun, me lad."

Heart hammering, hands shaky, knocking softly and the door opening, entering sixty-watt reality, and as I step through soft arms wrap around me, and Michelle is whispering in my ear, saying, "It's all here, baby, everything ya could ever want. Welcome home."

My eyes adjusting and taking in the diminutive blond from Billy's standing by the bed, hands on hips, wearing a smile and nothing else. Michelle's locking the door and pulling my T-shirt over my head, rubbing her tits against my back and softly kissing my neck.

As the little blonde glides towards me, Michelle whispering, "Tried to tell ya I'd do anything to make you happy. Here it is, baby, all for you. Got ten Preludins in the rig, we been waiting for you."

Looking in her already Preludin-sprung burning topaz eyes and knowing that her corruption has already gone too far to stop. When did she make that turn?

Accepting my unforgivable guilt and acknowledging, then embracing my damnation. She hands me a preloaded shot. Knowing that I have absolutely made my mind up to change my ways, knowing that I started this particular dance, feeling Michelle's soft/hard nipples against my back, feeling the blonde's breath against my lips as her eyes stare into mine.

Guilt and lust mixing, insane rhythm starting all by itself. Arguing with myself for a second and then laughing out loud, thinking that I am as crazy as anybody back at Bridgewater.

Fuck it.

Hold my left arm up and Michelle wraps her hands above the crook in my elbow and the needle glides home, the outfit fills with blood and the shot runs up my arm and into my soul, feel the etherlike fumes hit my lungs, and electric excitement fills me like 220 current running through a 110 line and the words *Eternal Damnation* echo through my head in time with the increasing speed of the music playing inside me.

Pull the works out and throw them into the corner, the needle quivering in the wall like a dart, as the music roaring behind my eyes goes motherfuckin' supersonic, the base and rhythm soaring as Michelle and the blonde and me descend into a lovely shared dark madness.